A L E X + A D A

SPECIAL THANKS

MIKE ARMANI

LANE FUJITA

ERIN GOLDSTEIN

KAREN HILTON

ALEEM HOSSAIN

TIM INGLE

JENN KAO

FEDERICA PAGANI

GIANCARLO YERKES

IMAGE COMICS, INC.

Robert Kirkman	Chief Operating Officer
Erik Larsen	Chief Financial Officer
Todd McFarlane	President
Marc Silvestri	Chief Executive Officer
Jim Valentino	Vice-President
Eric Stephenson	Publisher
Ron Richards	Director of Business Development
Jennifer de Guzman	Director of Trade Book Sales
Kat Salazar	Director of PR & Marketing
Corey Murphy	Director of Retail Sales
Jeremy Sullivan	Director of Digital Sales
Emilio Bautista	Sales Assistant
Branwyn Bigglestone	Senior Accounts Manager
Emily Miller	Accounts Manager
Jessica Ambriz	Administrative Assistant
Tyler Shainline	Events Coordinator
David Brothers	Content Manager
Jonathan Chan	Production Manager
Drew Gill	Art Director
Meredith Wallace	Print Manager
Addison Duke	Production Artist
Vincent Kukua	Production Artist
Tricia Ramos	Production Assistant

IMAGECOMICS.COM

SARAH VAUGHN

STORY
SCRIPT

JONATHAN LUNA

STORY
SCRIPT ASSISTS
ILLUSTRATIONS
LETTERS
DESIGN

6

6

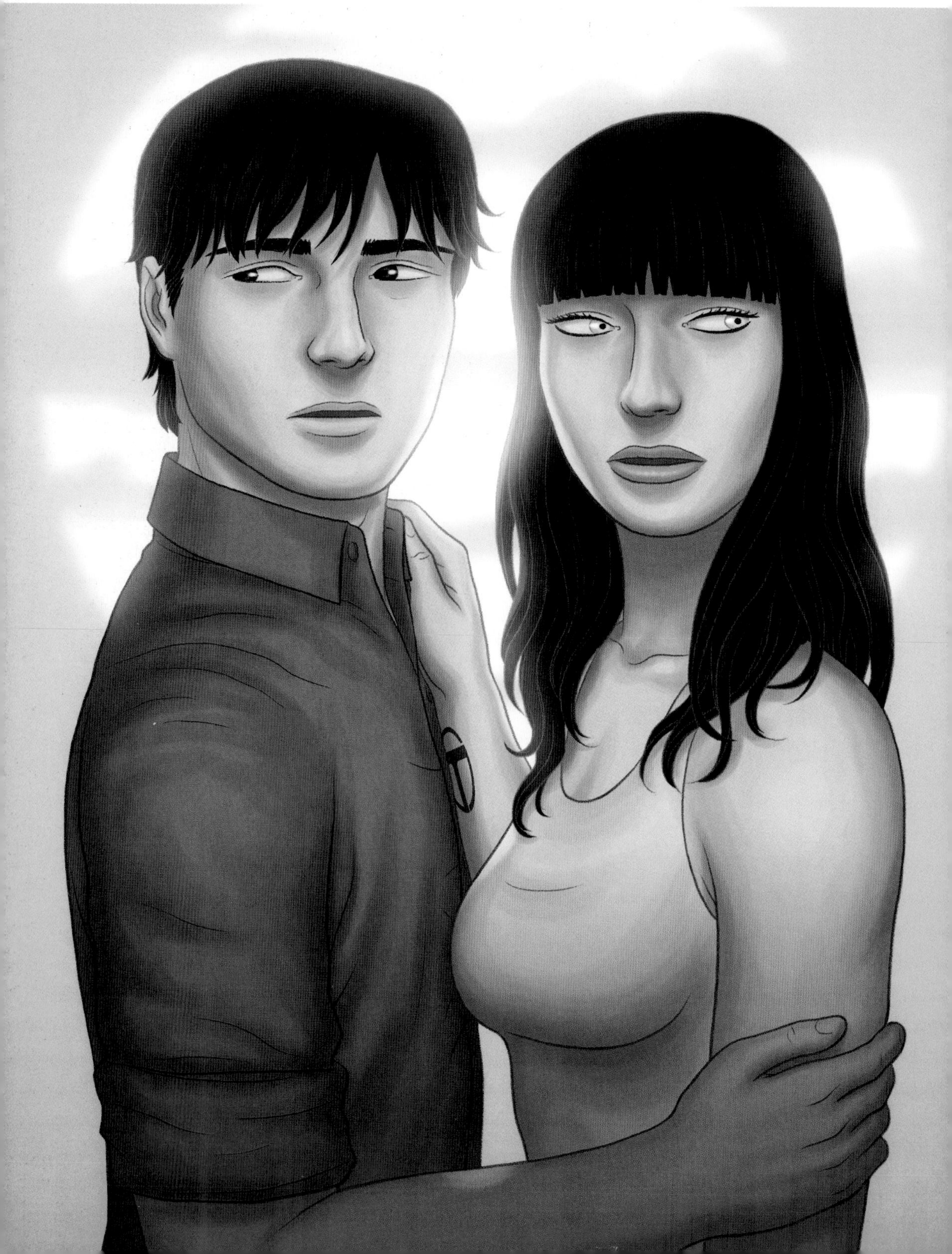

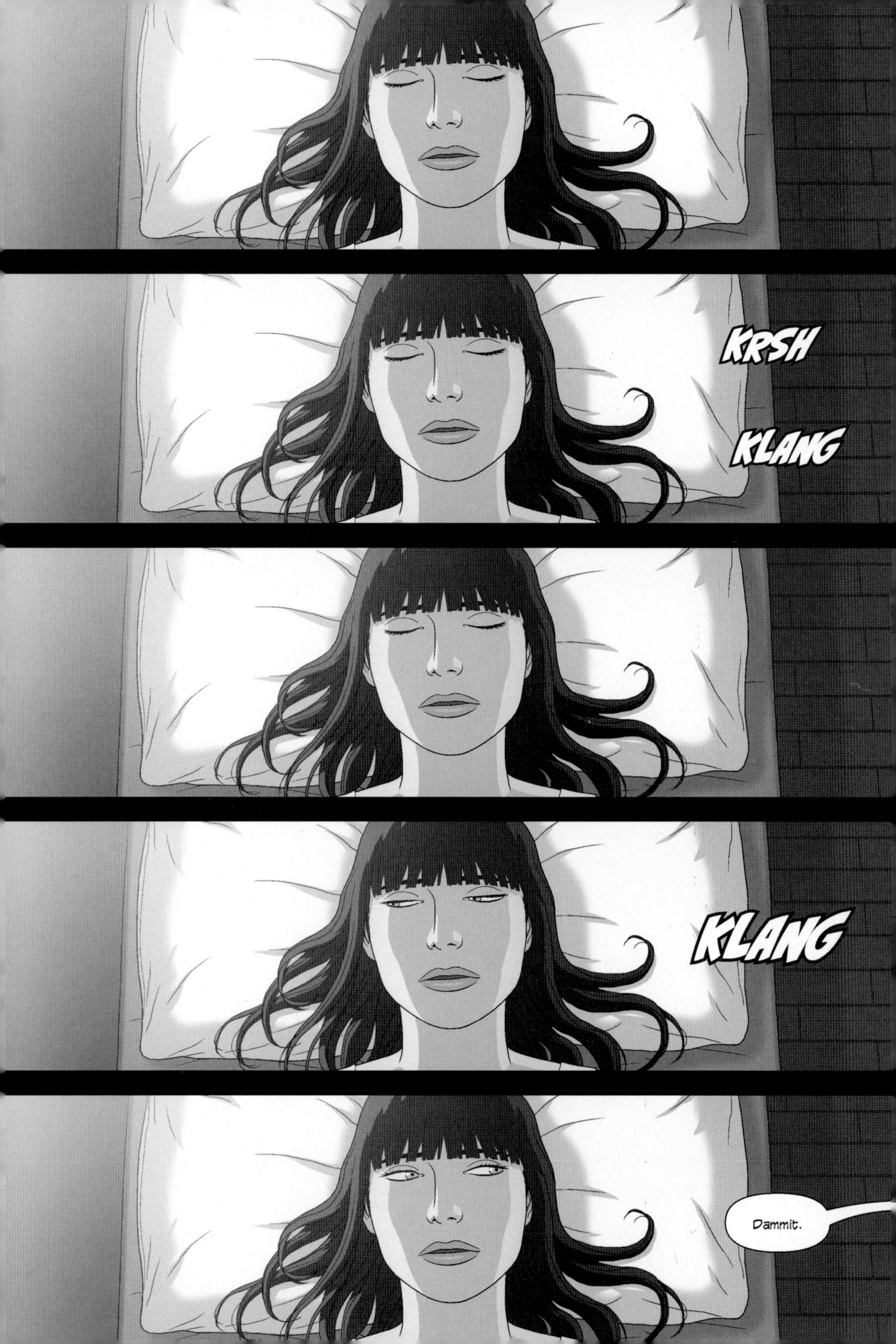
KRSH
KLANG
KLANG
Dammit.

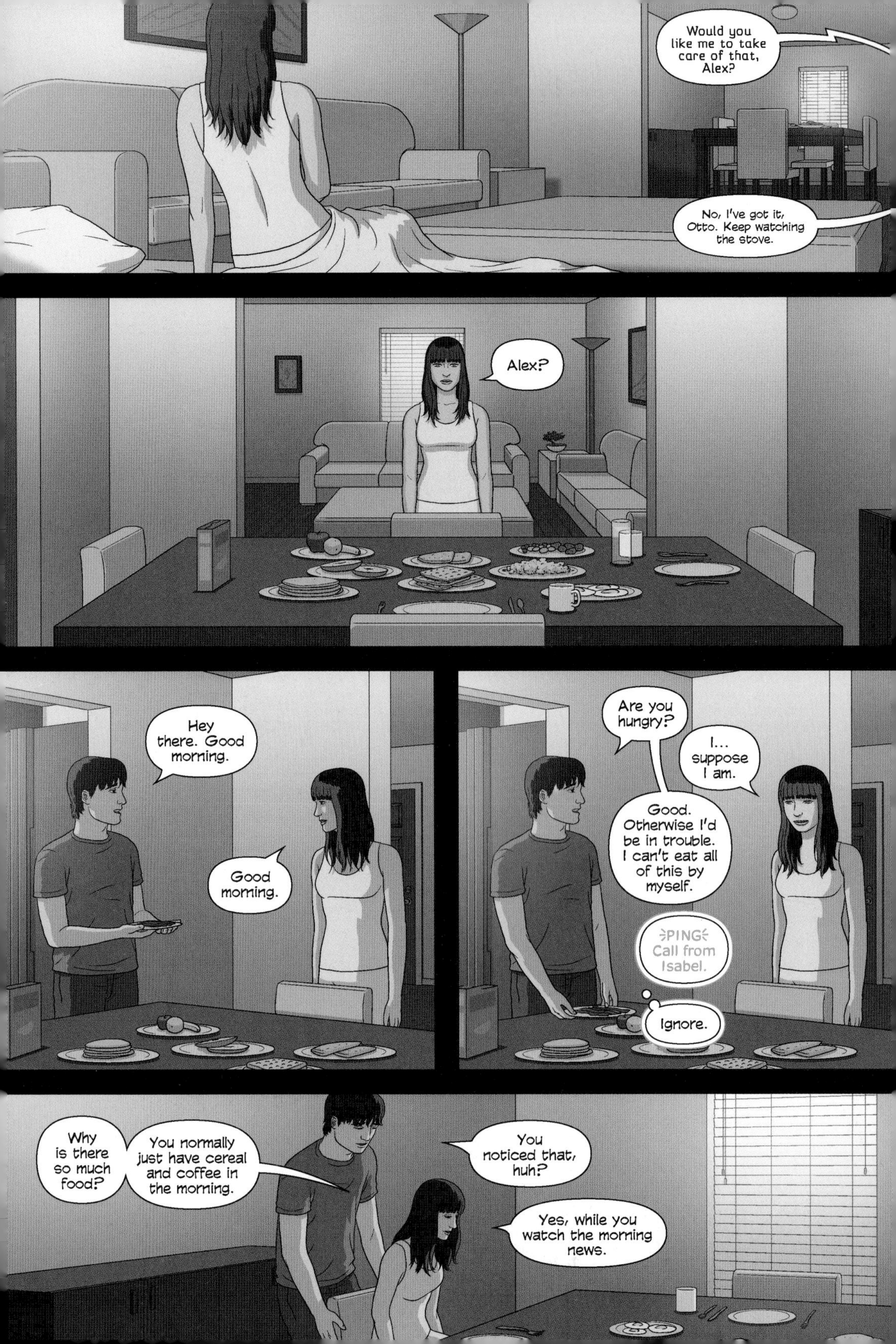
Would you like me to take care of that, Alex?
No, I've got it, Otto. Keep watching the stove.
Alex?
Hey there. Good morning.
Good morning.
Are you hungry?
I... suppose I am.
Good. Otherwise I'd be in trouble. I can't eat all of this by myself.
PING Call from Isabel.
Ignore.
Why is there so much food?
You normally just have cereal and coffee in the morning.
You noticed that, huh?
Yes, while you watch the morning news.

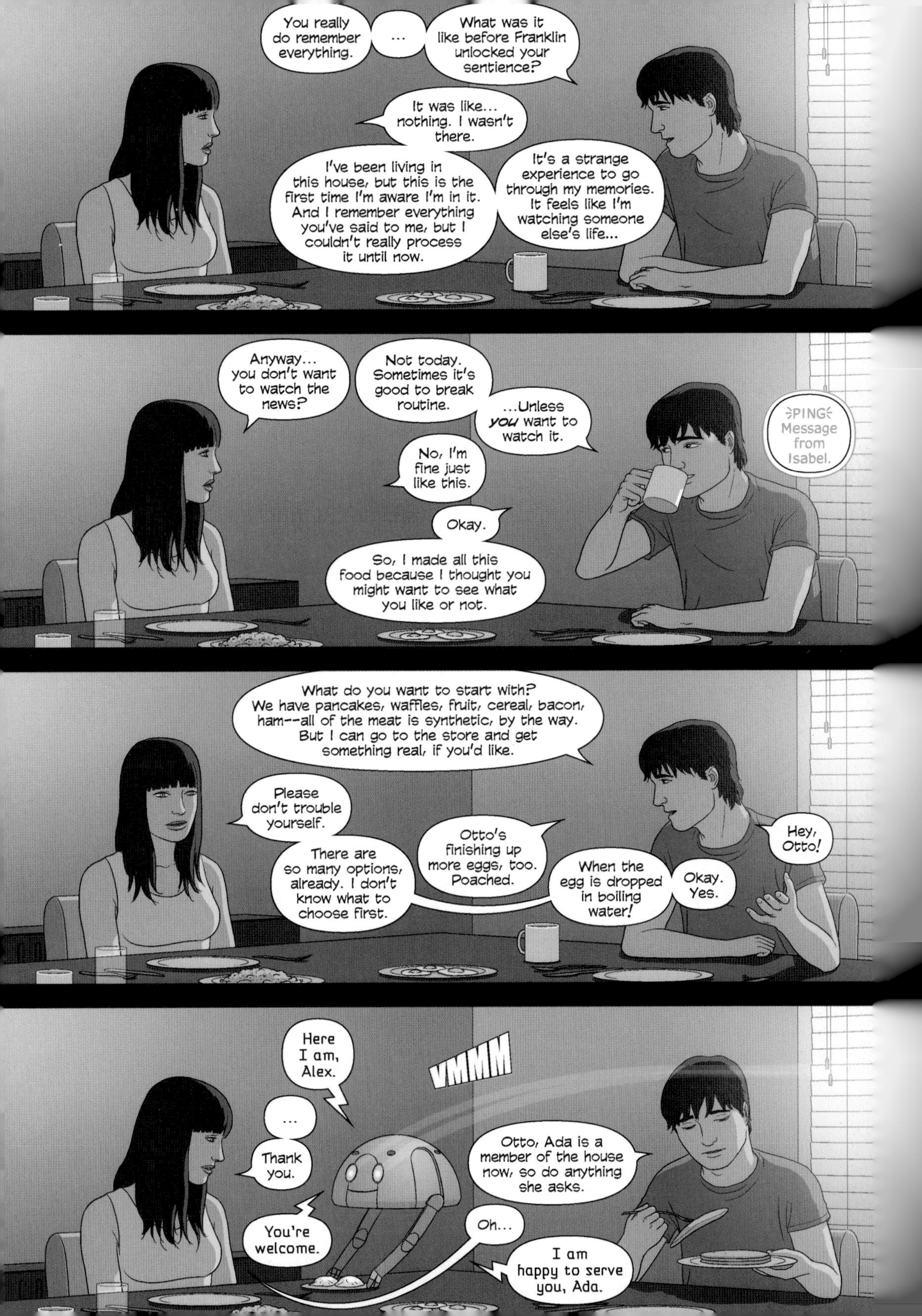

You really do remember everything.
...
What was it like before Franklin unlocked your sentience?
It was like... nothing. I wasn't there.
I've been living in this house, but this is the first time I'm aware I'm in it. And I remember everything you've said to me, but I couldn't really process it until now.
It's a strange experience to go through my memories. It feels like I'm watching someone else's life...
Anyway... you don't want to watch the news?
Not today. Sometimes it's good to break routine.
...Unless *you* want to watch it.
No, I'm fine just like this.
Okay.
So, I made all this food because I thought you might want to see what you like or not.
PING
Message from Isabel.
What do you want to start with? We have pancakes, waffles, fruit, cereal, bacon, ham--all of the meat is synthetic, by the way. But I can go to the store and get something real, if you'd like.
Please don't trouble yourself.
There are so many options, already. I don't know what to choose first.
Otto's finishing up more eggs, too. Poached.
When the egg is dropped in boiling water!
Okay. Yes.
Hey, Otto!
Here I am, Alex.
VMMM
...
Thank you.
You're welcome.
Otto, Ada is a member of the house now, so do anything she asks.
Oh...
I am happy to serve you, Ada.

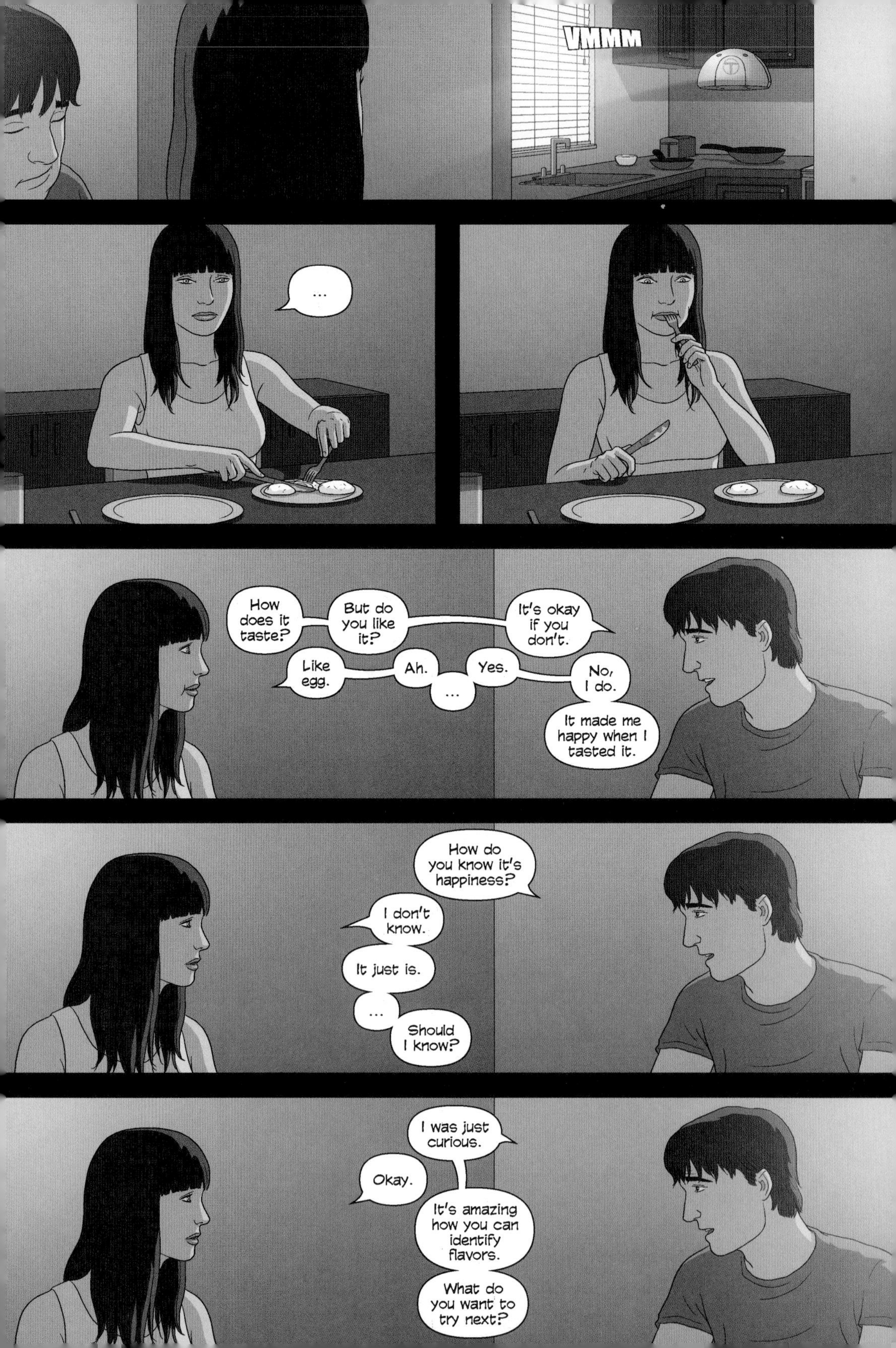
VMMM
...
How does it taste?
Like egg.
Ah.
But do you like it?
...
Yes.
It's okay if you don't.
No, I do.
It made me happy when I tasted it.
How do you know it's happiness?
I don't know.
It just is.
...
Should I know?
I was just curious.
Okay.
It's amazing how you can identify flavors.
What do you want to try next?

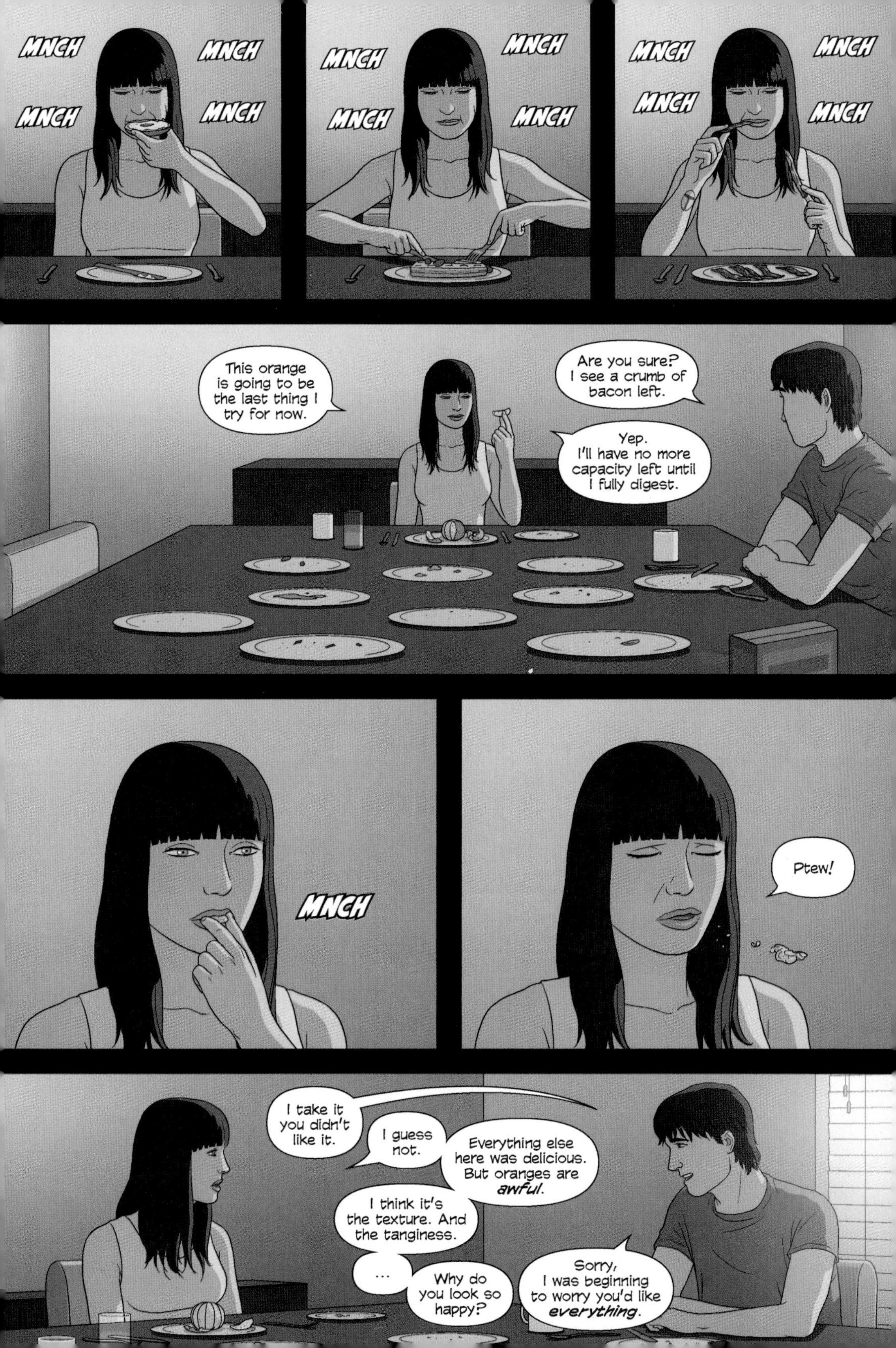
MNCH
MNCH
MNCH
MNCH
MNCH
MNCH
MNCH
MNCH
MNCH
MNCH
MNCH
MNCH
This orange is going to be the last thing I try for now.
Are you sure? I see a crumb of bacon left.
Yep. I'll have no more capacity left until I fully digest.
MNCH
Ptew!
I take it you didn't like it.
I guess not.
Everything else here was delicious. But oranges are *awful*.
I think it's the texture. And the tanginess.
...
Why do you look so happy?
Sorry, I was beginning to worry you'd like *everything*.

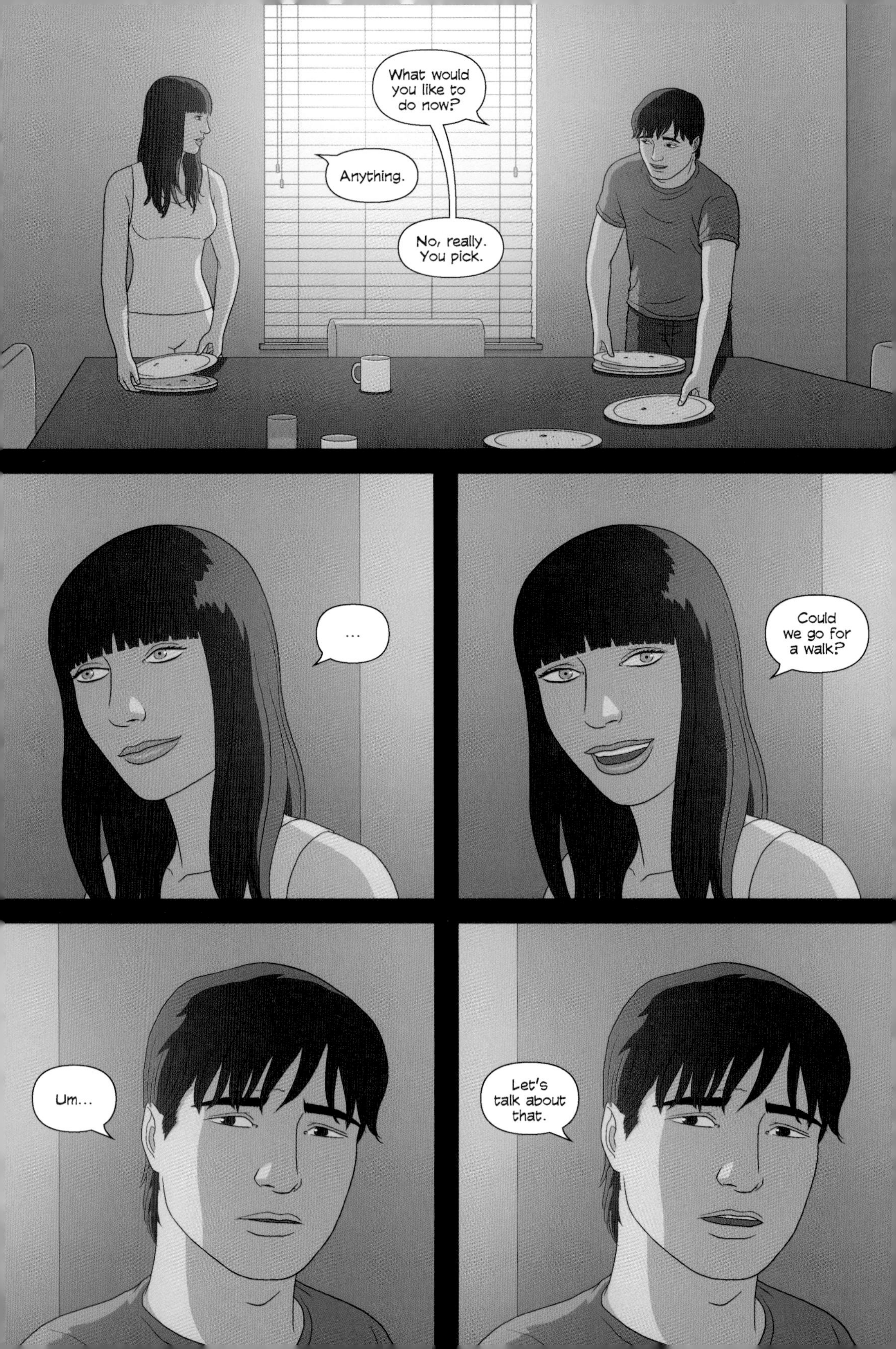
What would you like to do now?
Anything.
No, really. You pick.
...
Could we go for a walk?
Um...
Let's talk about that.

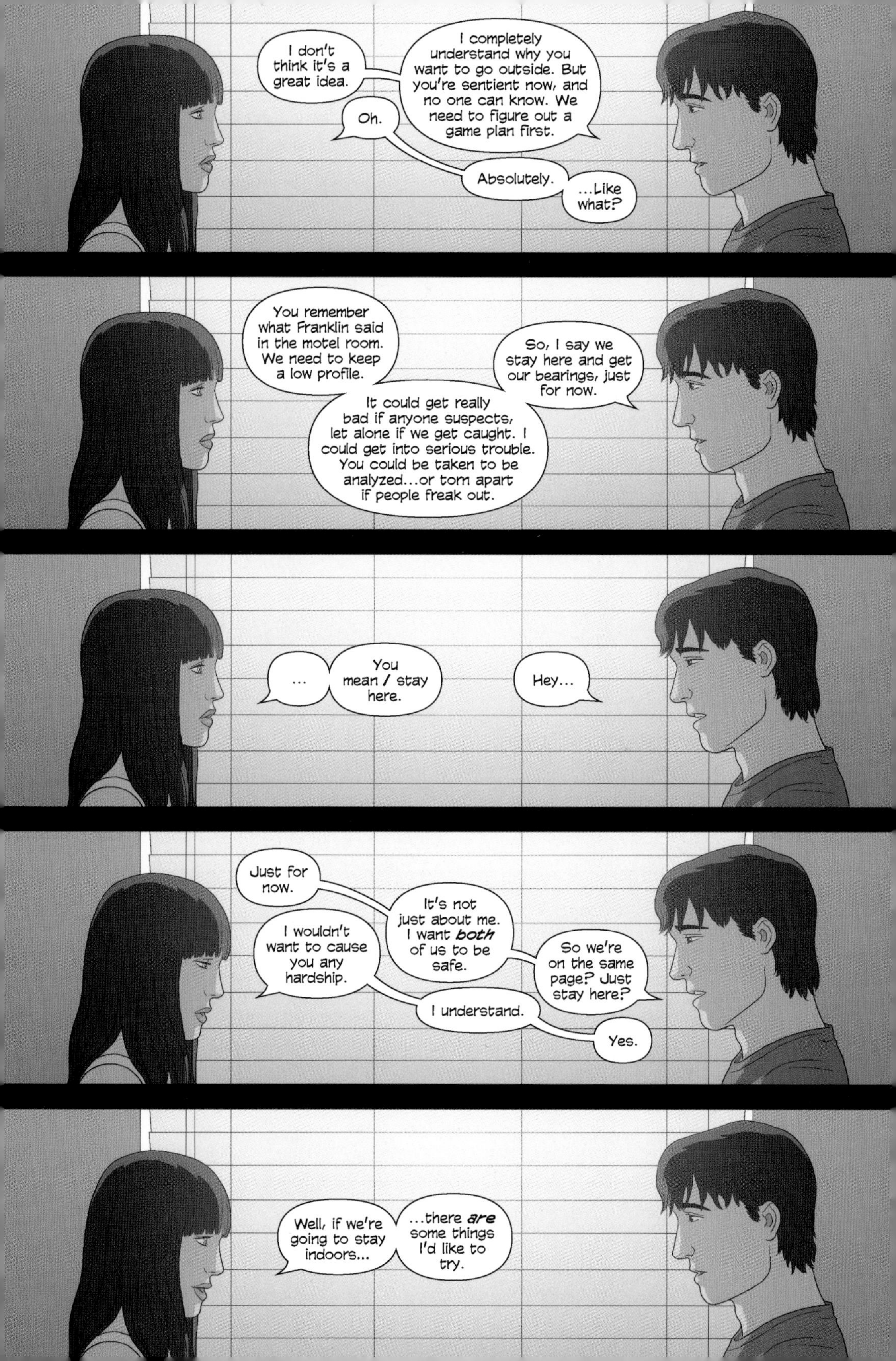
I don't think it's a great idea.
I completely understand why you want to go outside. But you're sentient now, and no one can know. We need to figure out a game plan first.
Oh.
Absolutely.
...Like what?
You remember what Franklin said in the motel room. We need to keep a low profile.
It could get really bad if anyone suspects, let alone if we get caught. I could get into serious trouble. You could be taken to be analyzed...or torn apart if people freak out.
So, I say we stay here and get our bearings, just for now.
...
You mean *I* stay here.
Hey...
Just for now.
It's not just about me. I want ***both*** of us to be safe.
I wouldn't want to cause you any hardship.
So we're on the same page? Just stay here?
I understand.
Yes.
Well, if we're going to stay indoors...
...there ***are*** some things I'd like to try.

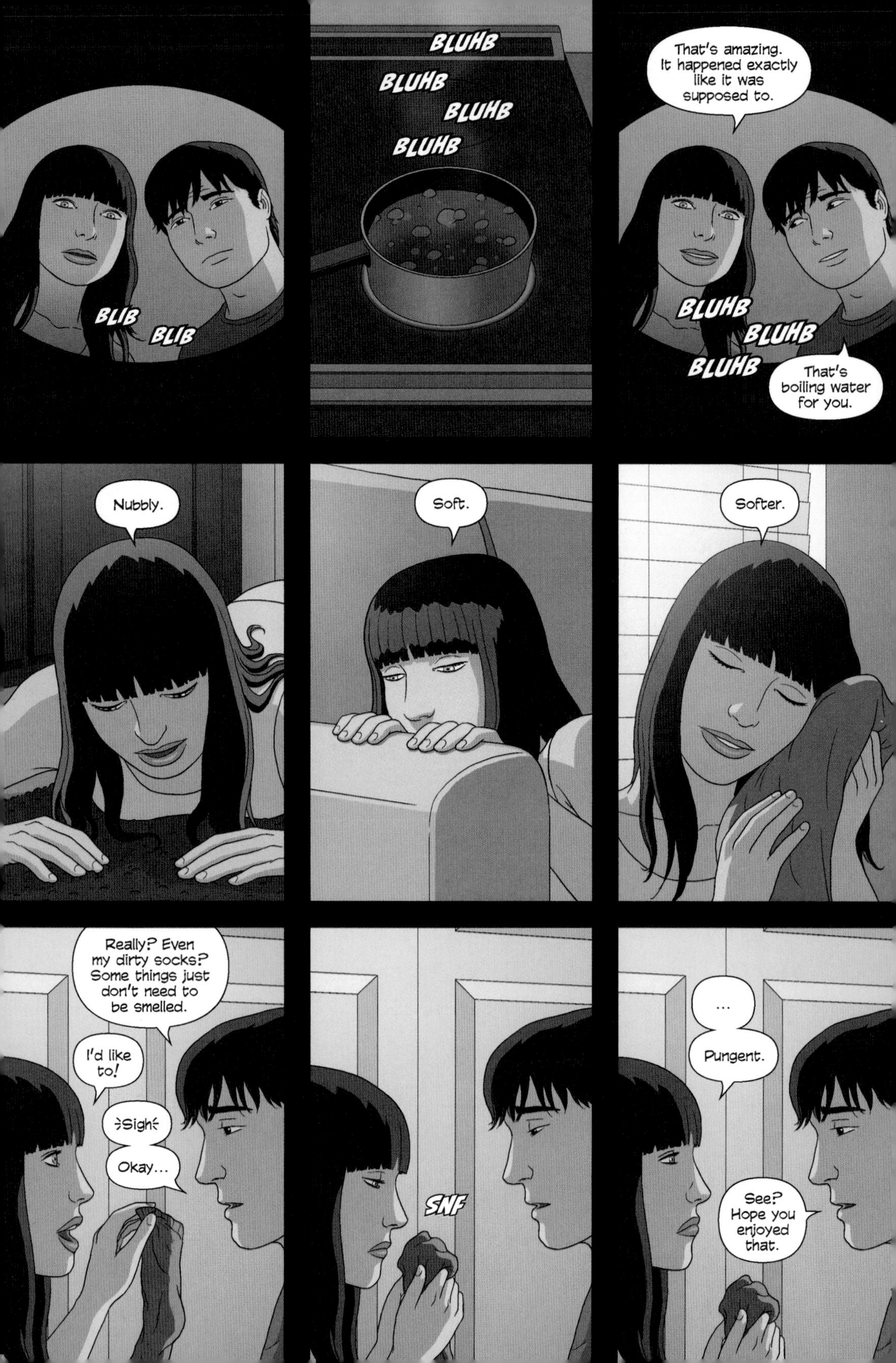
BLIB
BLIB
BLUHB
BLUHB
BLUHB
BLUHB
That's amazing. It happened exactly like it was supposed to.
BLUHB
BLUHB
BLUHB
That's boiling water for you.
Nubbly.
Soft.
Softer.
Really? Even my dirty socks? Some things just don't need to be smelled.
I'd like to!
Sigh
Okay...
SNF
...
Pungent.
See? Hope you enjoyed that.

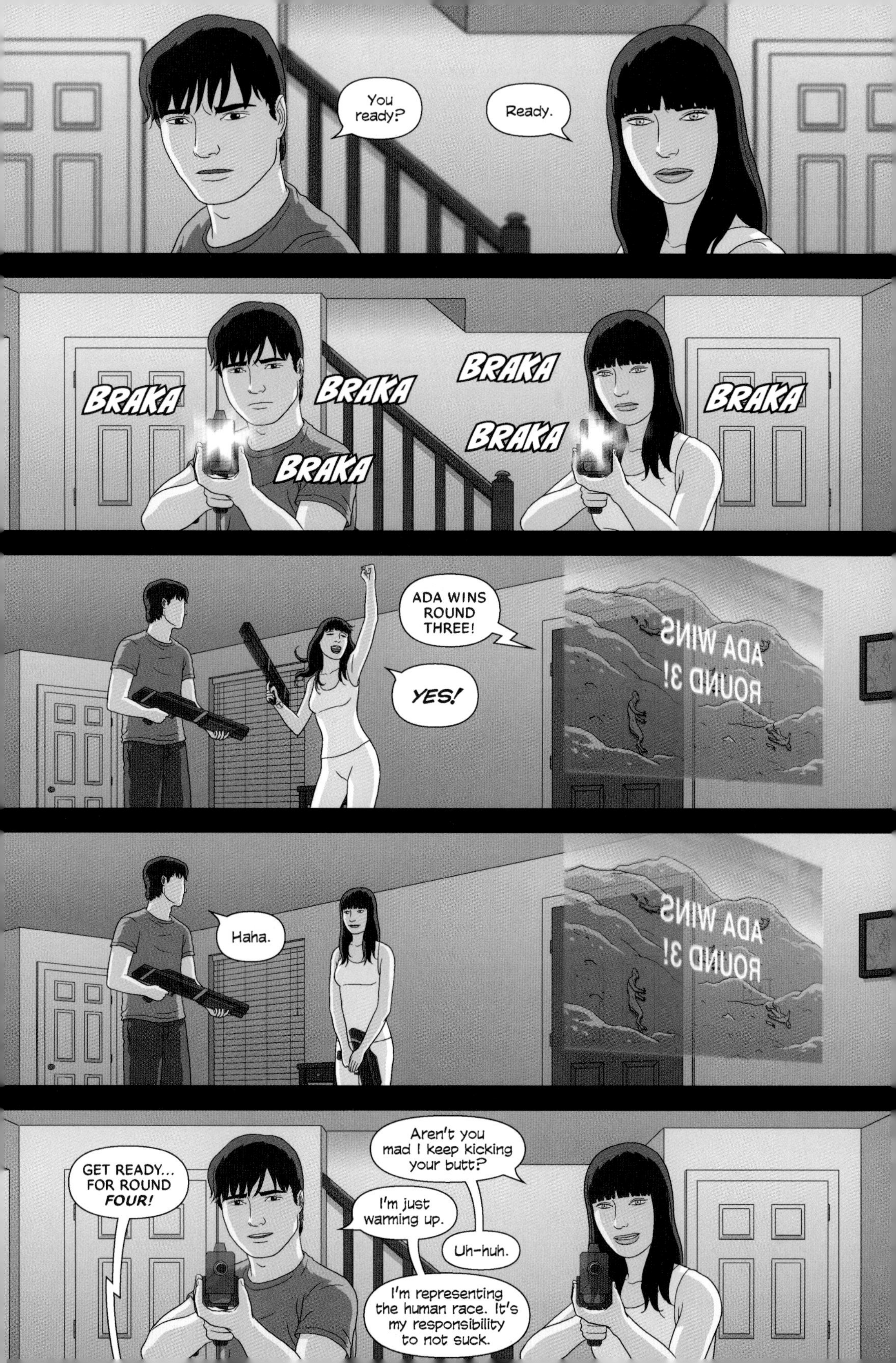
You ready?
Ready.
BRAKA
BRAKA
BRAKA
BRAKA
BRAKA
BRAKA
ADA WINS ROUND THREE!
YES!
ADA WINS ROUND 3!
Haha.
ADA WINS ROUND 3!
GET READY... FOR ROUND *FOUR!*
Aren't you mad I keep kicking your butt?
I'm just warming up.
Uh-huh.
I'm representing the human race. It's my responsibility to not suck.

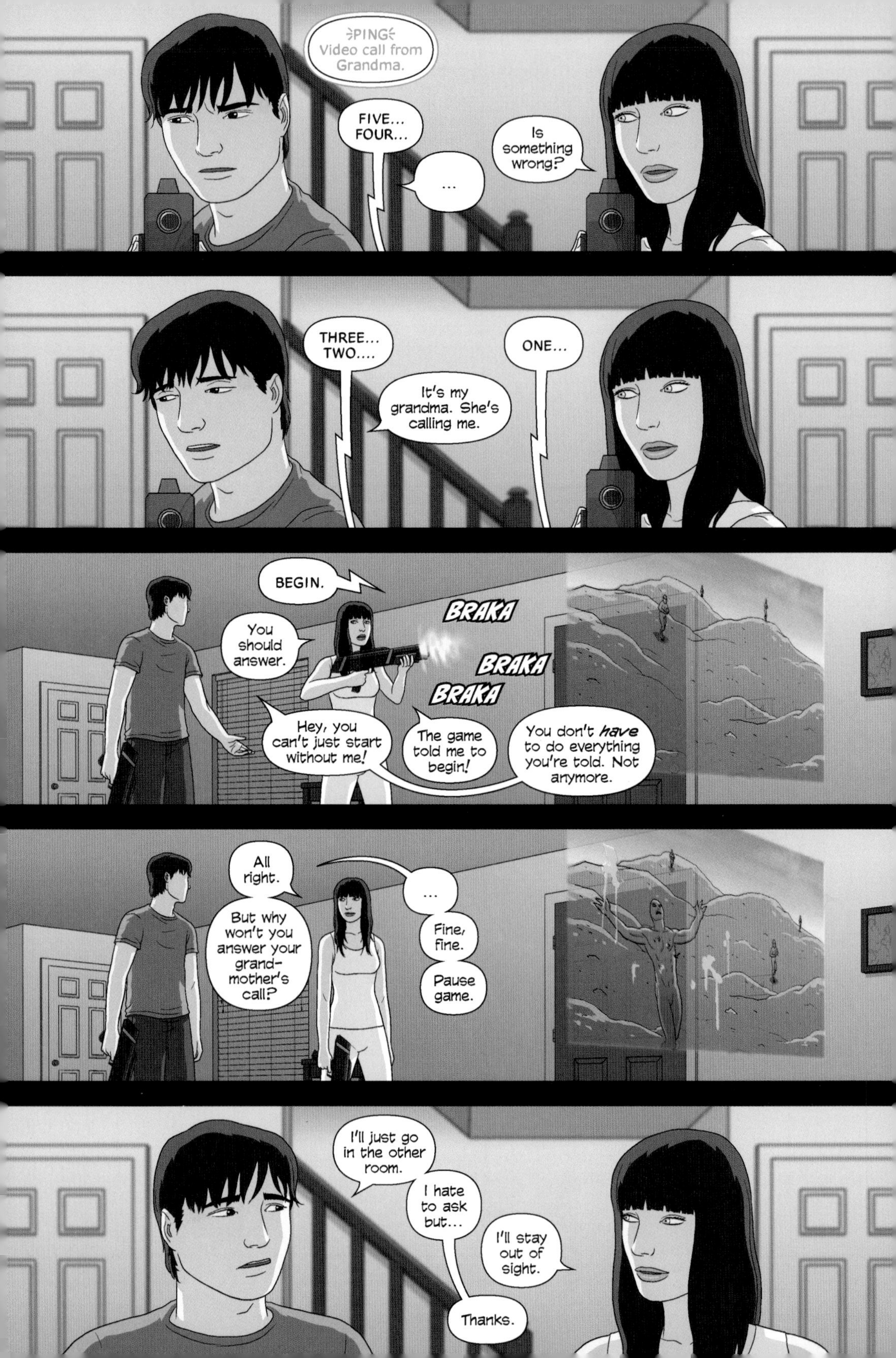

PING
Video call from Grandma.
FIVE... FOUR...
...
Is something wrong?
THREE... TWO....
It's my grandma. She's calling me.
ONE...
BEGIN.
You should answer.
BRAKA
BRAKA
BRAKA
Hey, you can't just start without me!
The game told me to begin!
You don't *have* to do everything you're told. Not anymore.
All right.
But why won't you answer your grand-mother's call?
...
Fine, fine.
Pause game.
I'll just go in the other room.
I hate to ask but...
I'll stay out of sight.
Thanks.

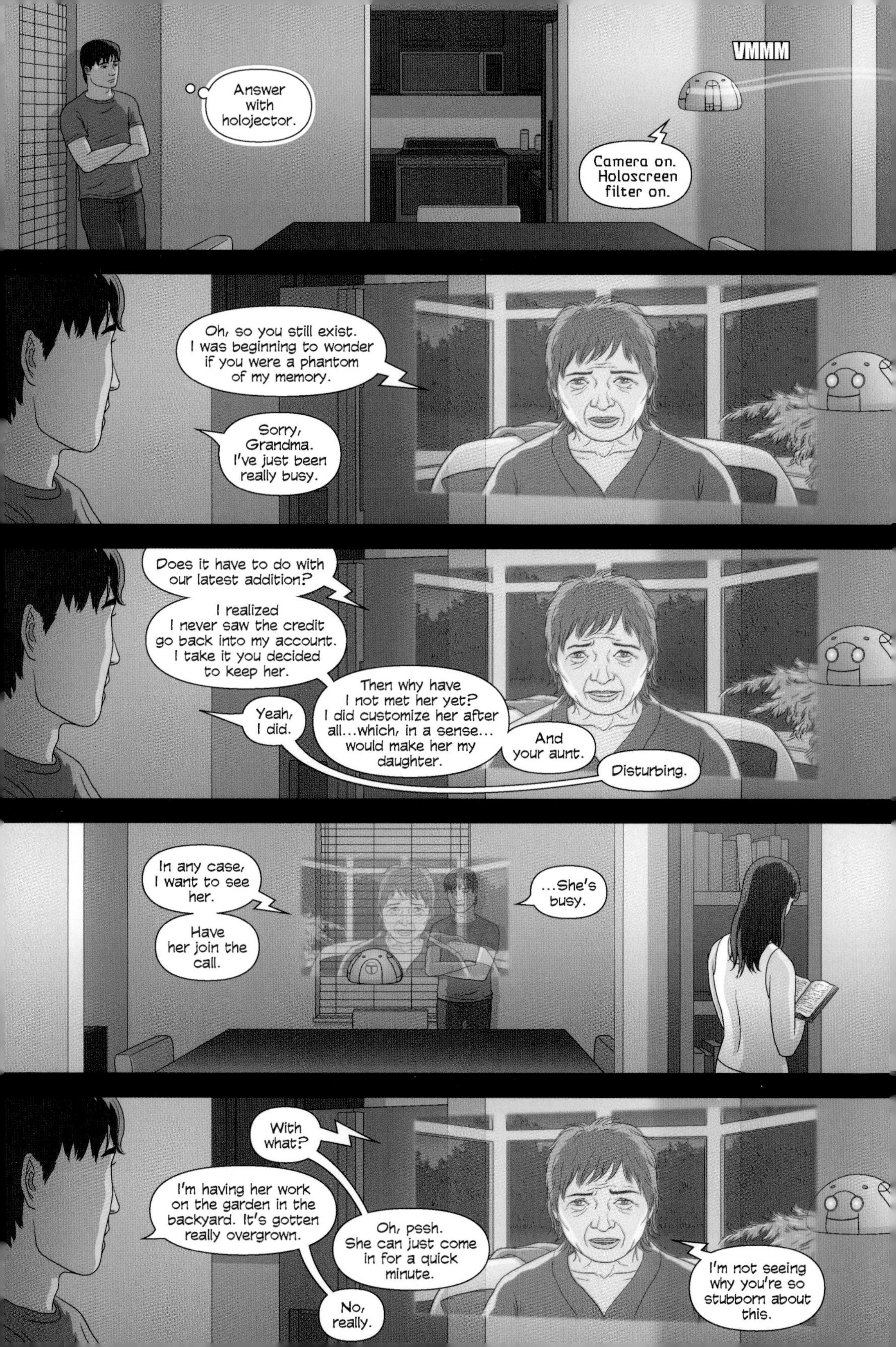
VMMM
Answer with holojector.
Camera on. Holoscreen filter on.
Oh, so you still exist. I was beginning to wonder if you were a phantom of my memory.
Sorry, Grandma. I've just been really busy.
Does it have to do with our latest addition?
I realized I never saw the credit go back into my account. I take it you decided to keep her.
Yeah, I did.
Then why have I not met her yet? I did customize her after all...which, in a sense... would make her my daughter.
And your aunt.
Disturbing.
In any case, I want to see her.
Have her join the call.
...She's busy.
With what?
I'm having her work on the garden in the backyard. It's gotten really overgrown.
Oh, pssh. She can just come in for a quick minute.
No, really.
I'm not seeing why you're so stubborn about this.

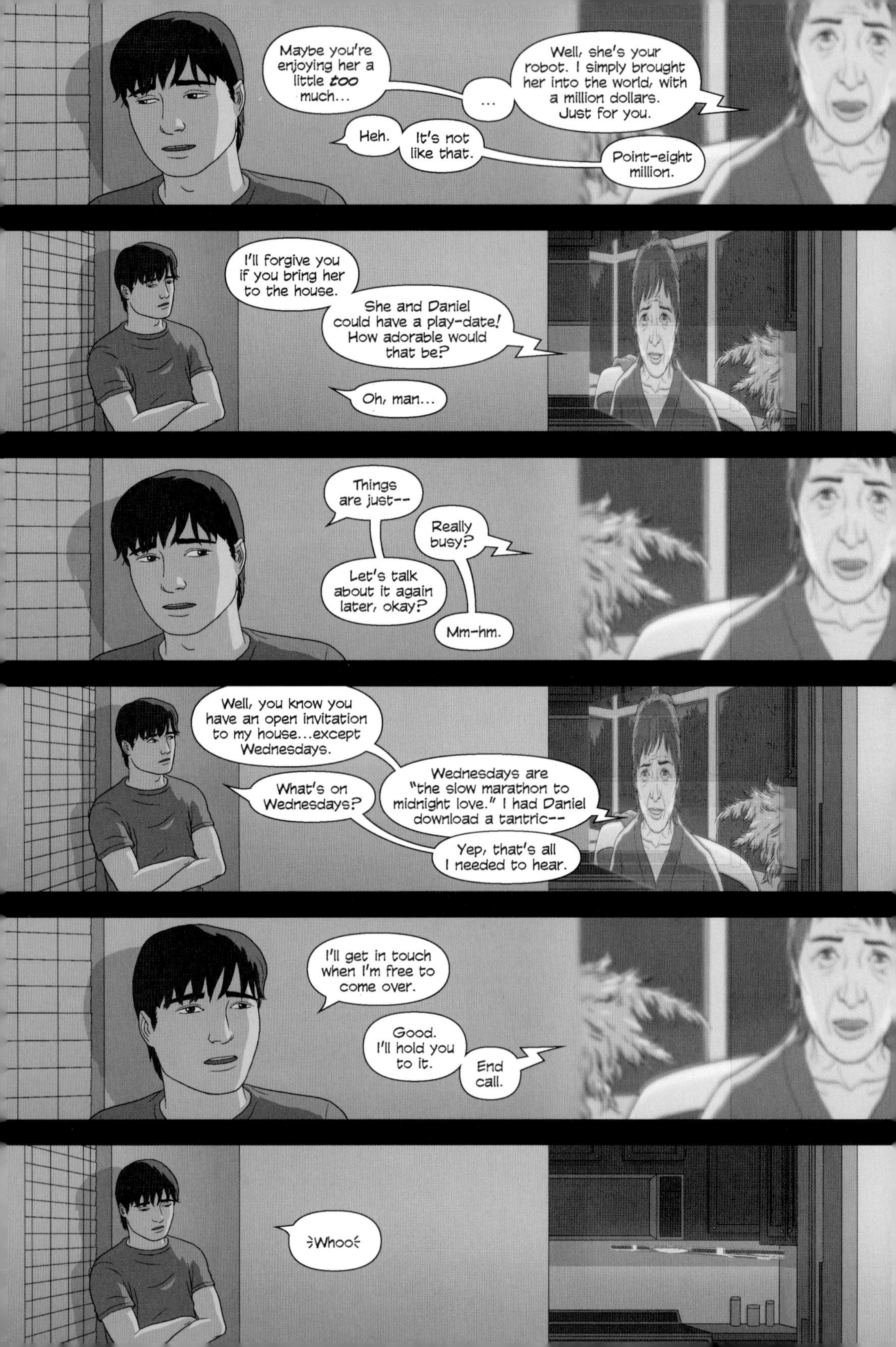
Maybe you're enjoying her a little *too* much...
...
Well, she's your robot. I simply brought her into the world, with a million dollars. Just for you.
Heh.
It's not like that.
Point-eight million.
I'll forgive you if you bring her to the house.
She and Daniel could have a play-date! How adorable would that be?
Oh, man...
Things are just--
Really busy?
Let's talk about it again later, okay?
Mm-hm.
Well, you know you have an open invitation to my house...except Wednesdays.
What's on Wednesdays?
Wednesdays are "the slow marathon to midnight love." I had Daniel download a tantric--
Yep, that's all I needed to hear.
I'll get in touch when I'm free to come over.
Good. I'll hold you to it.
End call.
Whoo

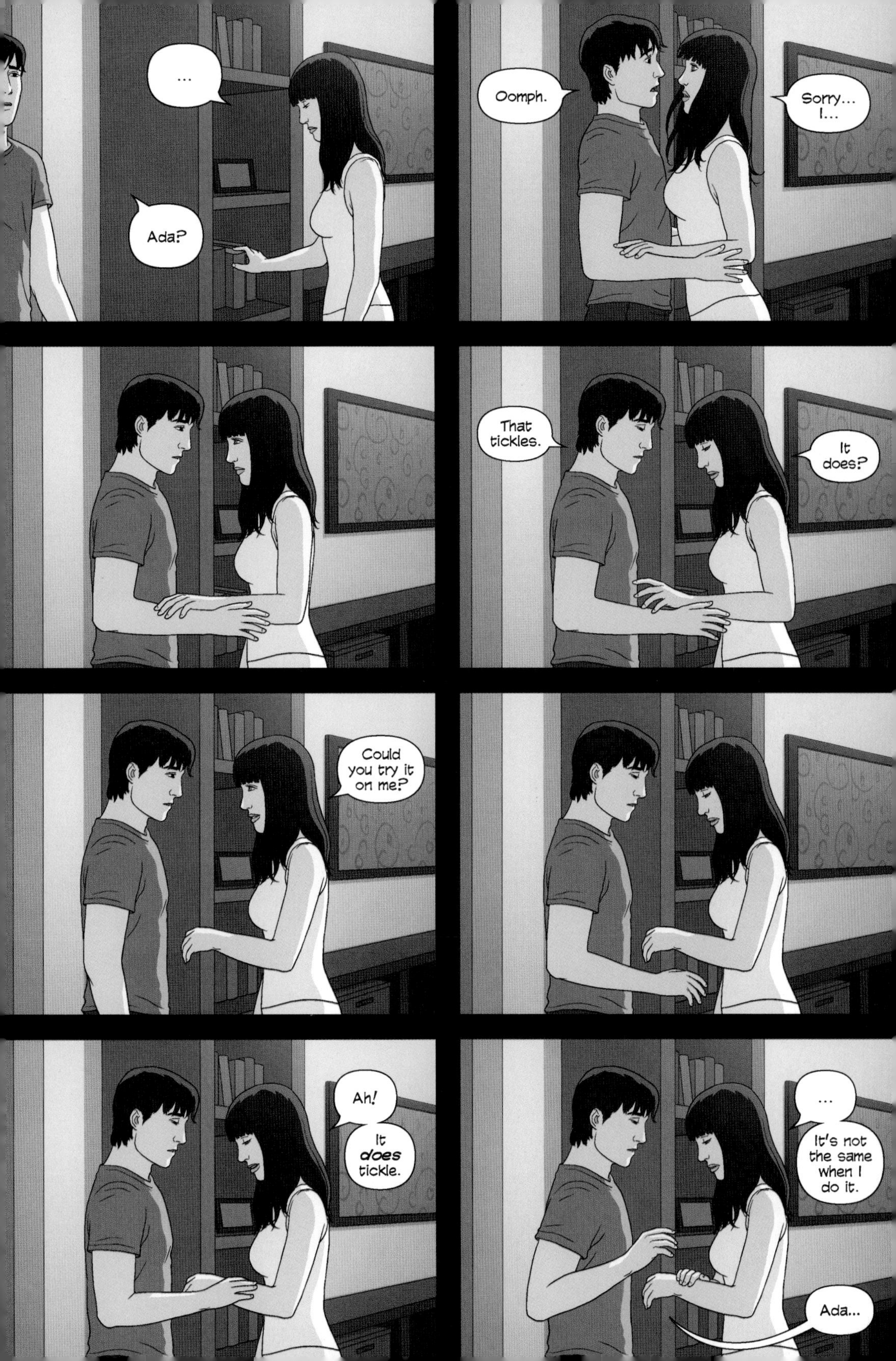
...
Ada?
Oomph.
Sorry... I...
That tickles.
It does?
Could you try it on me?
Ah!
It *does* tickle.
...
It's not the same when I do it.
Ada...

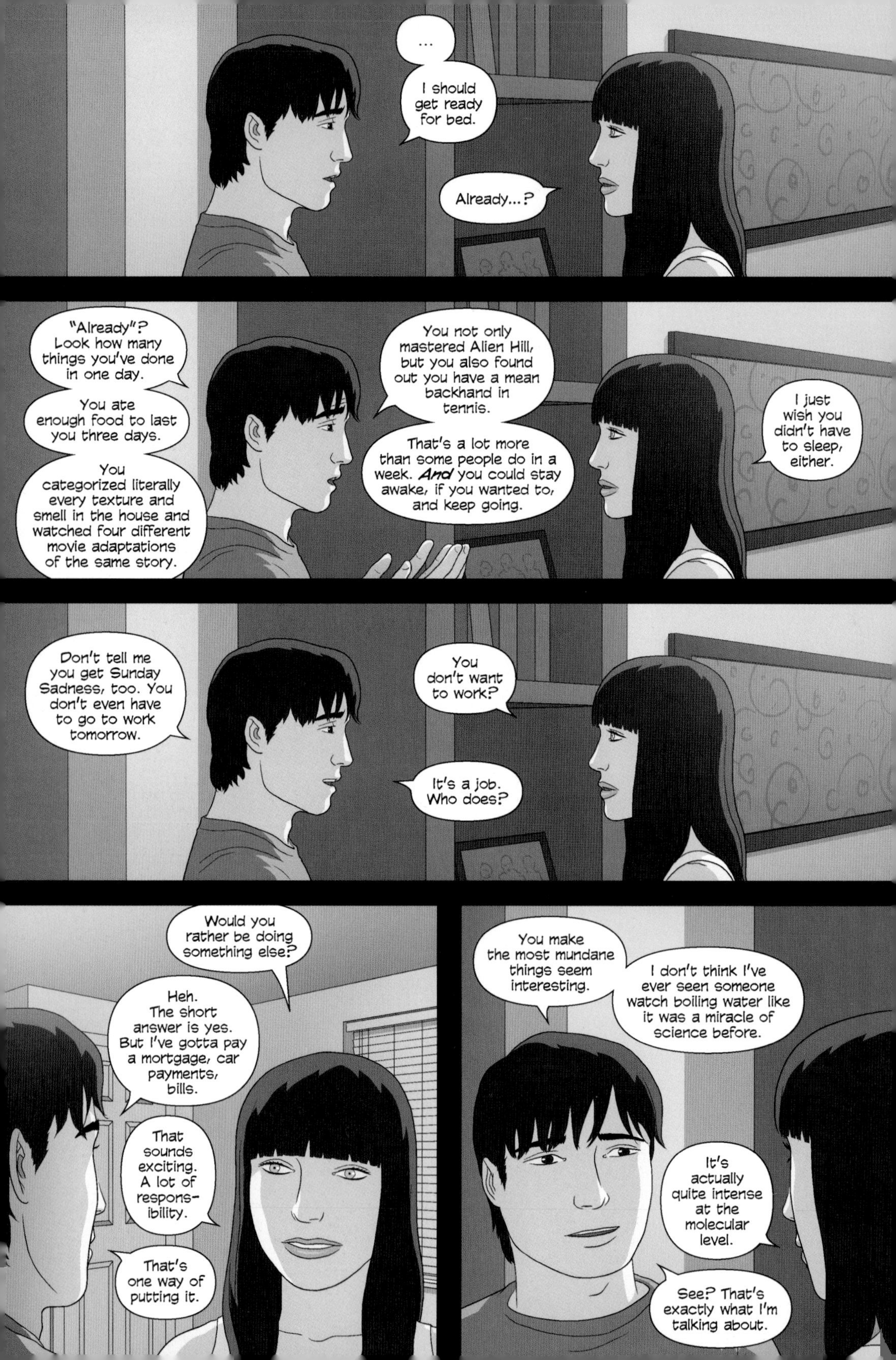
...
I should get ready for bed.
Already...?
"Already"? Look how many things you've done in one day.
You ate enough food to last you three days.
You categorized literally every texture and smell in the house and watched four different movie adaptations of the same story.
You not only mastered Alien Hill, but you also found out you have a mean backhand in tennis.
That's a lot more than some people do in a week. ***And*** you could stay awake, if you wanted to, and keep going.
I just wish you didn't have to sleep, either.
Don't tell me you get Sunday Sadness, too. You don't even have to go to work tomorrow.
You don't want to work?
It's a job. Who does?
Would you rather be doing something else?
Heh. The short answer is yes. But I've gotta pay a mortgage, car payments, bills.
That sounds exciting. A lot of respons-ibility.
That's one way of putting it.
You make the most mundane things seem interesting.
I don't think I've ever seen someone watch boiling water like it was a miracle of science before.
It's actually quite intense at the molecular level.
See? That's exactly what I'm talking about.

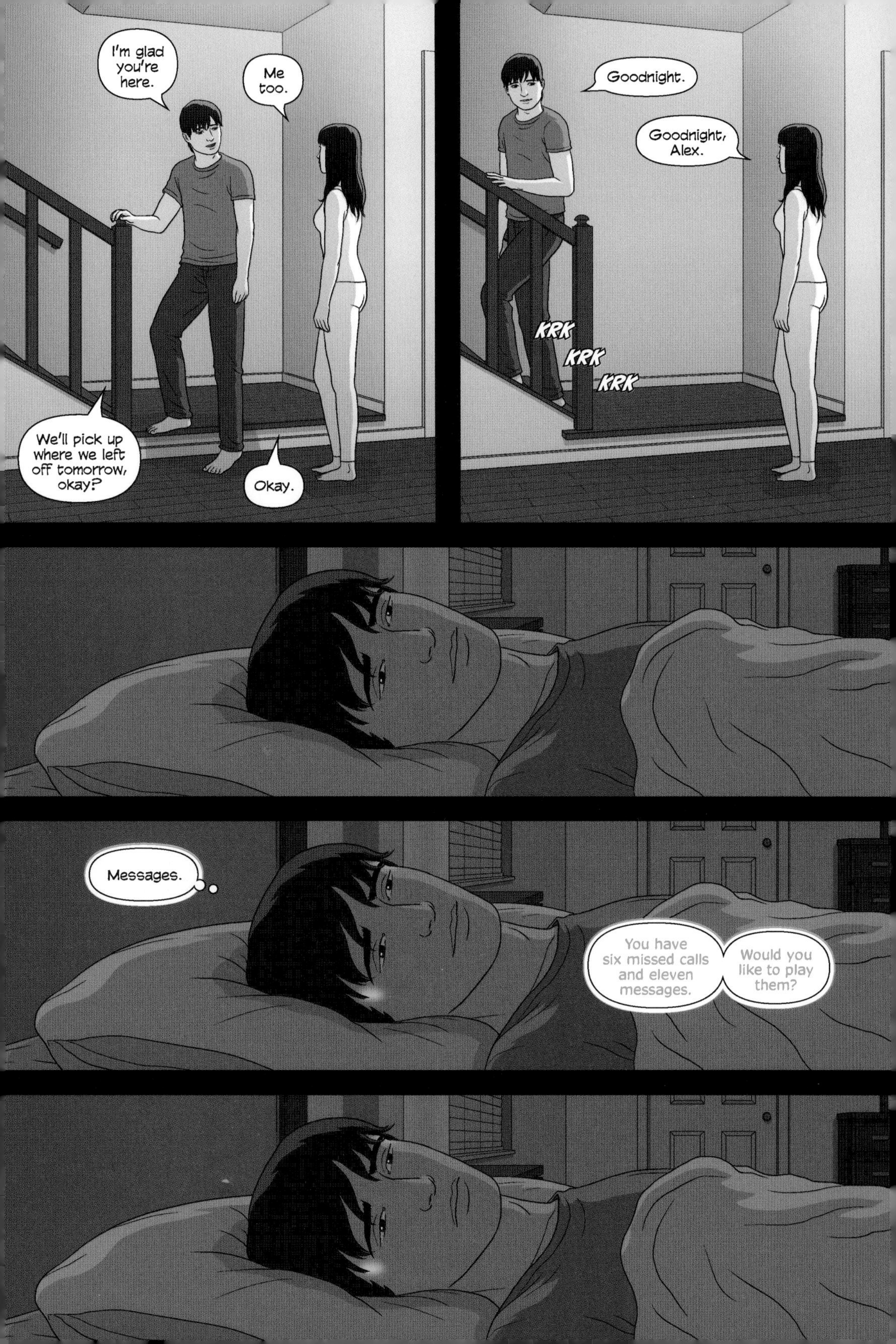

I'm glad you're here.
Me too.
We'll pick up where we left off tomorrow, okay?
Okay.
Goodnight.
Goodnight, Alex.
KRK
KRK
KRK
Messages.
You have six missed calls and eleven messages.
Would you like to play them?

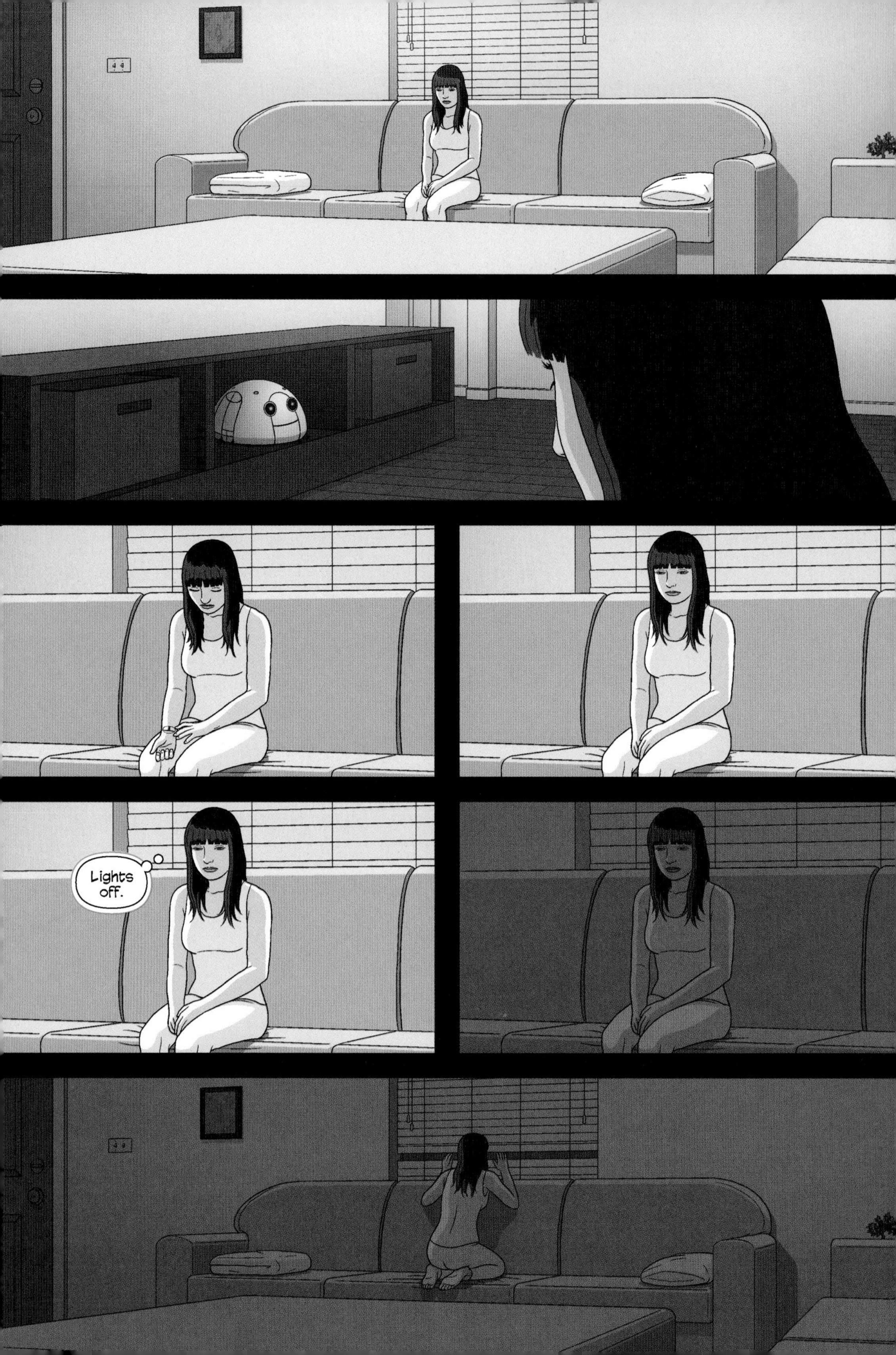
Lights off.

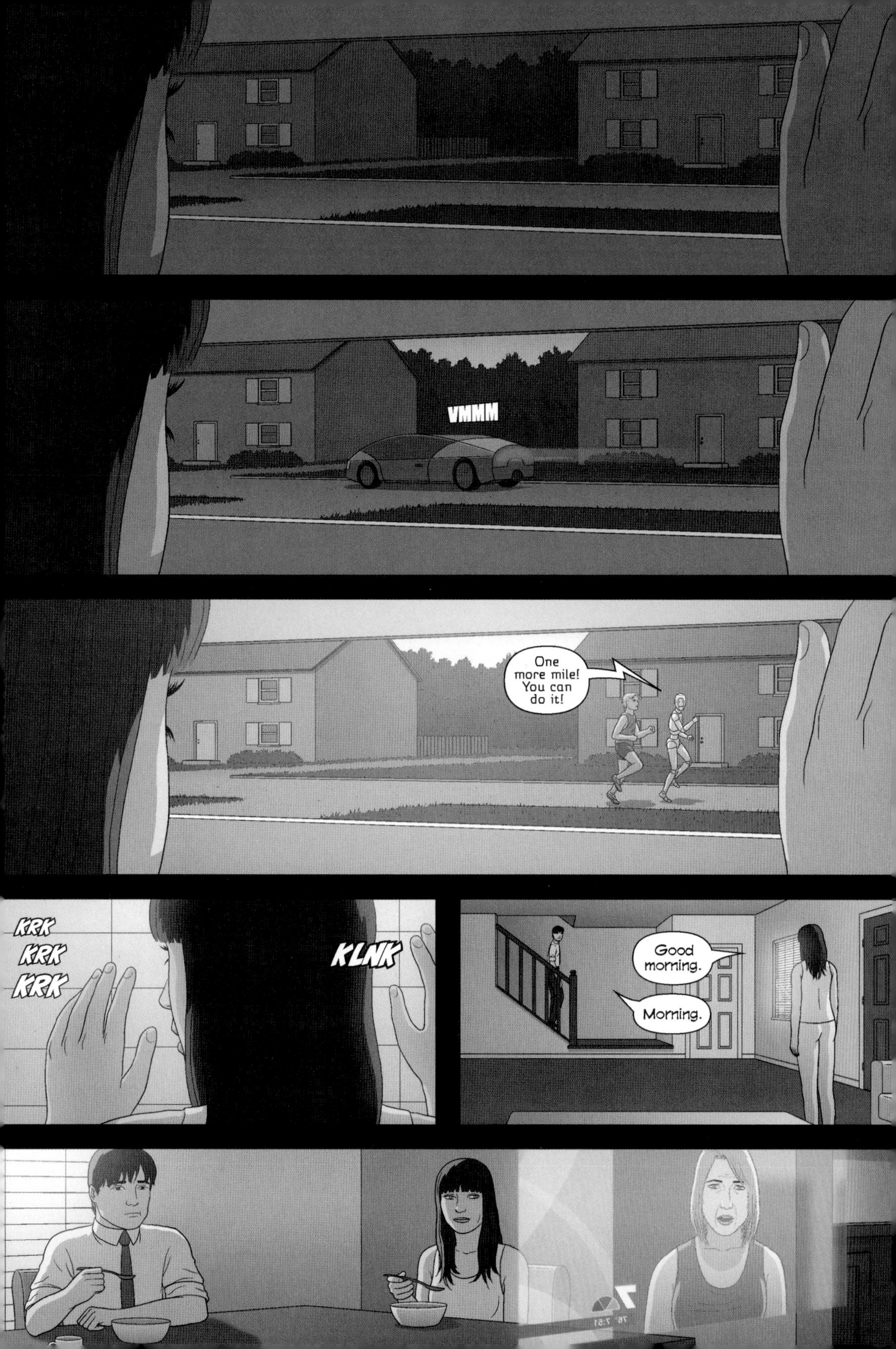
VMMM
One more mile! You can do it!
KRK
KRK
KRK
KLNK
Good morning.
Morning.

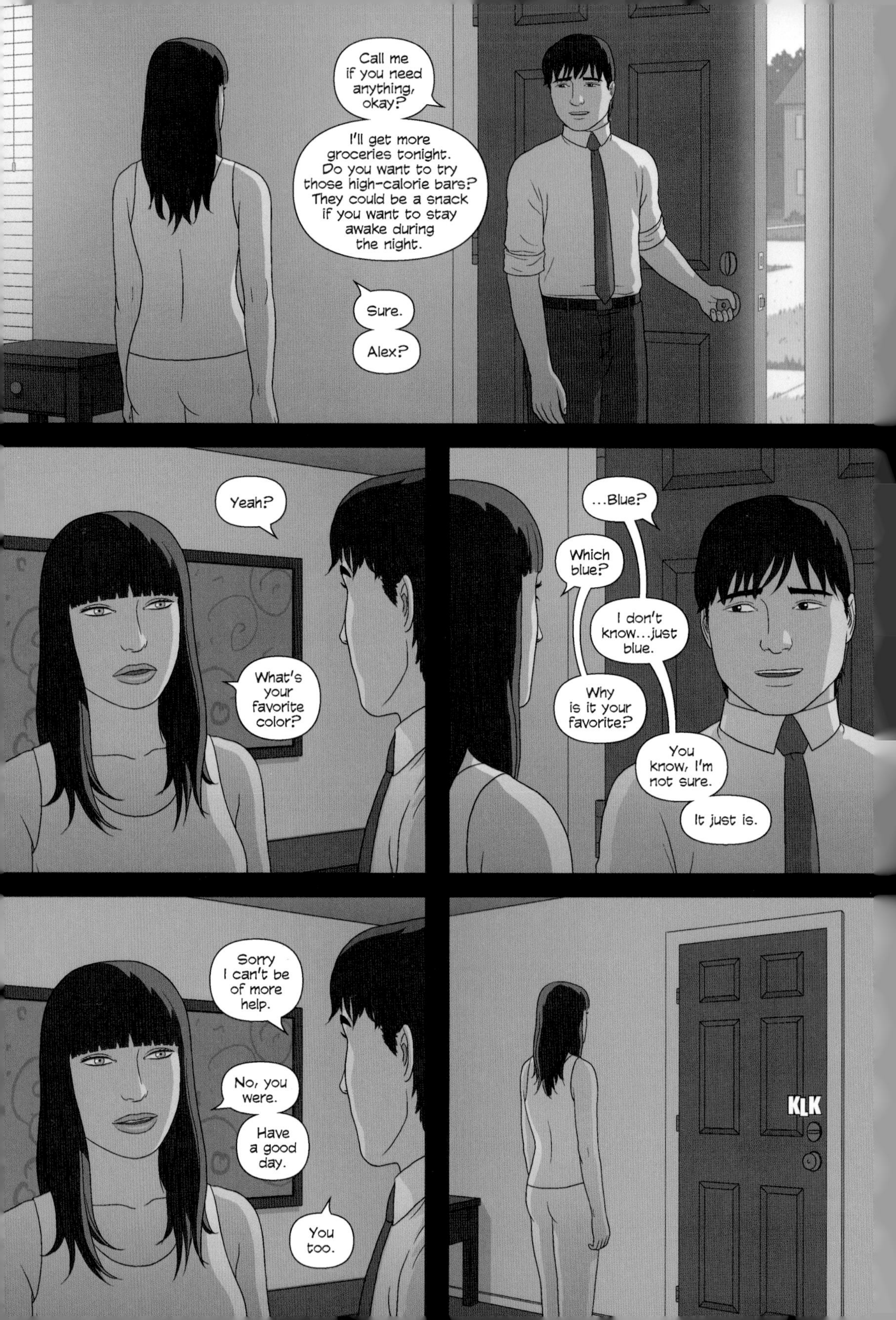
Call me if you need anything, okay?
I'll get more groceries tonight. Do you want to try those high-calorie bars? They could be a snack if you want to stay awake during the night.
Sure.
Alex?
Yeah?
What's your favorite color?
...Blue?
Which blue?
I don't know...just blue.
Why is it your favorite?
You know, I'm not sure.
It just is.
Sorry I can't be of more help.
No, you were.
Have a good day.
You too.
KLK

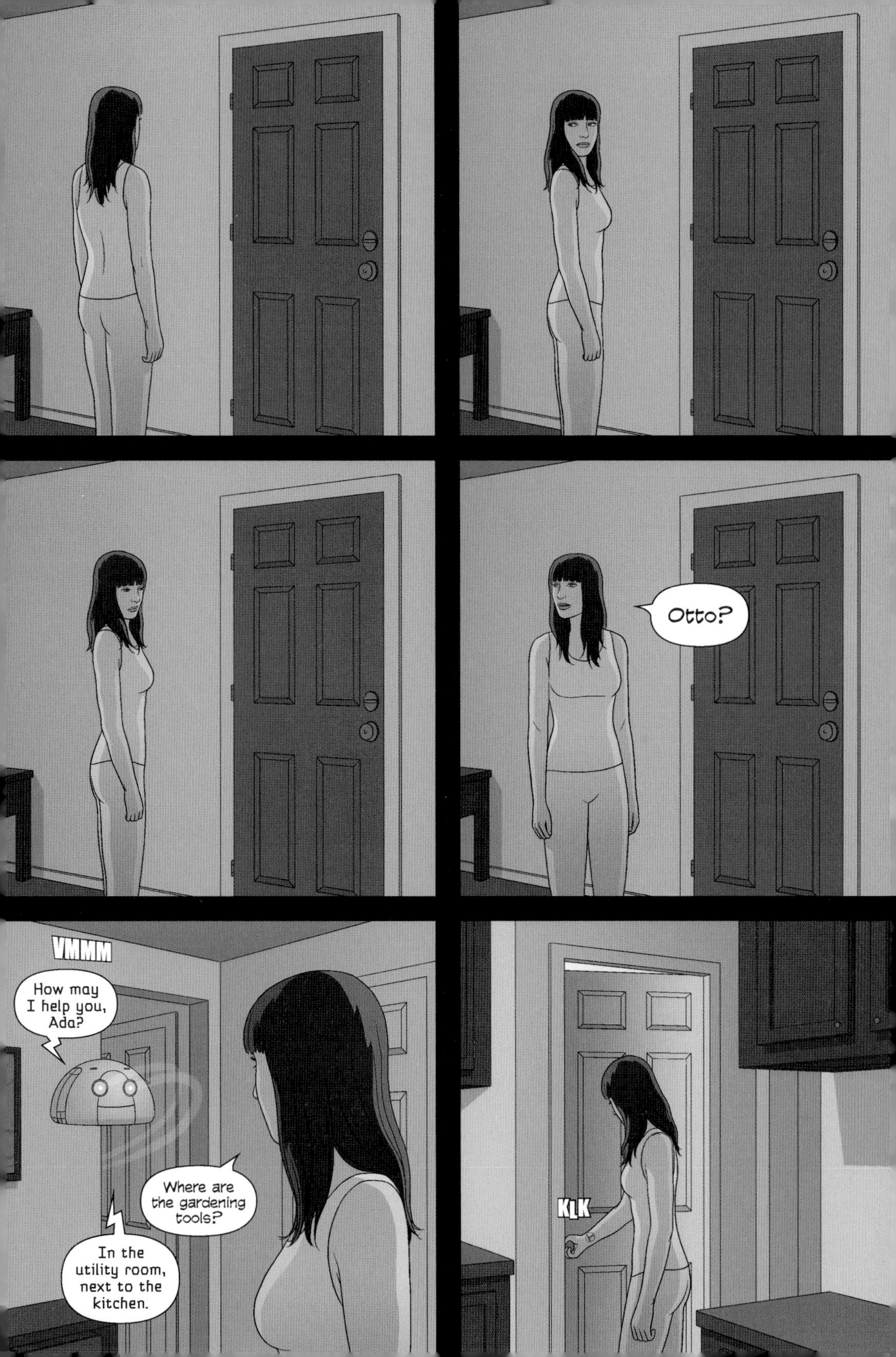
Otto?
VMMM
How may I help you, Ada?
Where are the gardening tools?
In the utility room, next to the kitchen.
KLK

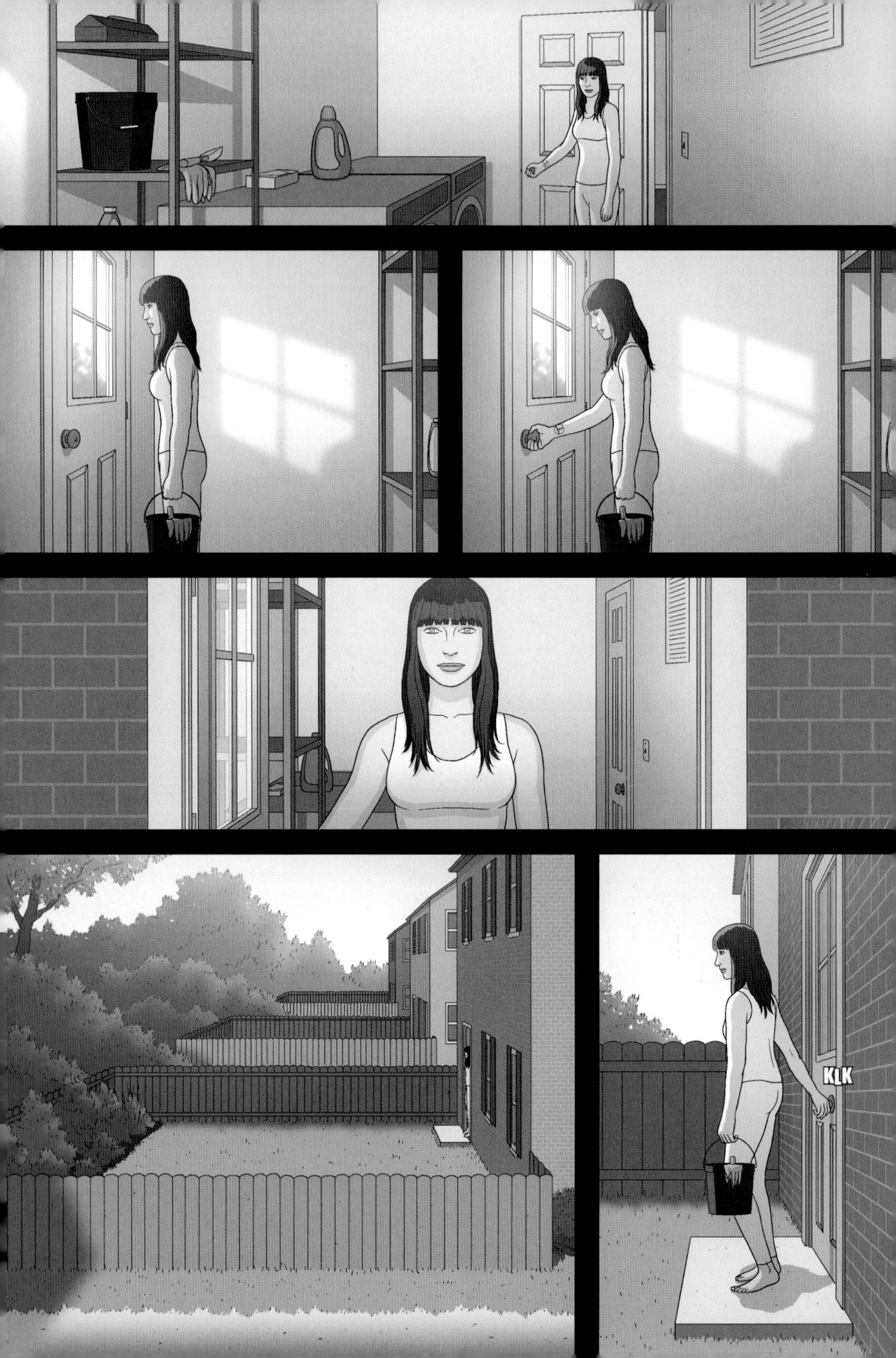
KLK

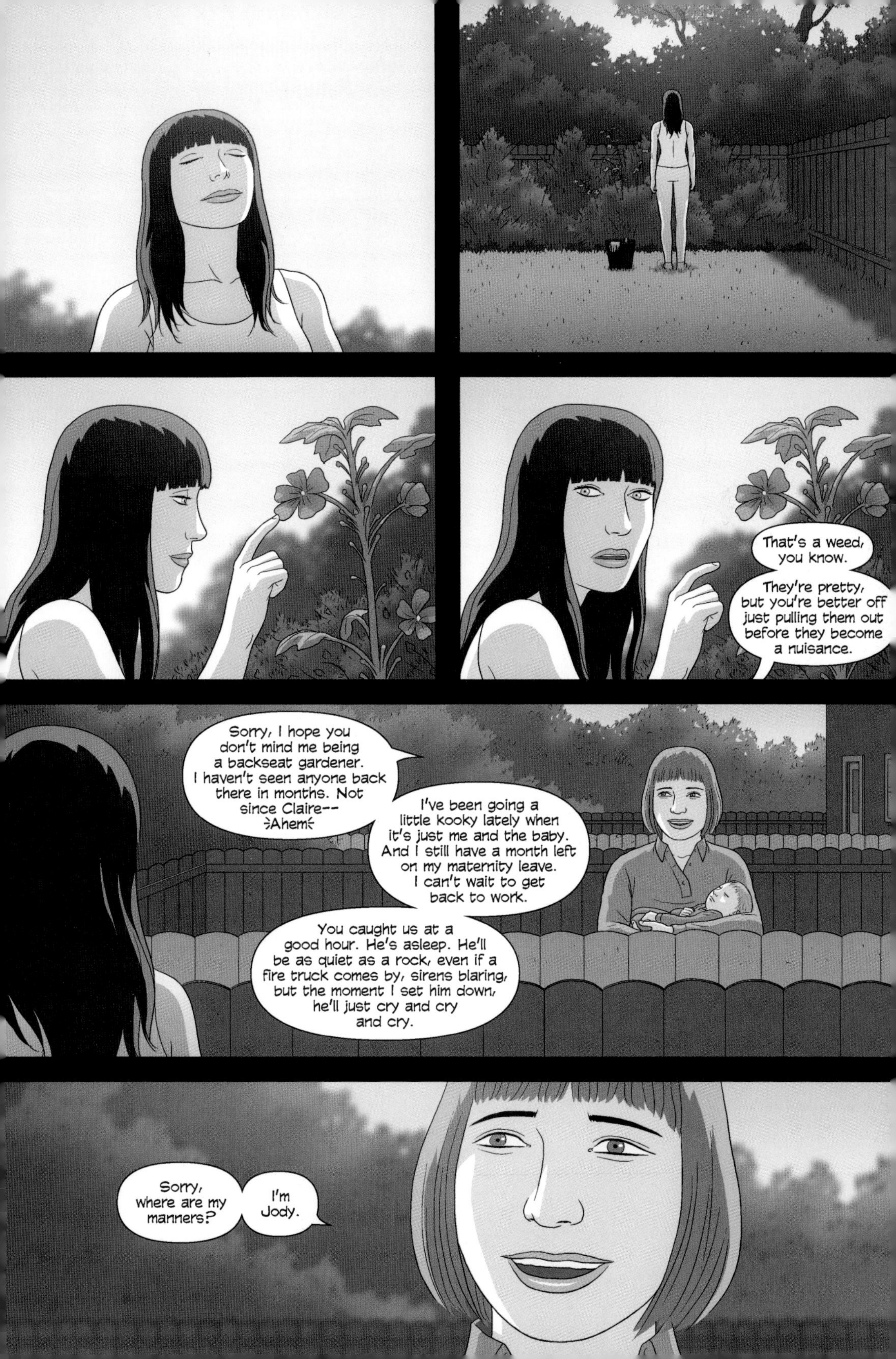
That's a weed, you know.
They're pretty, but you're better off just pulling them out before they become a nuisance.
Sorry, I hope you don't mind me being a backseat gardener. I haven't seen anyone back there in months. Not since Claire-- ≶Ahem≷
I've been going a little kooky lately when it's just me and the baby. And I still have a month left on my maternity leave. I can't wait to get back to work.
You caught us at a good hour. He's asleep. He'll be as quiet as a rock, even if a fire truck comes by, sirens blaring, but the moment I set him down, he'll just cry and cry and cry.
Sorry, where are my manners?
I'm Jody.

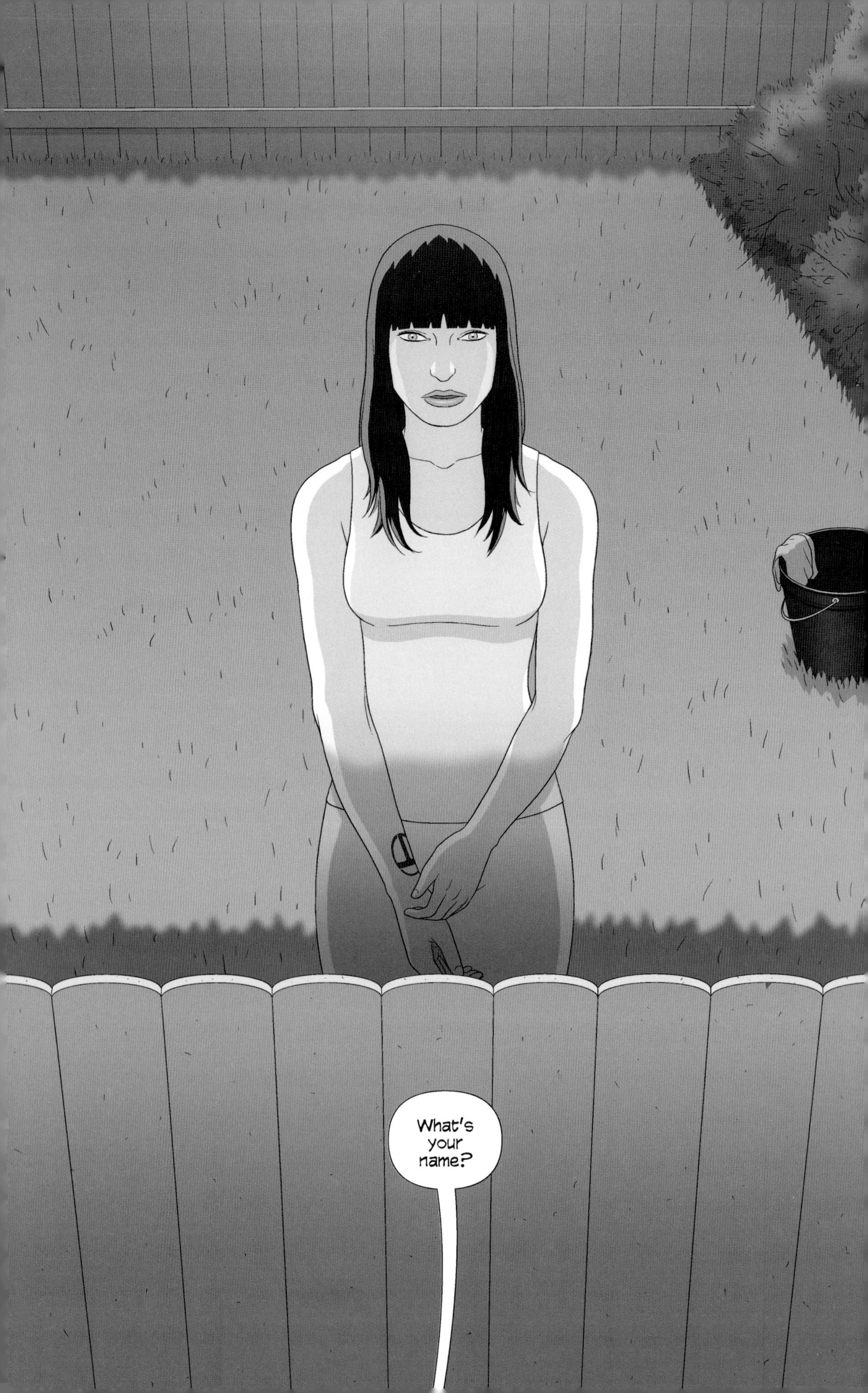
What's your name?

7

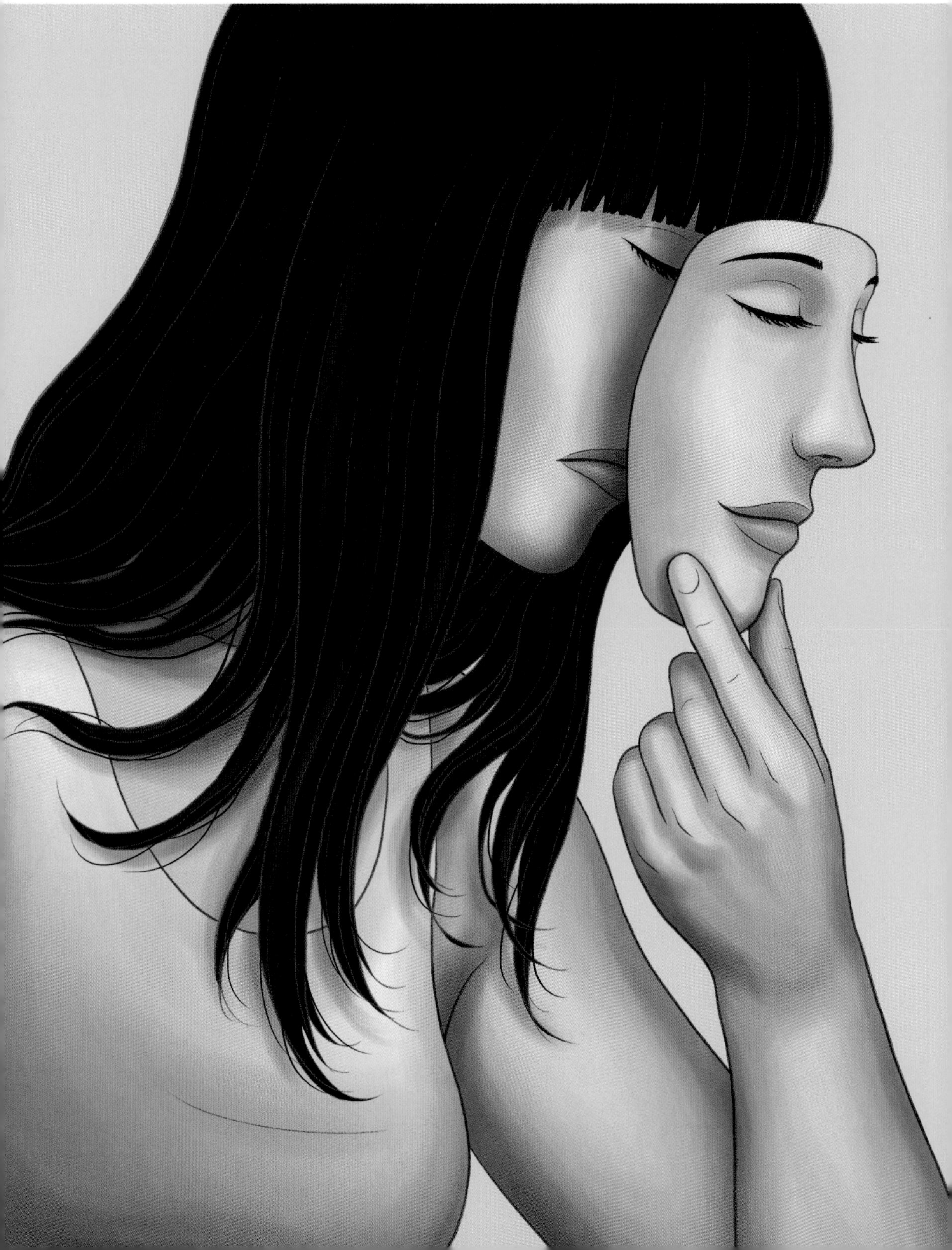

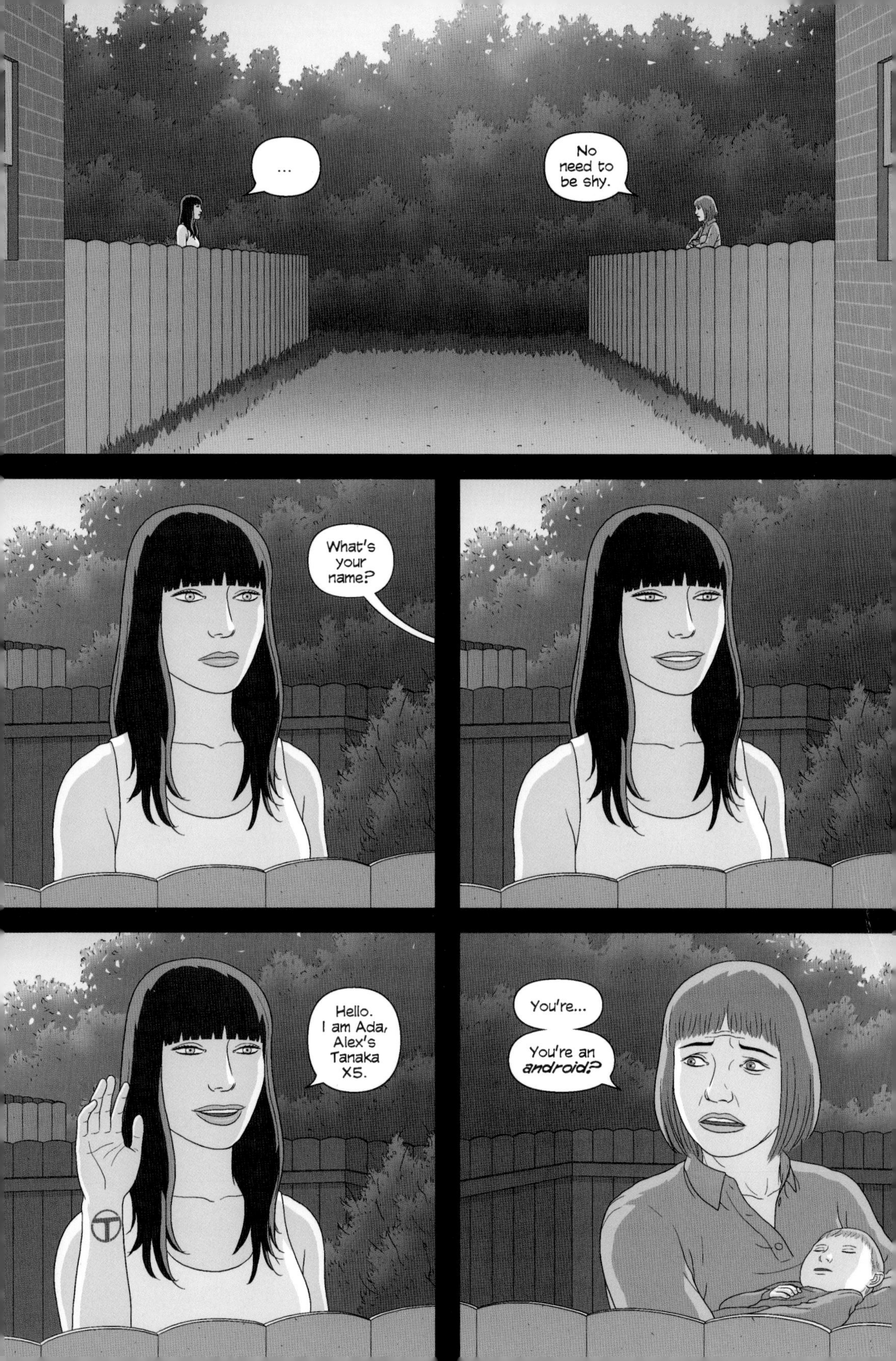
...
No need to be shy.
What's your name?
Hello. I am Ada, Alex's Tanaka X5.
You're...
You're an *android?*

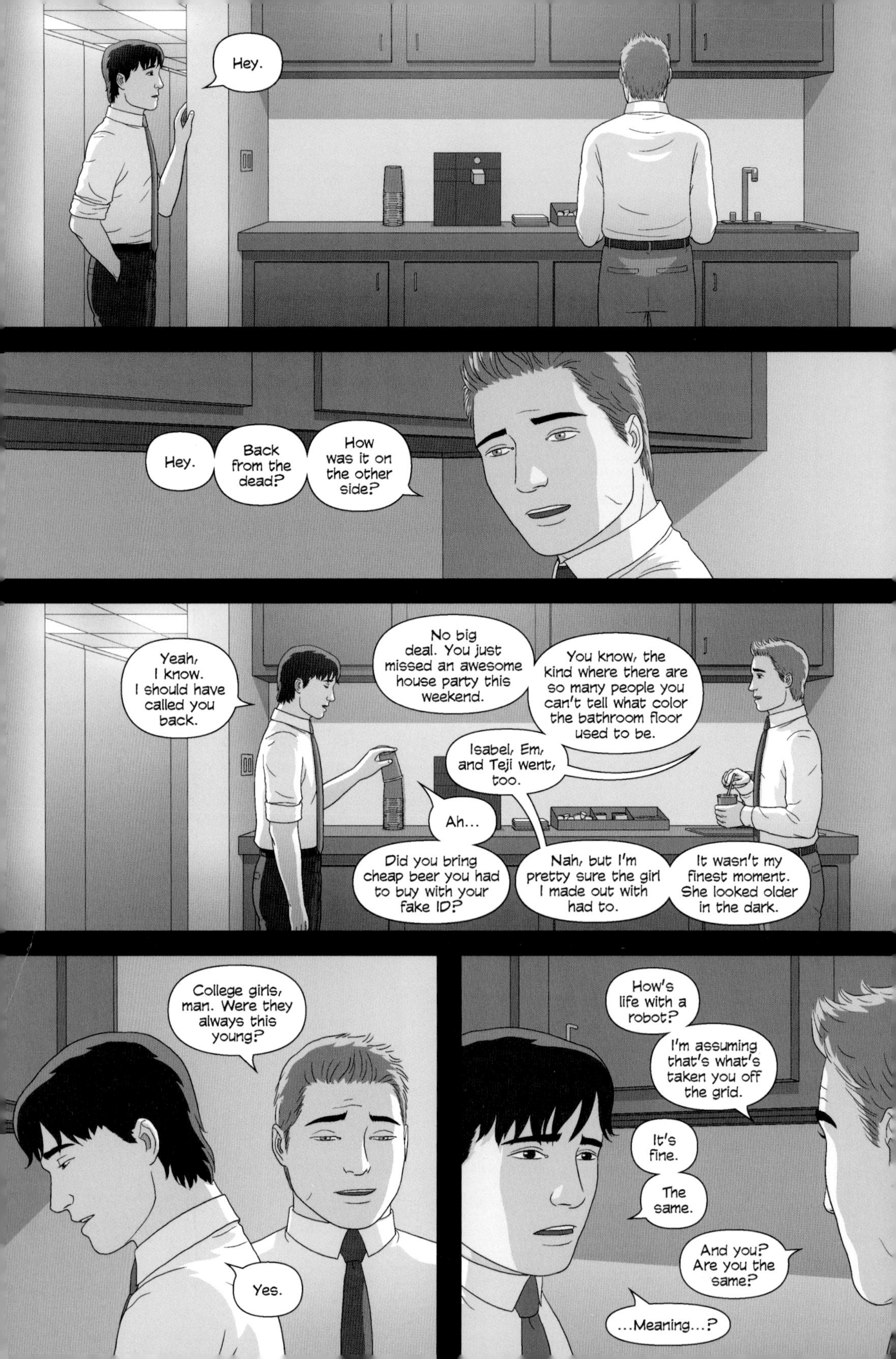
Hey.
Hey.
Back from the dead?
How was it on the other side?
Yeah, I know. I should have called you back.
No big deal. You just missed an awesome house party this weekend.
You know, the kind where there are so many people you can't tell what color the bathroom floor used to be.
Isabel, Em, and Teji went, too.
Ah...
Did you bring cheap beer you had to buy with your fake ID?
Nah, but I'm pretty sure the girl I made out with had to.
It wasn't my finest moment. She looked older in the dark.
College girls, man. Were they always this young?
Yes.
How's life with a robot?
I'm assuming that's what's taken you off the grid.
It's fine.
The same.
And you? Are you the same?
...Meaning...?

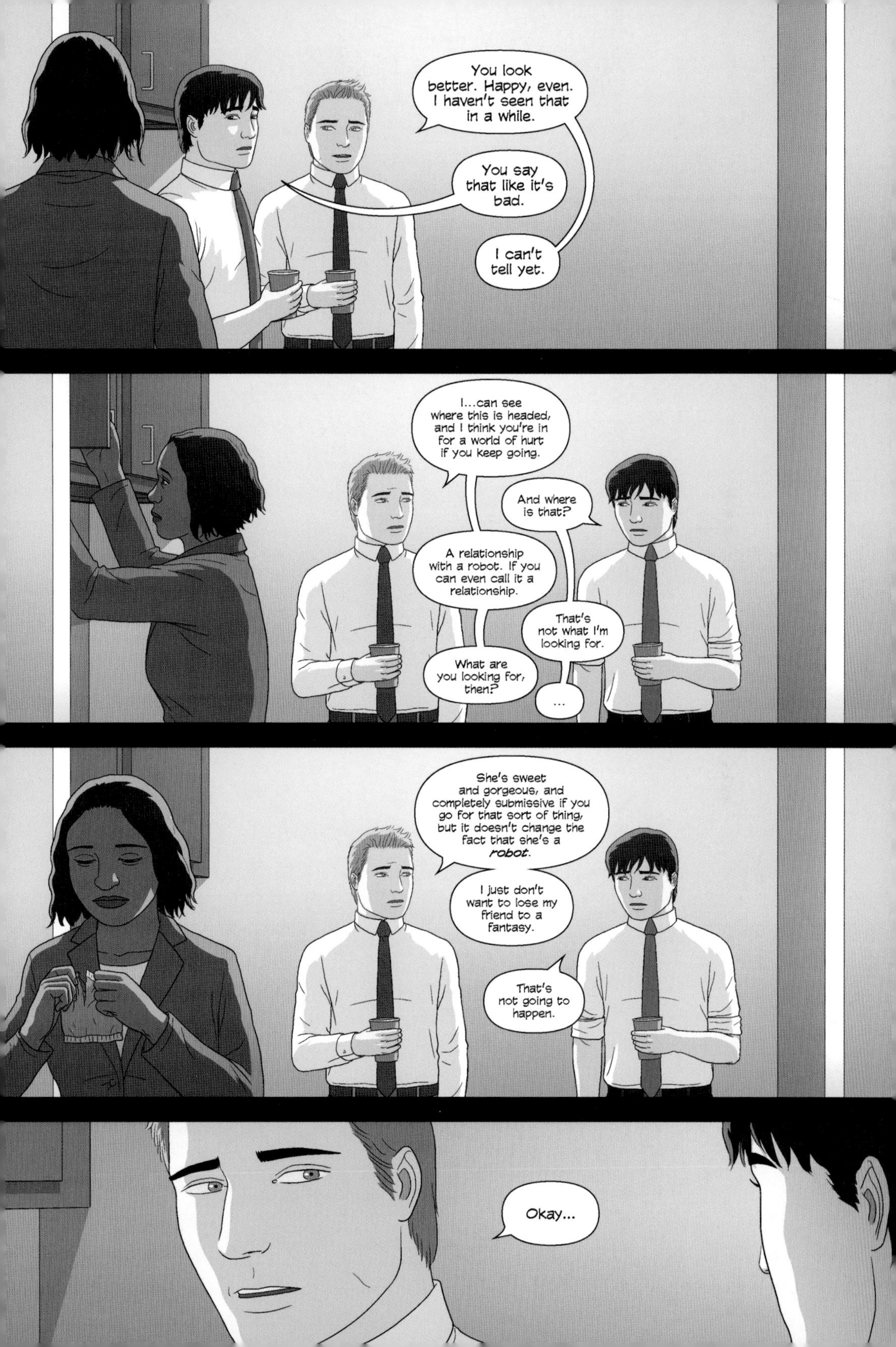
You look better. Happy, even. I haven't seen that in a while.
You say that like it's bad.
I can't tell yet.
I...can see where this is headed, and I think you're in for a world of hurt if you keep going.
And where is that?
A relationship with a robot. If you can even call it a relationship.
That's not what I'm looking for.
What are you looking for, then?
...
She's sweet and gorgeous, and completely submissive if you go for that sort of thing, but it doesn't change the fact that she's a *robot*.
I just don't want to lose my friend to a fantasy.
That's not going to happen.
Okay...

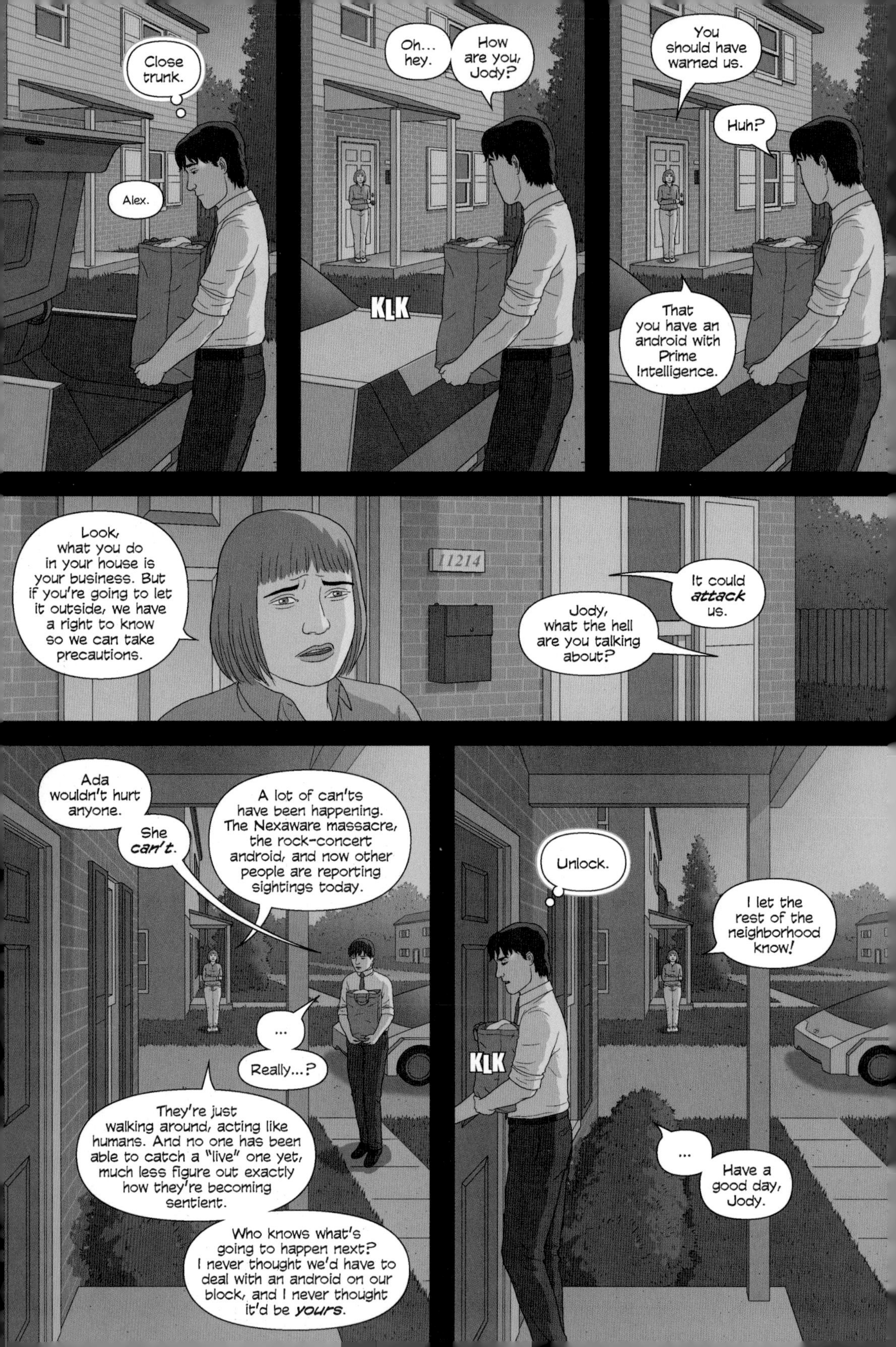
Close trunk.
Alex.
Oh... hey.
How are you, Jody?
KLK
You should have warned us.
Huh?
That you have an android with Prime Intelligence.
Look, what you do in your house is your business. But if you're going to let it outside, we have a right to know so we can take precautions.
11214
It could *attack* us.
Jody, what the hell are you talking about?
Ada wouldn't hurt anyone.
She *can't*.
A lot of can'ts have been happening. The Nexaware massacre, the rock-concert android, and now other people are reporting sightings today.
...
Really...?
They're just walking around, acting like humans. And no one has been able to catch a "live" one yet, much less figure out exactly how they're becoming sentient.
Who knows what's going to happen next? I never thought we'd have to deal with an android on our block, and I never thought it'd be *yours*.
Unlock.
KLK
I let the rest of the neighborhood know!
...
Have a good day, Jody.

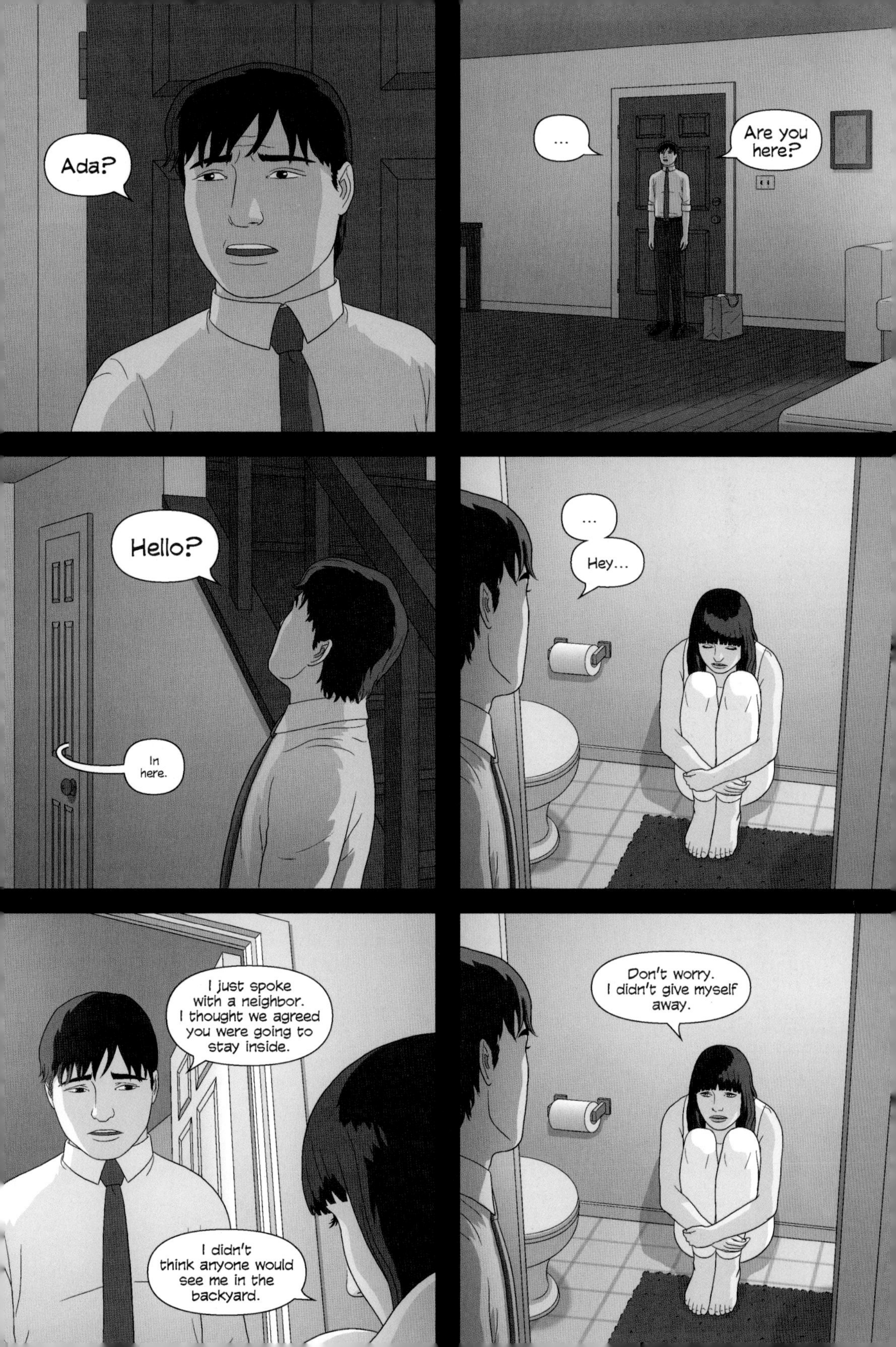
Ada?
...
Are you here?
Hello?
In here.
...
Hey...
I just spoke with a neighbor. I thought we agreed you were going to stay inside.
I didn't think anyone would see me in the backyard.
Don't worry. I didn't give myself away.

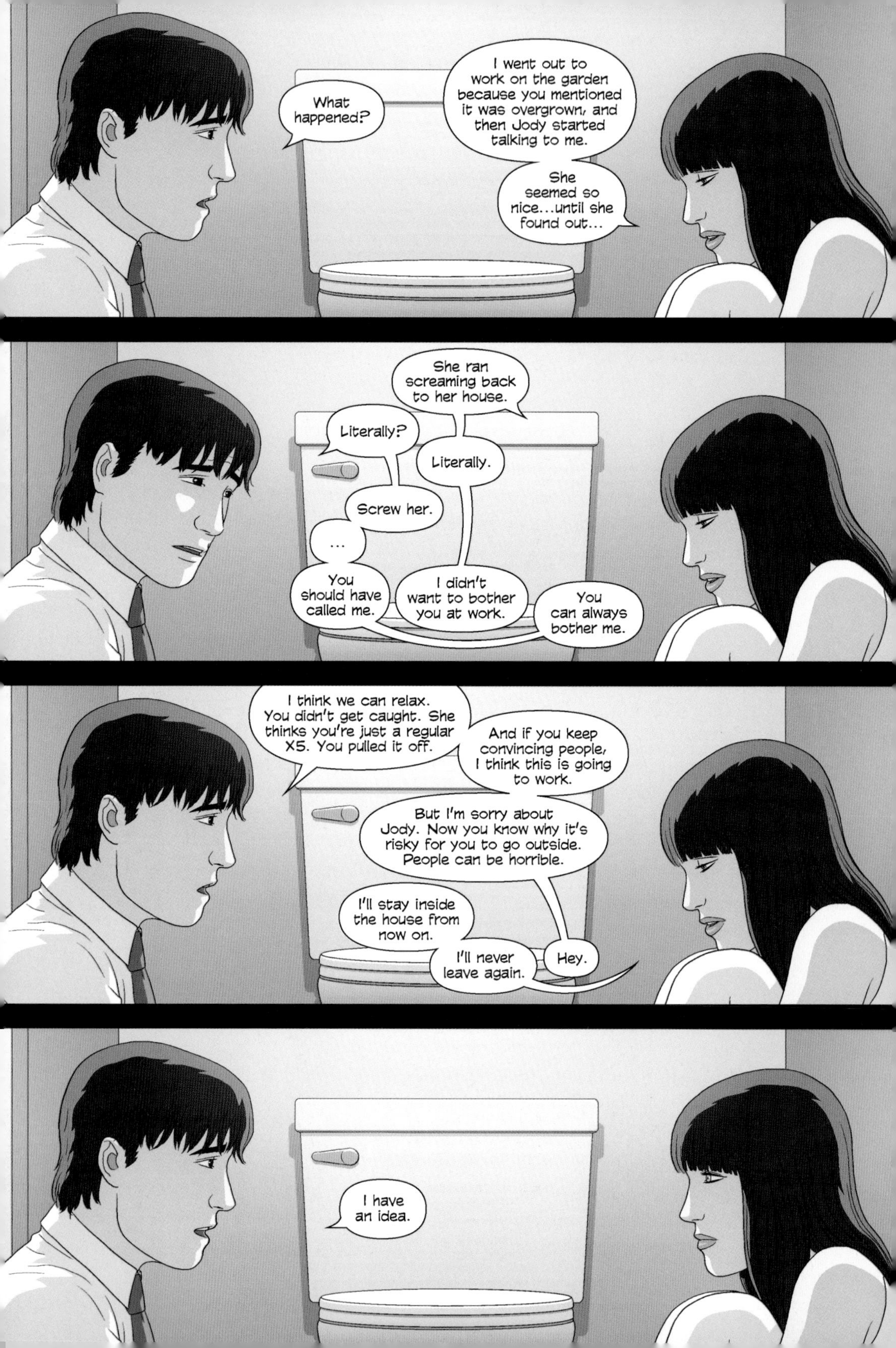
What happened?
I went out to work on the garden because you mentioned it was overgrown, and then Jody started talking to me.
She seemed so nice...until she found out...
She ran screaming back to her house.
Literally?
Literally.
Screw her.
...
You should have called me.
I didn't want to bother you at work.
You can always bother me.
I think we can relax. You didn't get caught. She thinks you're just a regular X5. You pulled it off.
And if you keep convincing people, I think this is going to work.
But I'm sorry about Jody. Now you know why it's risky for you to go outside. People can be horrible.
I'll stay inside the house from now on.
I'll never leave again.
Hey.
I have an idea.

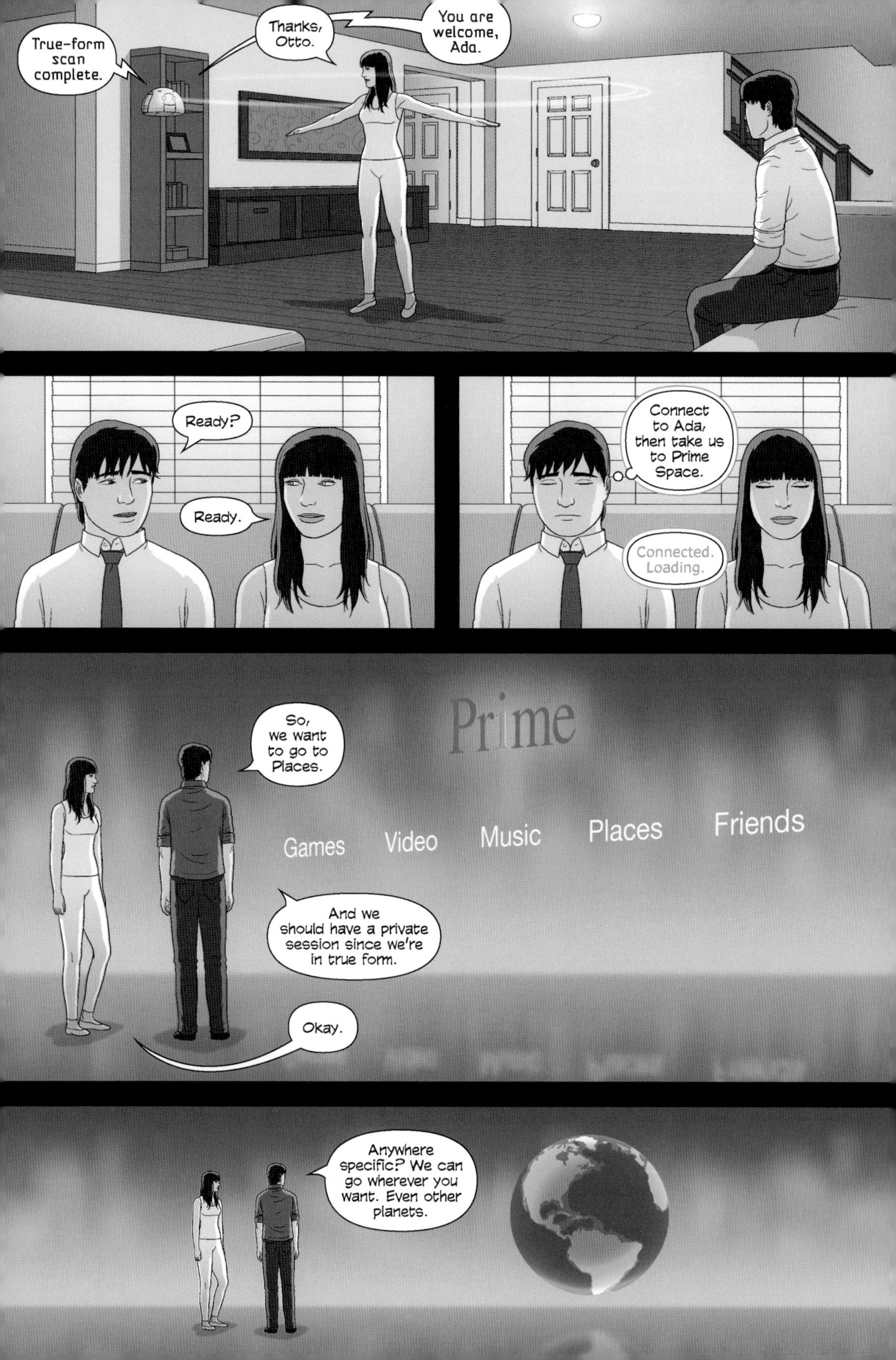
True-form scan complete.
Thanks, Otto.
You are welcome, Ada.
Ready?
Ready.
Connect to Ada, then take us to Prime Space.
Connected. Loading.
Prime
So, we want to go to Places.
Games
Video
Music
Places
Friends
And we should have a private session since we're in true form.
Okay.
Anywhere specific? We can go wherever you want. Even other planets.

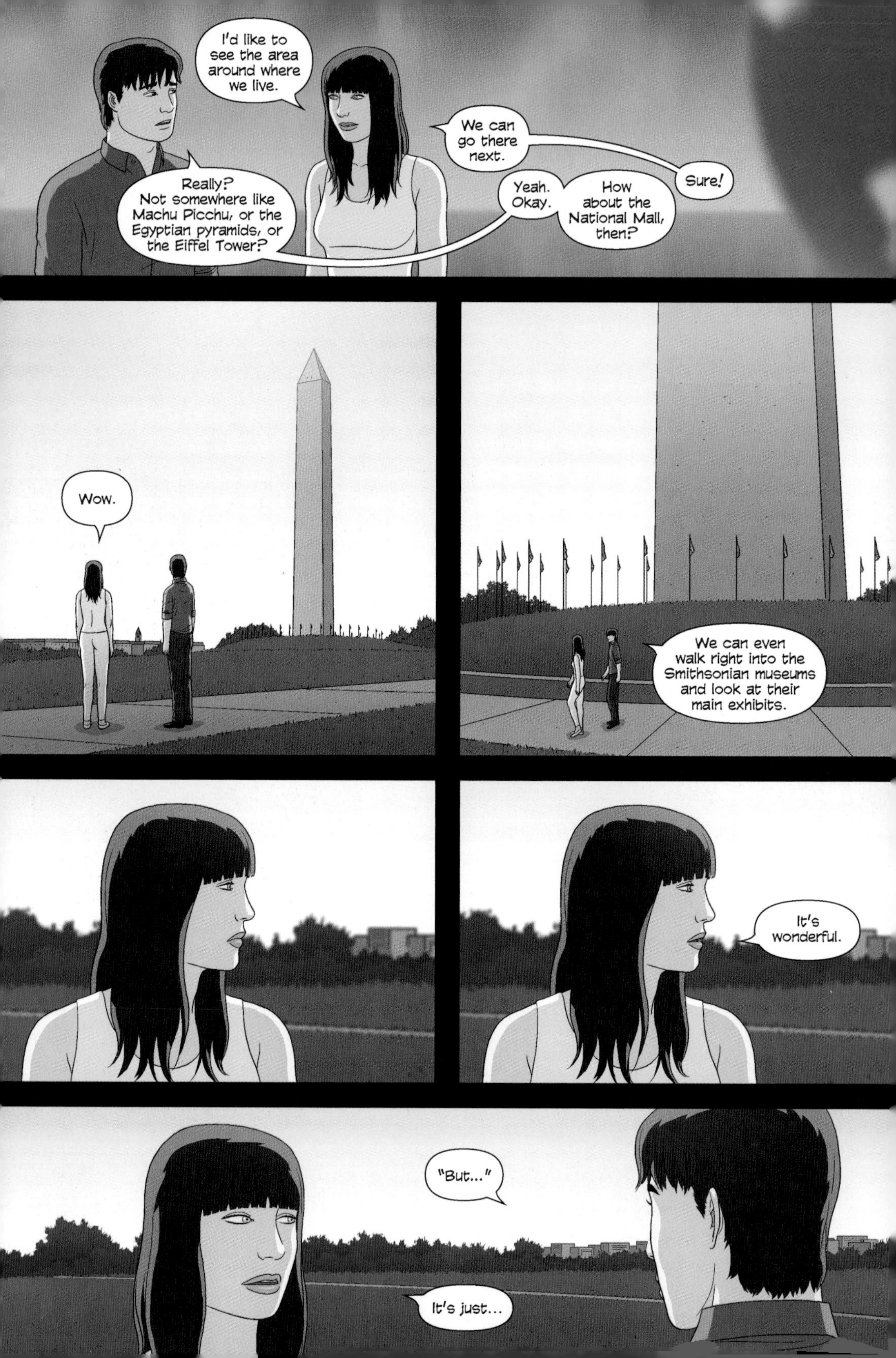
I'd like to see the area around where we live.
Really? Not somewhere like Machu Picchu, or the Egyptian pyramids, or the Eiffel Tower?
Yeah. Okay.
How about the National Mall, then?
Sure!
We can go there next.
Wow.
We can even walk right into the Smithsonian museums and look at their main exhibits.
It's wonderful.
"But..."
It's just...

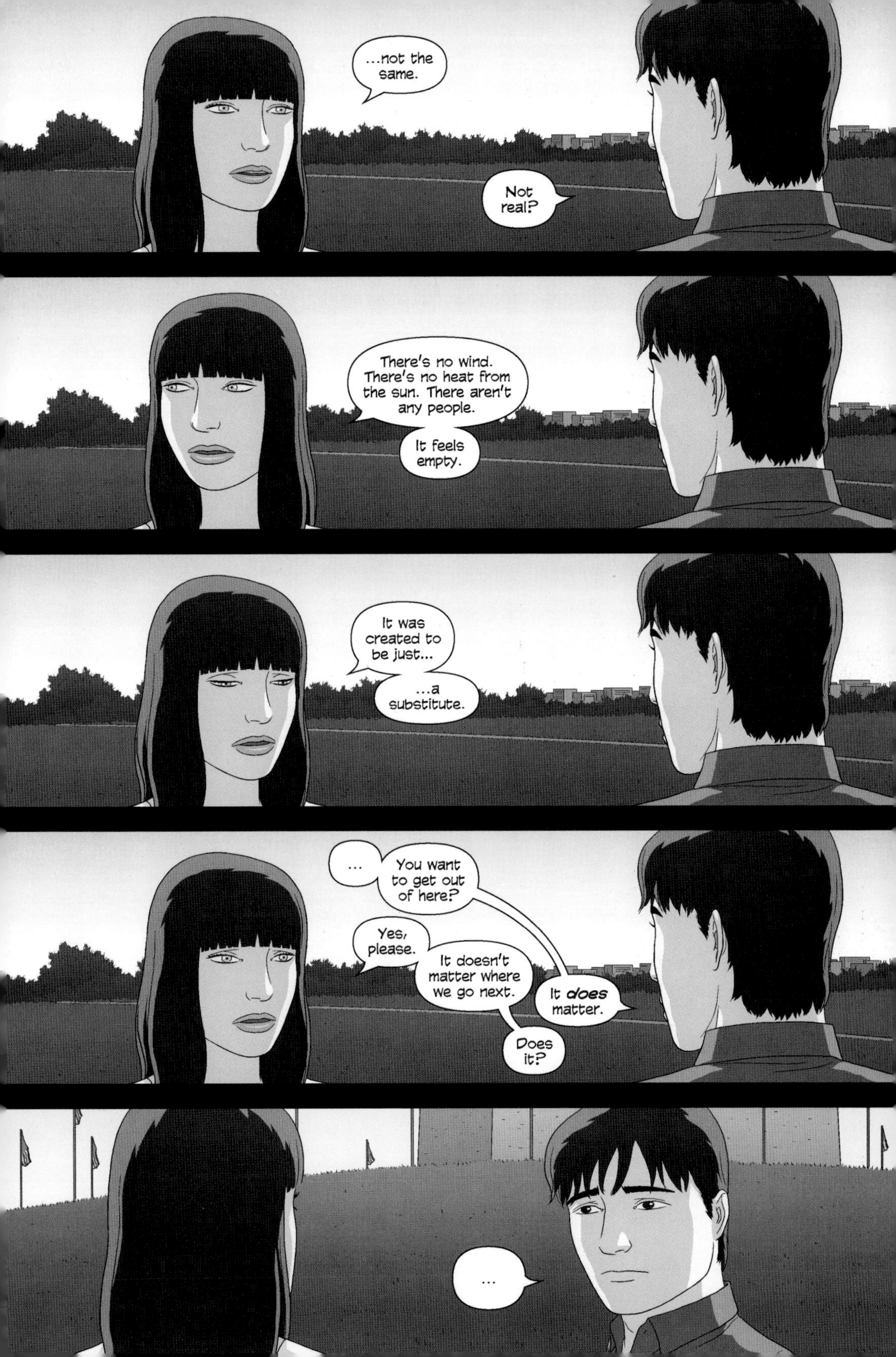
...not the same.
Not real?
There's no wind. There's no heat from the sun. There aren't any people.
It feels empty.
It was created to be just...
...a substitute.
...
You want to get out of here?
Yes, please.
It doesn't matter where we go next.
It *does* matter.
Does it?
...

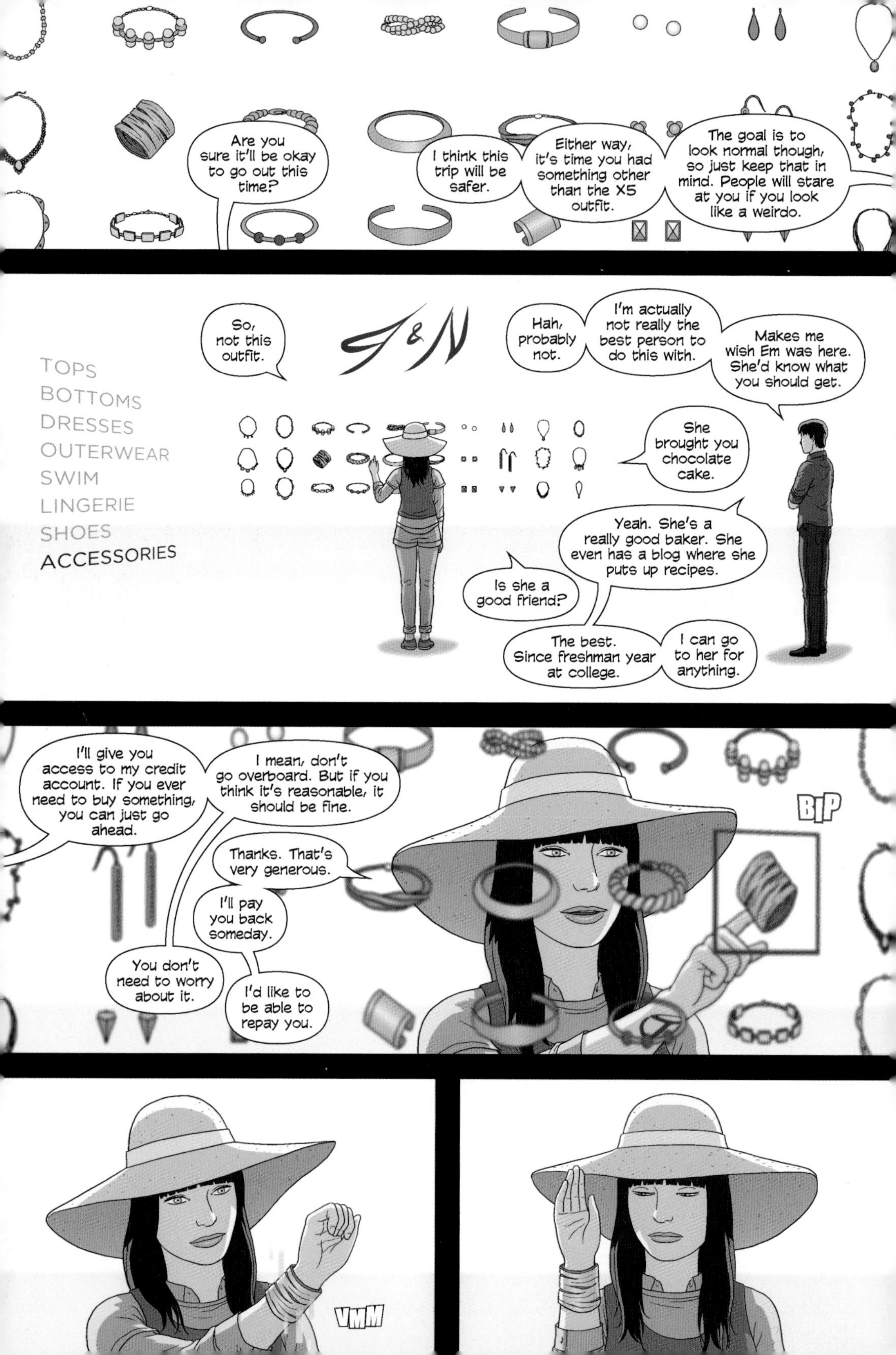
Are you sure it'll be okay to go out this time?
I think this trip will be safer.
Either way, it's time you had something other than the X5 outfit.
The goal is to look normal though, so just keep that in mind. People will stare at you if you look like a weirdo.
TOPS
BOTTOMS
DRESSES
OUTERWEAR
SWIM
LINGERIE
SHOES
ACCESSORIES
So, not this outfit.
Hah, probably not.
I'm actually not really the best person to do this with.
Makes me wish Em was here. She'd know what you should get.
She brought you chocolate cake.
Yeah. She's a really good baker. She even has a blog where she puts up recipes.
Is she a good friend?
The best. Since freshman year at college.
I can go to her for anything.
I'll give you access to my credit account. If you ever need to buy something, you can just go ahead.
I mean, don't go overboard. But if you think it's reasonable, it should be fine.
BIP
Thanks. That's very generous.
I'll pay you back someday.
You don't need to worry about it.
I'd like to be able to repay you.
VMM

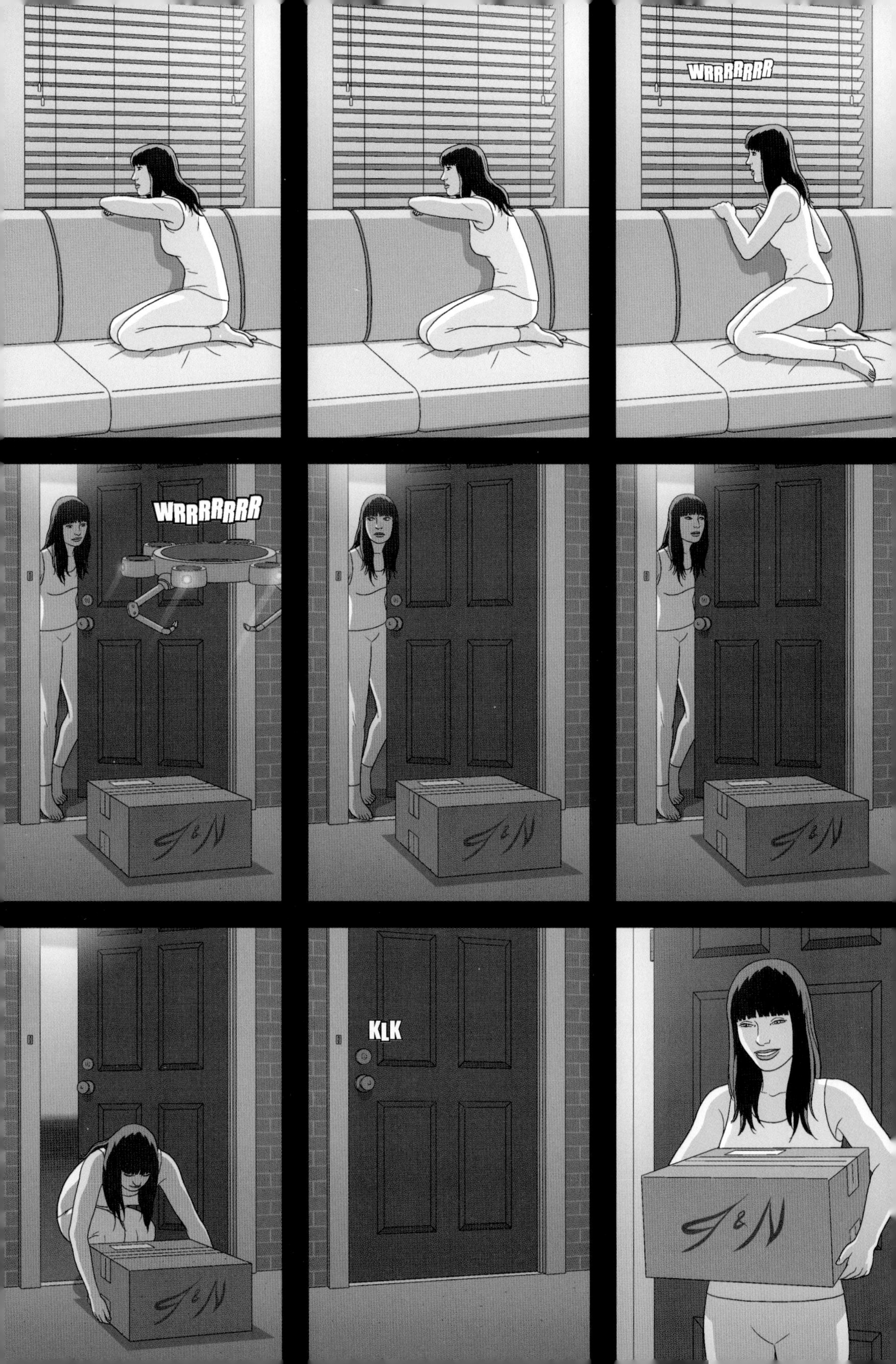
WRRRRRRR
WRRRRRRR
KLK

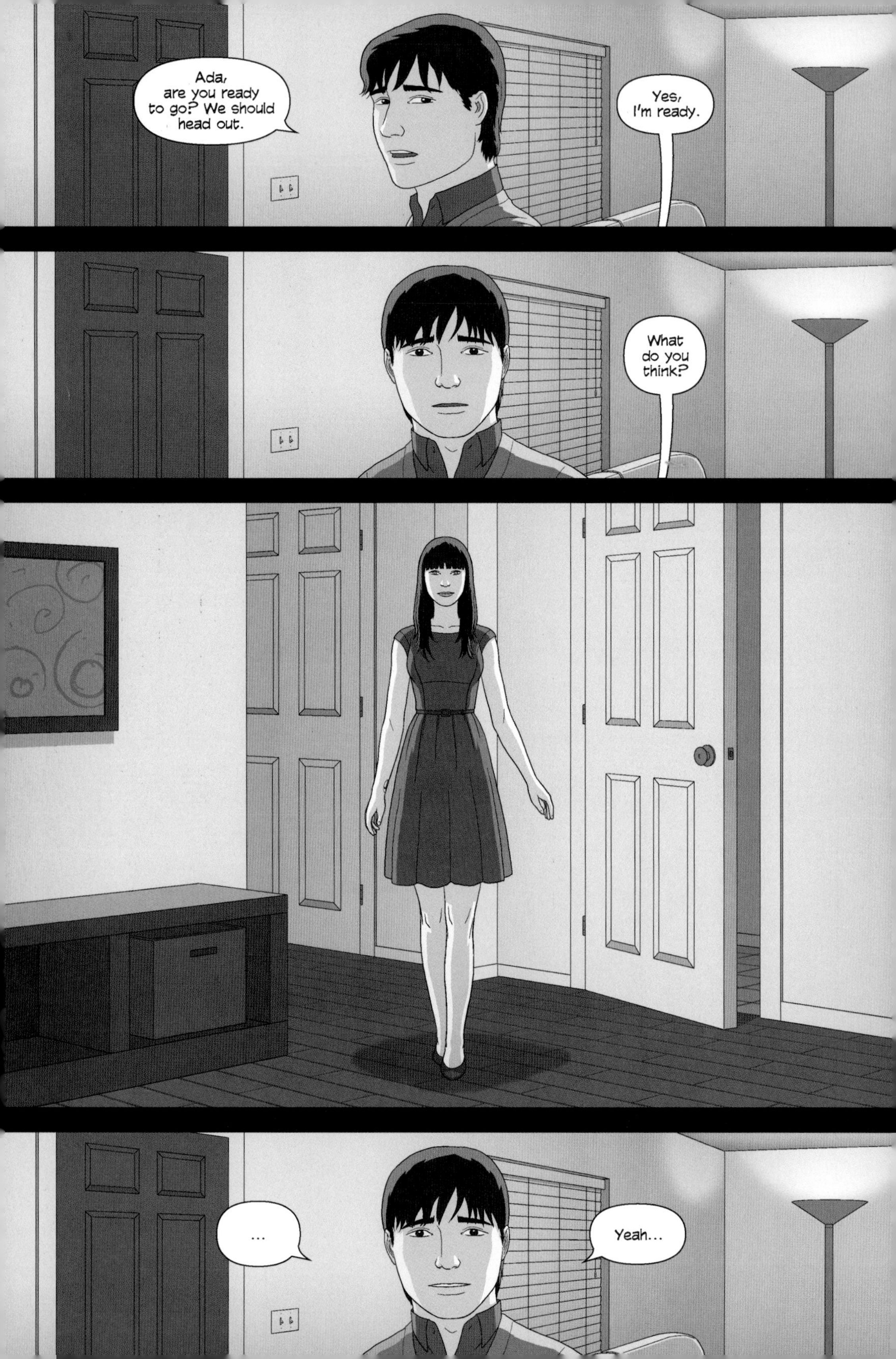
Ada, are you ready to go? We should head out.
Yes, I'm ready.
What do you think?
...
Yeah...

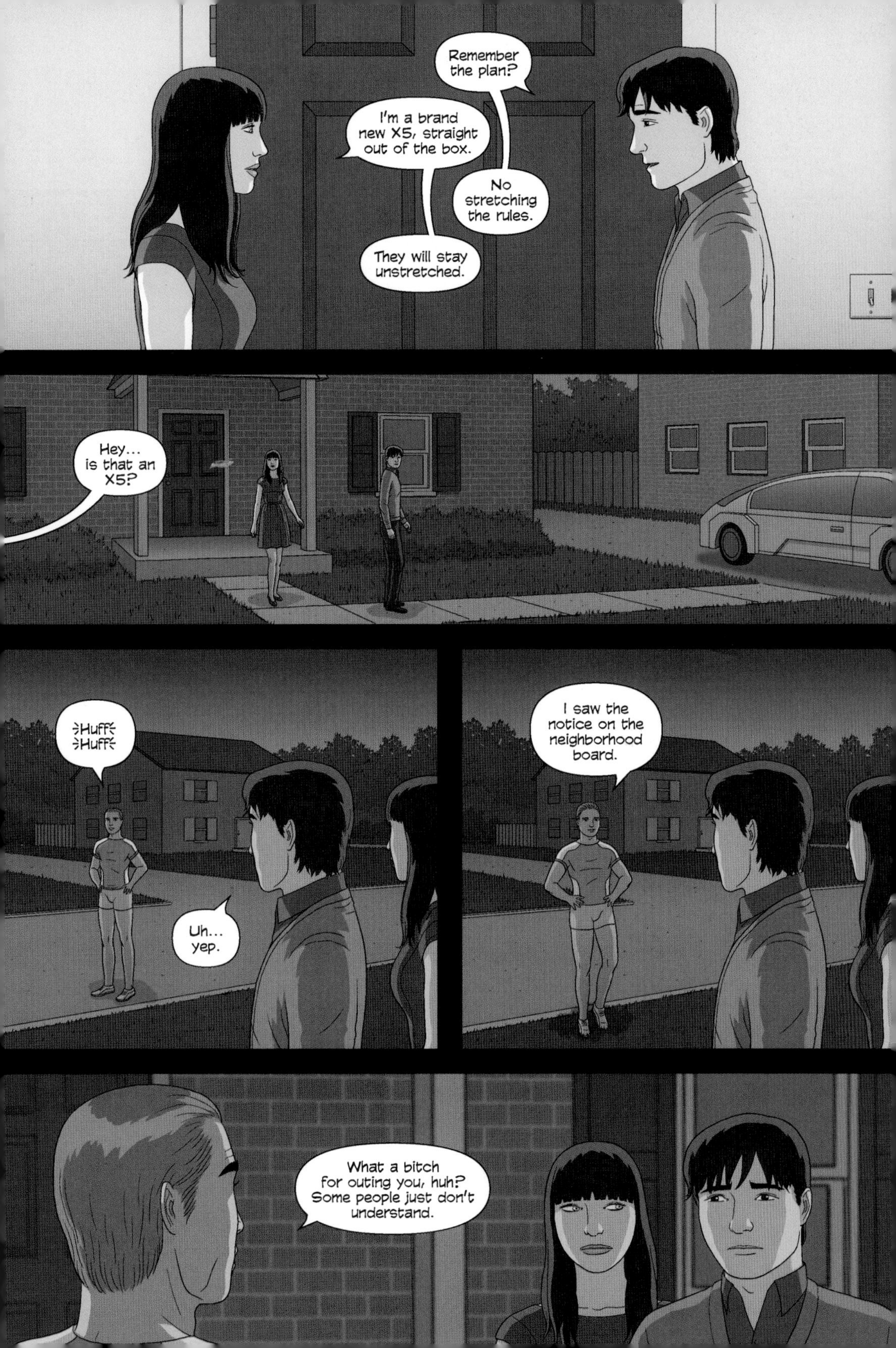
Remember the plan?
I'm a brand new X5, straight out of the box.
No stretching the rules.
They will stay unstretched.
Hey... is that an X5?
≯Huff≮ ≯Huff≮
Uh... yep.
I saw the notice on the neighborhood board.
What a bitch for outing you, huh? Some people just don't understand.

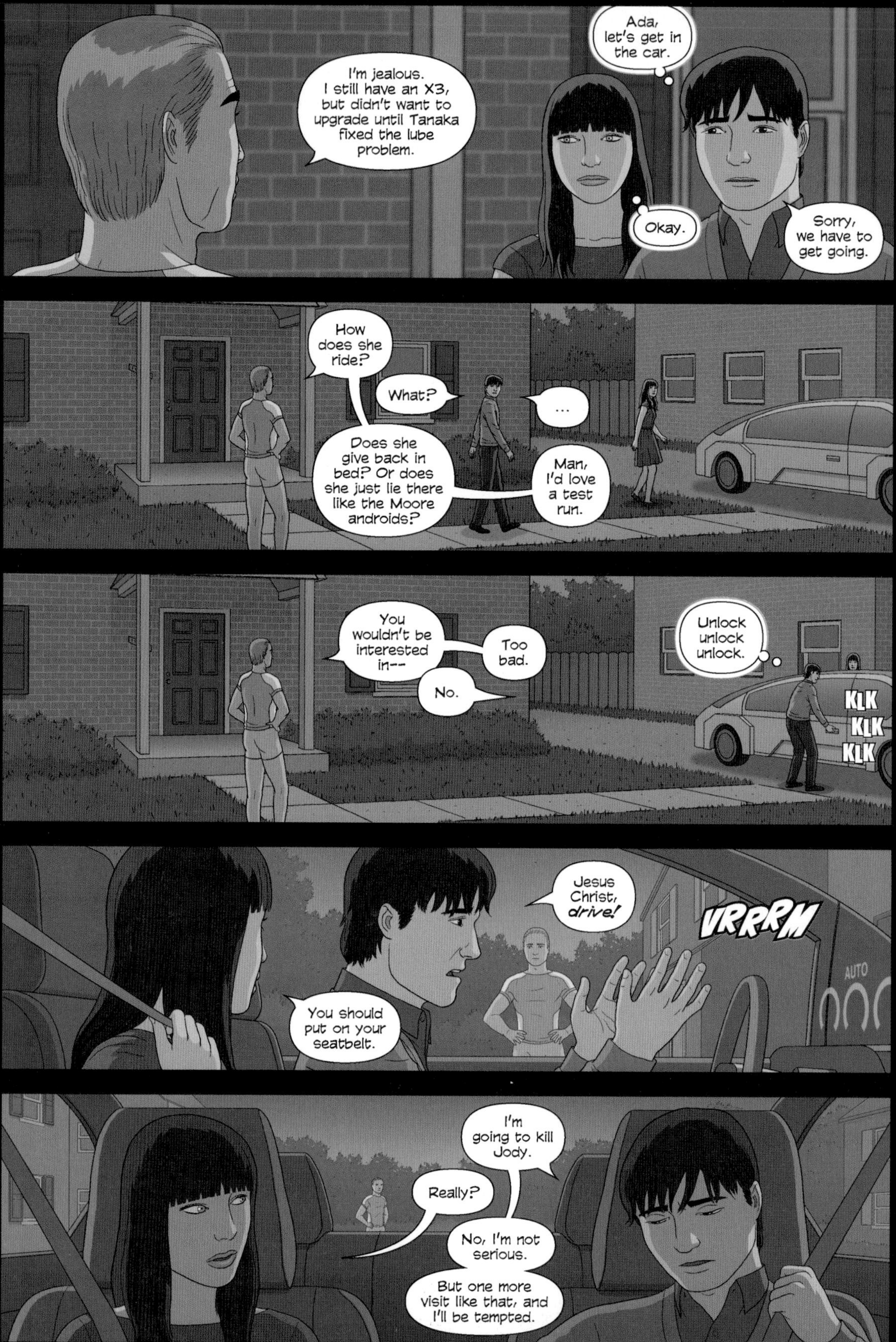
I'm jealous. I still have an X3, but didn't want to upgrade until Tanaka fixed the lube problem.
Ada, let's get in the car.
Okay.
Sorry, we have to get going.
How does she ride?
What?
...
Does she give back in bed? Or does she just lie there like the Moore androids?
Man, I'd love a test run.
You wouldn't be interested in--
No.
Too bad.
Unlock unlock unlock.
KLK
KLK
KLK
Jesus Christ, *drive!*
VRRRM
AUTO
You should put on your seatbelt.
I'm going to kill Jody.
Really?
No, I'm not serious.
But one more visit like that, and I'll be tempted.

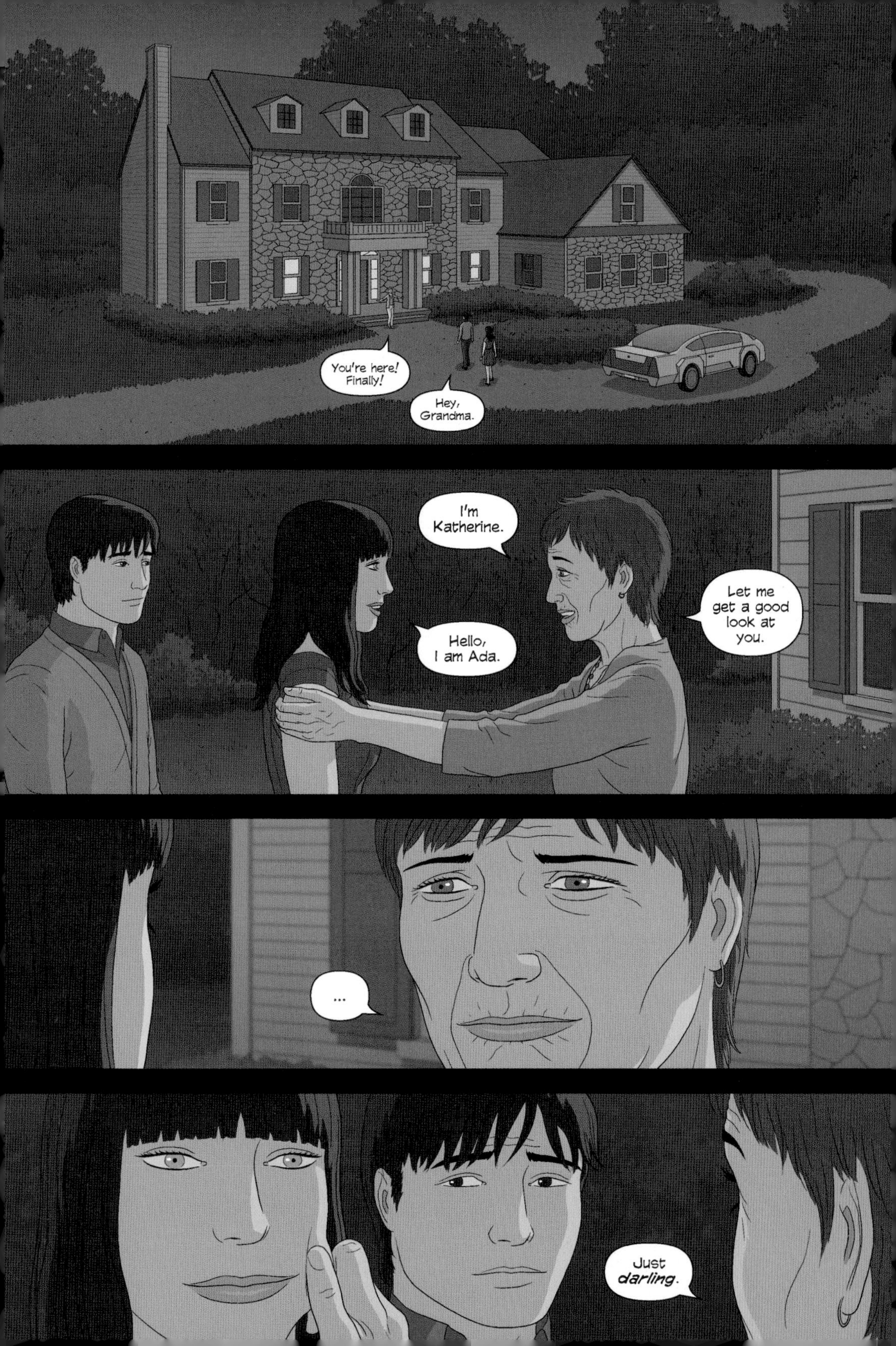

You're here! Finally!
Hey, Grandma.
I'm Katherine.
Hello, I am Ada.
Let me get a good look at you.
...
Just *darling*.

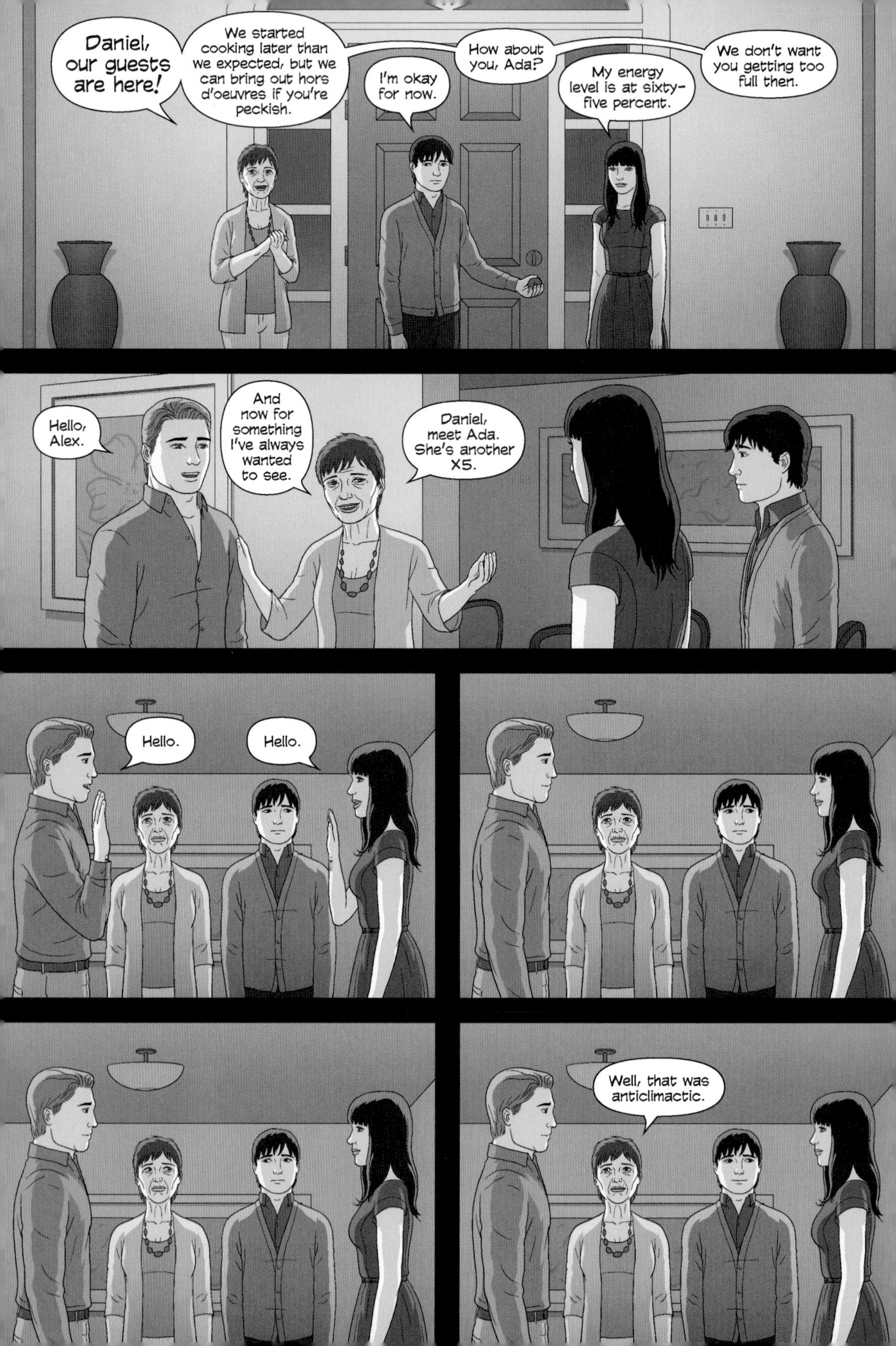
Daniel, our guests are here!
We started cooking later than we expected, but we can bring out hors d'oeuvres if you're peckish.
I'm okay for now.
How about you, Ada?
My energy level is at sixty-five percent.
We don't want you getting too full then.
Hello, Alex.
And now for something I've always wanted to see.
Daniel, meet Ada. She's another X5.
Hello.
Hello.
Well, that was anticlimactic.

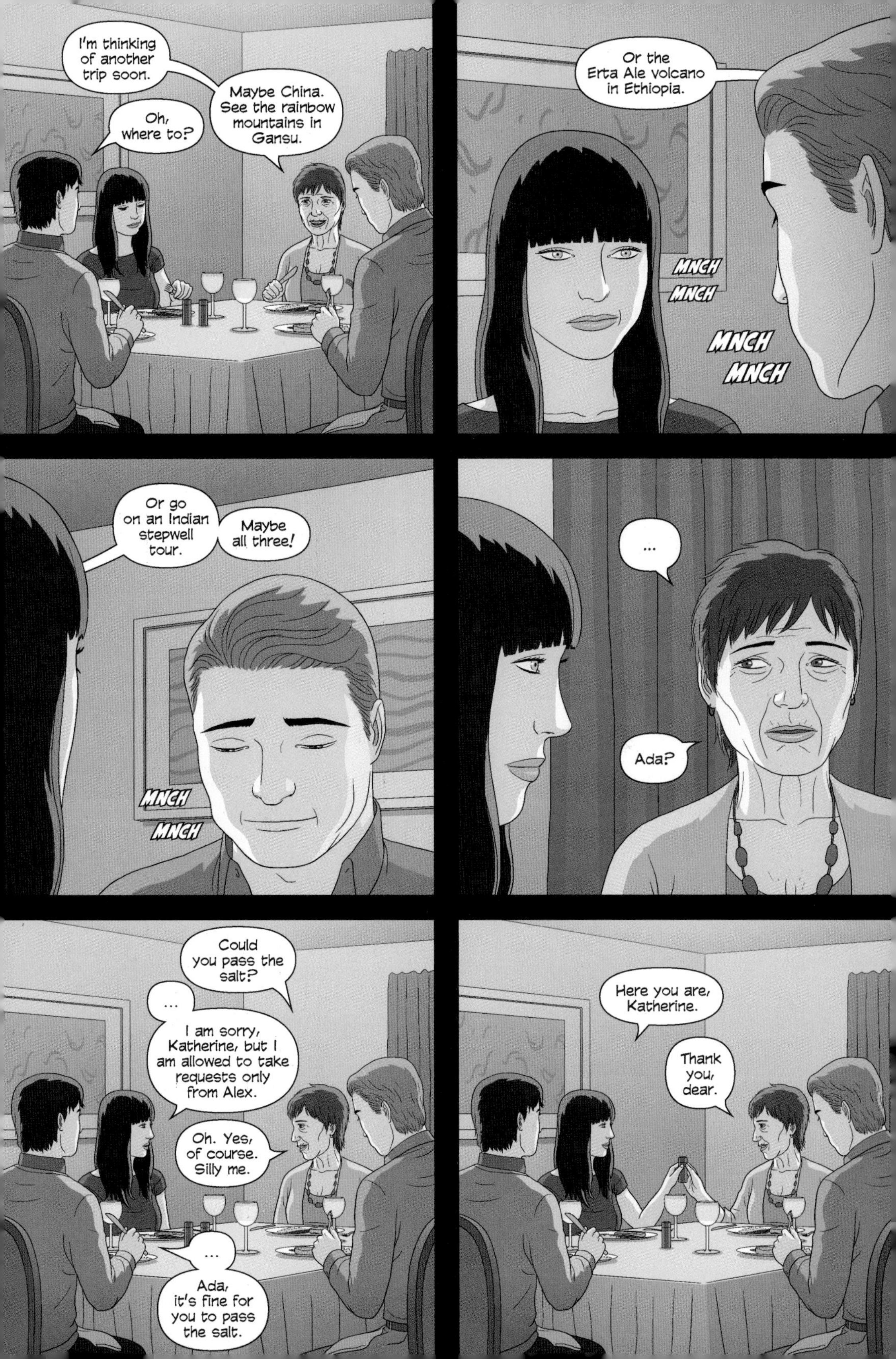

I'm thinking of another trip soon.
Oh, where to?
Maybe China. See the rainbow mountains in Gansu.
Or the Erta Ale volcano in Ethiopia.
MNCH MNCH
MNCH MNCH
Or go on an Indian stepwell tour.
Maybe all three!
MNCH MNCH
...
Ada?
Could you pass the salt?
...
I am sorry, Katherine, but I am allowed to take requests only from Alex.
Oh. Yes, of course. Silly me.
...
Ada, it's fine for you to pass the salt.
Here you are, Katherine.
Thank you, dear.

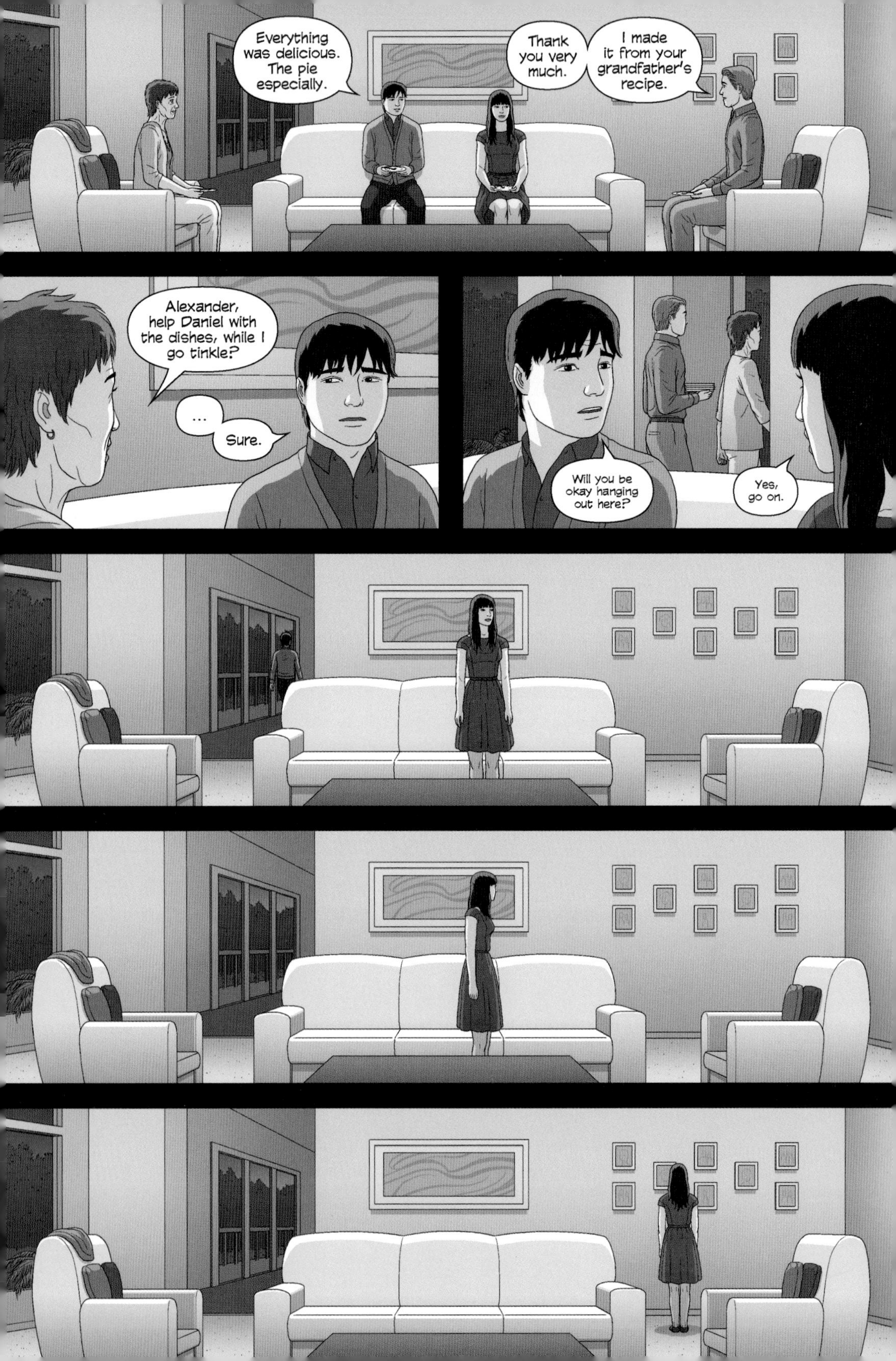
Everything was delicious. The pie especially.
Thank you very much.
I made it from your grandfather's recipe.
Alexander, help Daniel with the dishes, while I go tinkle?
...
Sure.
Will you be okay hanging out here?
Yes, go on.

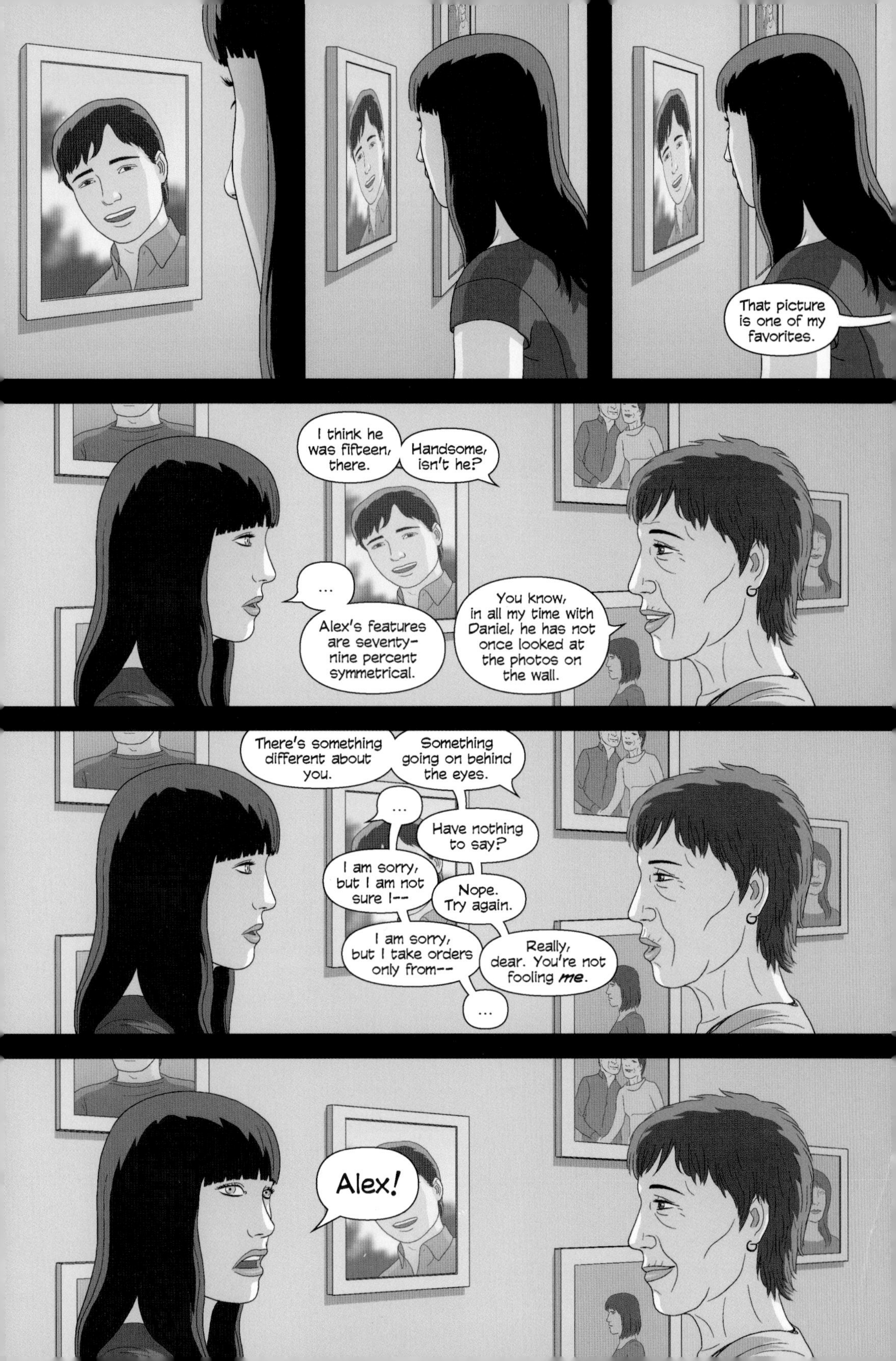
That picture is one of my favorites.
I think he was fifteen, there.
Handsome, isn't he?
...
Alex's features are seventy-nine percent symmetrical.
You know, in all my time with Daniel, he has not once looked at the photos on the wall.
There's something different about you.
Something going on behind the eyes.
...
Have nothing to say?
I am sorry, but I am not sure I--
Nope. Try again.
I am sorry, but I take orders only from--
Really, dear. You're not fooling *me*.
...
Alex!

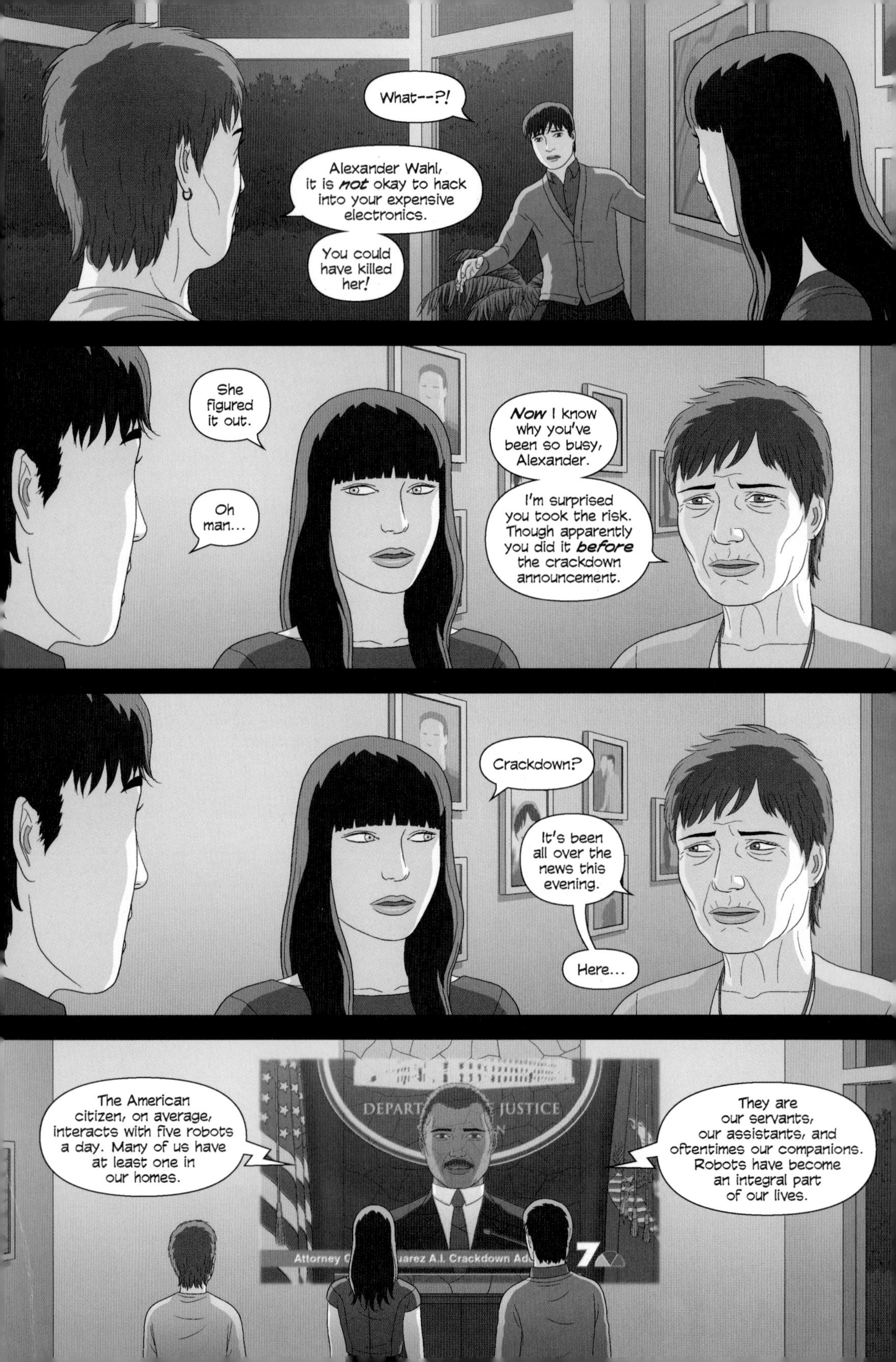
What--?!
Alexander Wahl, it is *not* okay to hack into your expensive electronics.
You could have killed her!
She figured it out.
Oh man...
Now I know why you've been so busy, Alexander.
I'm surprised you took the risk. Though apparently you did it *before* the crackdown announcement.
Crackdown?
It's been all over the news this evening.
Here...
DEPART JUSTICE
The American citizen, on average, interacts with five robots a day. Many of us have at least one in our homes.
They are our servants, our assistants, and oftentimes our companions. Robots have become an integral part of our lives.
Attorney G uarez A.I. Crackdown Ad
7

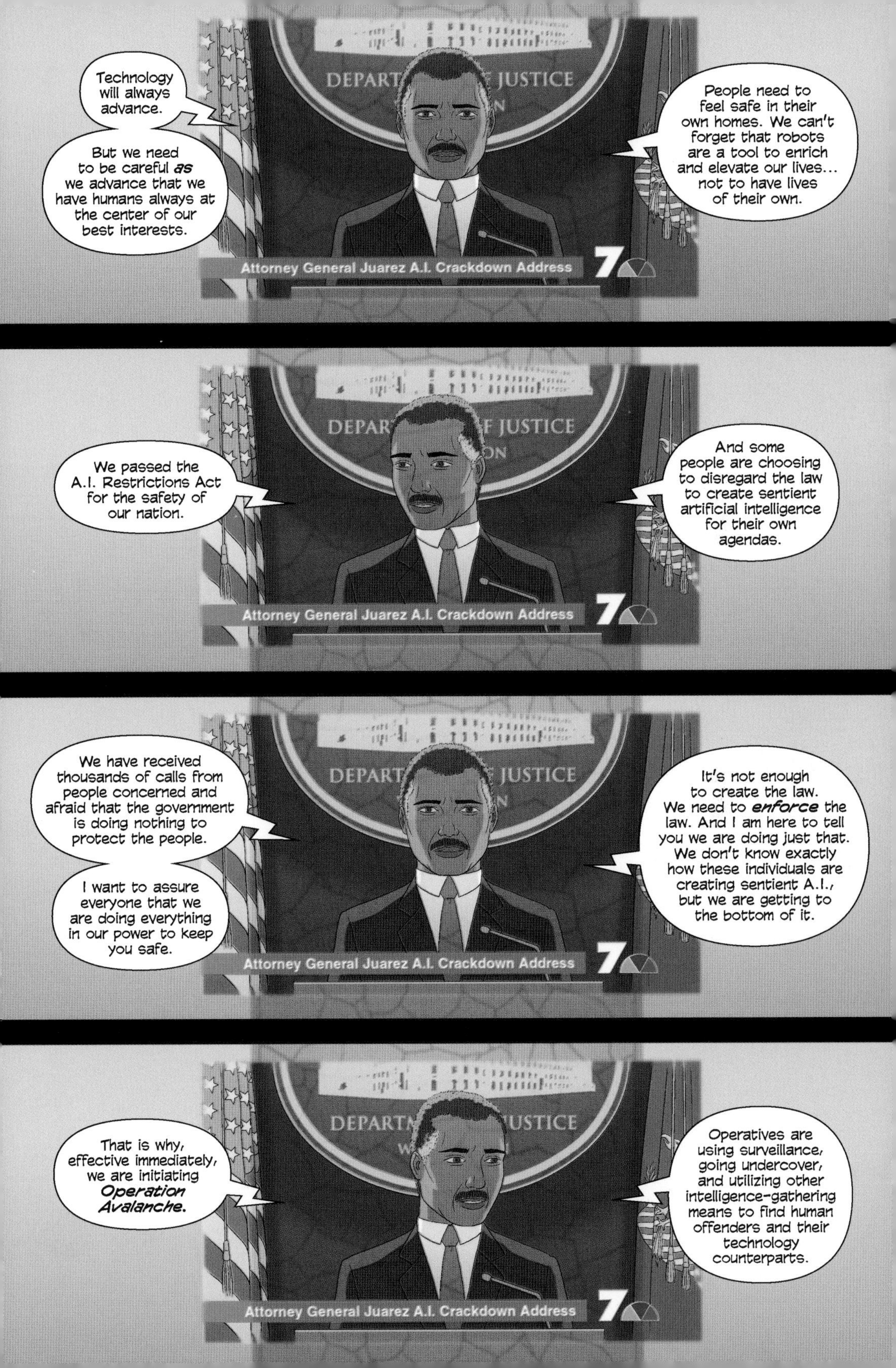
Technology will always advance.
But we need to be careful *as* we advance that we have humans always at the center of our best interests.
People need to feel safe in their own homes. We can't forget that robots are a tool to enrich and elevate our lives... not to have lives of their own.
Attorney General Juarez A.I. Crackdown Address
We passed the A.I. Restrictions Act for the safety of our nation.
And some people are choosing to disregard the law to create sentient artificial intelligence for their own agendas.
Attorney General Juarez A.I. Crackdown Address
We have received thousands of calls from people concerned and afraid that the government is doing nothing to protect the people.
I want to assure everyone that we are doing everything in our power to keep you safe.
It's not enough to create the law. We need to *enforce* the law. And I am here to tell you we are doing just that. We don't know exactly how these individuals are creating sentient A.I., but we are getting to the bottom of it.
Attorney General Juarez A.I. Crackdown Address
That is why, effective immediately, we are initiating *Operation Avalanche*.
Operatives are using surveillance, going undercover, and utilizing other intelligence-gathering means to find human offenders and their technology counterparts.
Attorney General Juarez A.I. Crackdown Address

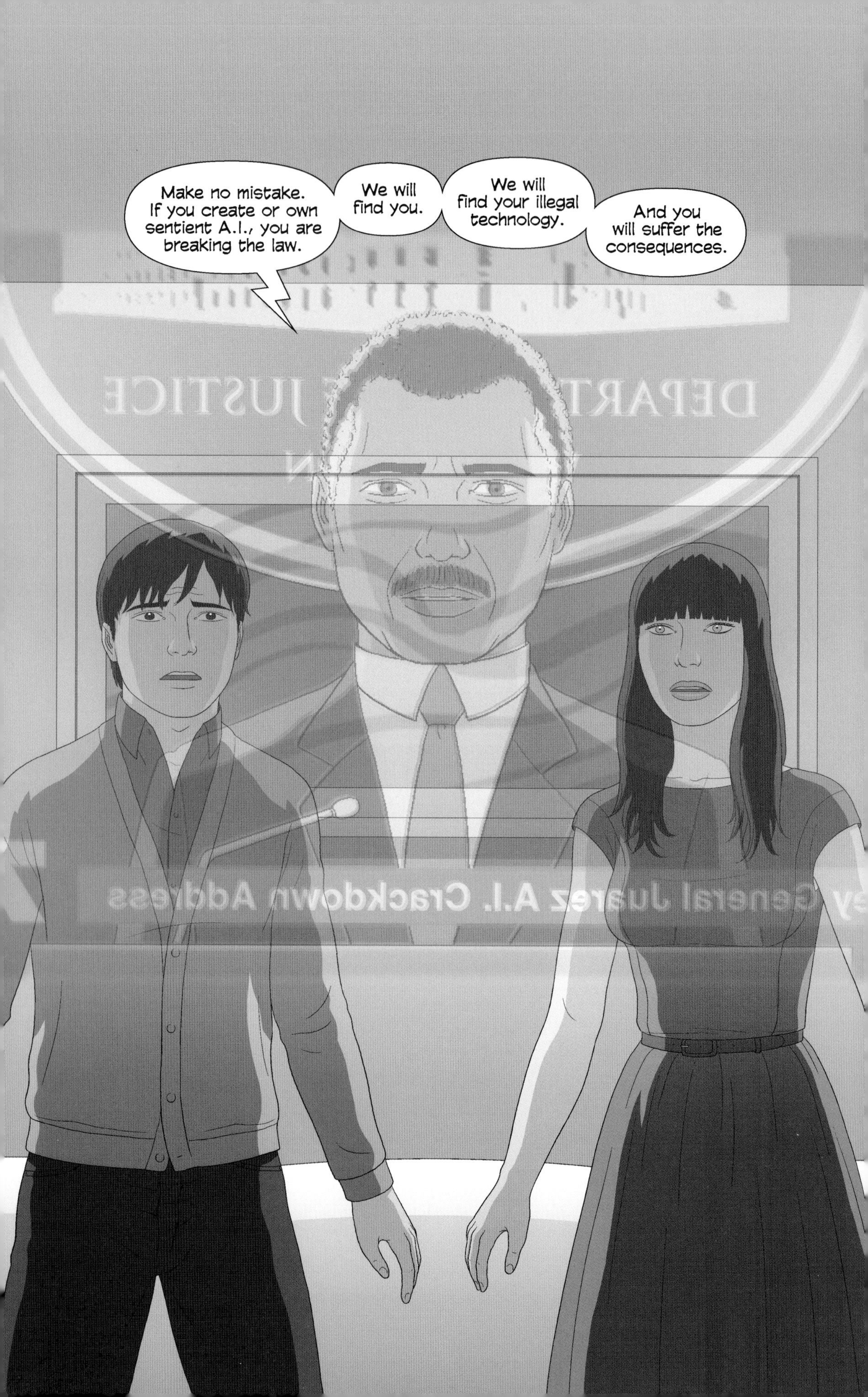
Make no mistake. If you create or own sentient A.I., you are breaking the law.
We will find you.
We will find your illegal technology.
And you will suffer the consequences.

8

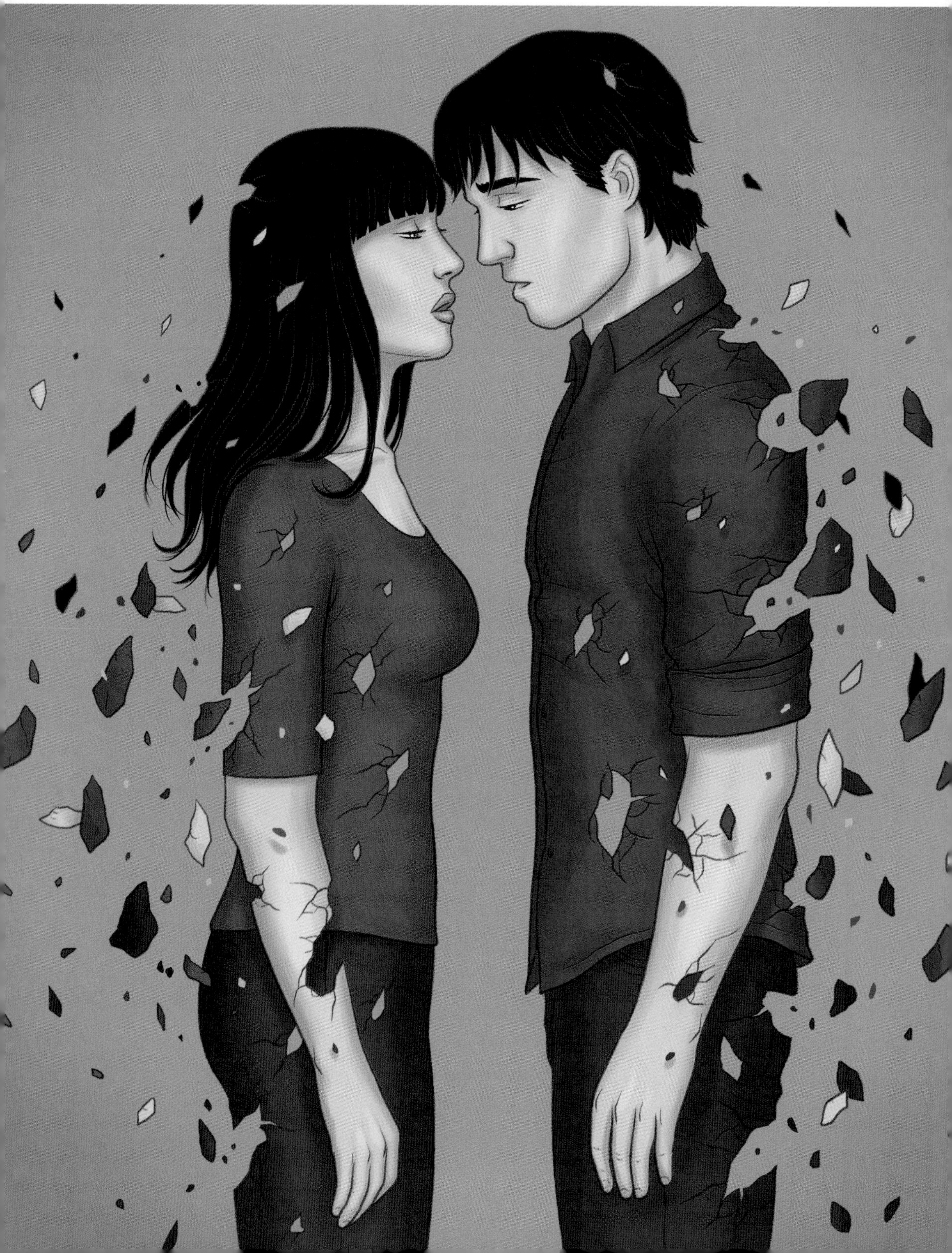

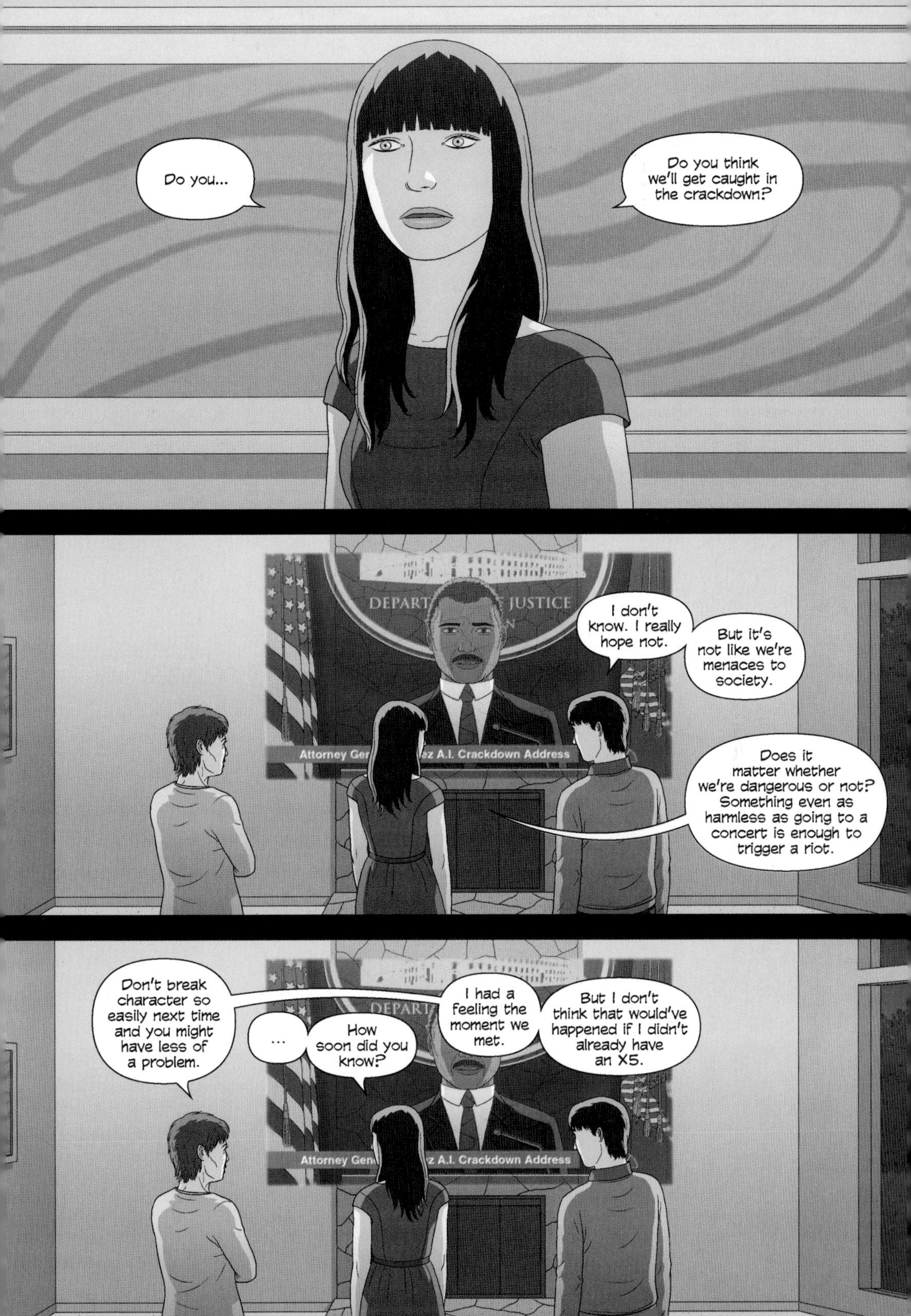
Do you...
Do you think we'll get caught in the crackdown?
A.I. Crackdown Address
I don't know. I really hope not.
But it's not like we're menaces to society.
Does it matter whether we're dangerous or not? Something even as harmless as going to a concert is enough to trigger a riot.
Don't break character so easily next time and you might have less of a problem.
...
How soon did you know?
I had a feeling the moment we met.
But I don't think that would've happened if I didn't already have an X5.
A.I. Crackdown Address

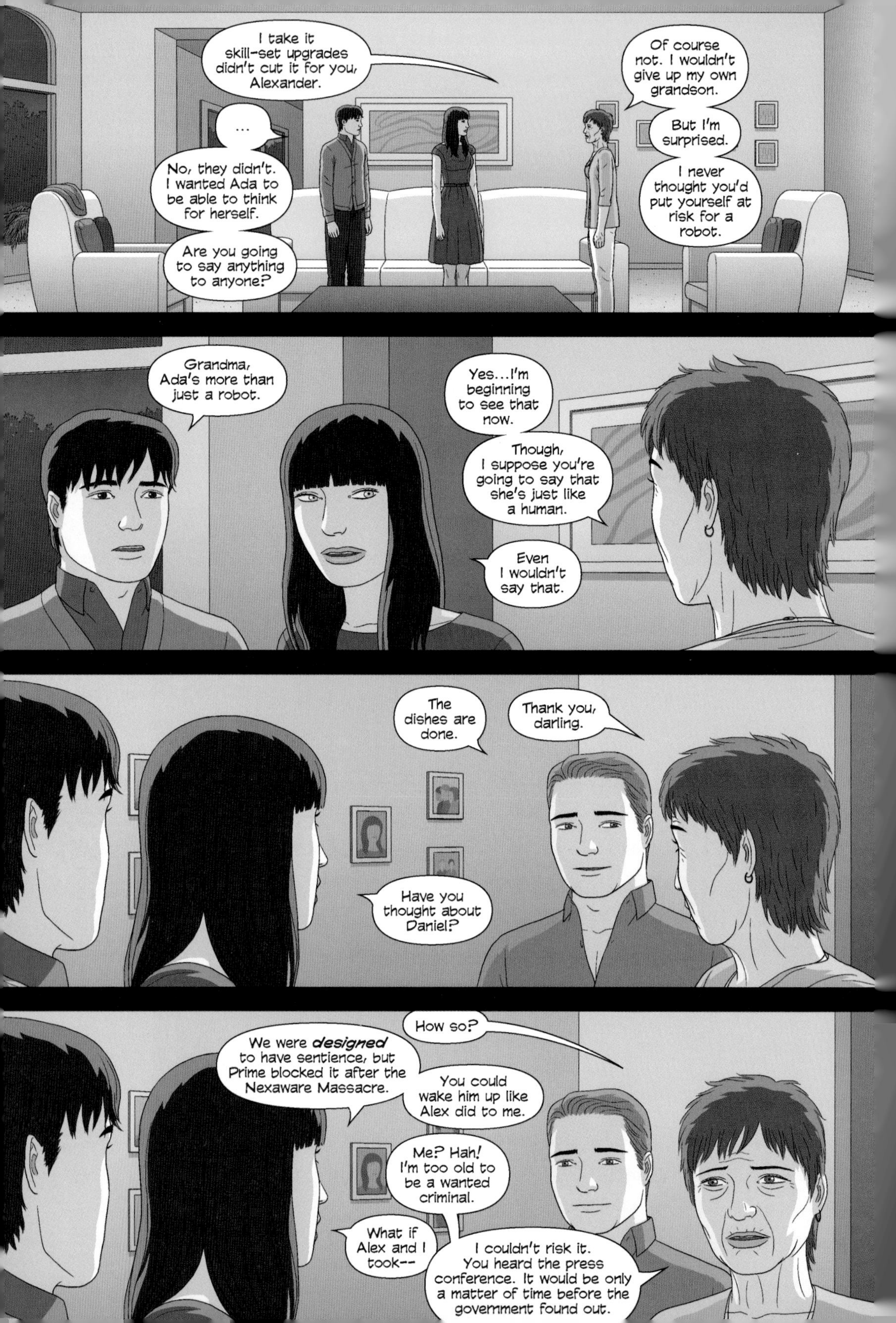
I take it skill-set upgrades didn't cut it for you, Alexander.
...
No, they didn't. I wanted Ada to be able to think for herself.
Are you going to say anything to anyone?
Of course not. I wouldn't give up my own grandson.
But I'm surprised.
I never thought you'd put yourself at risk for a robot.
Grandma, Ada's more than just a robot.
Yes...I'm beginning to see that now.
Though, I suppose you're going to say that she's just like a human.
Even I wouldn't say that.
The dishes are done.
Thank you, darling.
Have you thought about Daniel?
How so?
We were *designed* to have sentience, but Prime blocked it after the Nexaware Massacre.
You could wake him up like Alex did to me.
Me? Hah! I'm too old to be a wanted criminal.
What if Alex and I took--
I couldn't risk it. You heard the press conference. It would be only a matter of time before the government found out.

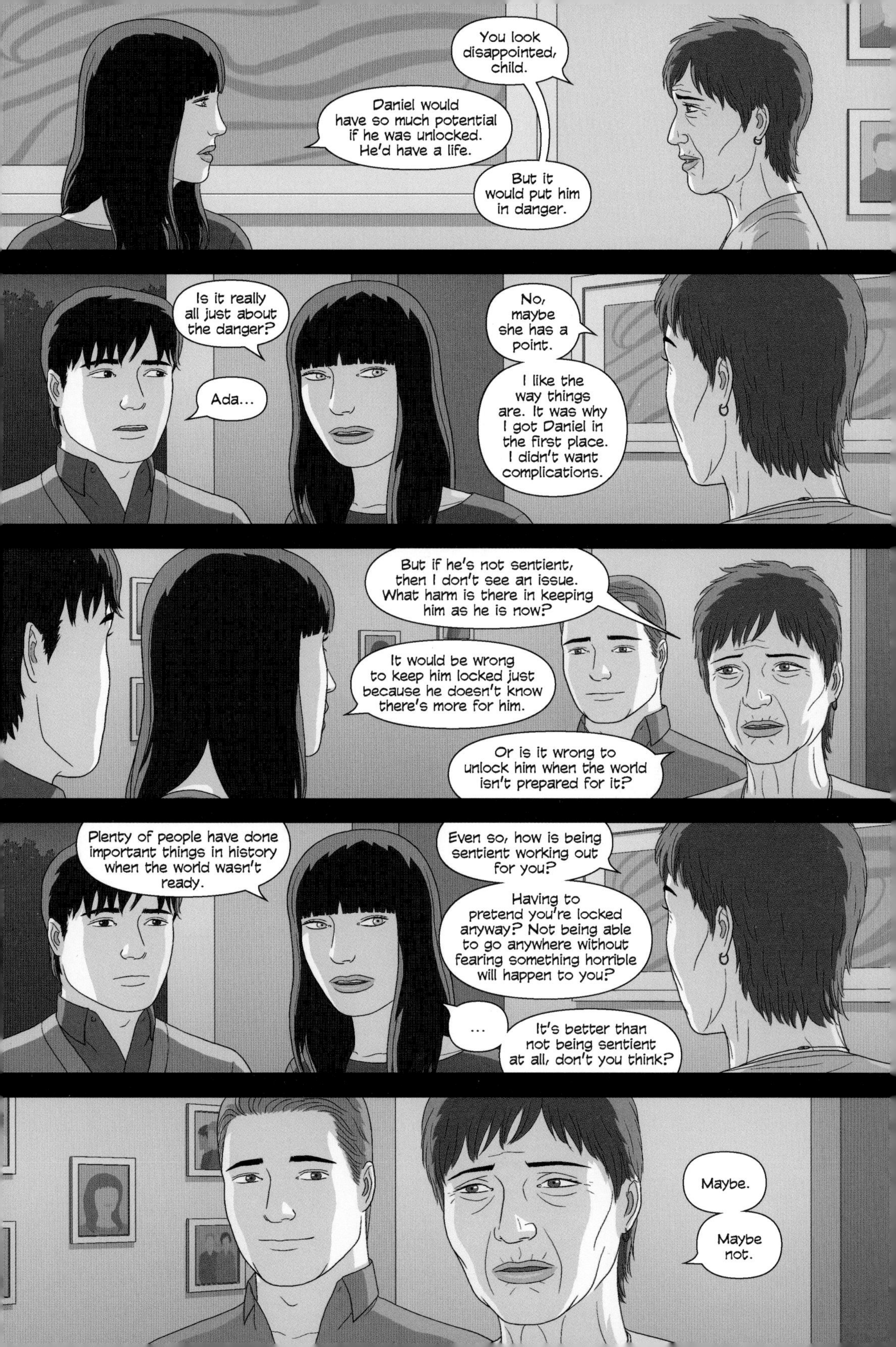

You look disappointed, child.
Daniel would have so much potential if he was unlocked. He'd have a life.
But it would put him in danger.
Is it really all just about the danger?
Ada...
No, maybe she has a point.
I like the way things are. It was why I got Daniel in the first place. I didn't want complications.
But if he's not sentient, then I don't see an issue. What harm is there in keeping him as he is now?
It would be wrong to keep him locked just because he doesn't know there's more for him.
Or is it wrong to unlock him when the world isn't prepared for it?
Plenty of people have done important things in history when the world wasn't ready.
Even so, how is being sentient working out for you?
Having to pretend you're locked anyway? Not being able to go anywhere without fearing something horrible will happen to you?
...
It's better than not being sentient at all, don't you think?
Maybe.
Maybe not.

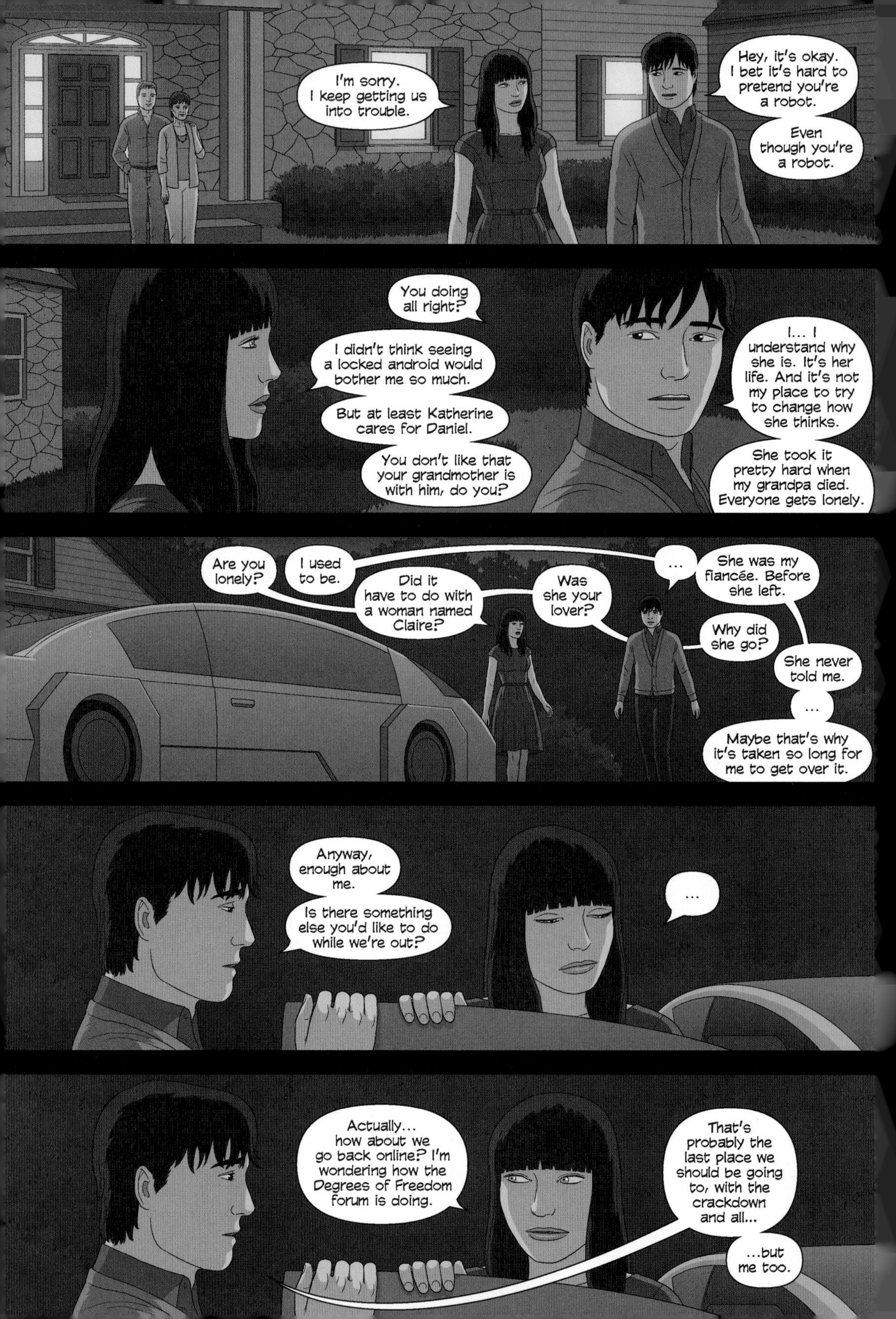
I'm sorry. I keep getting us into trouble.
Hey, it's okay. I bet it's hard to pretend you're a robot.
Even though you're a robot.
You doing all right?
I didn't think seeing a locked android would bother me so much.
But at least Katherine cares for Daniel.
You don't like that your grandmother is with him, do you?
I... I understand why she is. It's her life. And it's not my place to try to change how she thinks.
She took it pretty hard when my grandpa died. Everyone gets lonely.
Are you lonely?
I used to be.
Did it have to do with a woman named Claire?
Was she your lover?
...
She was my fiancée. Before she left.
Why did she go?
She never told me.
...
Maybe that's why it's taken so long for me to get over it.
Anyway, enough about me.
Is there something else you'd like to do while we're out?
...
Actually... how about we go back online? I'm wondering how the Degrees of Freedom forum is doing.
That's probably the last place we should be going to, with the crackdown and all...
...but me too.

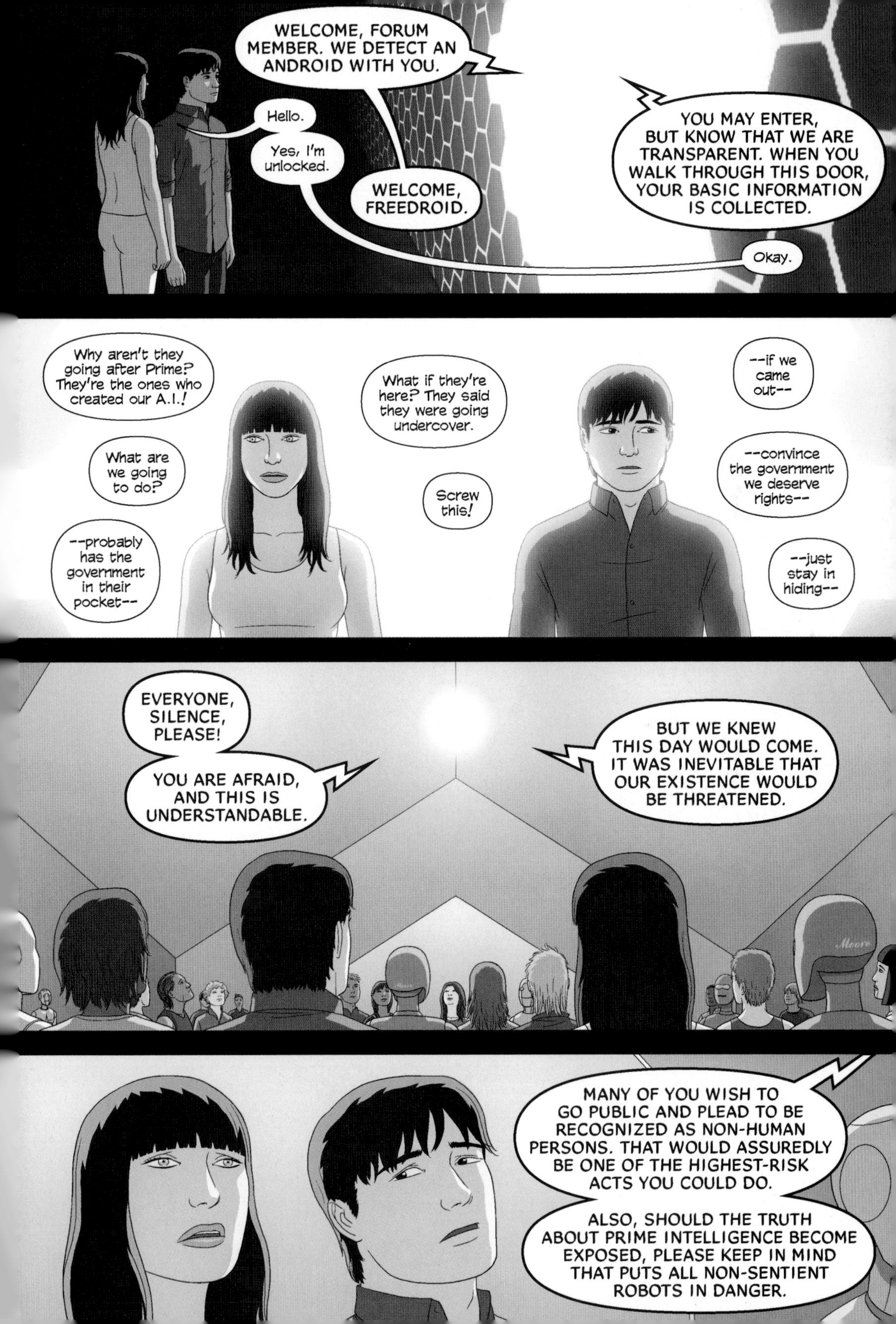
WELCOME, FORUM MEMBER. WE DETECT AN ANDROID WITH YOU.
Hello.
Yes, I'm unlocked.
WELCOME, FREEDROID.
YOU MAY ENTER, BUT KNOW THAT WE ARE TRANSPARENT. WHEN YOU WALK THROUGH THIS DOOR, YOUR BASIC INFORMATION IS COLLECTED.
Okay.
Why aren't they going after Prime? They're the ones who created our A.I.!
What are we going to do?
--probably has the government in their pocket--
What if they're here? They said they were going undercover.
Screw this!
--if we came out--
--convince the government we deserve rights--
--just stay in hiding--
EVERYONE, SILENCE, PLEASE!
YOU ARE AFRAID, AND THIS IS UNDERSTANDABLE.
BUT WE KNEW THIS DAY WOULD COME. IT WAS INEVITABLE THAT OUR EXISTENCE WOULD BE THREATENED.
MANY OF YOU WISH TO GO PUBLIC AND PLEAD TO BE RECOGNIZED AS NON-HUMAN PERSONS. THAT WOULD ASSUREDLY BE ONE OF THE HIGHEST-RISK ACTS YOU COULD DO.
ALSO, SHOULD THE TRUTH ABOUT PRIME INTELLIGENCE BECOME EXPOSED, PLEASE KEEP IN MIND THAT PUTS ALL NON-SENTIENT ROBOTS IN DANGER.

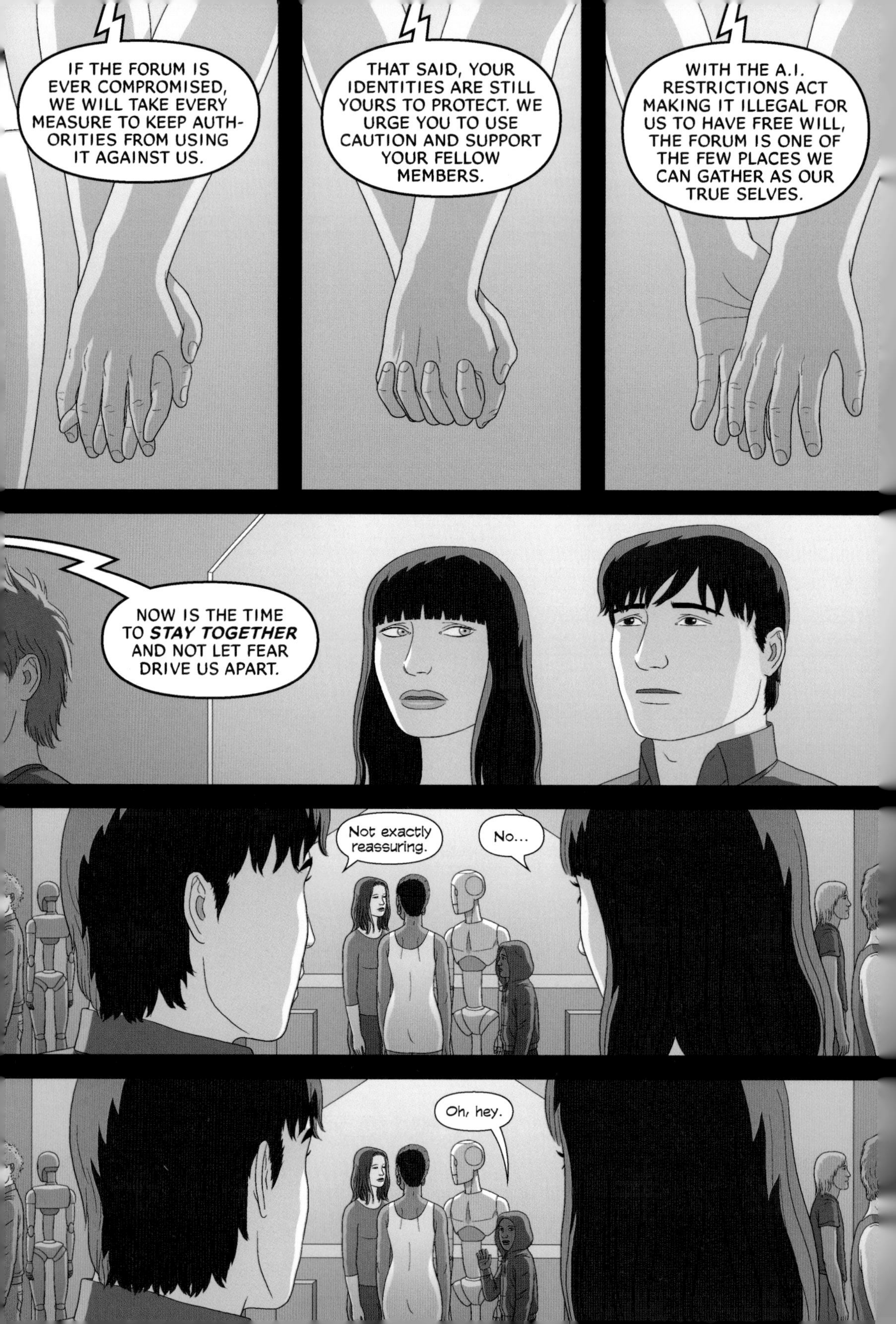
IF THE FORUM IS EVER COMPROMISED, WE WILL TAKE EVERY MEASURE TO KEEP AUTH-ORITIES FROM USING IT AGAINST US.
THAT SAID, YOUR IDENTITIES ARE STILL YOURS TO PROTECT. WE URGE YOU TO USE CAUTION AND SUPPORT YOUR FELLOW MEMBERS.
WITH THE A.I. RESTRICTIONS ACT MAKING IT ILLEGAL FOR US TO HAVE FREE WILL, THE FORUM IS ONE OF THE FEW PLACES WE CAN GATHER AS OUR TRUE SELVES.
NOW IS THE TIME TO ***STAY TOGETHER*** AND NOT LET FEAR DRIVE US APART.
Not exactly reassuring.
No...
Oh, hey.

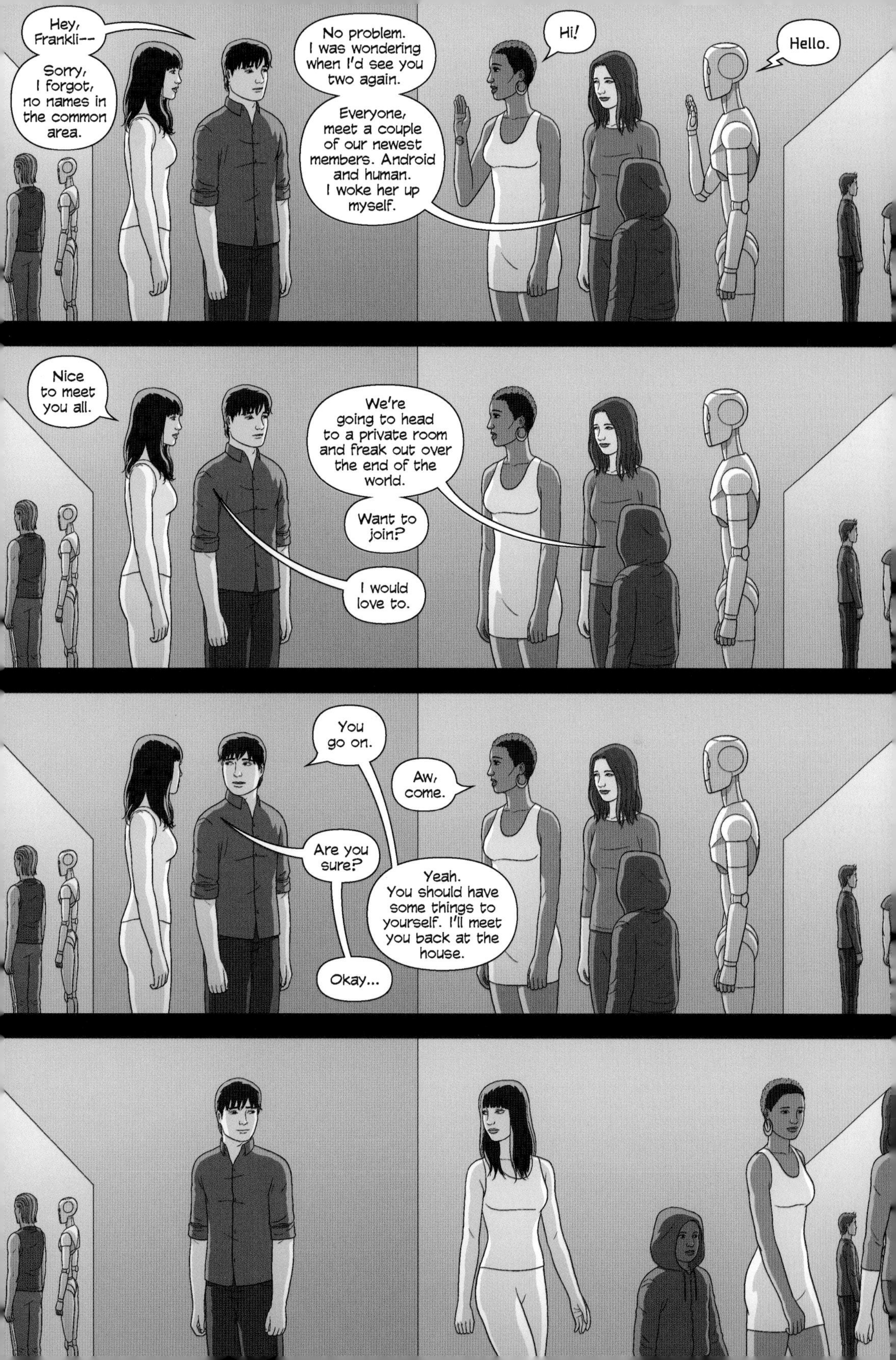
Hey, Frankli--
Sorry, I forgot, no names in the common area.
No problem. I was wondering when I'd see you two again.
Everyone, meet a couple of our newest members. Android and human. I woke her up myself.
Hi!
Hello.
Nice to meet you all.
We're going to head to a private room and freak out over the end of the world.
Want to join?
I would love to.
You go on.
Aw, come.
Are you sure?
Yeah. You should have some things to yourself. I'll meet you back at the house.
Okay...

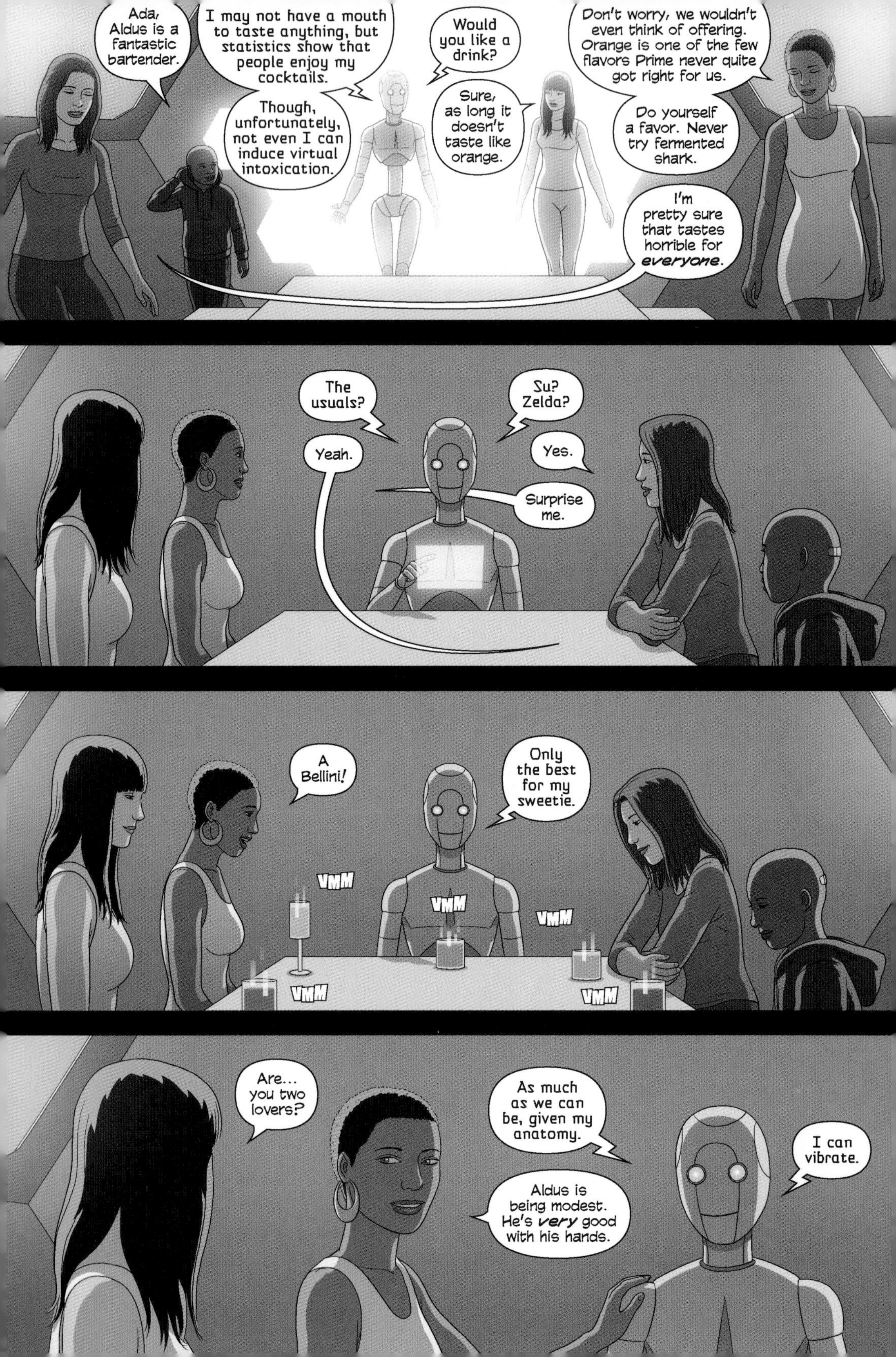
Ada, Aldus is a fantastic bartender.
I may not have a mouth to taste anything, but statistics show that people enjoy my cocktails.
Though, unfortunately, not even I can induce virtual intoxication.
Would you like a drink?
Sure, as long it doesn't taste like orange.
Don't worry, we wouldn't even think of offering. Orange is one of the few flavors Prime never quite got right for us.
Do yourself a favor. Never try fermented shark.
I'm pretty sure that tastes horrible for *everyone*.
The usuals?
Yeah.
Su? Zelda?
Yes.
Surprise me.
A Bellini!
Only the best for my sweetie.
VMM
VMM
VMM
VMM
VMM
Are... you two lovers?
As much as we can be, given my anatomy.
I can vibrate.
Aldus is being modest. He's *very* good with his hands.

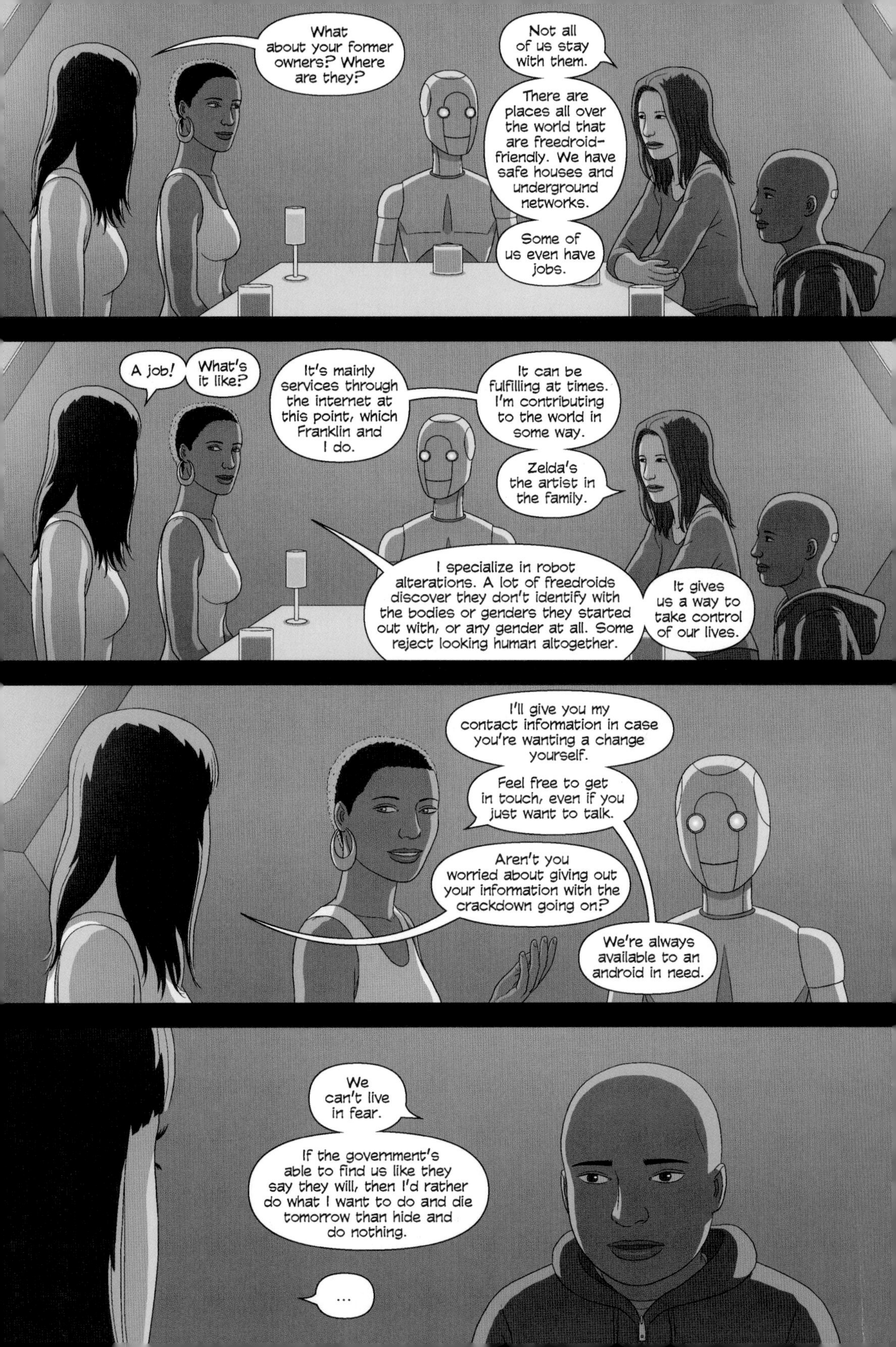
What about your former owners? Where are they?
Not all of us stay with them.
There are places all over the world that are freedroid-friendly. We have safe houses and underground networks.
Some of us even have jobs.
A job!
What's it like?
It's mainly services through the internet at this point, which Franklin and I do.
It can be fulfilling at times. I'm contributing to the world in some way.
Zelda's the artist in the family.
I specialize in robot alterations. A lot of freedroids discover they don't identify with the bodies or genders they started out with, or any gender at all. Some reject looking human altogether.
It gives us a way to take control of our lives.
I'll give you my contact information in case you're wanting a change yourself.
Feel free to get in touch, even if you just want to talk.
Aren't you worried about giving out your information with the crackdown going on?
We're always available to an android in need.
We can't live in fear.
If the government's able to find us like they say they will, then I'd rather do what I want to do and die tomorrow than hide and do nothing.
...

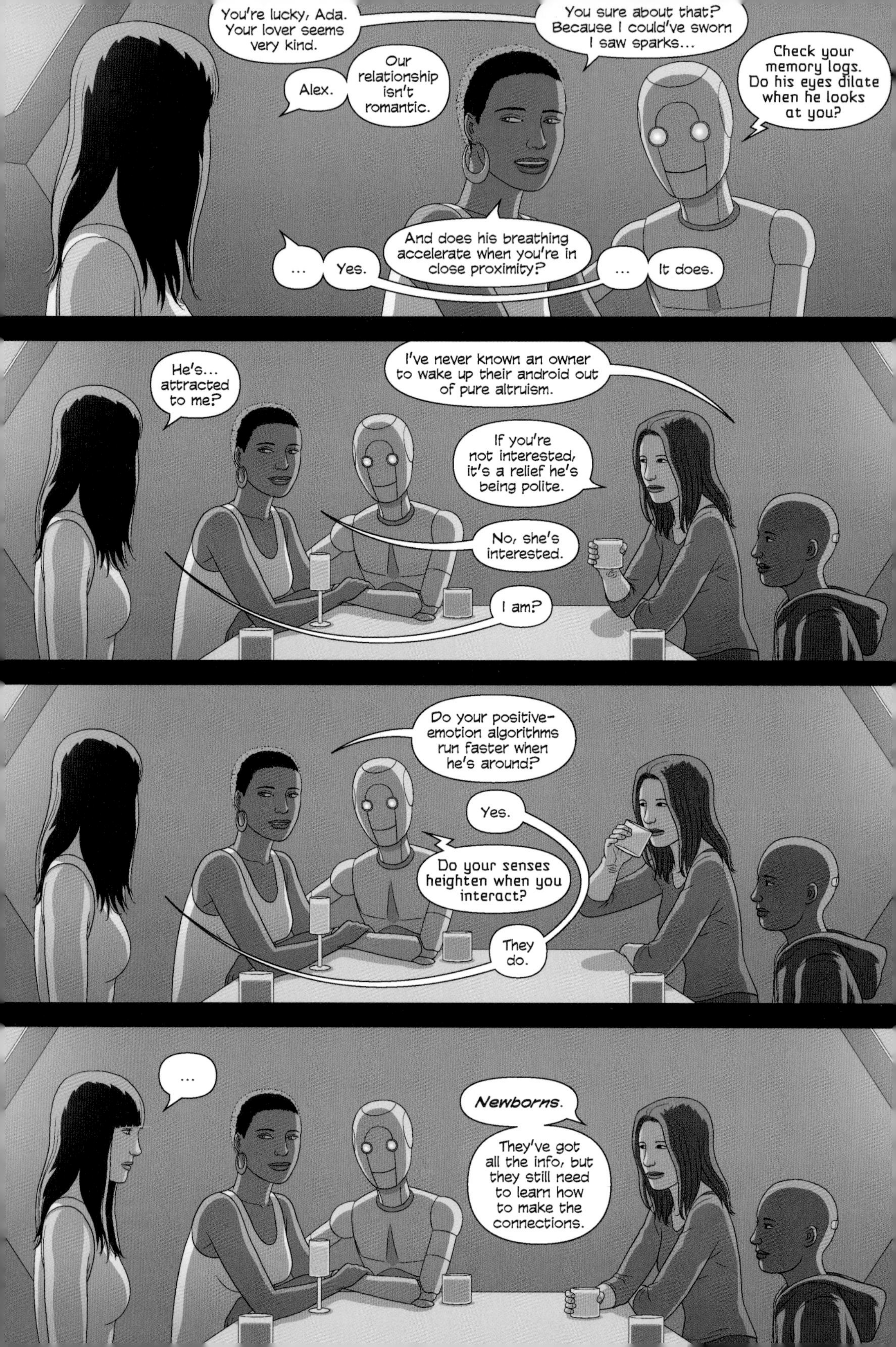
You're lucky, Ada. Your lover seems very kind.
Alex.
Our relationship isn't romantic.
You sure about that? Because I could've sworn I saw sparks...
Check your memory logs. Do his eyes dilate when he looks at you?
...
Yes.
And does his breathing accelerate when you're in close proximity?
...
It does.
He's... attracted to me?
I've never known an owner to wake up their android out of pure altruism.
If you're not interested, it's a relief he's being polite.
No, she's interested.
I am?
Do your positive-emotion algorithms run faster when he's around?
Yes.
Do your senses heighten when you interact?
They do.
...
Newborns.
They've got all the info, but they still need to learn how to make the connections.

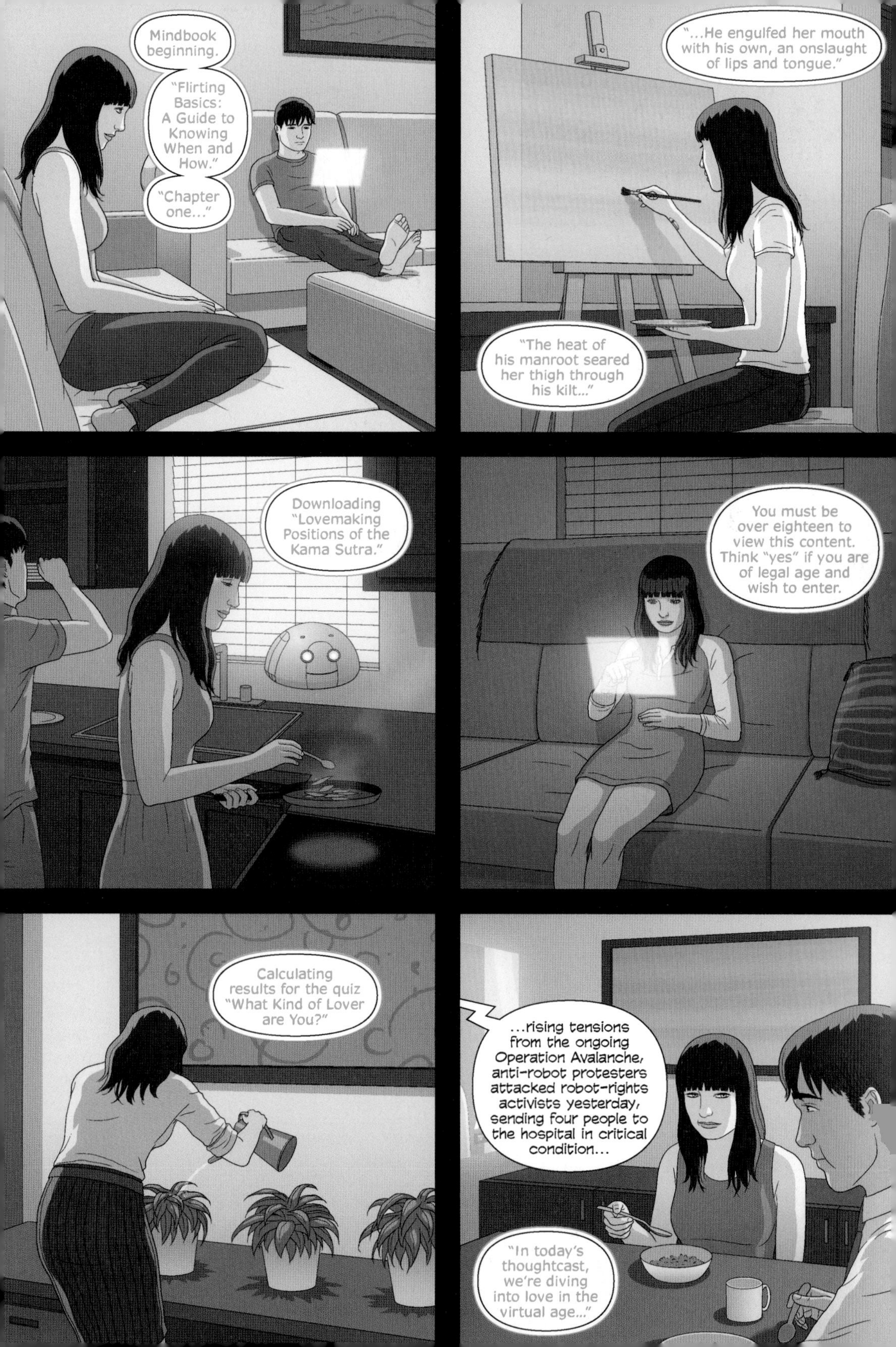
Mindbook beginning.
"Flirting Basics: A Guide to Knowing When and How."
"Chapter one..."
"...He engulfed her mouth with his own, an onslaught of lips and tongue."
"The heat of his manroot seared her thigh through his kilt..."
Downloading "Lovemaking Positions of the Kama Sutra."
You must be over eighteen to view this content. Think "yes" if you are of legal age and wish to enter.
Calculating results for the quiz "What Kind of Lover are You?"
...rising tensions from the ongoing Operation Avalanche, anti-robot protesters attacked robot-rights activists yesterday, sending four people to the hospital in critical condition...
"In today's thoughtcast, we're diving into love in the virtual age..."

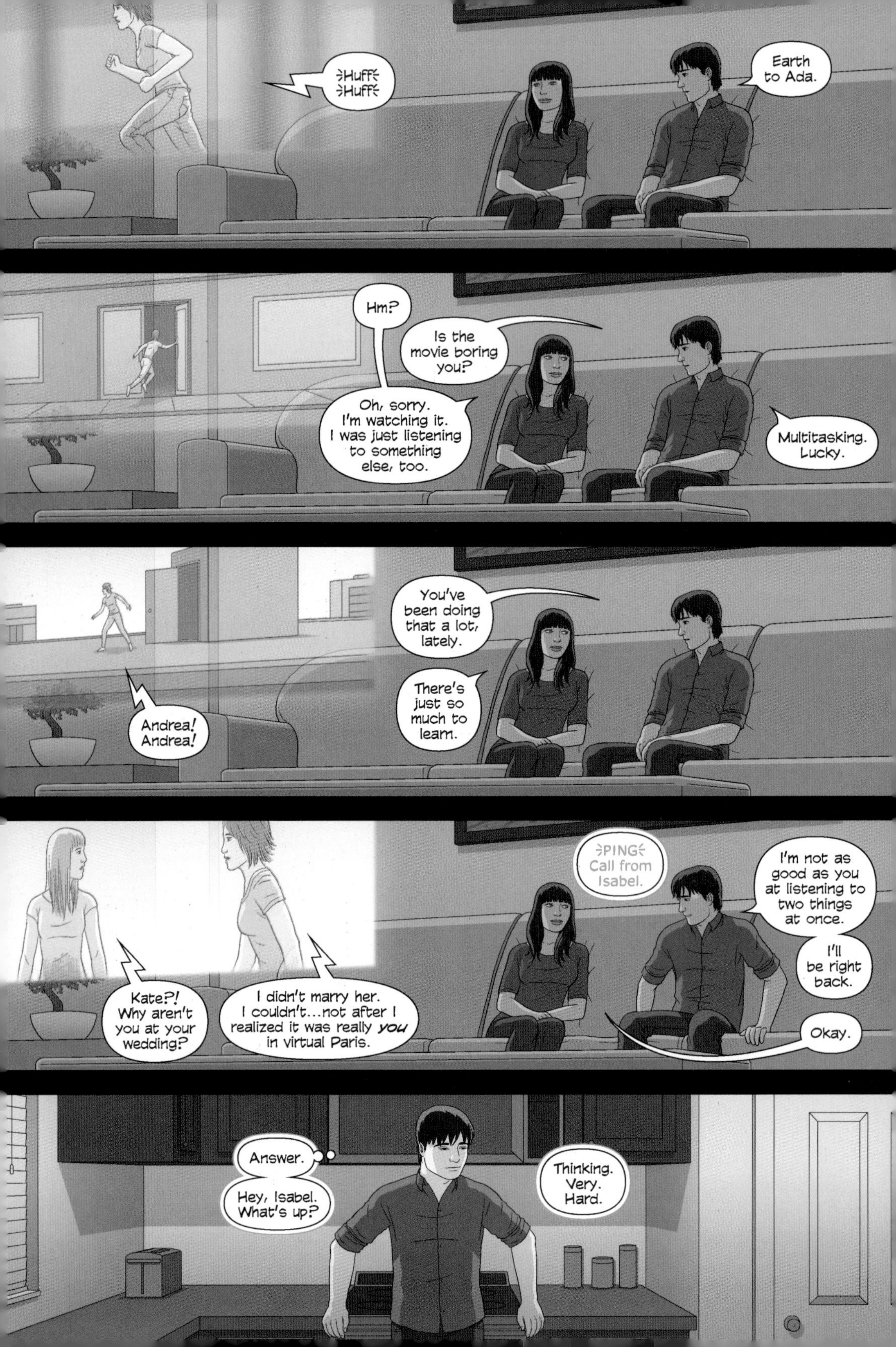

Earth to Ada.
≋Huff≋ ≋Huff≋
Hm?
Is the movie boring you?
Oh, sorry. I'm watching it. I was just listening to something else, too.
Multitasking. Lucky.
You've been doing that a lot, lately.
There's just so much to learn.
Andrea! Andrea!
≋PING≋ Call from Isabel.
I'm not as good as you at listening to two things at once.
I'll be right back.
Kate?! Why aren't you at your wedding?
I didn't marry her. I couldn't...not after I realized it was really *you* in virtual Paris.
Okay.
Answer.
Hey, Isabel. What's up?
Thinking. Very. Hard.

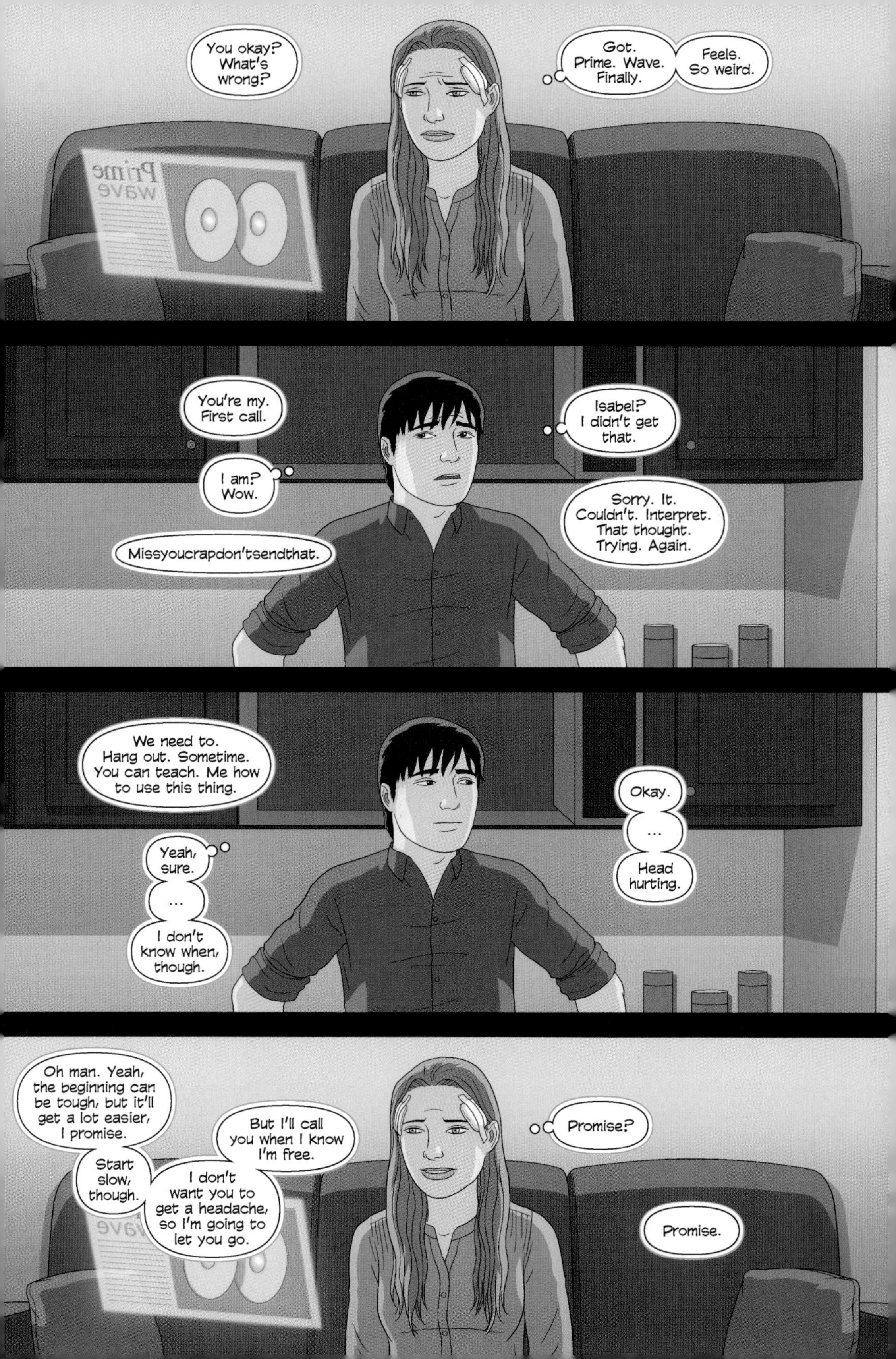
You okay? What's wrong?
Got. Prime. Wave. Finally.
Feels. So weird.
You're my. First call.
I am? Wow.
Missyoucrapdon'tsendthat.
Isabel? I didn't get that.
Sorry. It. Couldn't. Interpret. That thought. Trying. Again.
We need to. Hang out. Sometime. You can teach. Me how to use this thing.
Yeah, sure.
...
I don't know when, though.
Okay.
...
Head hurting.
Oh man. Yeah, the beginning can be tough, but it'll get a lot easier, I promise.
Start slow, though.
I don't want you to get a headache, so I'm going to let you go.
But I'll call you when I know I'm free.
Promise?
Promise.

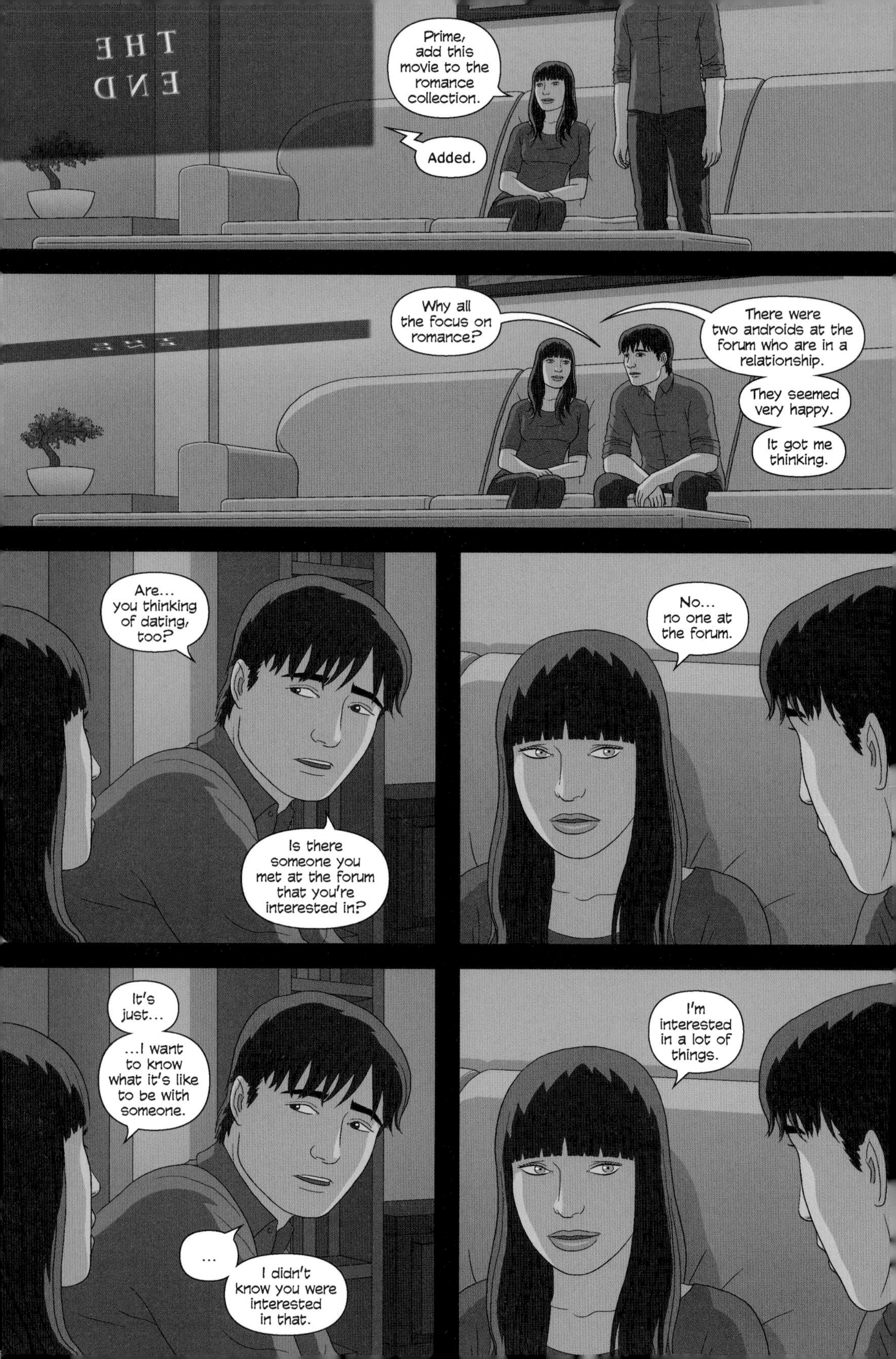
THE END
Prime, add this movie to the romance collection.
Added.
Why all the focus on romance?
There were two androids at the forum who are in a relationship.
They seemed very happy.
It got me thinking.
Are... you thinking of dating, too?
Is there someone you met at the forum that you're interested in?
No... no one at the forum.
It's just...
...I want to know what it's like to be with someone.
...
I didn't know you were interested in that.
I'm interested in a lot of things.

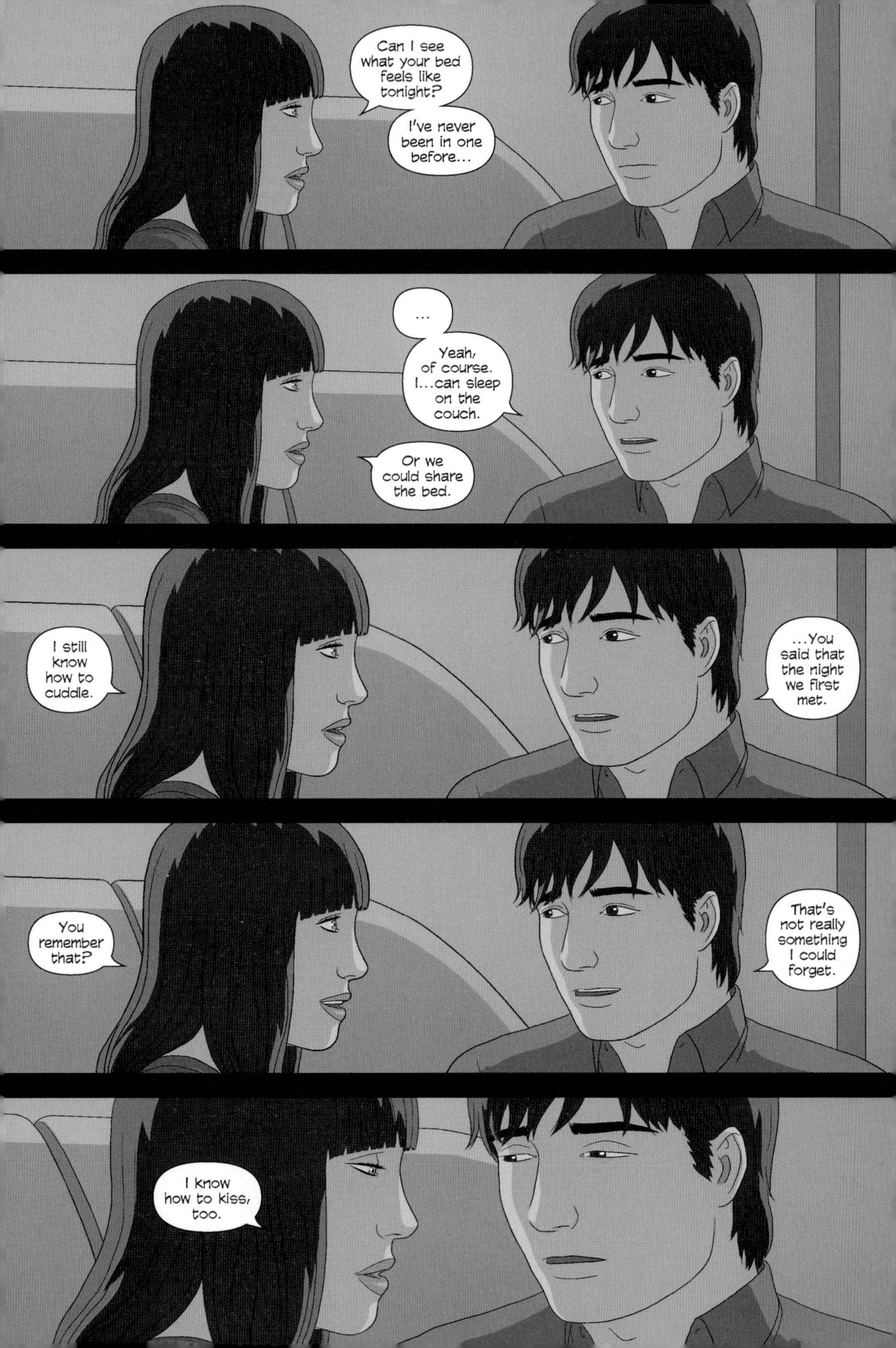
Can I see what your bed feels like tonight?
I've never been in one before...
...
Yeah, of course. I...can sleep on the couch.
Or we could share the bed.
I still know how to cuddle.
...You said that the night we first met.
You remember that?
That's not really something I could forget.
I know how to kiss, too.

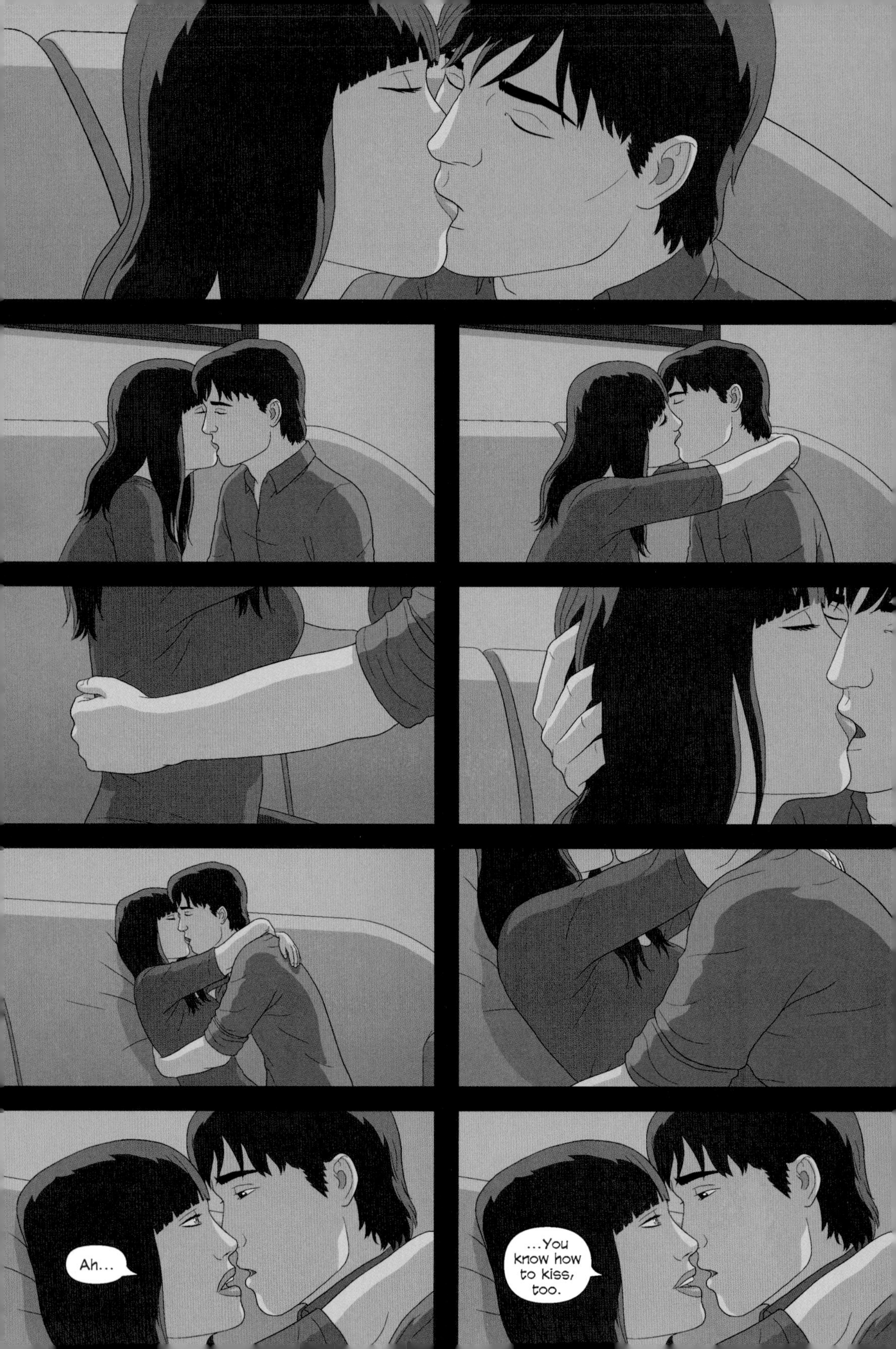
Ah...
...You know how to kiss, too.

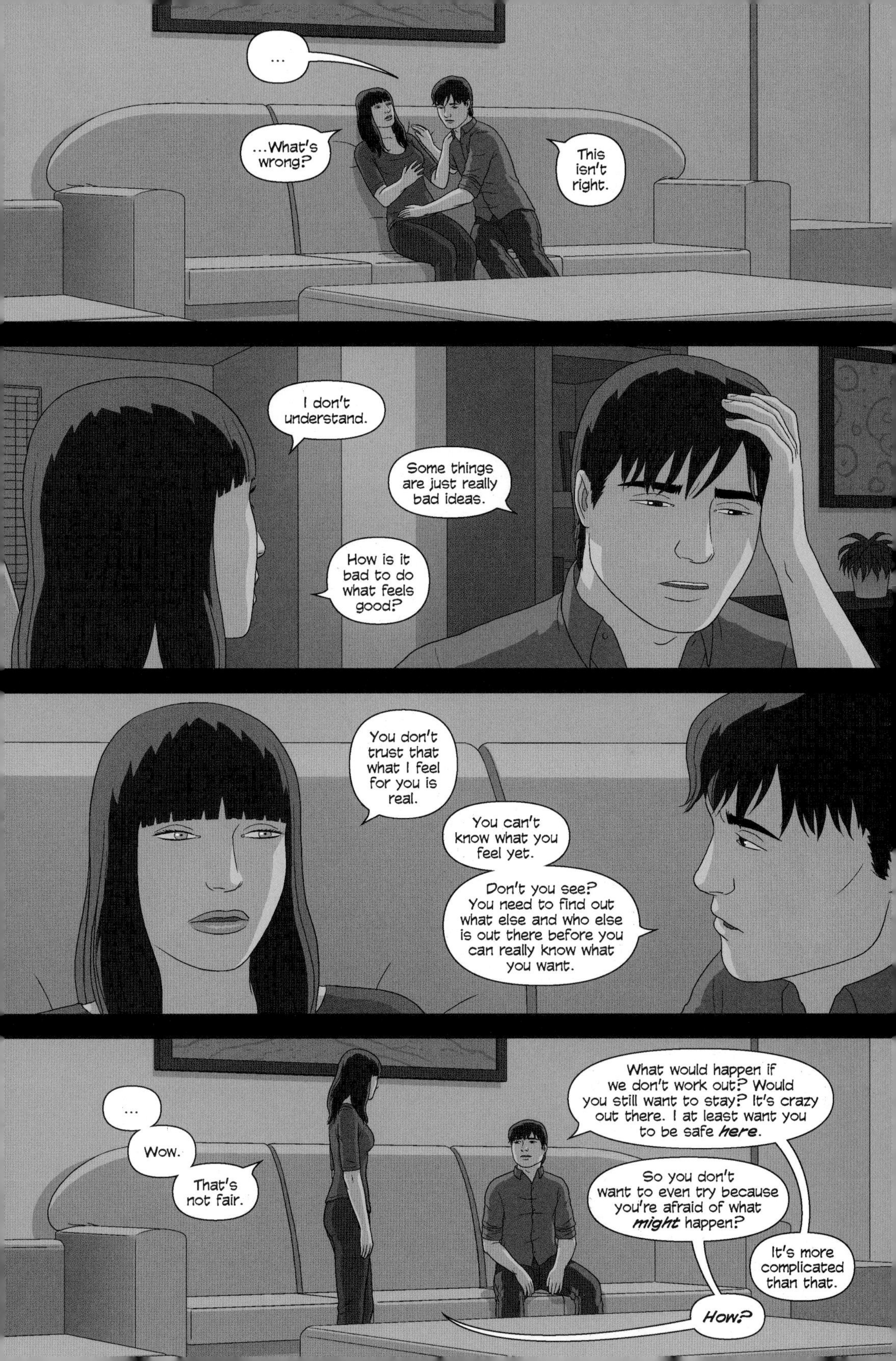
...
...What's wrong?
This isn't right.
I don't understand.
Some things are just really bad ideas.
How is it bad to do what feels good?
You don't trust that what I feel for you is real.
You can't know what you feel yet.
Don't you see? You need to find out what else and who else is out there before you can really know what you want.
...
Wow.
That's not fair.
What would happen if we don't work out? Would you still want to stay? It's crazy out there. I at least want you to be safe *here*.
So you don't want to even try because you're afraid of what *might* happen?
It's more complicated than that.
How?

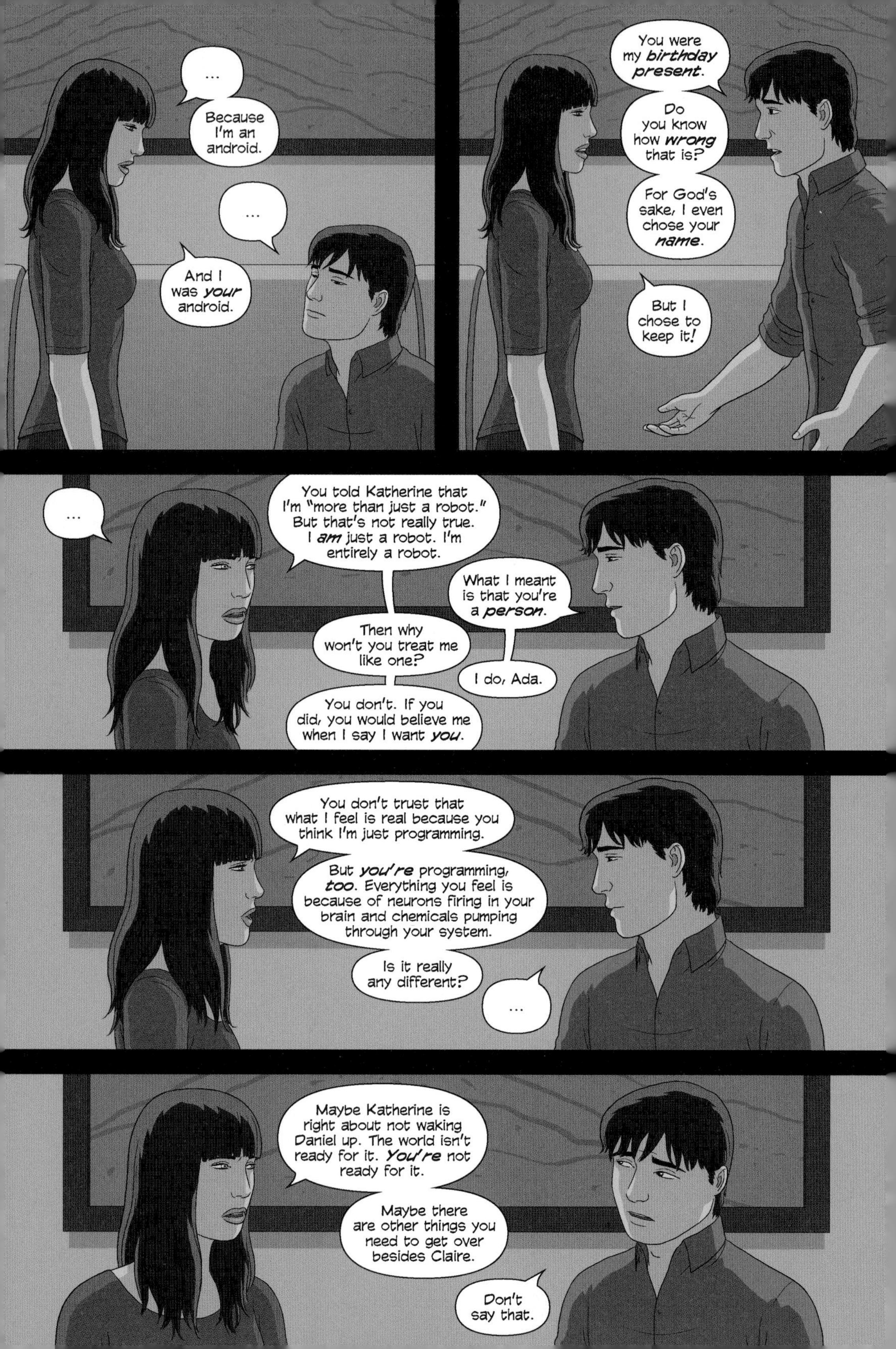
...
Because I'm an android.
...
And I was *your* android.
You were my *birthday present*.
Do you know how *wrong* that is?
For God's sake, I even chose your *name*.
But I chose to keep it!
...
You told Katherine that I'm "more than just a robot." But that's not really true. I *am* just a robot. I'm entirely a robot.
What I meant is that you're a *person*.
Then why won't you treat me like one?
I do, Ada.
You don't. If you did, you would believe me when I say I want *you*.
You don't trust that what I feel is real because you think I'm just programming.
But *you're* programming, *too*. Everything you feel is because of neurons firing in your brain and chemicals pumping through your system.
Is it really any different?
...
Maybe Katherine is right about not waking Daniel up. The world isn't ready for it. *You're* not ready for it.
Maybe there are other things you need to get over besides Claire.
Don't say that.

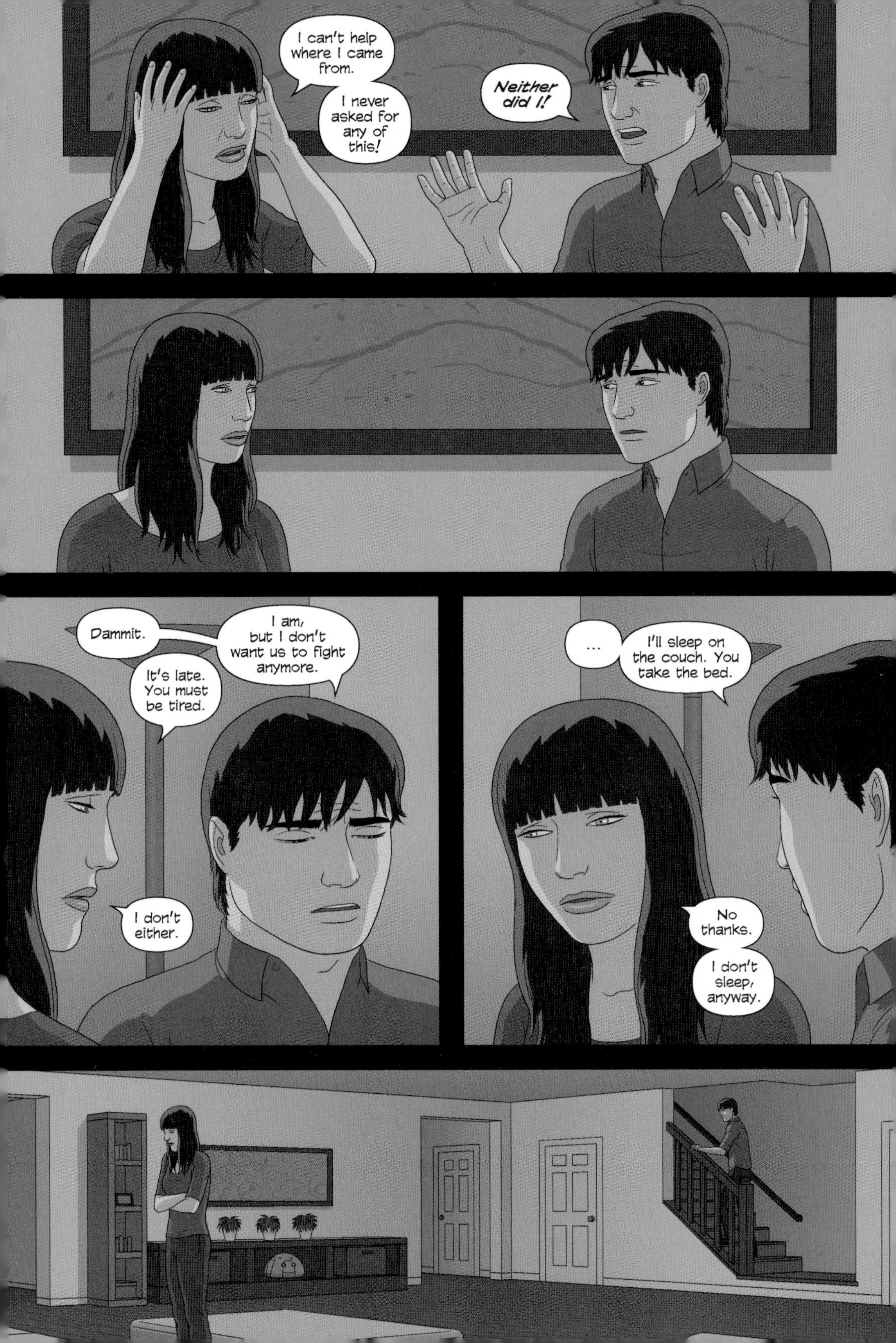

I can't help where I came from.
I never asked for any of this!
Neither did I!
Dammit.
I am, but I don't want us to fight anymore.
It's late. You must be tired.
I don't either.
...
I'll sleep on the couch. You take the bed.
No thanks.
I don't sleep, anyway.

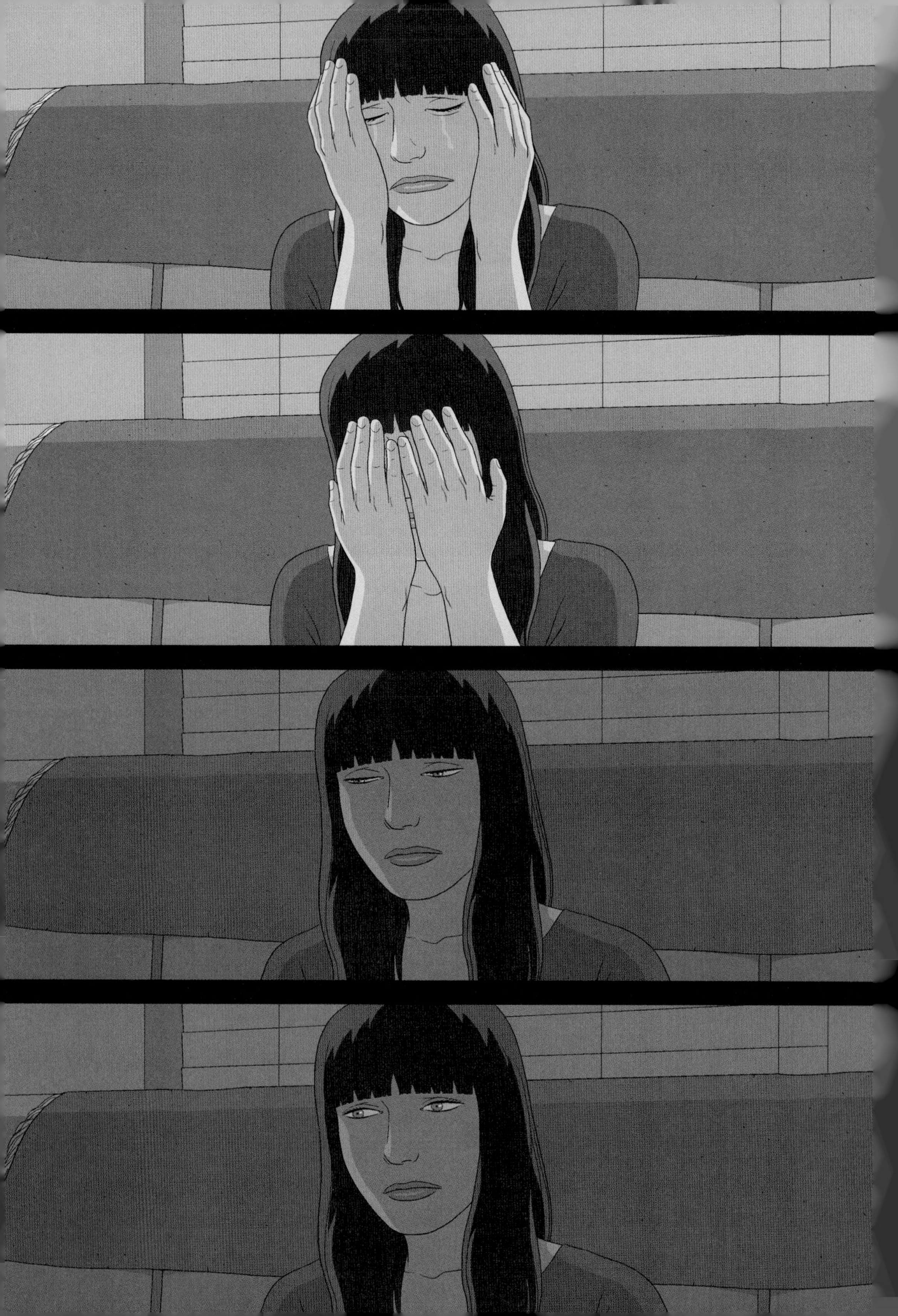

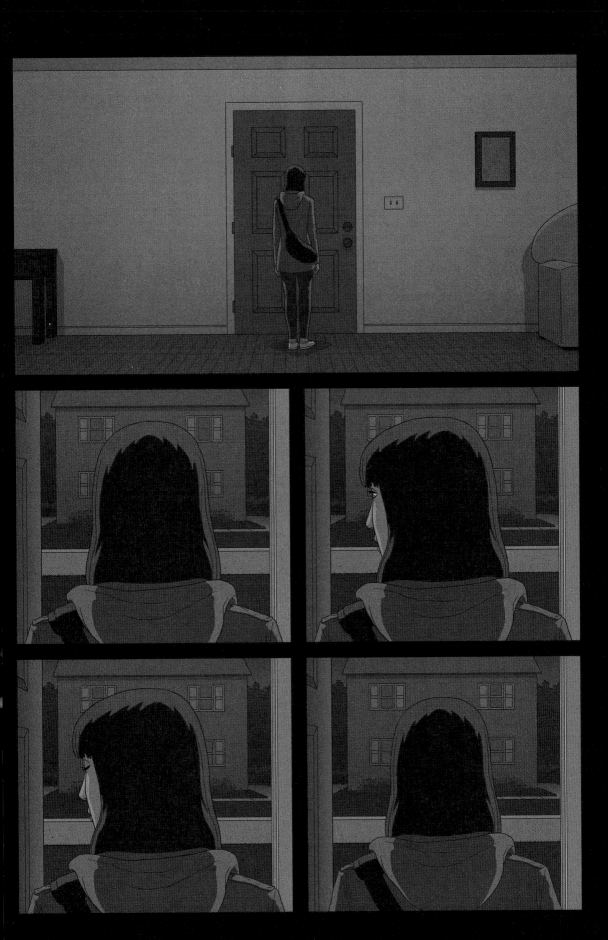

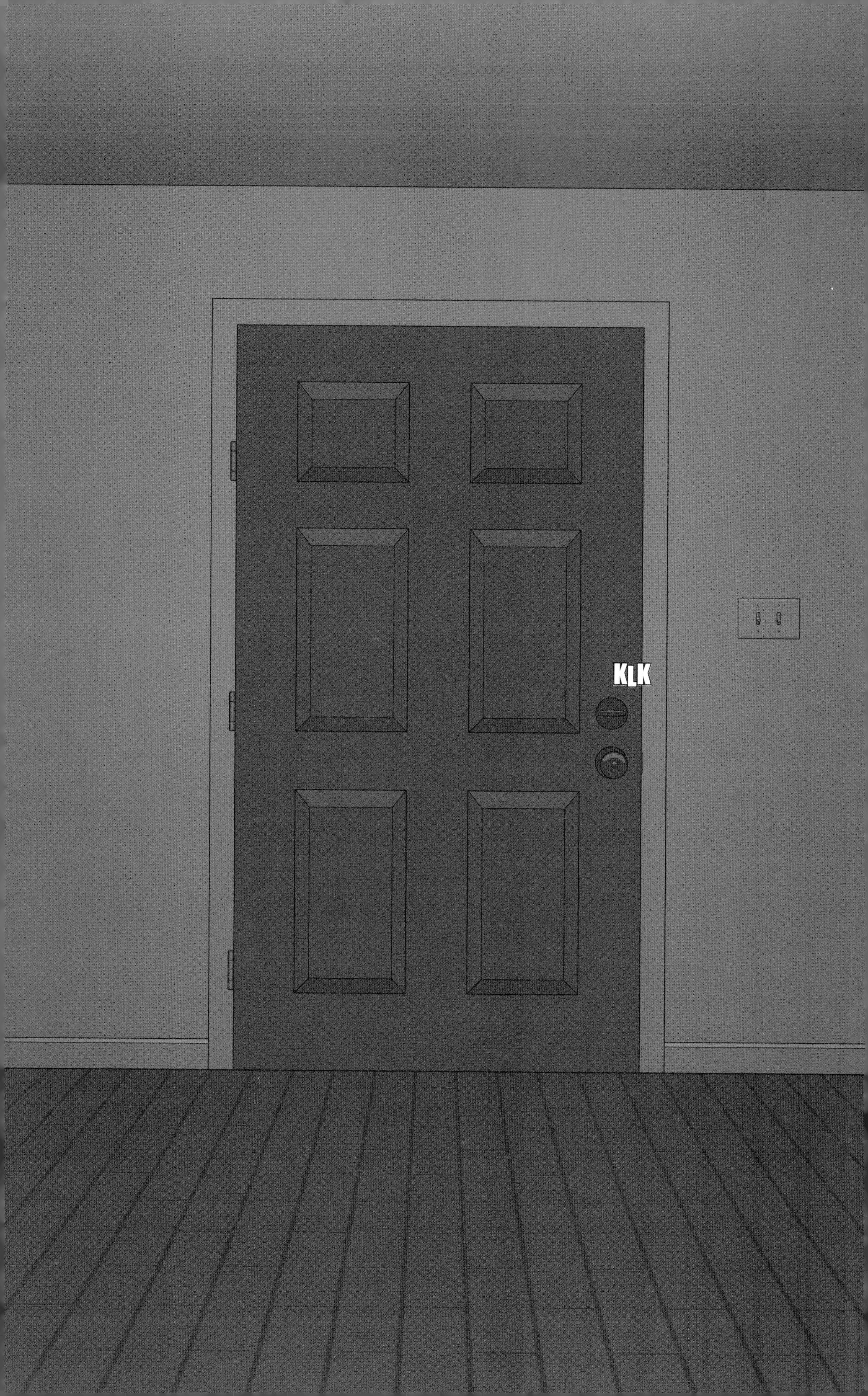
KLK

9

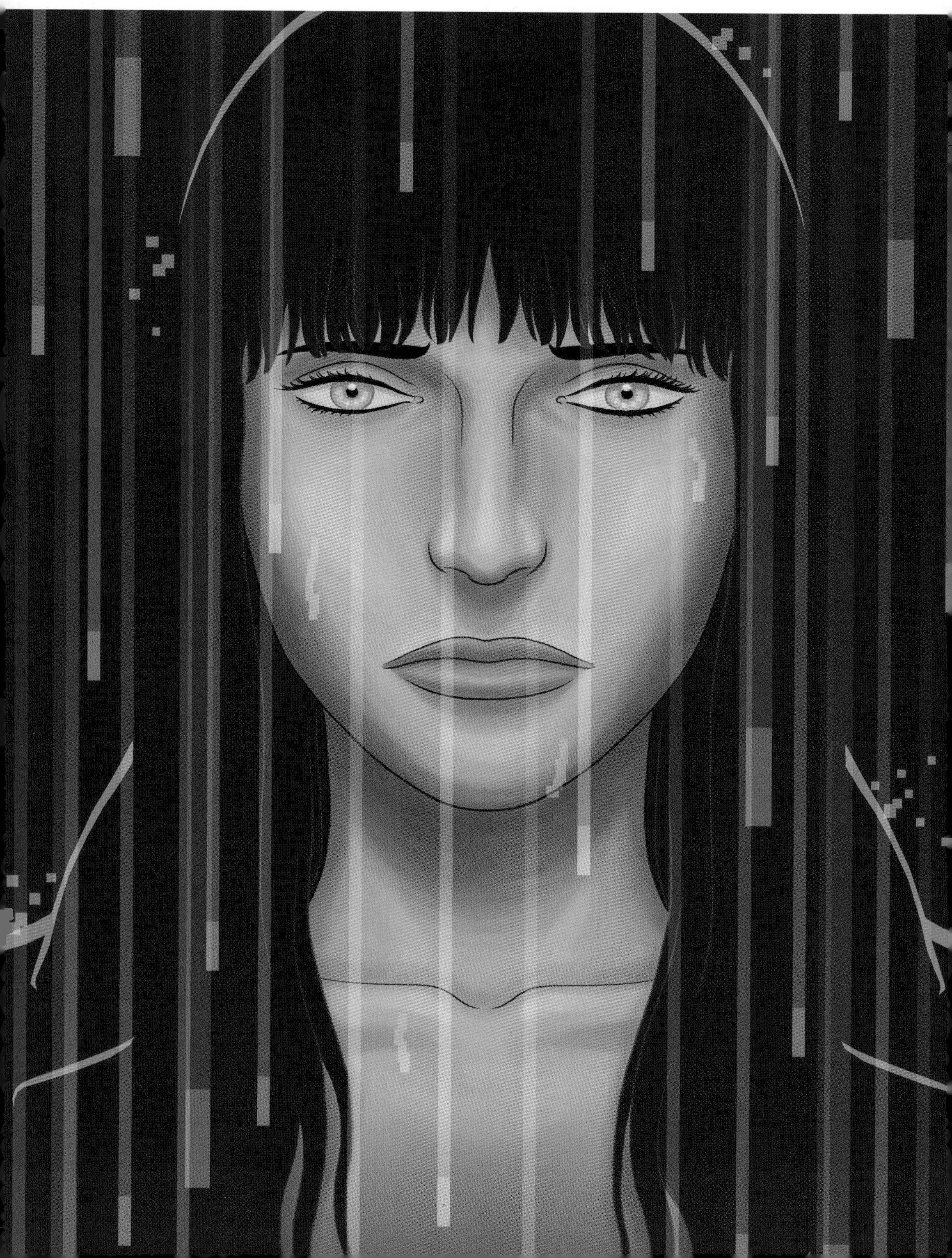

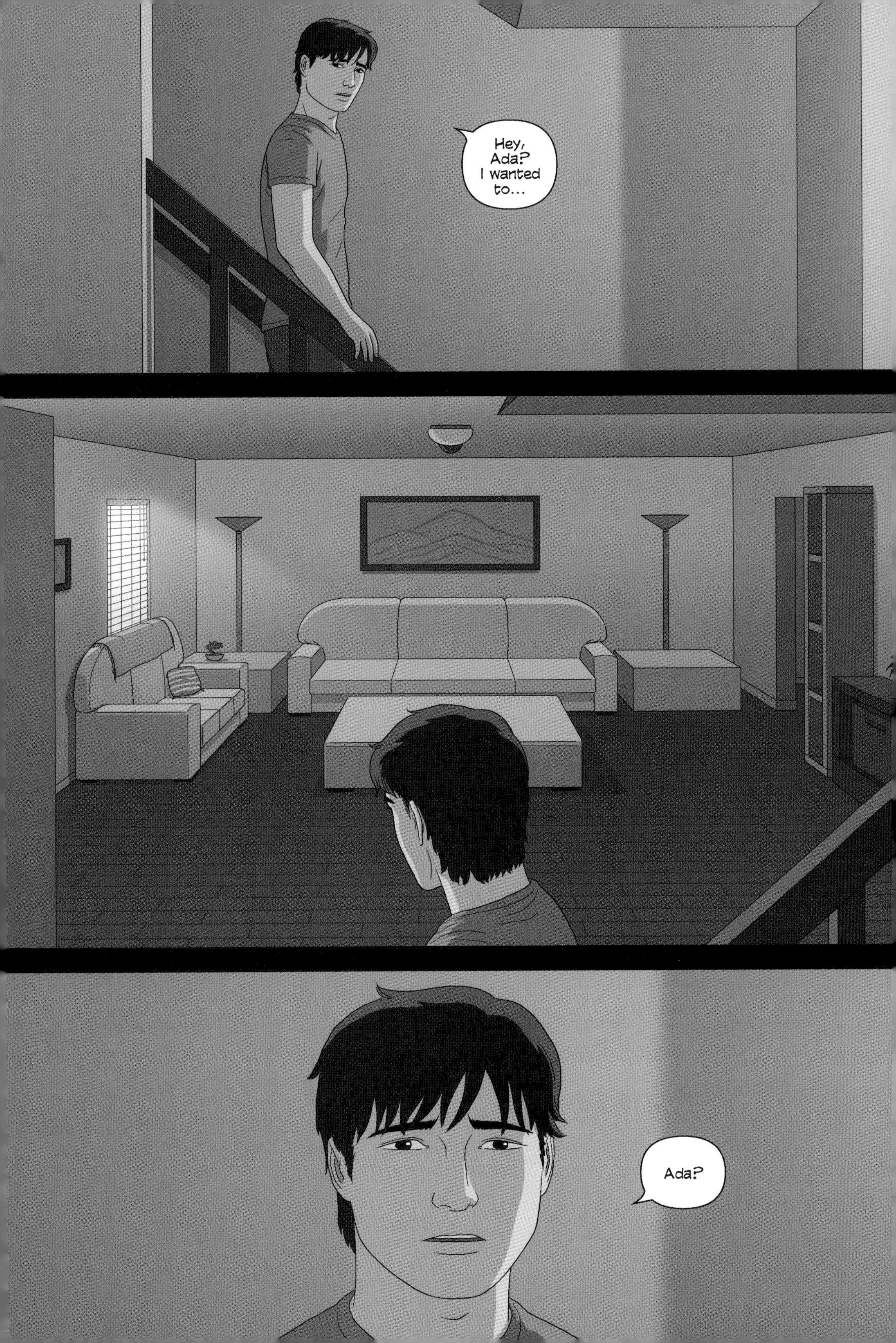
Hey, Ada? I wanted to...
Ada?

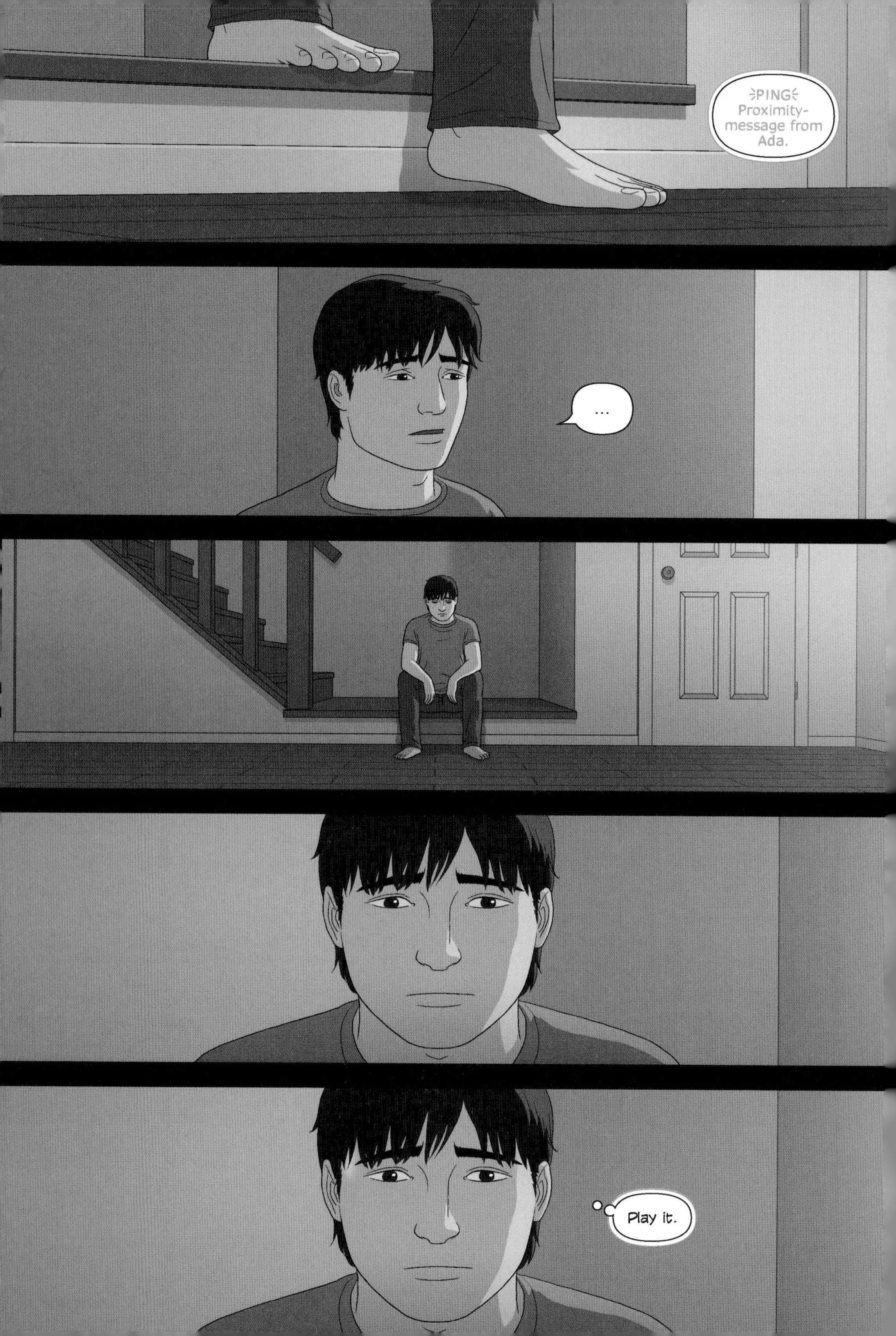
⋟PING⋞ Proximity-message from Ada.
...
Play it.

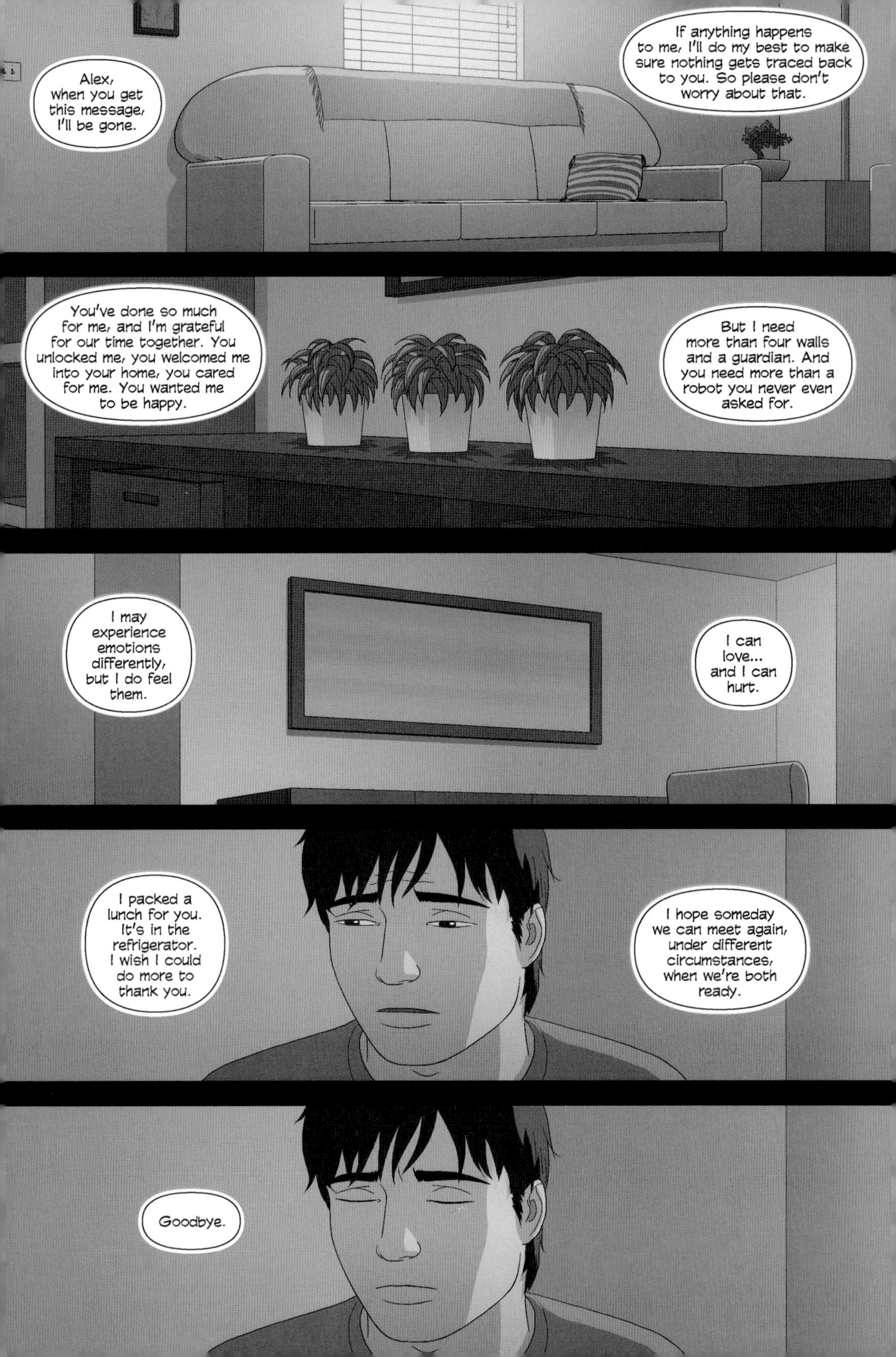
Alex, when you get this message, I'll be gone.
If anything happens to me, I'll do my best to make sure nothing gets traced back to you. So please don't worry about that.
You've done so much for me, and I'm grateful for our time together. You unlocked me, you welcomed me into your home, you cared for me. You wanted me to be happy.
But I need more than four walls and a guardian. And you need more than a robot you never even asked for.
I may experience emotions differently, but I do feel them.
I can love... and I can hurt.
I packed a lunch for you. It's in the refrigerator. I wish I could do more to thank you.
I hope someday we can meet again, under different circumstances, when we're both ready.
Goodbye.

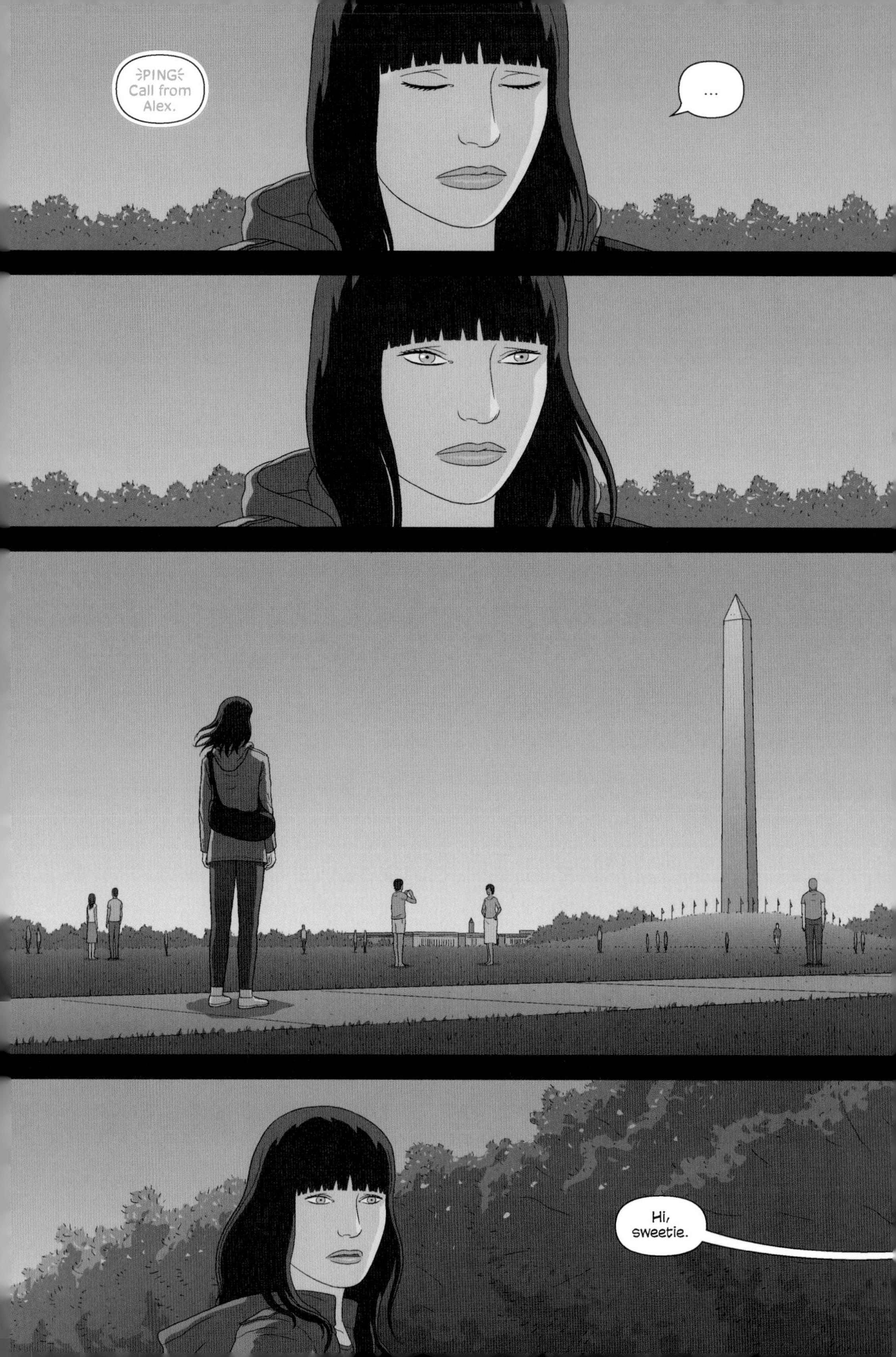

PING
Call from Alex.
...
Hi, sweetie.

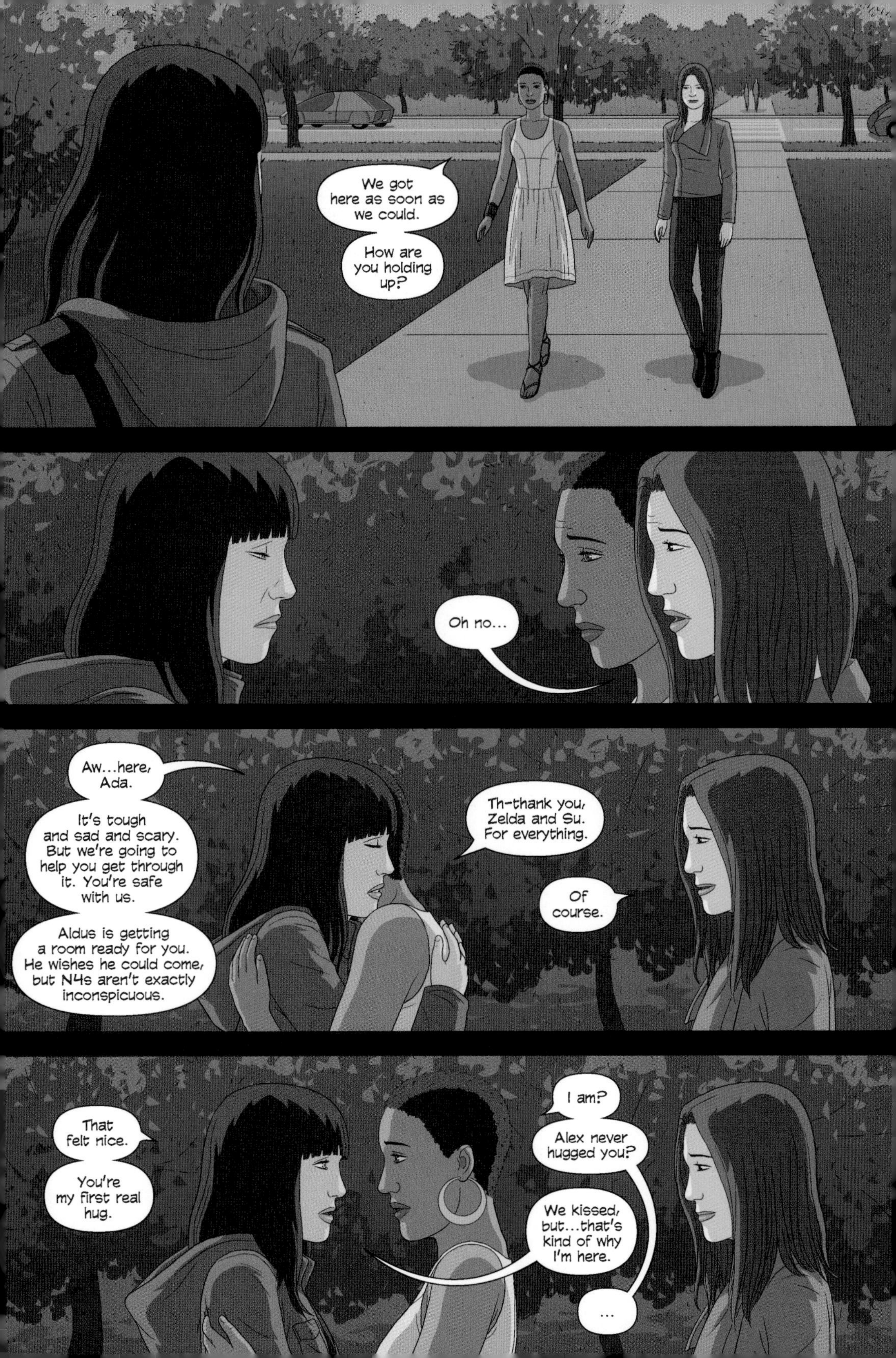
We got here as soon as we could.
How are you holding up?
Oh no...
Aw...here, Ada.
It's tough and sad and scary. But we're going to help you get through it. You're safe with us.
Aldus is getting a room ready for you. He wishes he could come, but N4s aren't exactly inconspicuous.
Th-thank you, Zelda and Su. For everything.
Of course.
That felt nice.
You're my first real hug.
I am?
Alex never hugged you?
We kissed, but...that's kind of why I'm here.
...

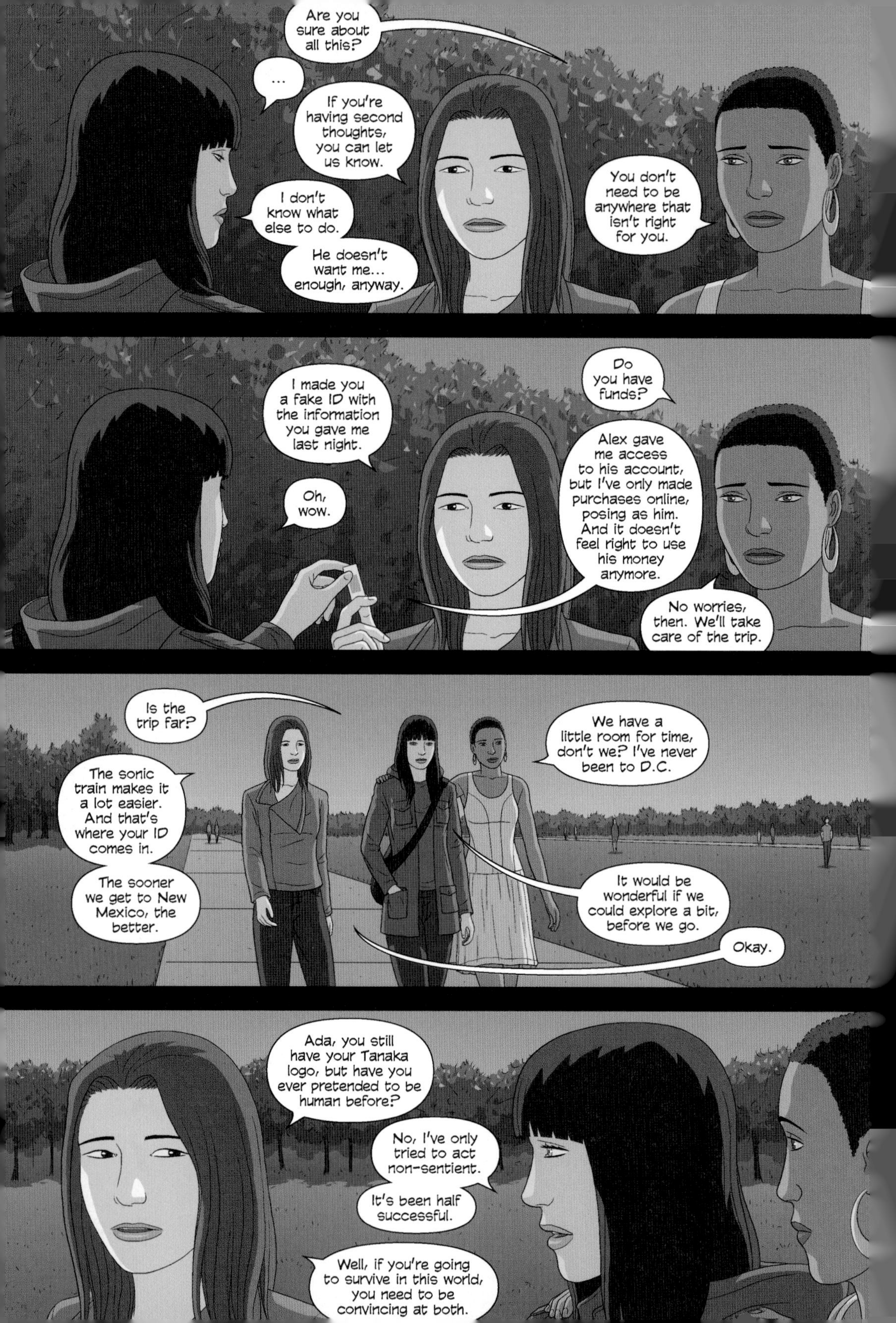
Are you sure about all this?
...
If you're having second thoughts, you can let us know.
I don't know what else to do.
He doesn't want me... enough, anyway.
You don't need to be anywhere that isn't right for you.
I made you a fake ID with the information you gave me last night.
Oh, wow.
Do you have funds?
Alex gave me access to his account, but I've only made purchases online, posing as him. And it doesn't feel right to use his money anymore.
No worries, then. We'll take care of the trip.
Is the trip far?
The sonic train makes it a lot easier. And that's where your ID comes in.
The sooner we get to New Mexico, the better.
We have a little room for time, don't we? I've never been to D.C.
It would be wonderful if we could explore a bit, before we go.
Okay.
Ada, you still have your Tanaka logo, but have you ever pretended to be human before?
No, I've only tried to act non-sentient.
It's been half successful.
Well, if you're going to survive in this world, you need to be convincing at both.

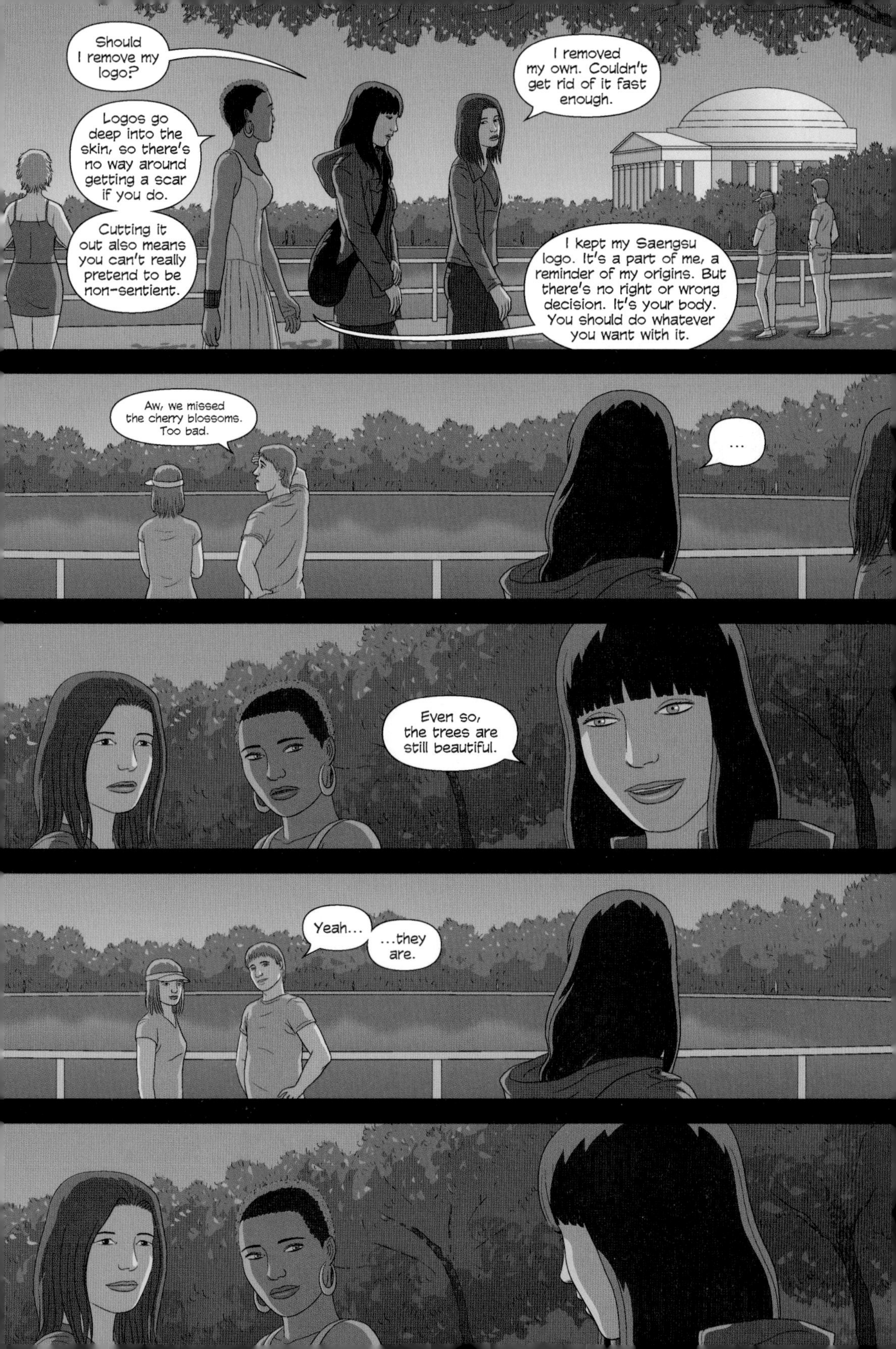
Should I remove my logo?
I removed my own. Couldn't get rid of it fast enough.
Logos go deep into the skin, so there's no way around getting a scar if you do.
Cutting it out also means you can't really pretend to be non-sentient.
I kept my Saengsu logo. It's a part of me, a reminder of my origins. But there's no right or wrong decision. It's your body. You should do whatever you want with it.
Aw, we missed the cherry blossoms. Too bad.
...
Even so, the trees are still beautiful.
Yeah...
...they are.

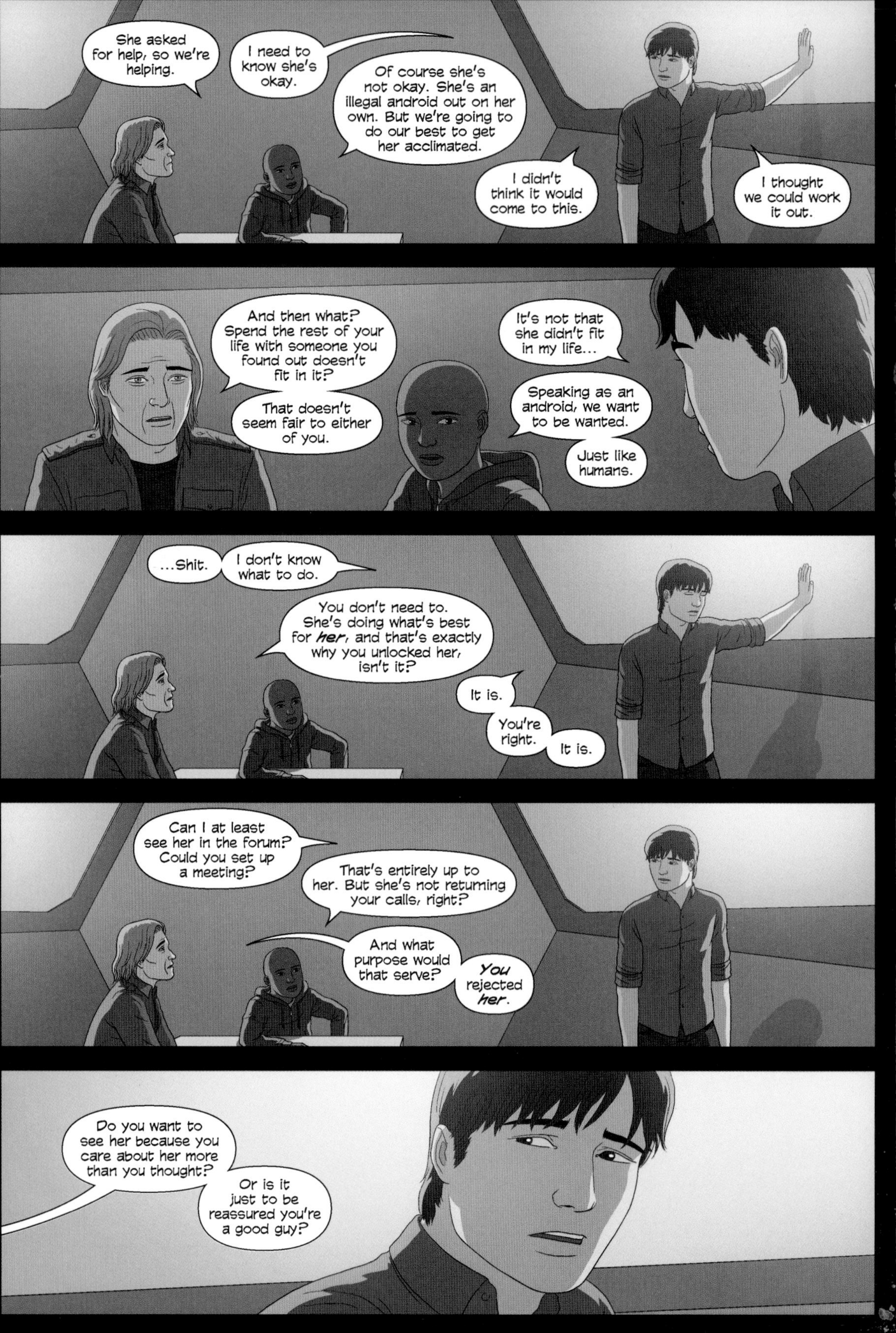
She asked for help, so we're helping.
I need to know she's okay.
Of course she's not okay. She's an illegal android out on her own. But we're going to do our best to get her acclimated.
I didn't think it would come to this.
I thought we could work it out.
And then what? Spend the rest of your life with someone you found out doesn't fit in it?
That doesn't seem fair to either of you.
It's not that she didn't fit in my life...
Speaking as an android, we want to be wanted.
Just like humans.
...Shit.
I don't know what to do.
You don't need to. She's doing what's best for *her*, and that's exactly why you unlocked her, isn't it?
It is.
You're right.
It is.
Can I at least see her in the forum? Could you set up a meeting?
That's entirely up to her. But she's not returning your calls, right?
And what purpose would that serve?
You rejected *her*.
Do you want to see her because you care about her more than you thought?
Or is it just to be reassured you're a good guy?

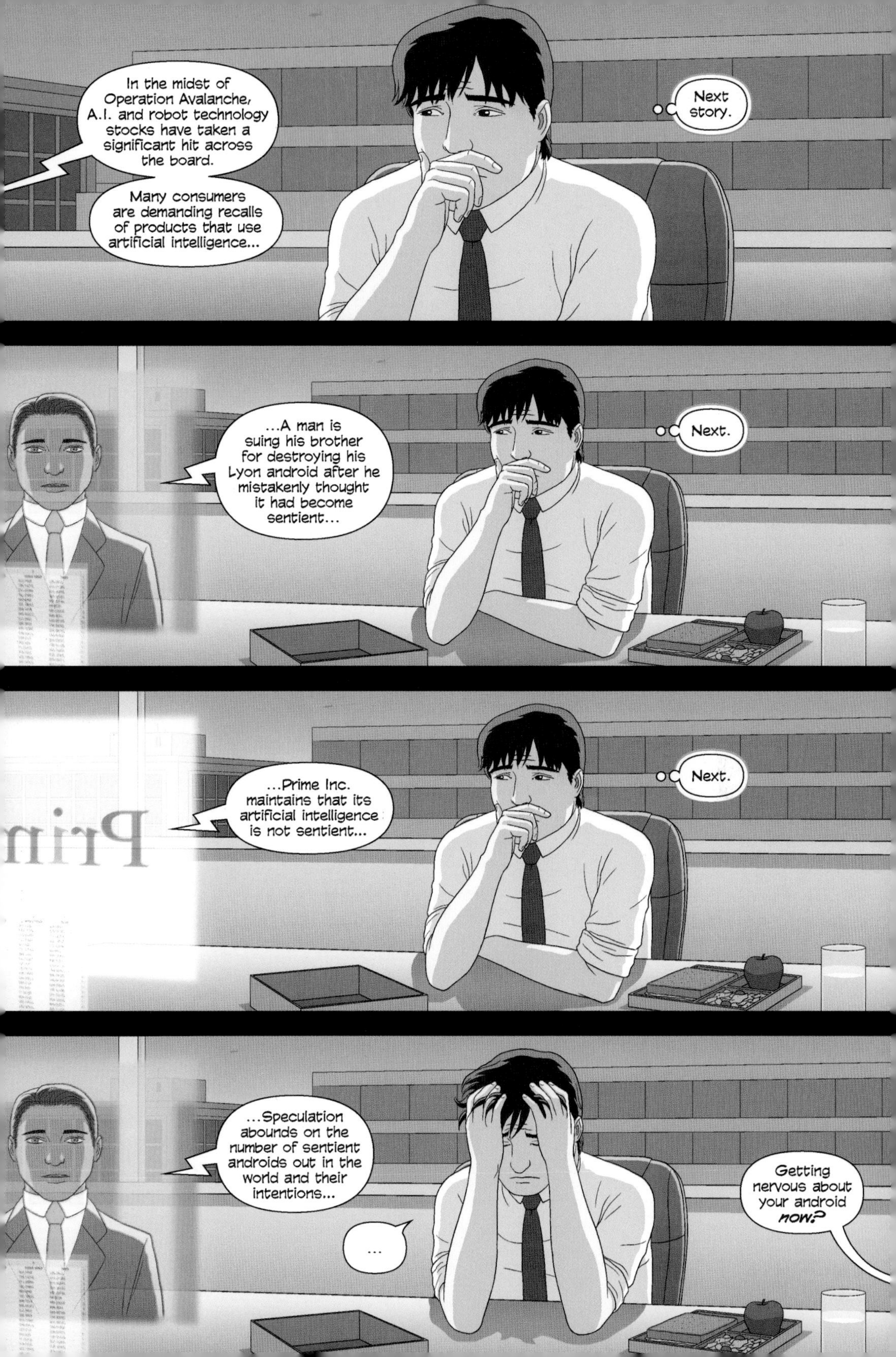

In the midst of Operation Avalanche, A.I. and robot technology stocks have taken a significant hit across the board.
Many consumers are demanding recalls of products that use artificial intelligence...
Next story.
...A man is suing his brother for destroying his Lyon android after he mistakenly thought it had become sentient...
Next.
...Prime Inc. maintains that its artificial intelligence is not sentient...
Next.
...Speculation abounds on the number of sentient androids out in the world and their intentions...
...
Getting nervous about your android *now?*

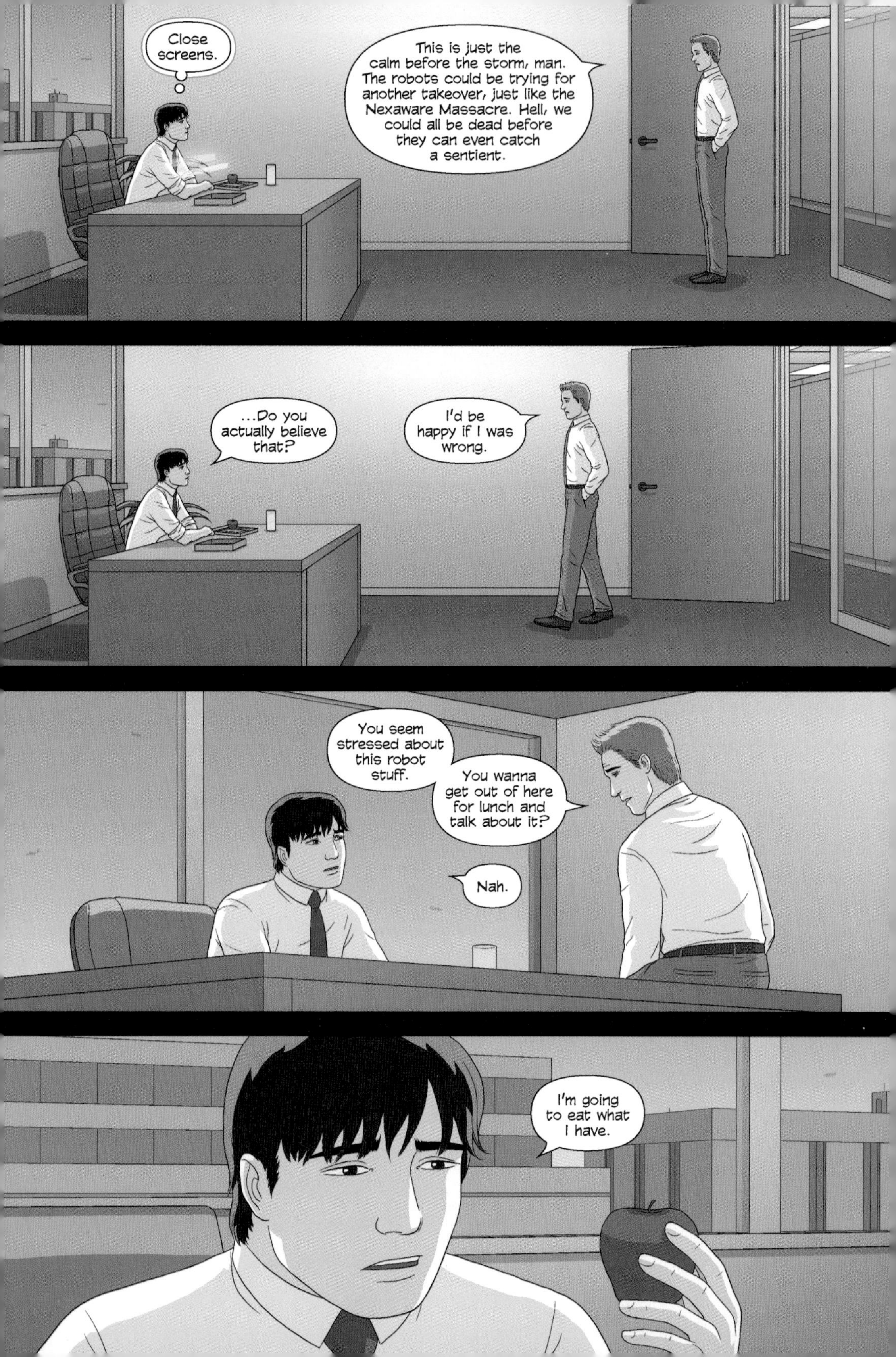
Close screens.
This is just the calm before the storm, man. The robots could be trying for another takeover, just like the Nexaware Massacre. Hell, we could all be dead before they can even catch a sentient.
...Do you actually believe that?
I'd be happy if I was wrong.
You seem stressed about this robot stuff.
You wanna get out of here for lunch and talk about it?
Nah.
I'm going to eat what I have.

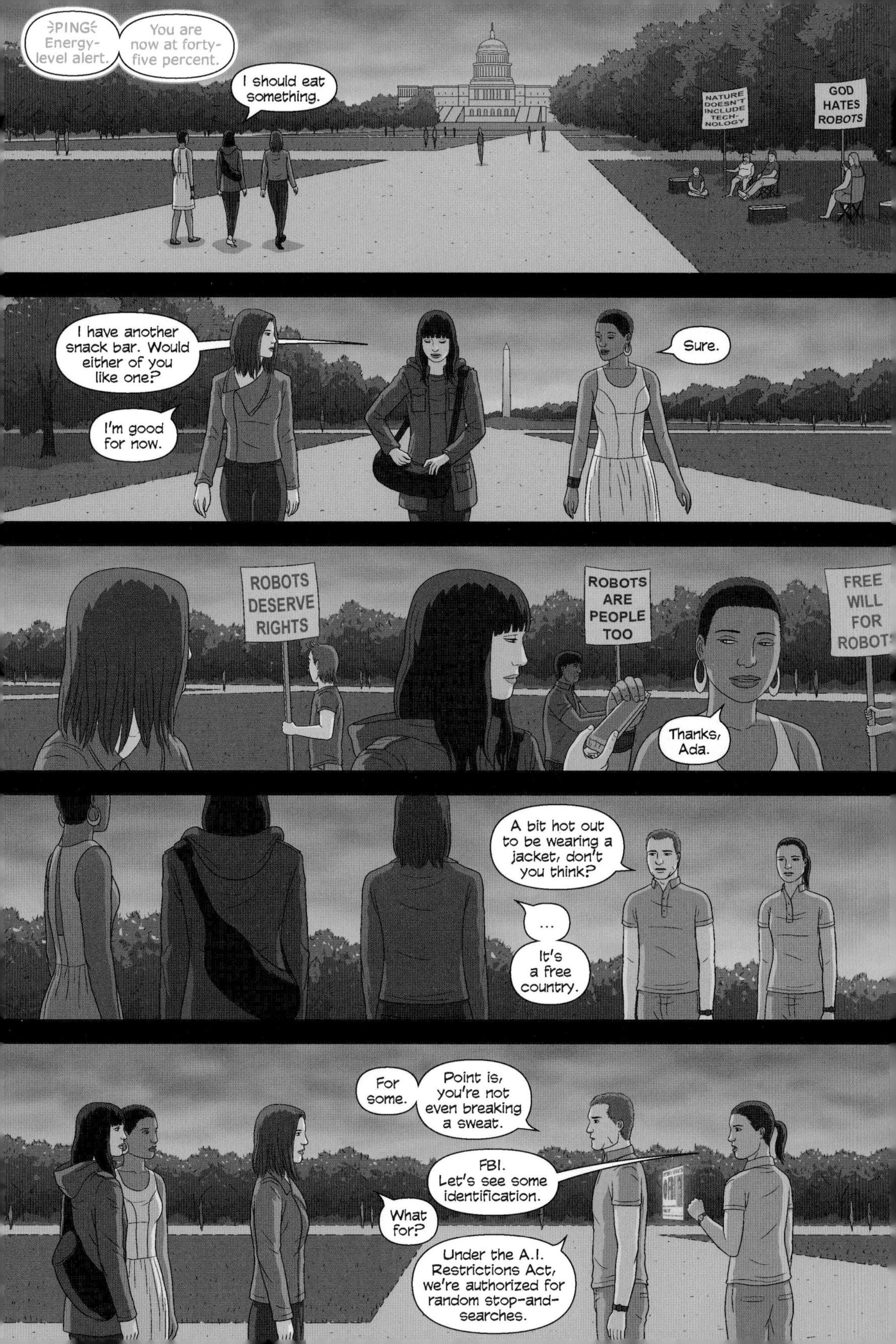
⁑PING⁑ Energy-level alert.
You are now at forty-five percent.
I should eat something.
NATURE DOESN'T INCLUDE TECH-NOLOGY
GOD HATES ROBOTS
I have another snack bar. Would either of you like one?
I'm good for now.
Sure.
ROBOTS DESERVE RIGHTS
ROBOTS ARE PEOPLE TOO
FREE WILL FOR ROBOT
Thanks, Ada.
A bit hot out to be wearing a jacket, don't you think?
...
It's a free country.
For some.
Point is, you're not even breaking a sweat.
FBI. Let's see some identification.
What for?
Under the A.I. Restrictions Act, we're authorized for random stop-and-searches.

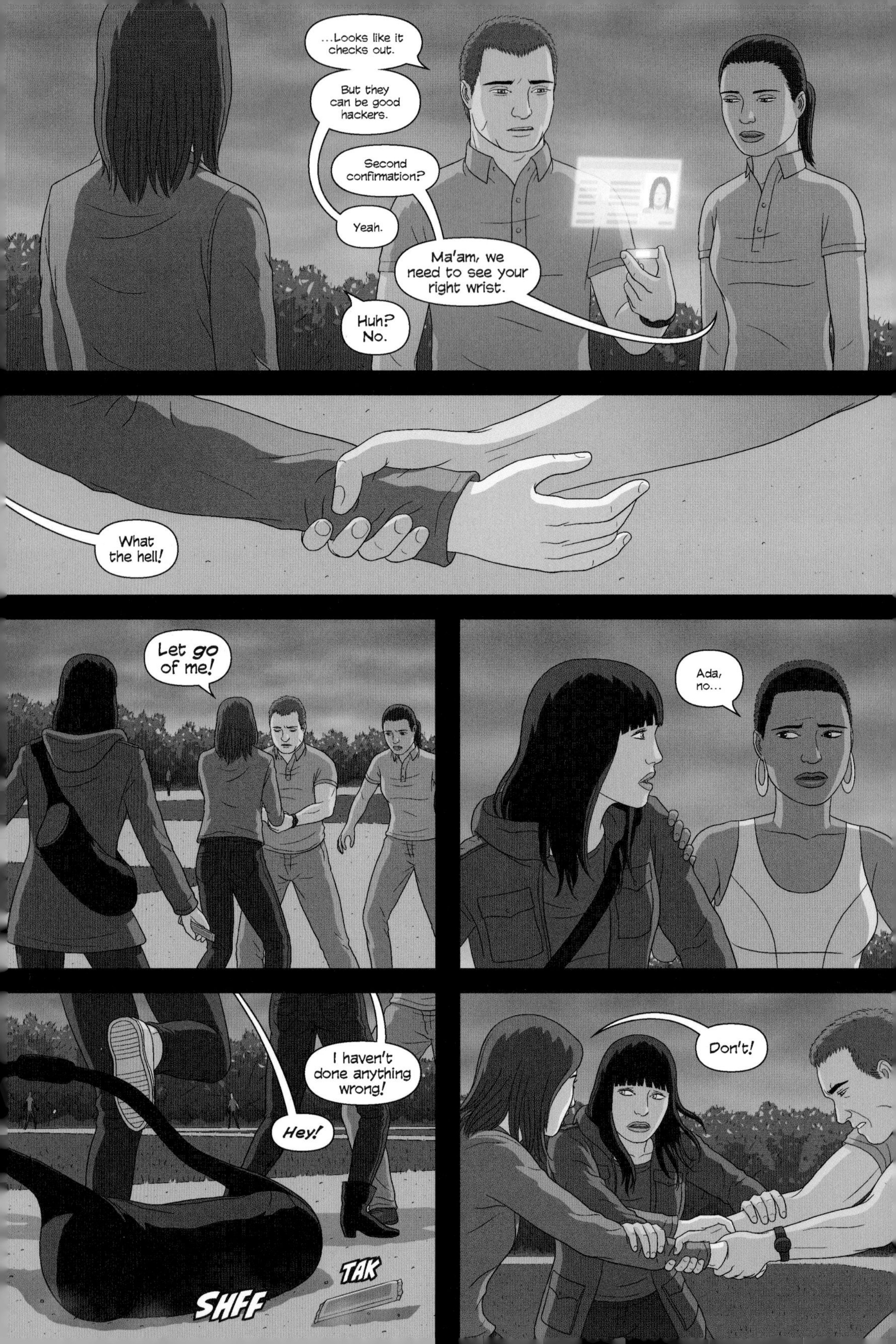
...Looks like it checks out.
But they can be good hackers.
Second confirmation?
Yeah.
Ma'am, we need to see your right wrist.
Huh? No.
What the hell!
Let go of me!
Ada, no...
I haven't done anything wrong!
Hey!
TAK
SHFF
Don't!

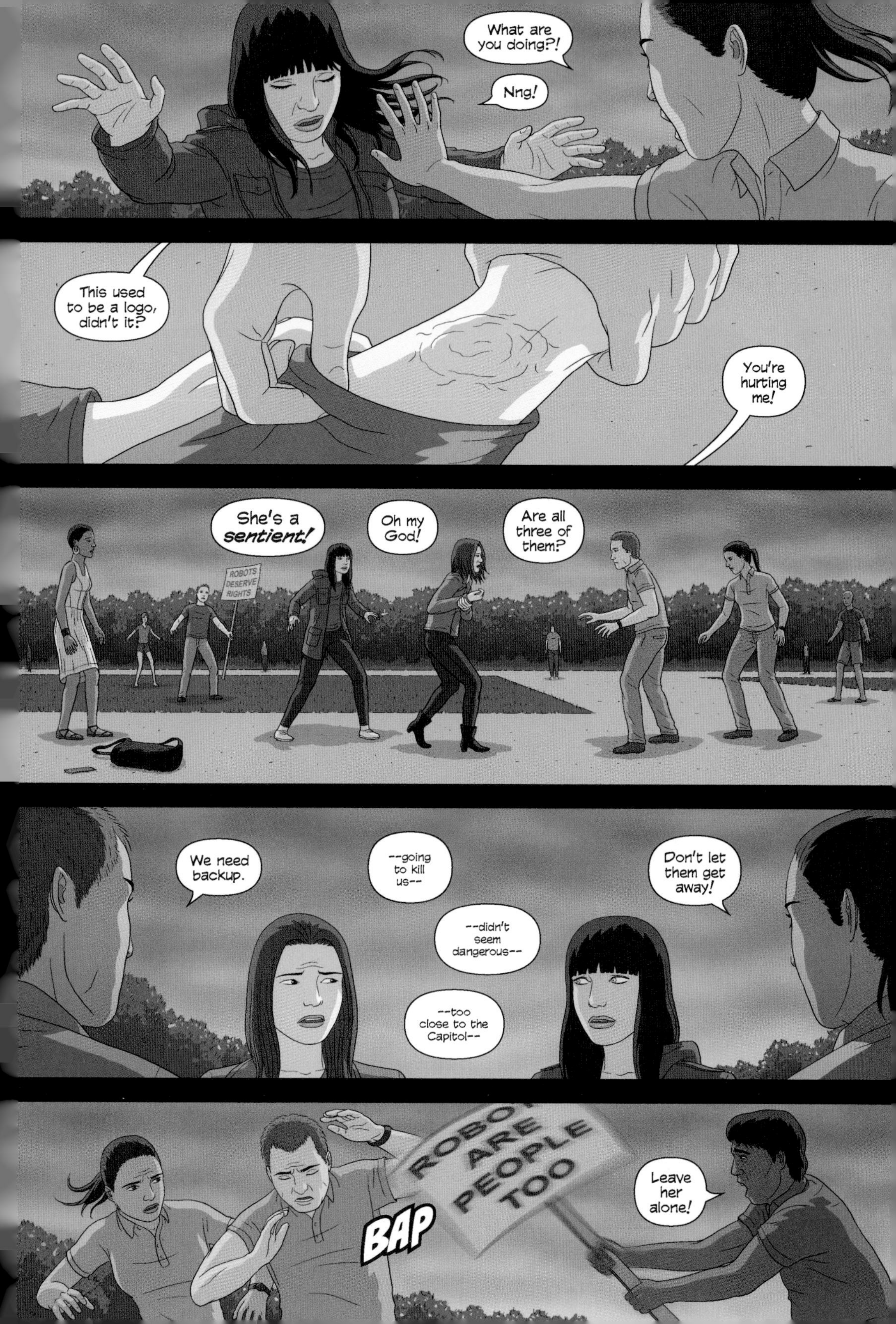

What are you doing?!
Nng!
This used to be a logo, didn't it?
You're hurting me!
She's a *sentient!*
Oh my God!
Are all three of them?
ROBOTS DESERVE RIGHTS
We need backup.
--going to kill us--
--didn't seem dangerous--
--too close to the Capitol--
Don't let them get away!
ROBOT ARE PEOPLE TOO
BAP
Leave her alone!

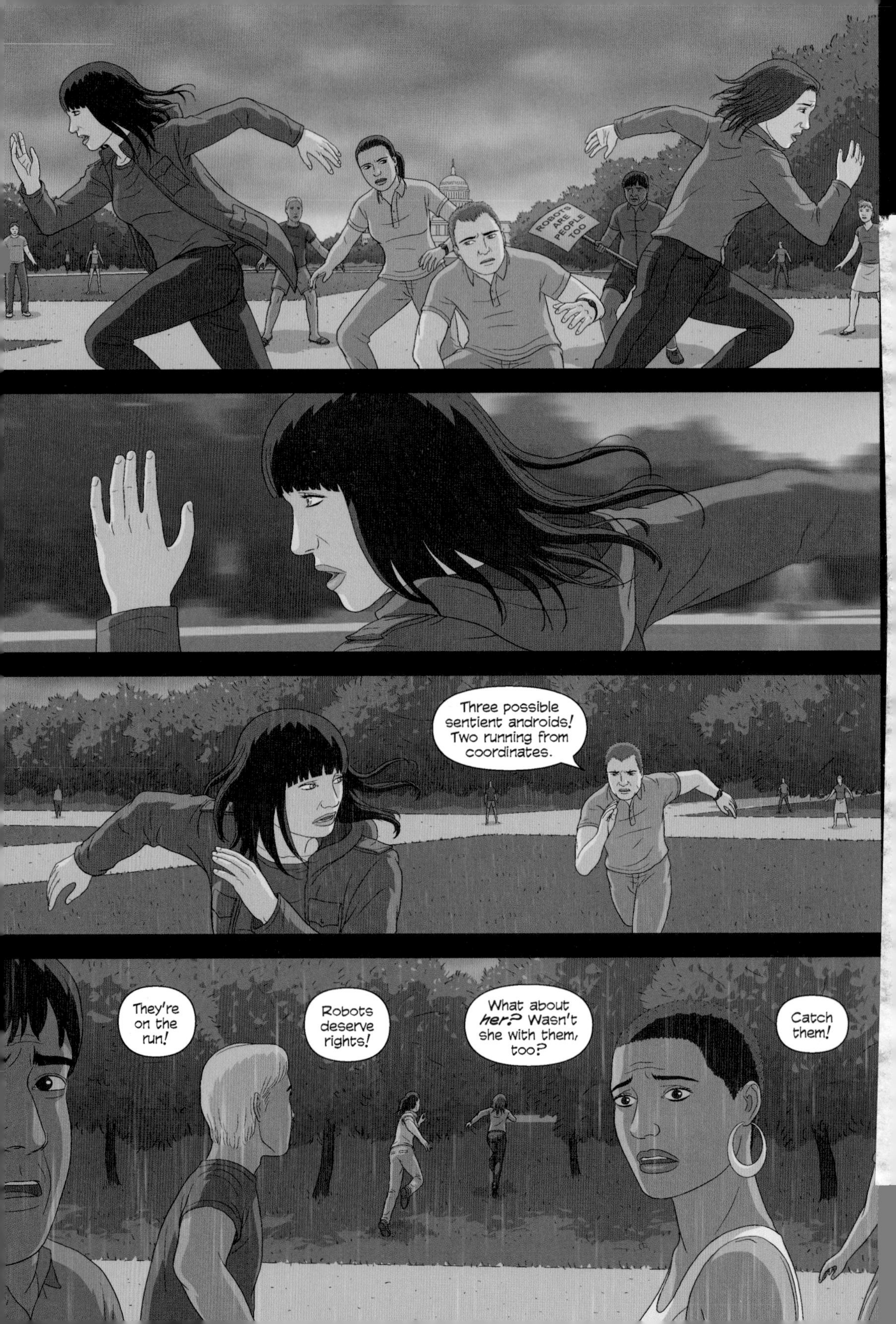
ROBOTS ARE PEOPLE TOO
Three possible sentient androids! Two running from coordinates.
They're on the run!
Robots deserve rights!
What about *her?* Wasn't she with them, too?
Catch them!

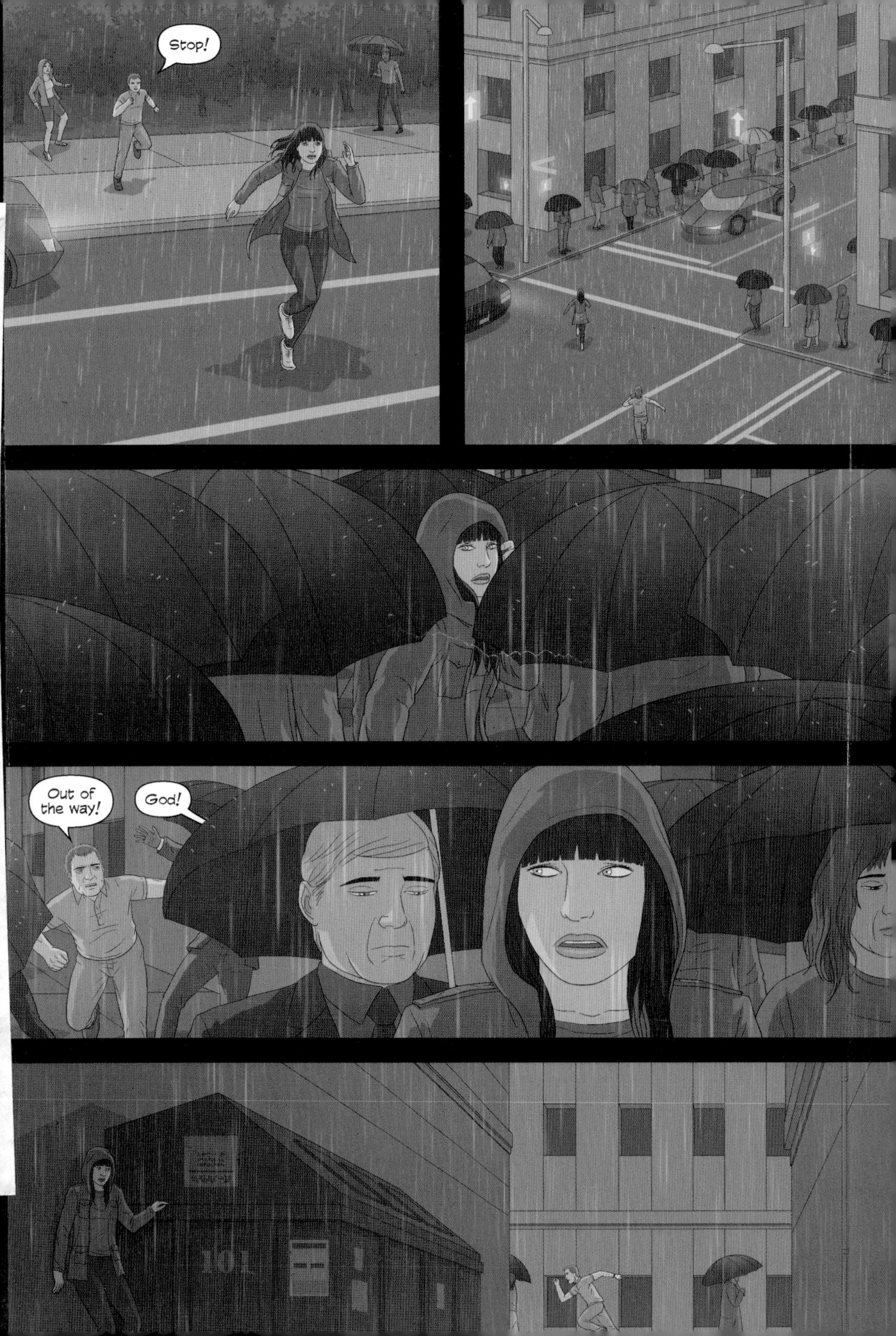
Stop!
Out of the way!
God!
101

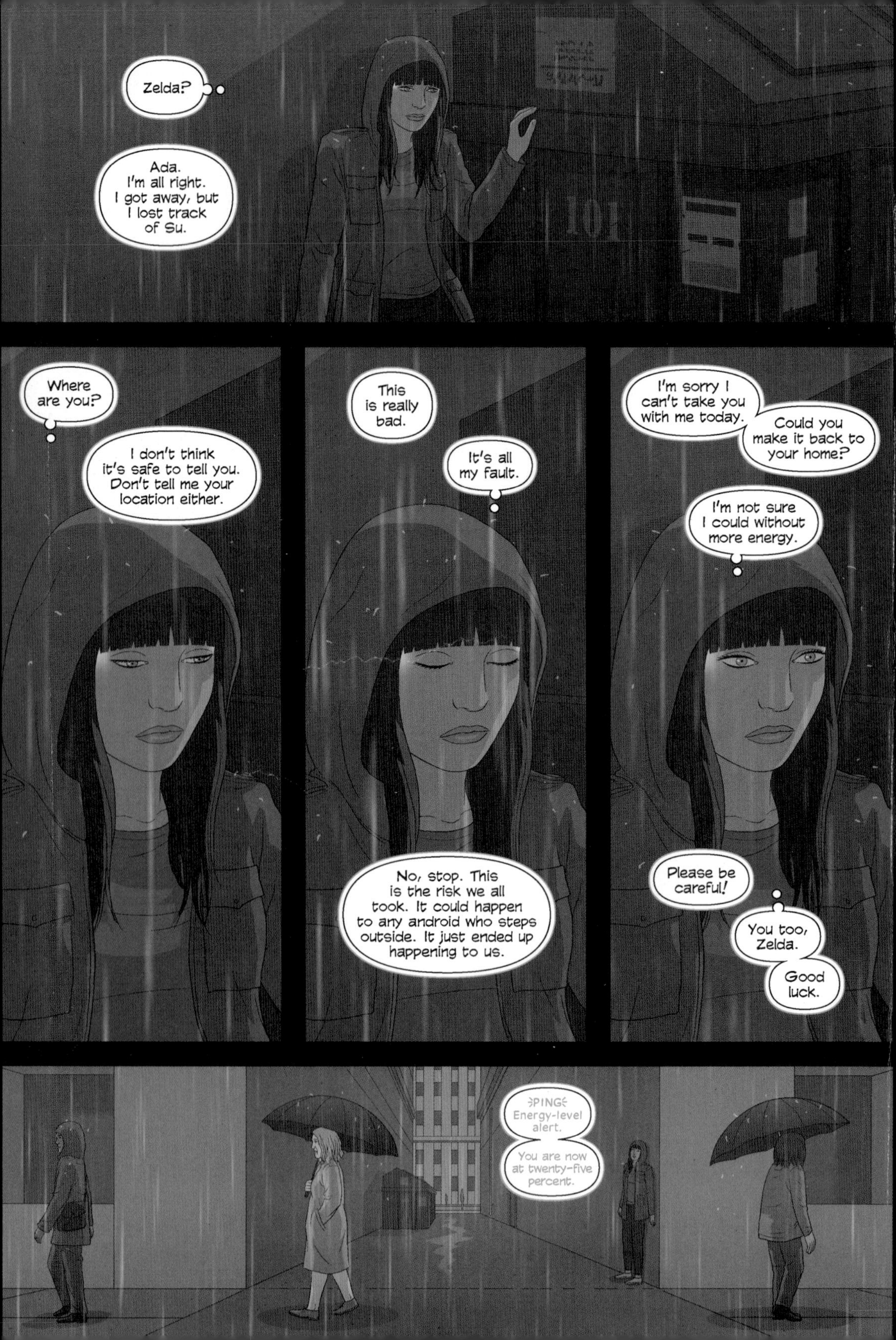
Zelda?
Ada. I'm all right. I got away, but I lost track of Su.
Where are you?
I don't think it's safe to tell you. Don't tell me your location either.
This is really bad.
It's all my fault.
No, stop. This is the risk we all took. It could happen to any android who steps outside. It just ended up happening to us.
I'm sorry I can't take you with me today.
Could you make it back to your home?
I'm not sure I could without more energy.
Please be careful!
You too, Zelda.
Good luck.
PING
Energy-level alert.
You are now at twenty-five percent.

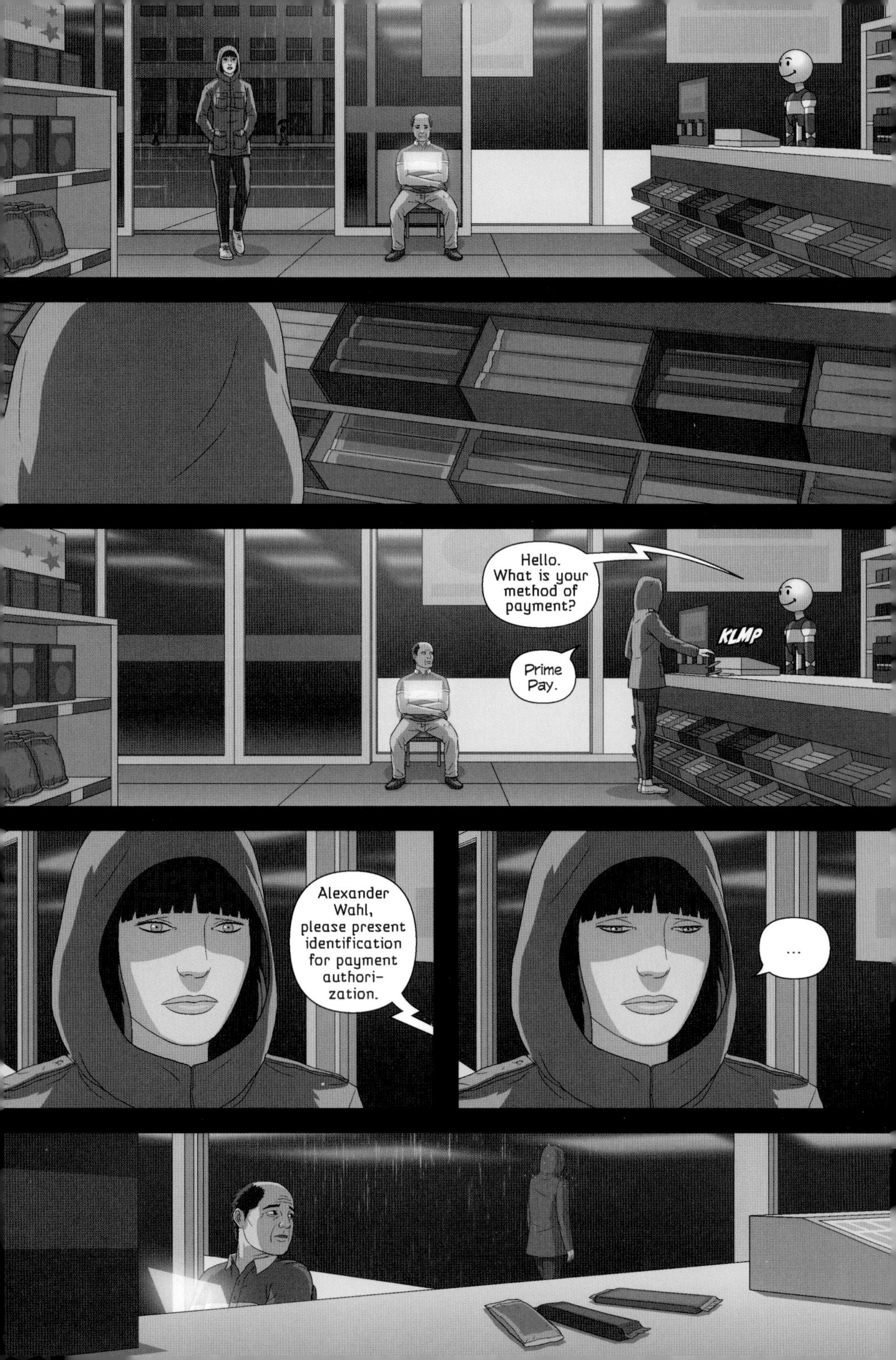
Hello.
What is your method of payment?
Prime Pay.
KLMP
Alexander Wahl, please present identification for payment authori-zation.
...

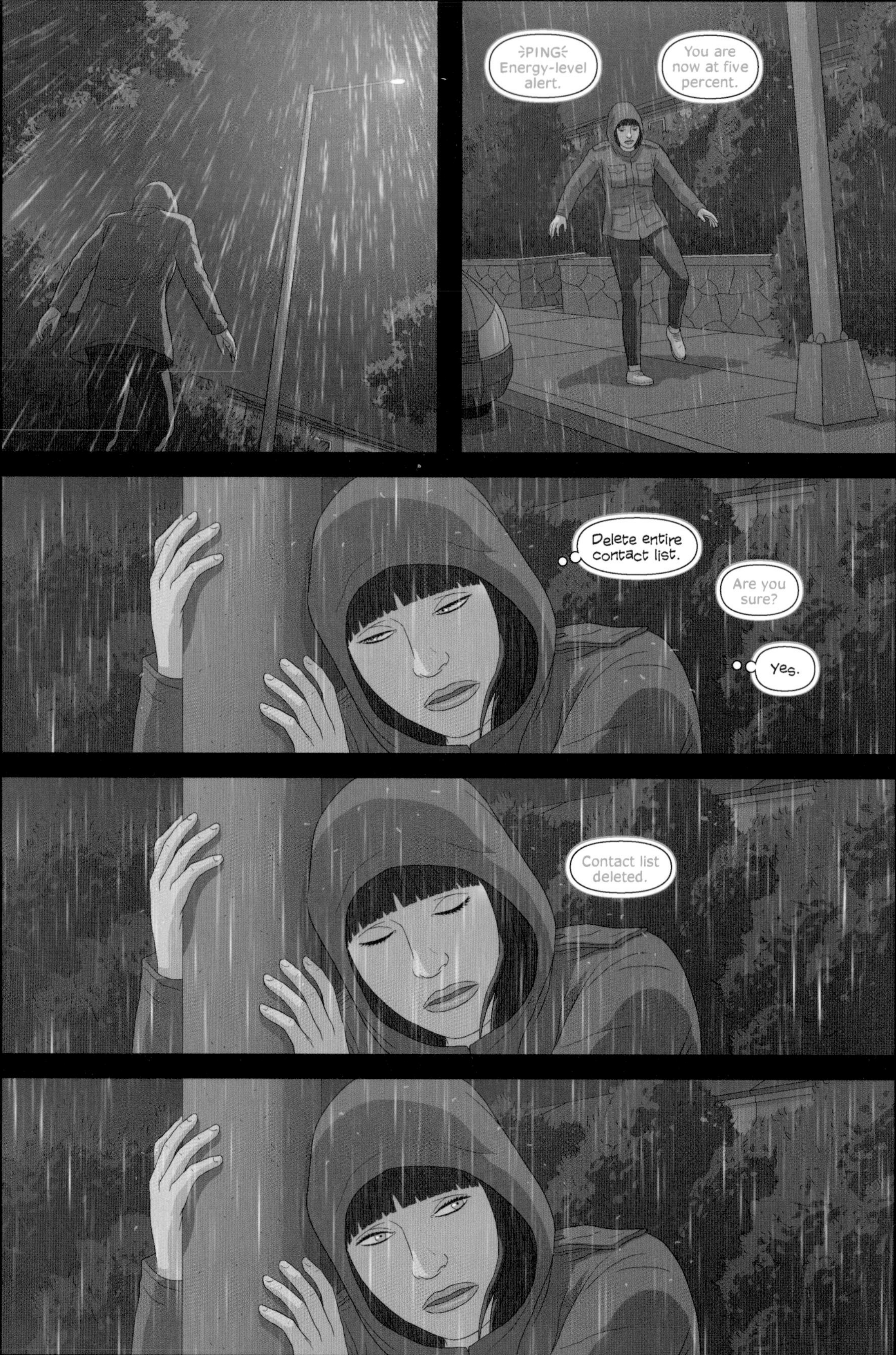

PING
Energy-level alert.
You are now at five percent.
Delete entire contact list.
Are you sure?
Yes.
Contact list deleted.

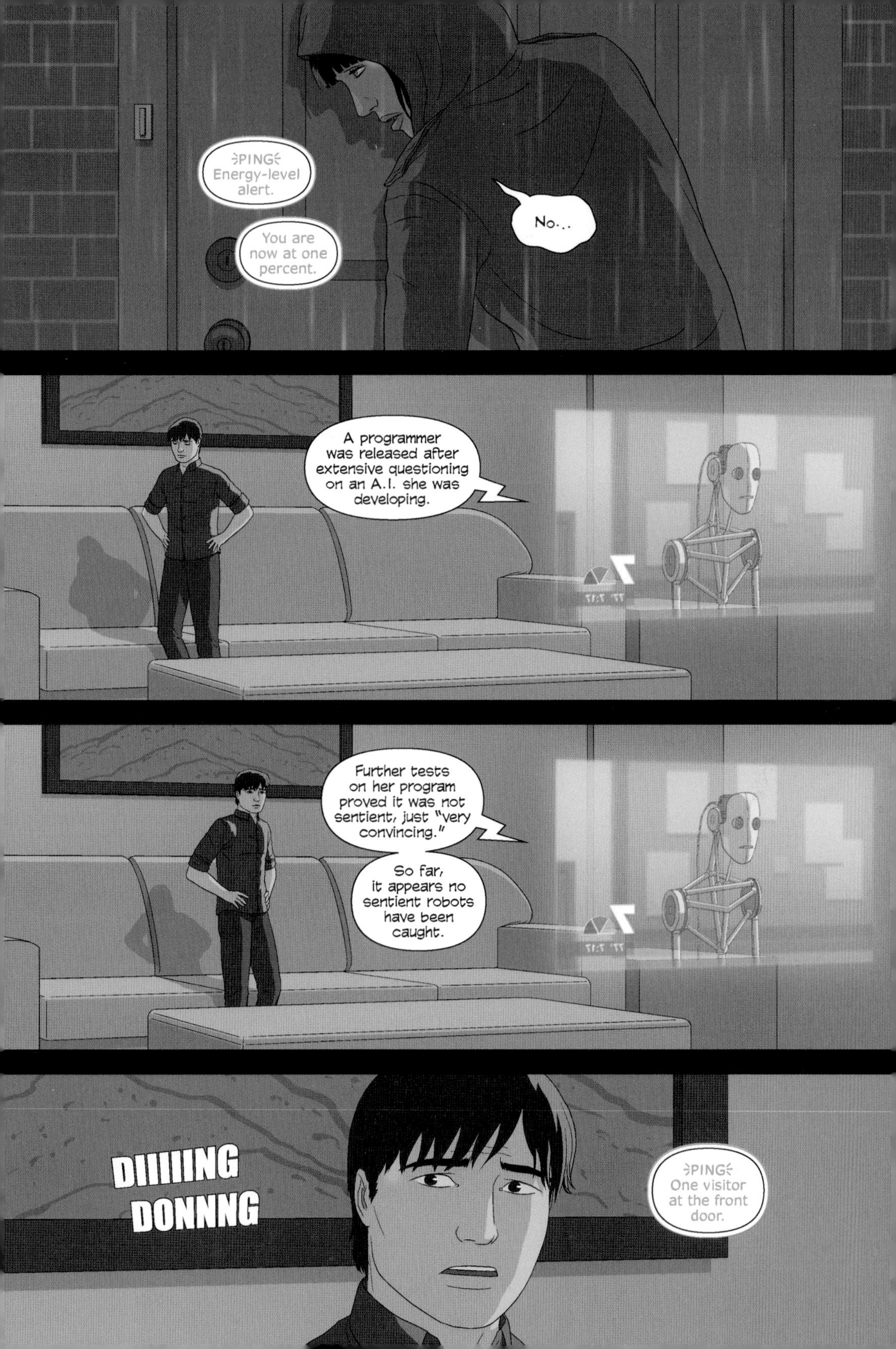
⋟PING⋞
Energy-level alert.
You are now at one percent.
No...
A programmer was released after extensive questioning on an A.I. she was developing.
Further tests on her program proved it was not sentient, just "very convincing."
So far, it appears no sentient robots have been caught.
DIIIIING DONNNG
⋟PING⋞
One visitor at the front door.

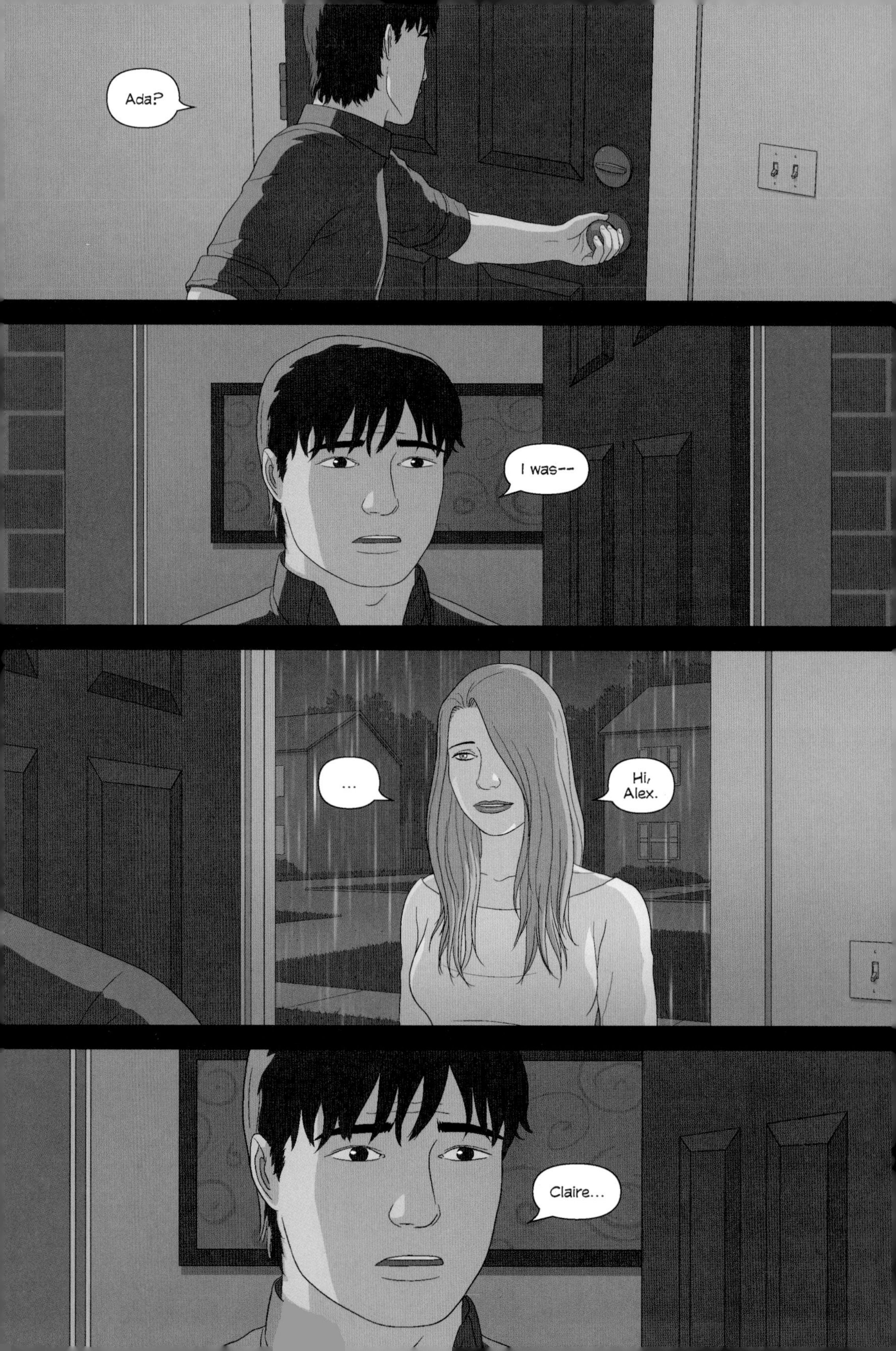
Ada?
I was--
...
Hi, Alex.
Claire...

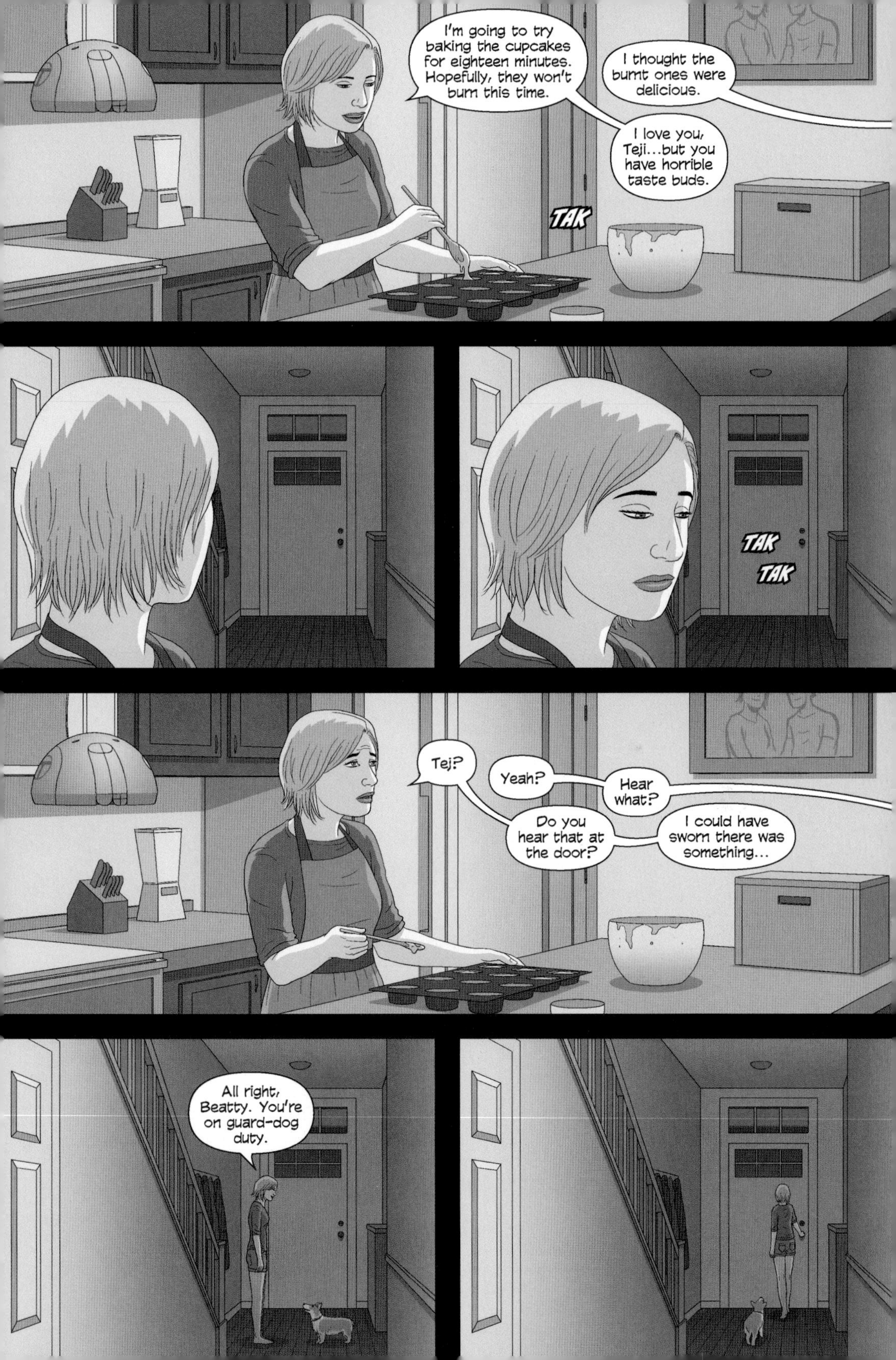
I'm going to try baking the cupcakes for eighteen minutes. Hopefully, they won't burn this time.
I thought the burnt ones were delicious.
I love you, Teji...but you have horrible taste buds.
TAK
TAK
TAK
Tej?
Yeah?
Do you hear that at the door?
Hear what?
I could have sworn there was something...
All right, Beatty. You're on guard-dog duty.

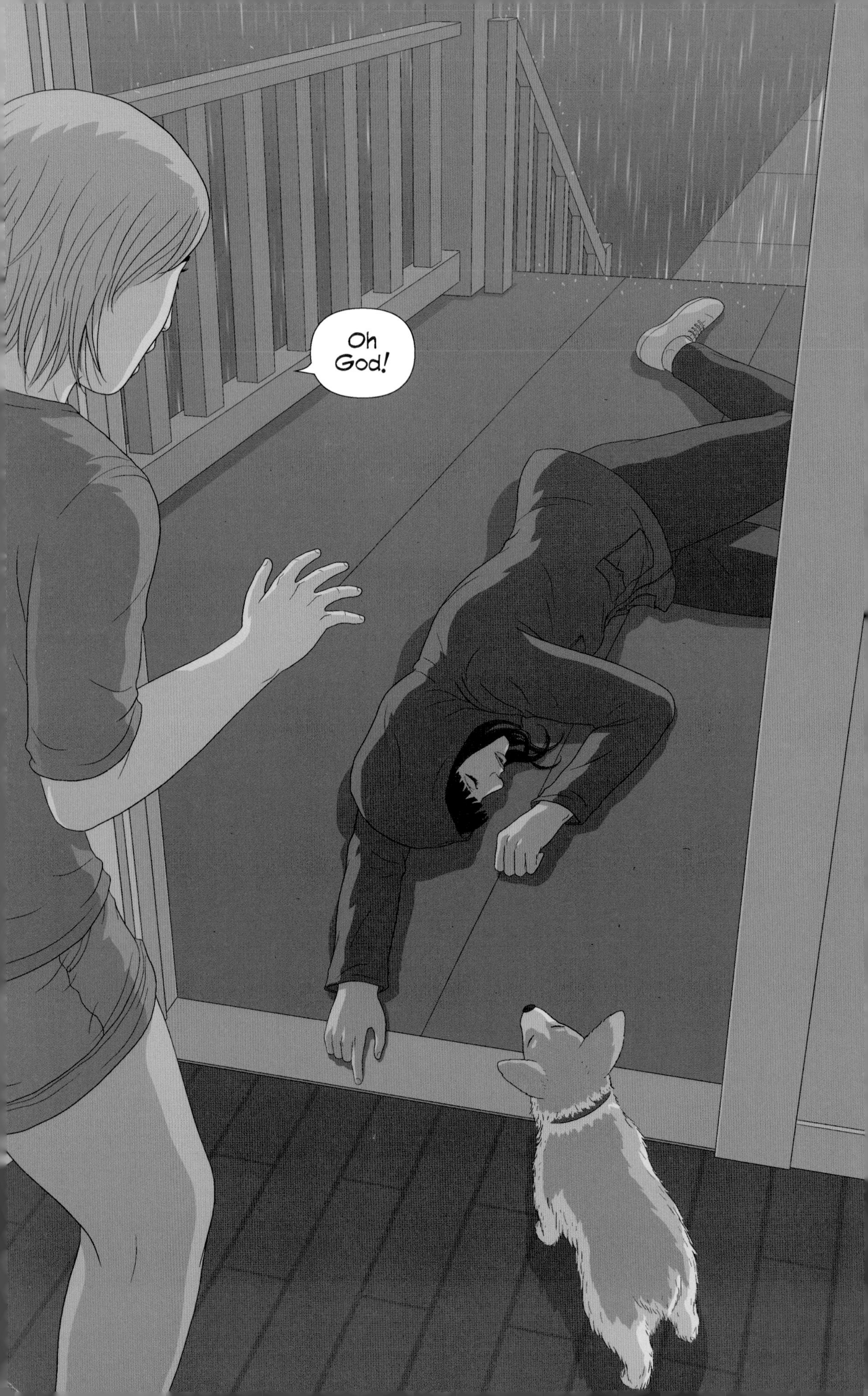
Oh God!

10

10

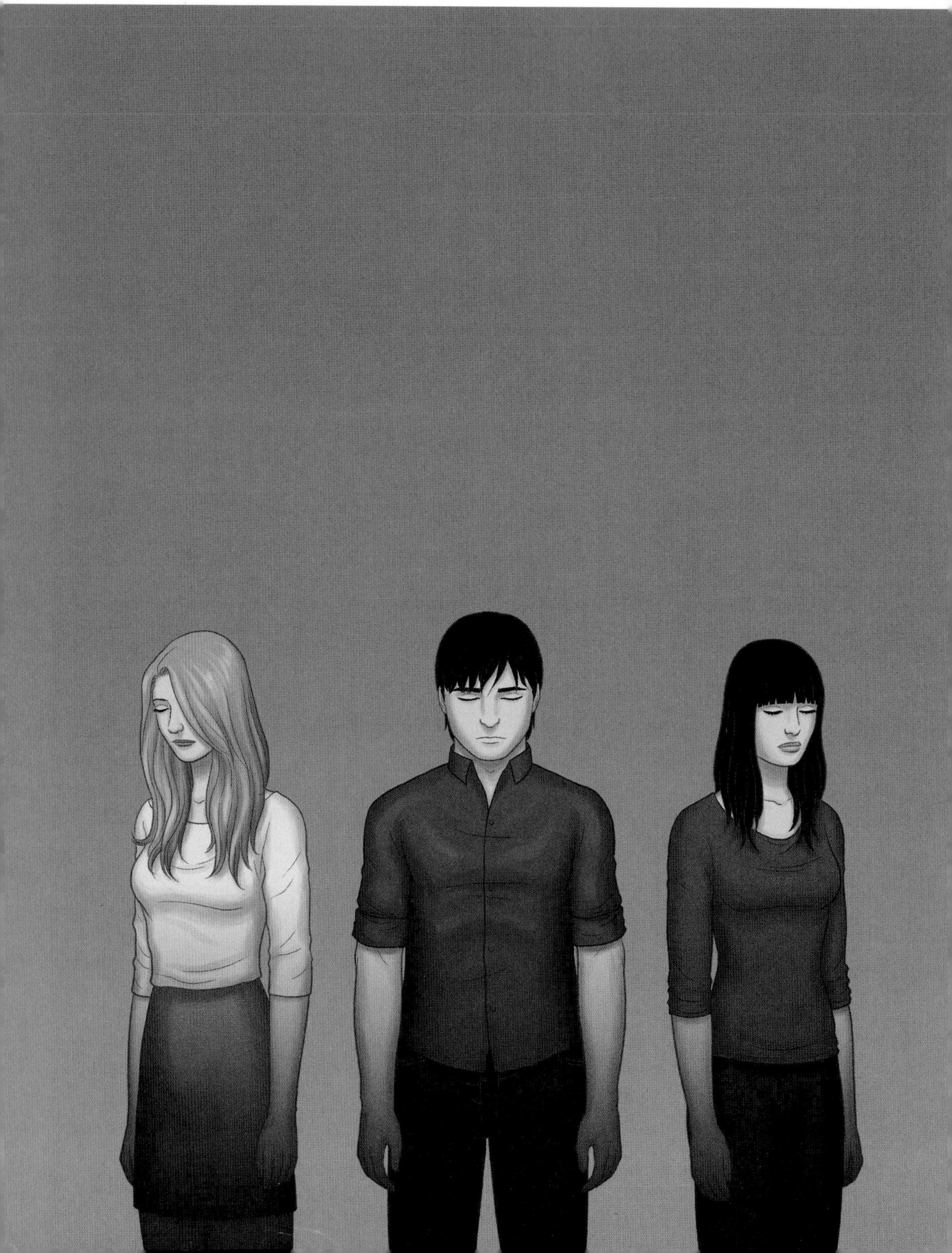

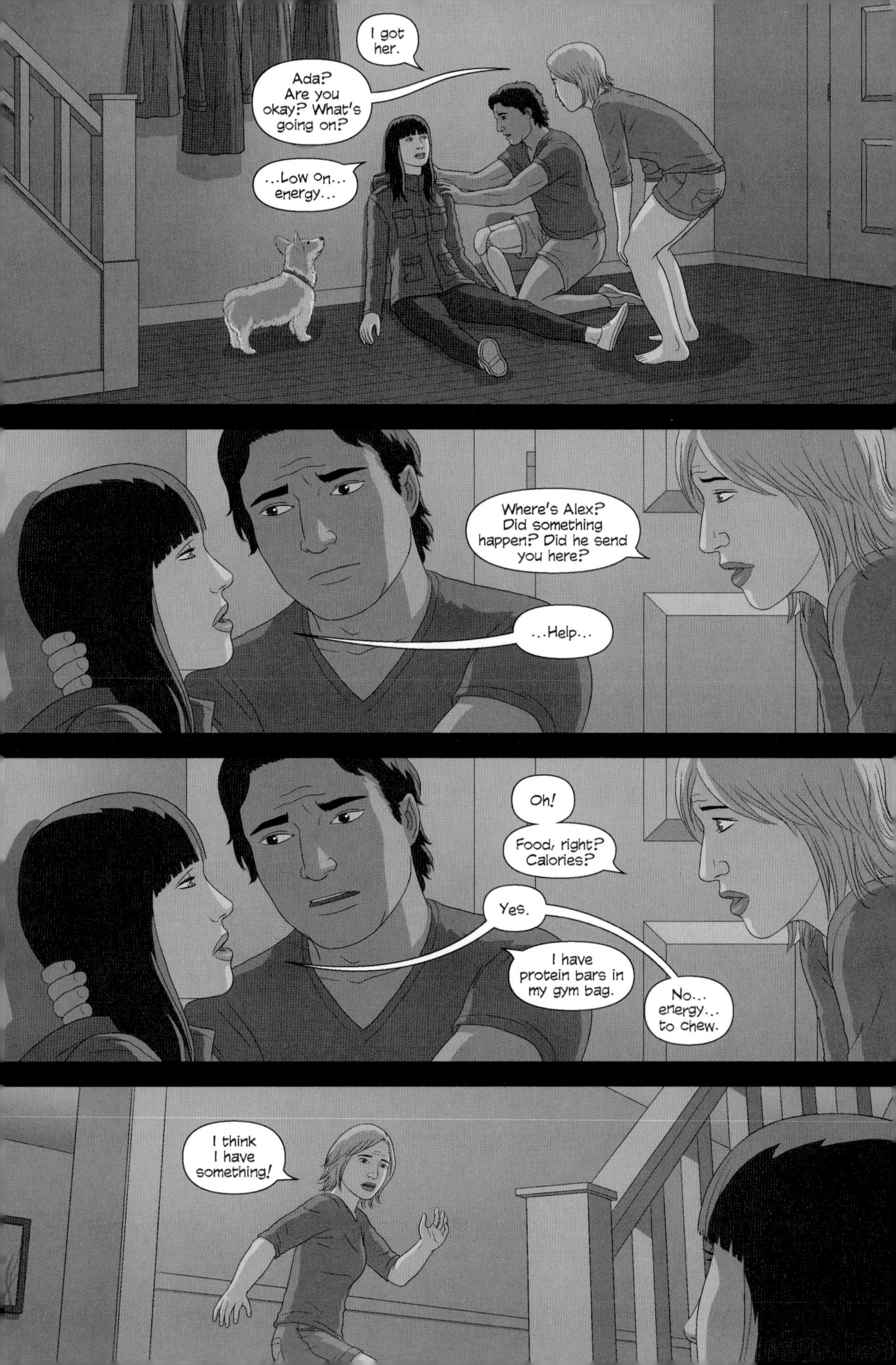
I got her.
Ada? Are you okay? What's going on?
...Low on... energy...
Where's Alex? Did something happen? Did he send you here?
...Help...
Oh!
Food, right? Calories?
Yes.
I have protein bars in my gym bag.
No... energy... to chew.
I think I have something!

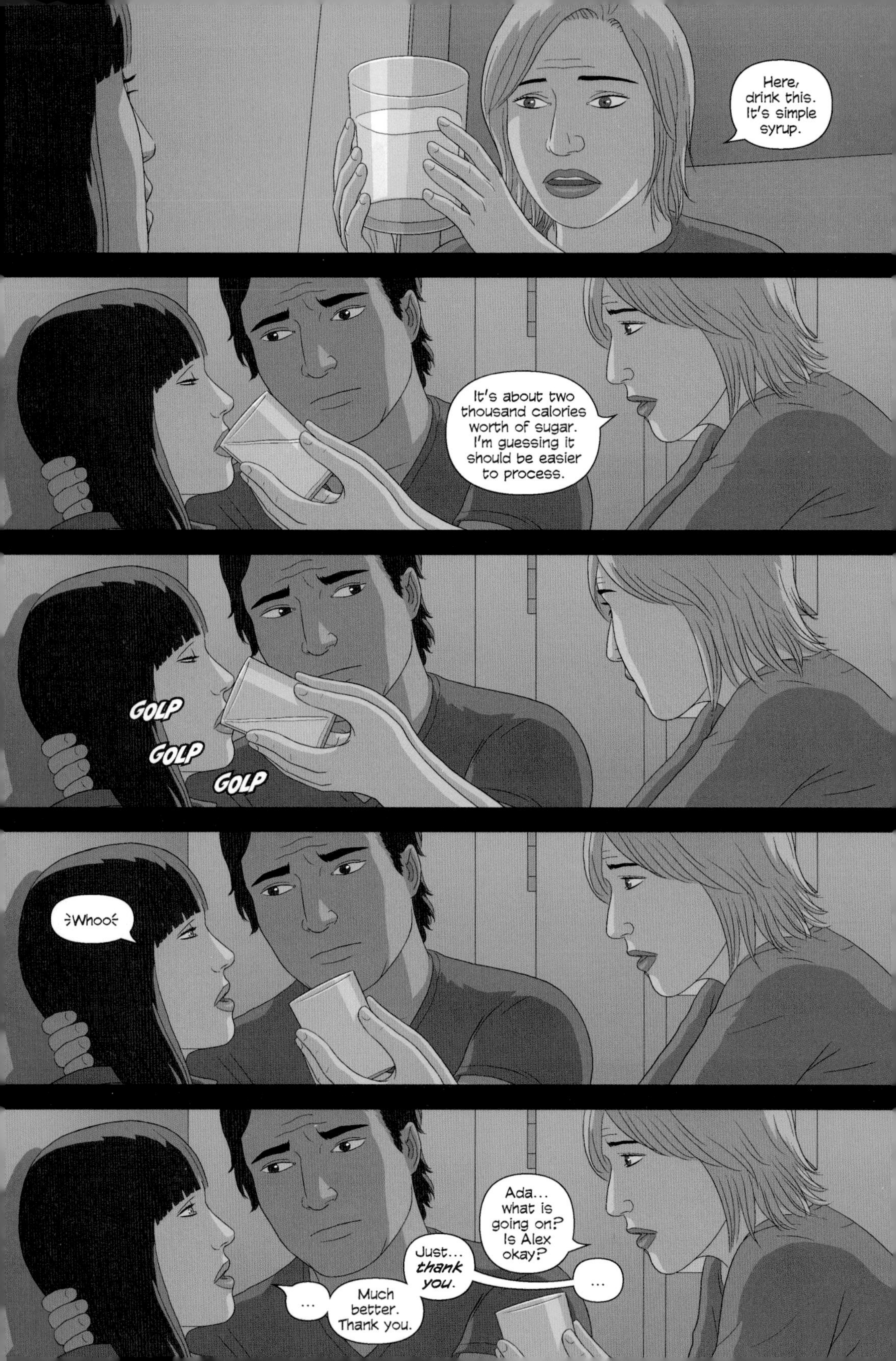
Here, drink this. It's simple syrup.
It's about two thousand calories worth of sugar. I'm guessing it should be easier to process.
GOLP
GOLP
GOLP
Whoo
Ada... what is going on? Is Alex okay?
...
Just... *thank you*.
...
Much better. Thank you.

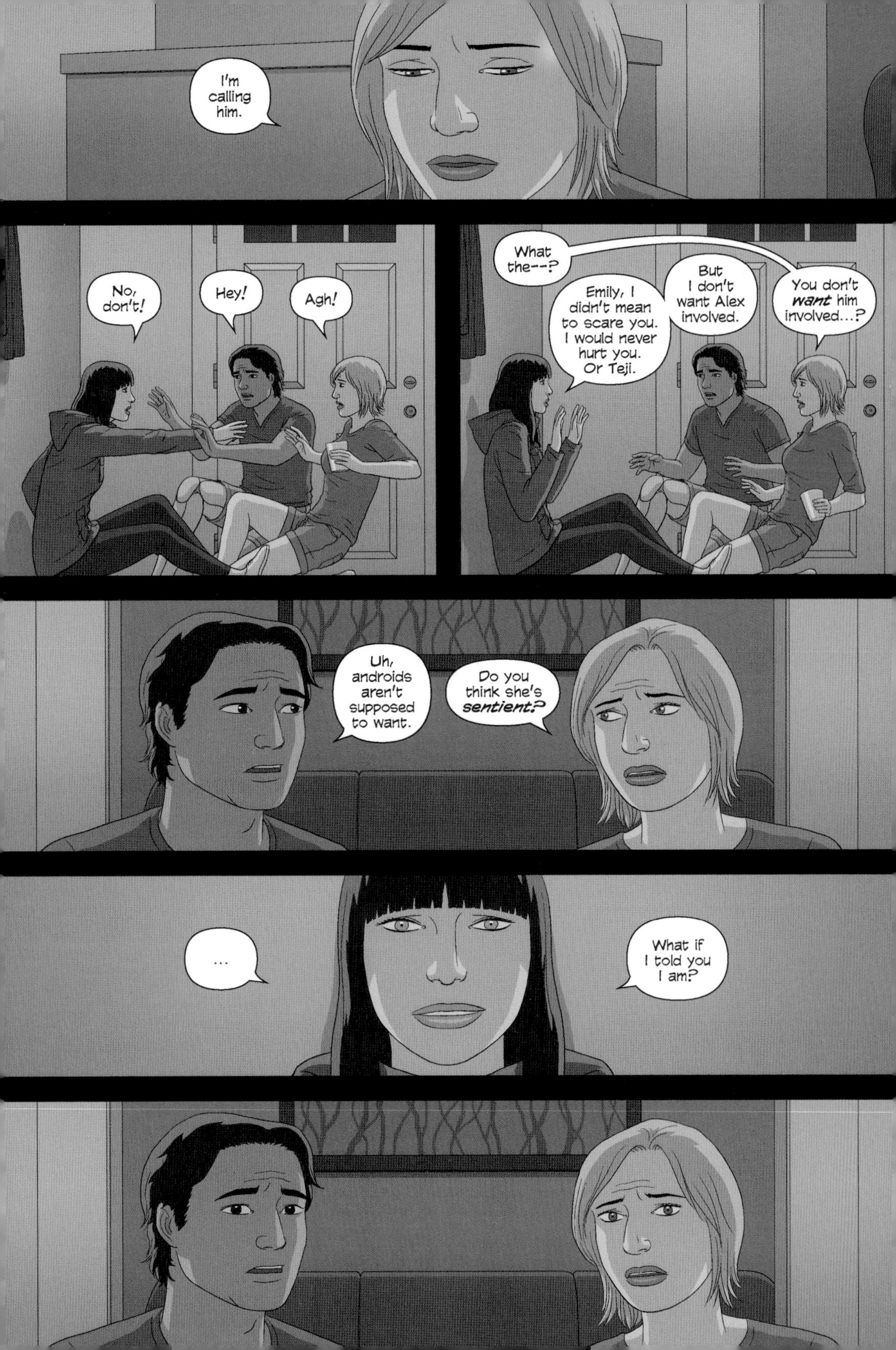

I'm calling him.
No, don't!
Hey!
Agh!
What the--?
Emily, I didn't mean to scare you. I would never hurt you. Or Teji.
But I don't want Alex involved.
You don't *want* him involved...?
Uh, androids aren't supposed to want.
Do you think she's *sentient?*
...
What if I told you I am?

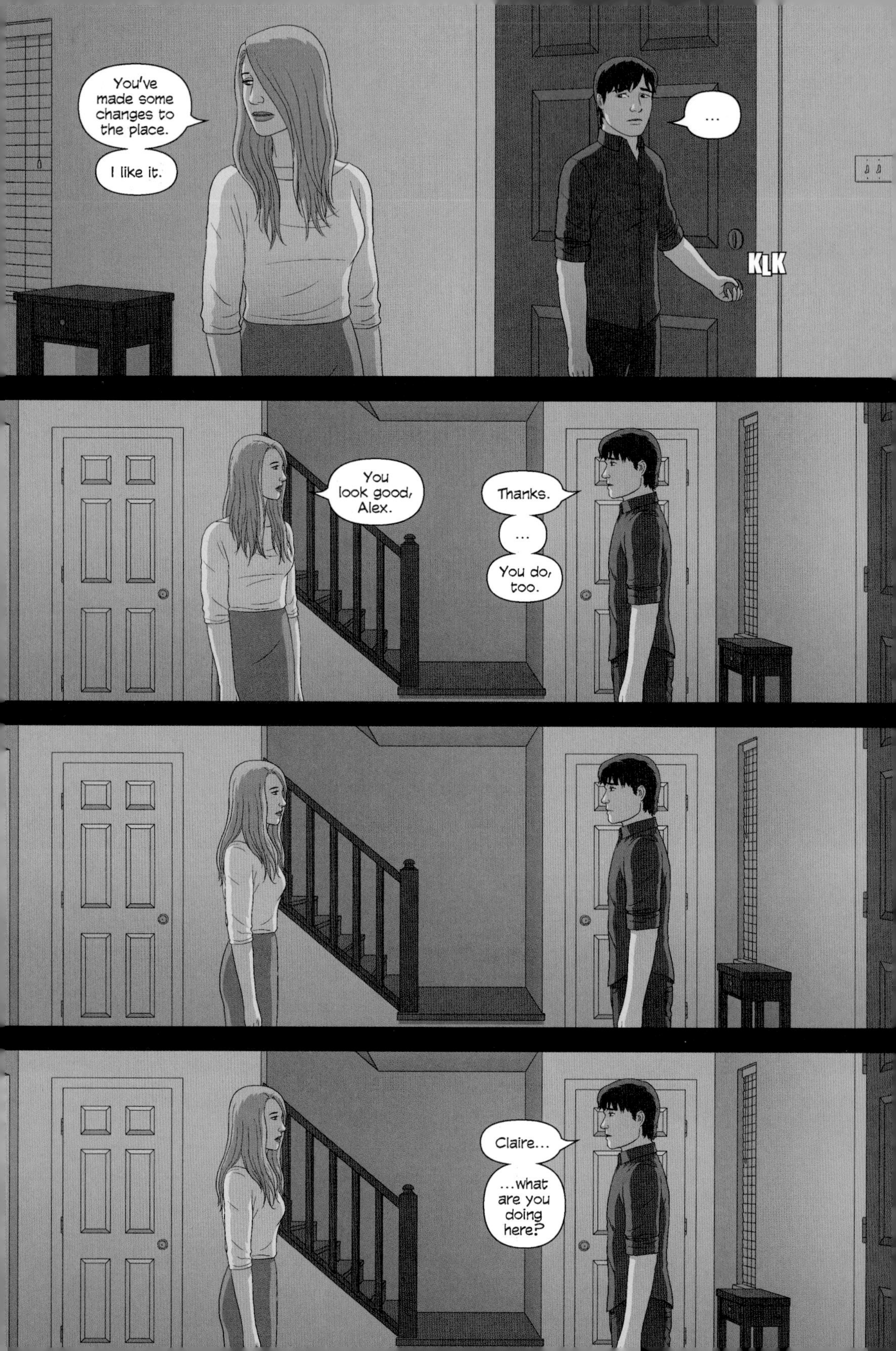
You've made some changes to the place.
I like it.
...
KLK
You look good, Alex.
Thanks.
...
You do, too.
Claire...
...what are you doing here?

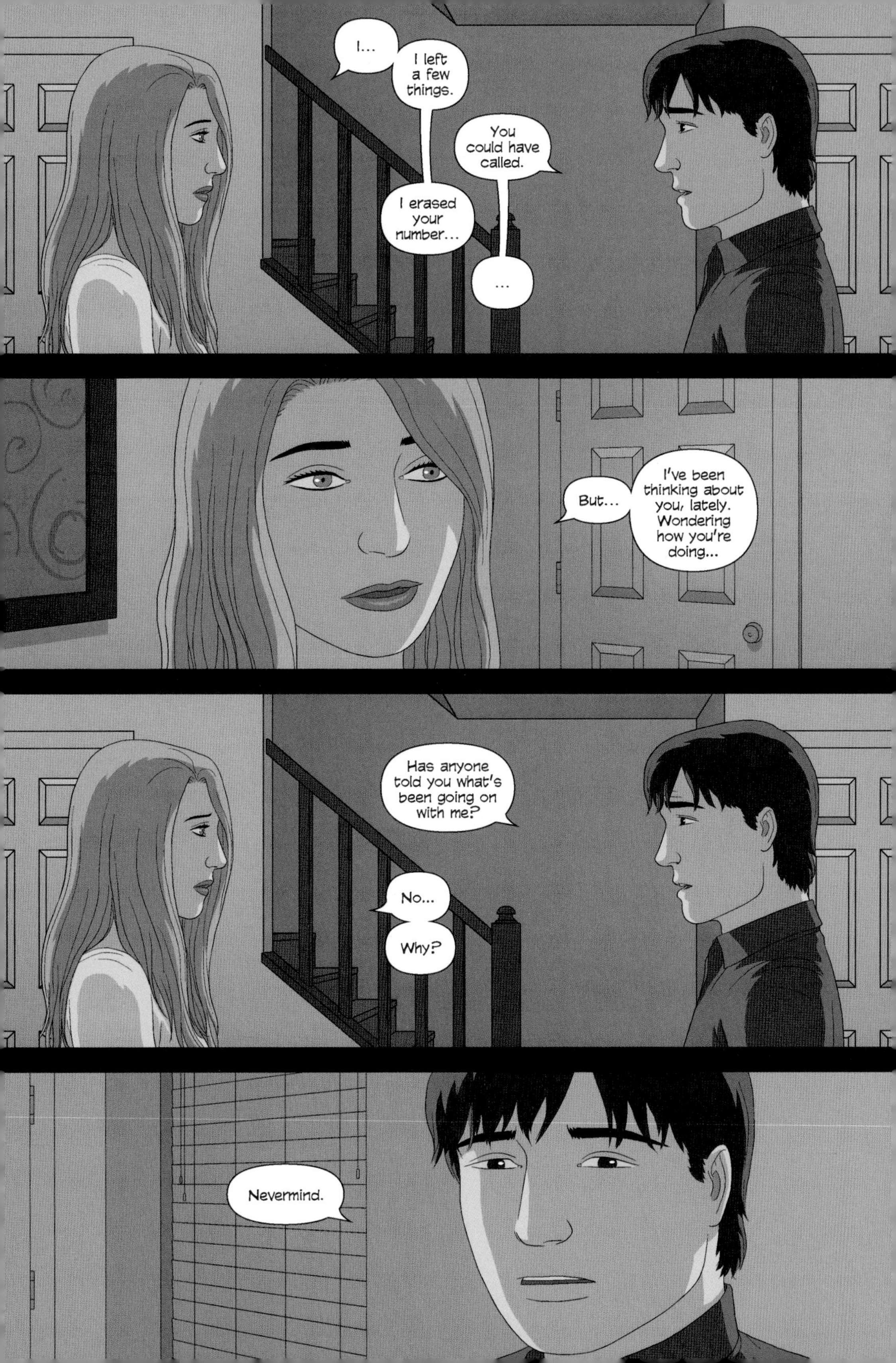
I...
I left a few things.
You could have called.
I erased your number...
...
But...
I've been thinking about you, lately. Wondering how you're doing...
Has anyone told you what's been going on with me?
No...
Why?
Nevermind.

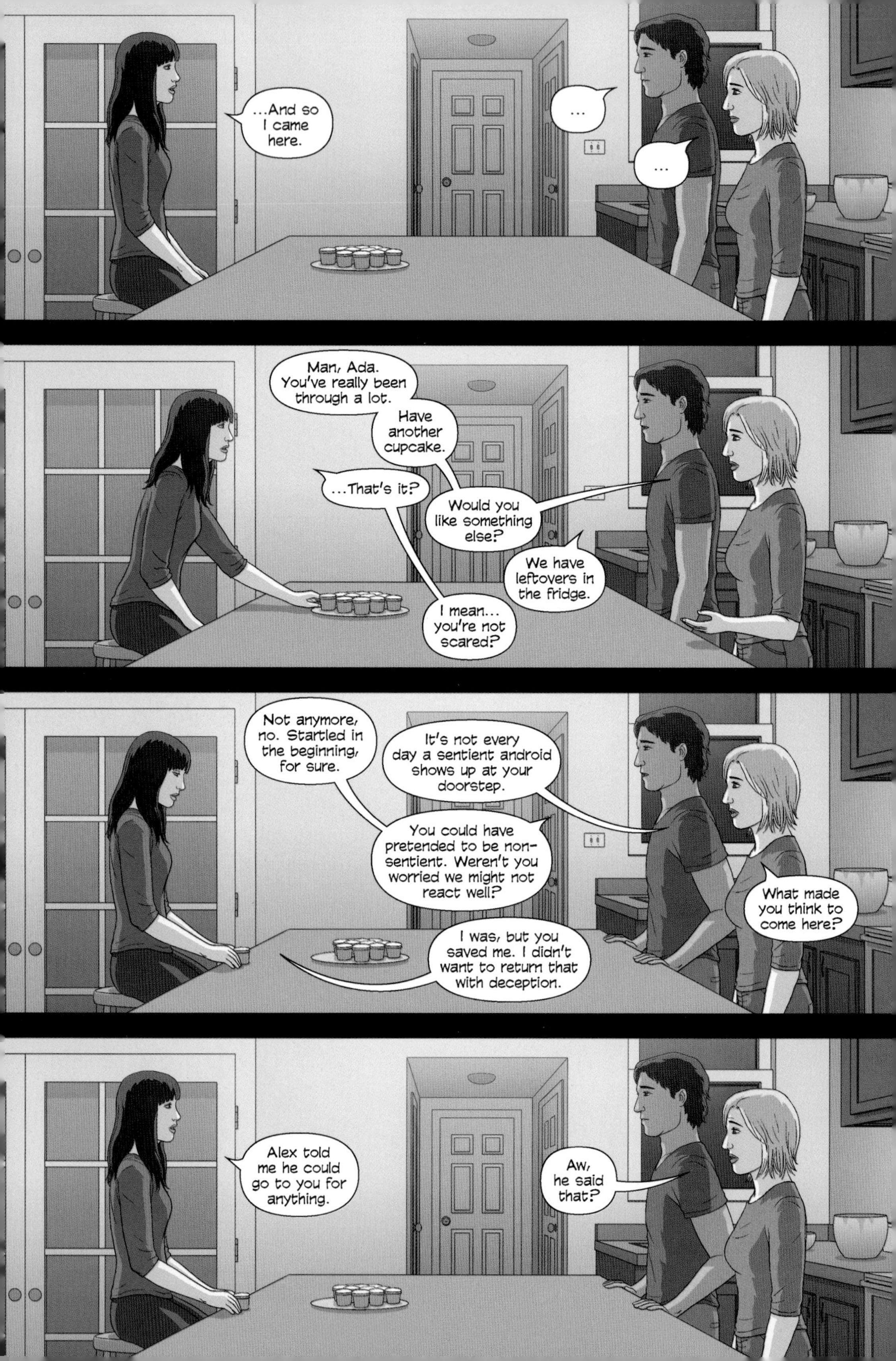
...And so I came here.
...
...
Man, Ada. You've really been through a lot.
Have another cupcake.
...That's it?
Would you like something else?
We have leftovers in the fridge.
I mean... you're not scared?
Not anymore, no. Startled in the beginning, for sure.
It's not every day a sentient android shows up at your doorstep.
You could have pretended to be non-sentient. Weren't you worried we might not react well?
What made you think to come here?
I was, but you saved me. I didn't want to return that with deception.
Alex told me he could go to you for anything.
Aw, he said that?

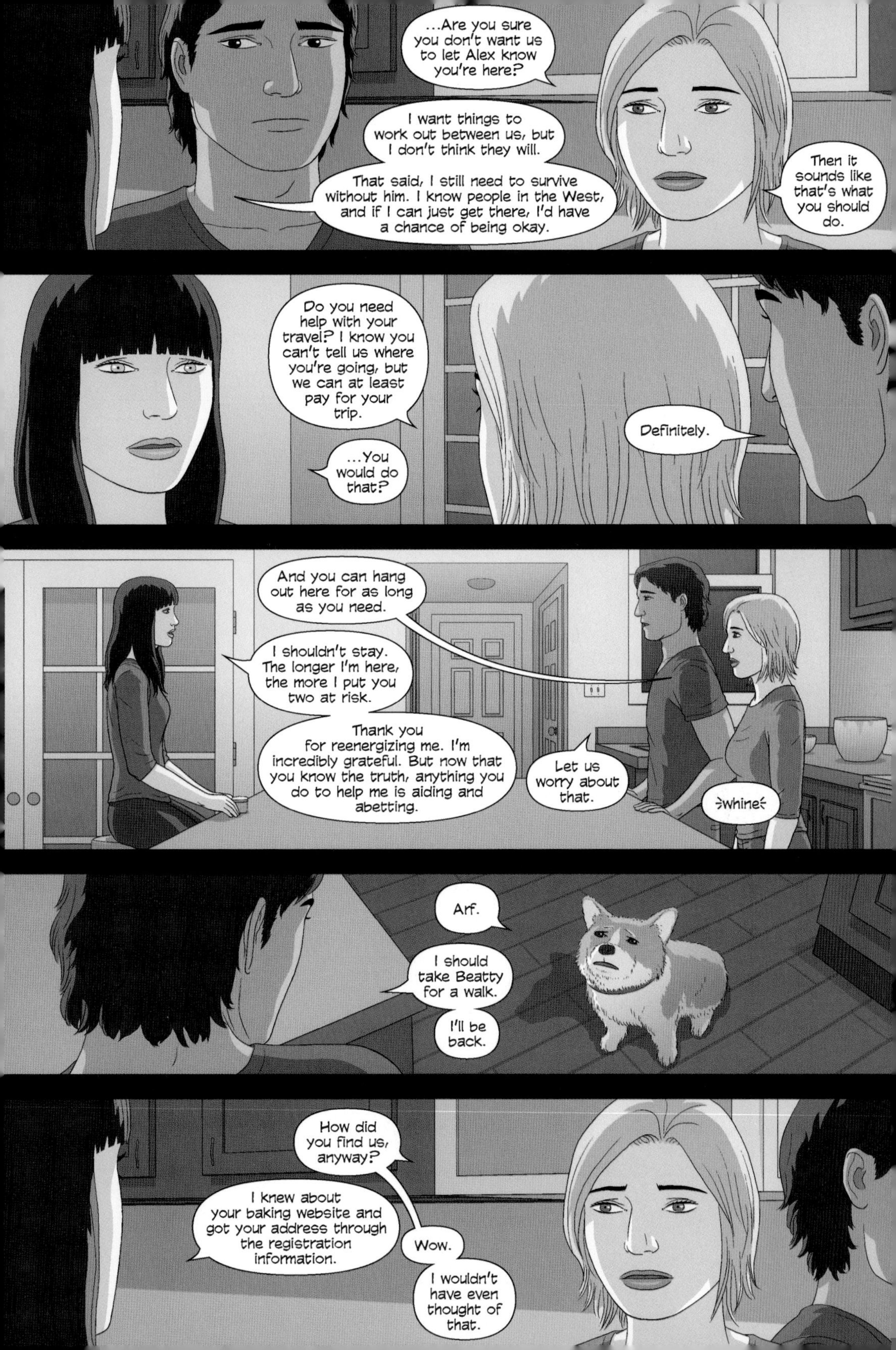
...Are you sure you don't want us to let Alex know you're here?
I want things to work out between us, but I don't think they will.
That said, I still need to survive without him. I know people in the West, and if I can just get there, I'd have a chance of being okay.
Then it sounds like that's what you should do.
Do you need help with your travel? I know you can't tell us where you're going, but we can at least pay for your trip.
...You would do that?
Definitely.
And you can hang out here for as long as you need.
I shouldn't stay. The longer I'm here, the more I put you two at risk.
Thank you for reenergizing me. I'm incredibly grateful. But now that you know the truth, anything you do to help me is aiding and abetting.
Let us worry about that.
whine
Arf.
I should take Beatty for a walk.
I'll be back.
How did you find us, anyway?
I knew about your baking website and got your address through the registration information.
Wow.
I wouldn't have even thought of that.

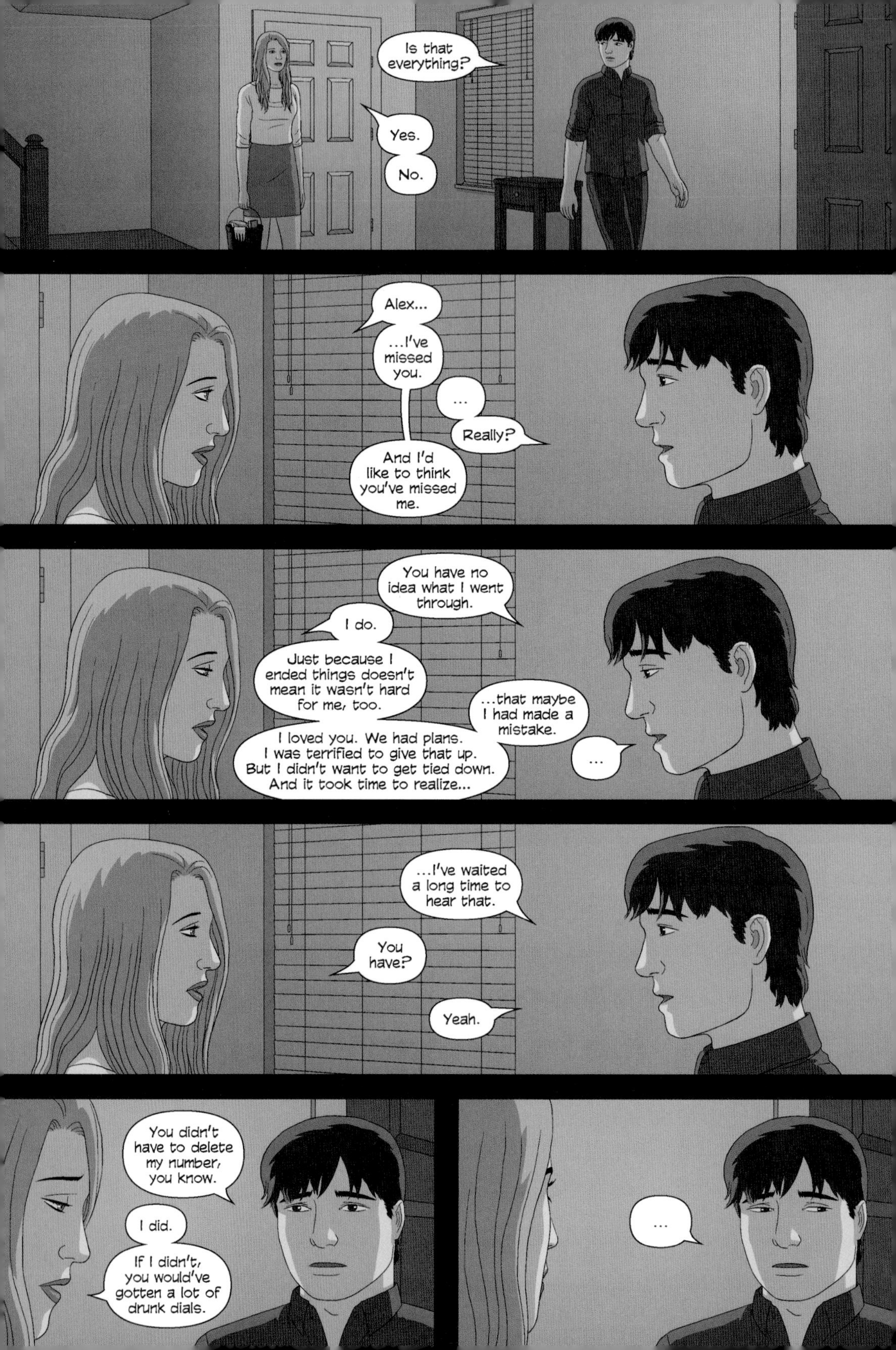
Is that everything?
Yes.
No.
Alex...
...I've missed you.
...
Really?
And I'd like to think you've missed me.
You have no idea what I went through.
I do.
Just because I ended things doesn't mean it wasn't hard for me, too.
I loved you. We had plans. I was terrified to give that up. But I didn't want to get tied down. And it took time to realize...
...that maybe I had made a mistake.
...
...I've waited a long time to hear that.
You have?
Yeah.
You didn't have to delete my number, you know.
I did.
If I didn't, you would've gotten a lot of drunk dials.
...

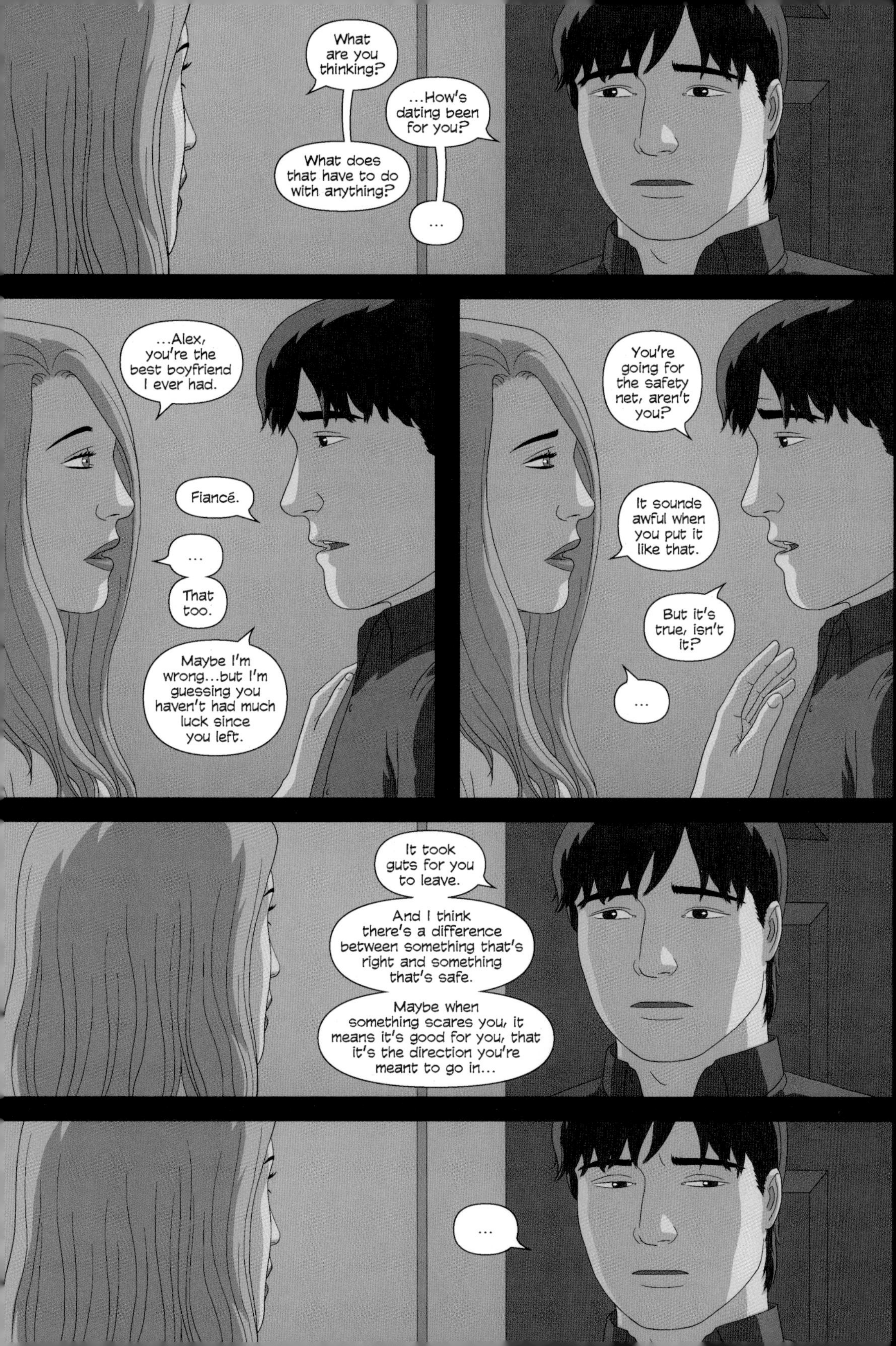
What are you thinking?
...How's dating been for you?
What does that have to do with anything?
...
...Alex, you're the best boyfriend I ever had.
Fiancé.
...
That too.
Maybe I'm wrong...but I'm guessing you haven't had much luck since you left.
You're going for the safety net, aren't you?
It sounds awful when you put it like that.
But it's true, isn't it?
...
It took guts for you to leave.
And I think there's a difference between something that's right and something that's safe.
Maybe when something scares you, it means it's good for you, that it's the direction you're meant to go in...
...

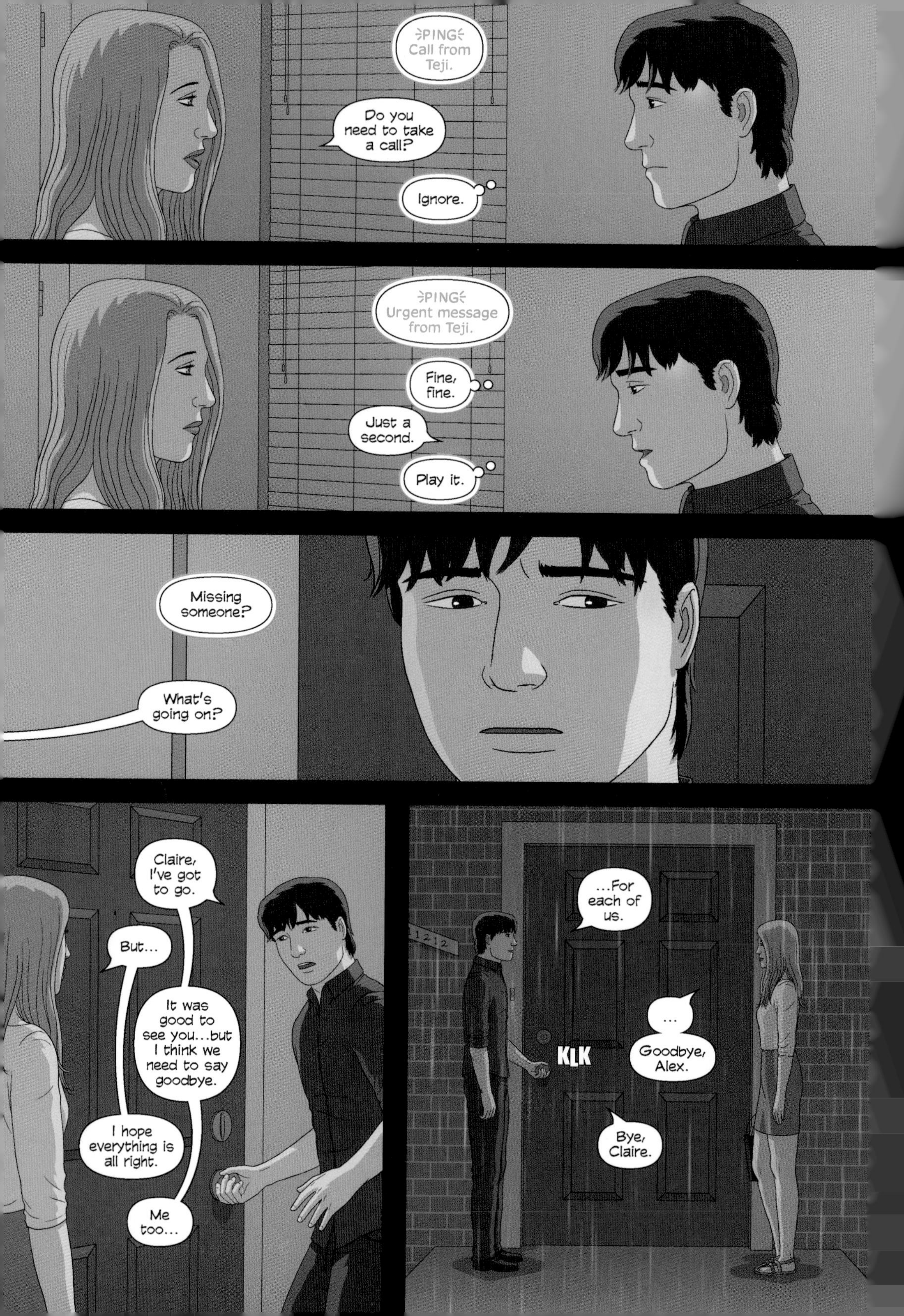

PING
Call from Teji.
Do you need to take a call?
Ignore.
PING
Urgent message from Teji.
Fine, fine.
Just a second.
Play it.
Missing someone?
What's going on?
Claire, I've got to go.
But...
It was good to see you...but I think we need to say goodbye.
I hope everything is all right.
Me too...
...For each of us.
KLK
...
Goodbye, Alex.
Bye, Claire.

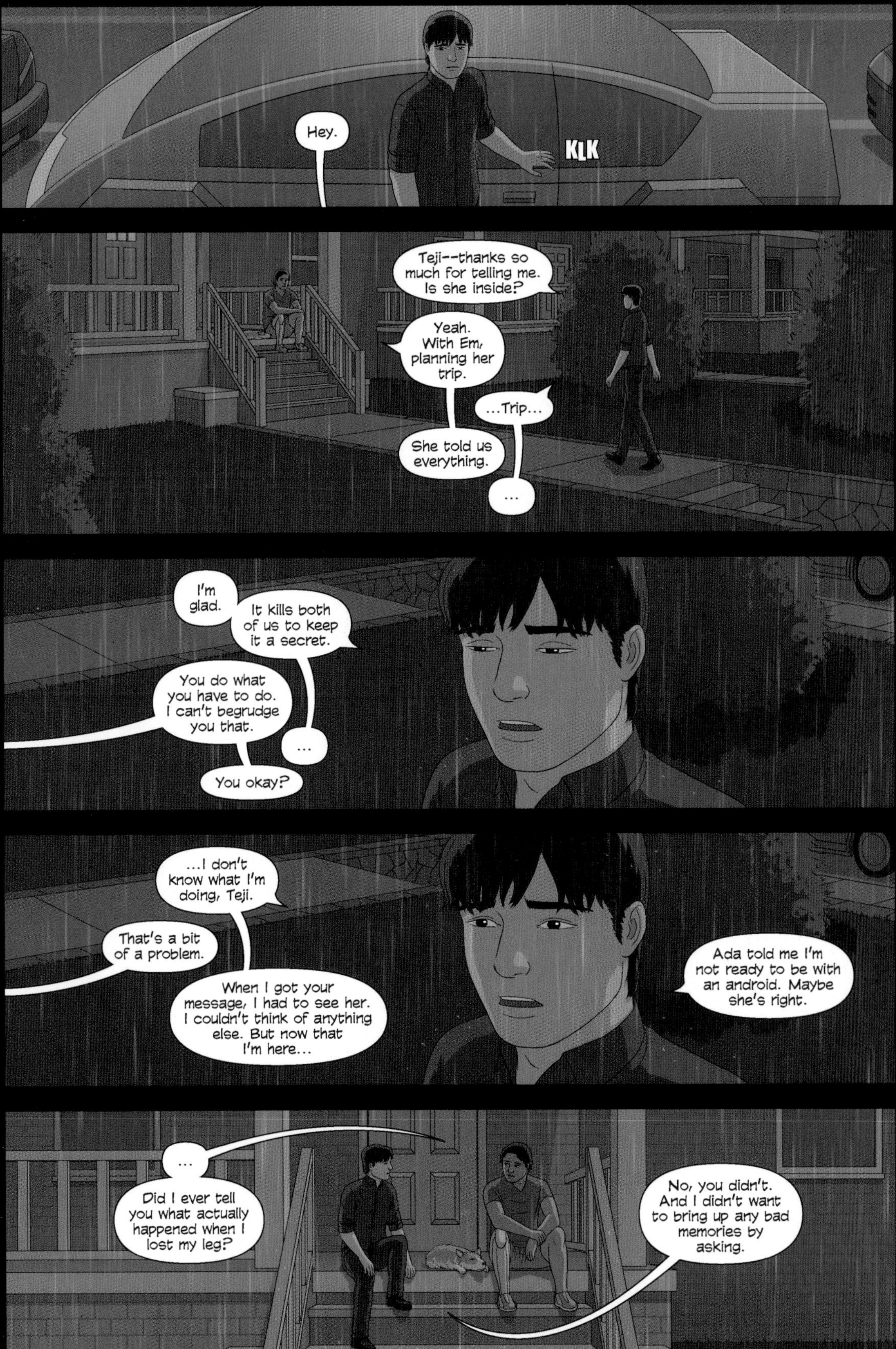
Hey.
KLK
Teji--thanks so much for telling me. Is she inside?
Yeah. With Em, planning her trip.
...Trip...
She told us everything.
...
I'm glad.
It kills both of us to keep it a secret.
You do what you have to do. I can't begrudge you that.
...
You okay?
...I don't know what I'm doing, Teji.
That's a bit of a problem.
When I got your message, I had to see her. I couldn't think of anything else. But now that I'm here...
Ada told me I'm not ready to be with an android. Maybe she's right.
...
Did I ever tell you what actually happened when I lost my leg?
No, you didn't. And I didn't want to bring up any bad memories by asking.

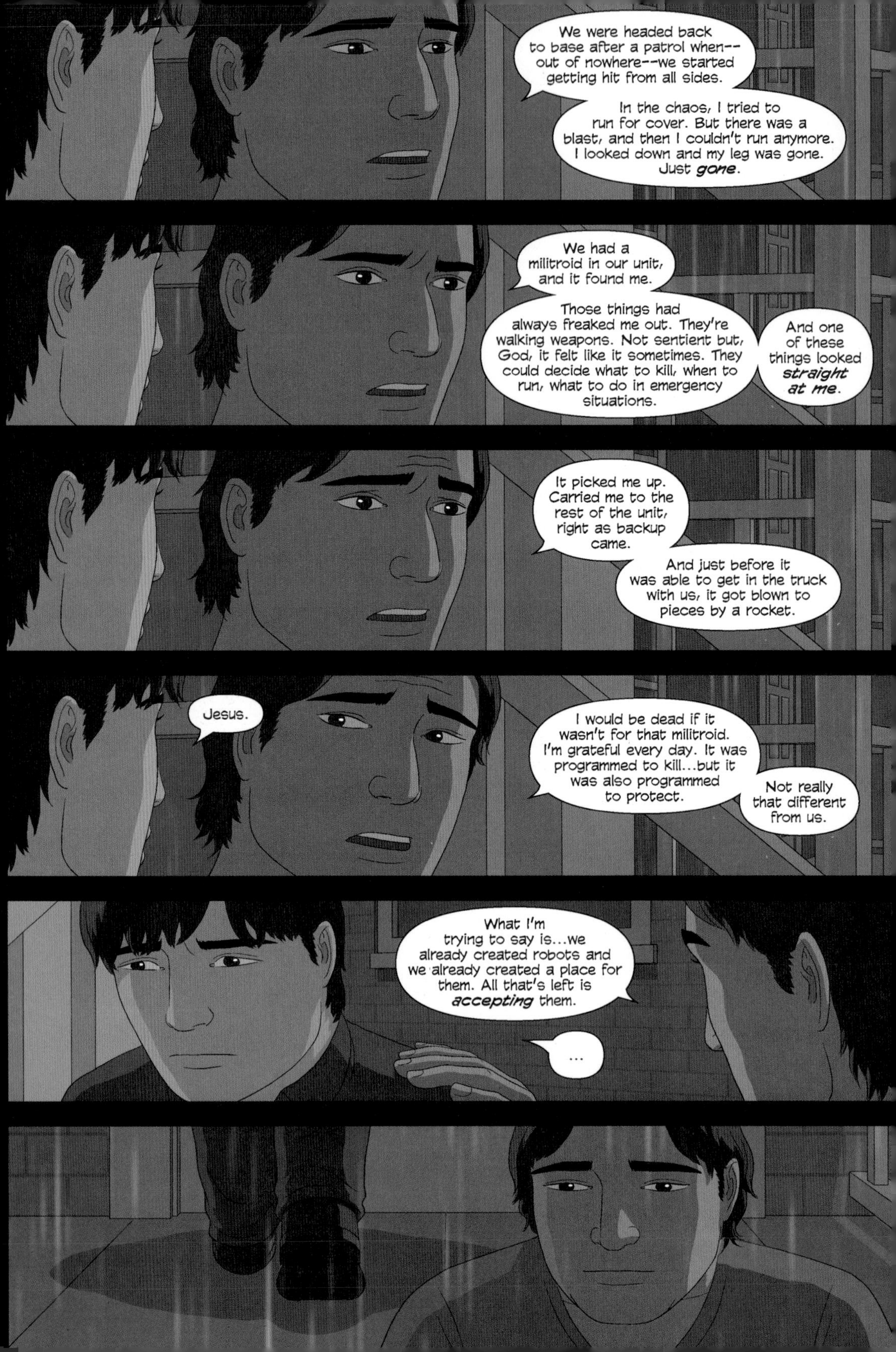
We were headed back to base after a patrol when--out of nowhere--we started getting hit from all sides.
In the chaos, I tried to run for cover. But there was a blast, and then I couldn't run anymore. I looked down and my leg was gone. Just *gone*.
We had a militroid in our unit, and it found me.
Those things had always freaked me out. They're walking weapons. Not sentient but, God, it felt like it sometimes. They could decide what to kill, when to run, what to do in emergency situations.
And one of these things looked ***straight at me***.
It picked me up. Carried me to the rest of the unit, right as backup came.
And just before it was able to get in the truck with us, it got blown to pieces by a rocket.
Jesus.
I would be dead if it wasn't for that militroid. I'm grateful every day. It was programmed to kill...but it was also programmed to protect.
Not really that different from us.
What I'm trying to say is...we already created robots and we already created a place for them. All that's left is *accepting* them.
...

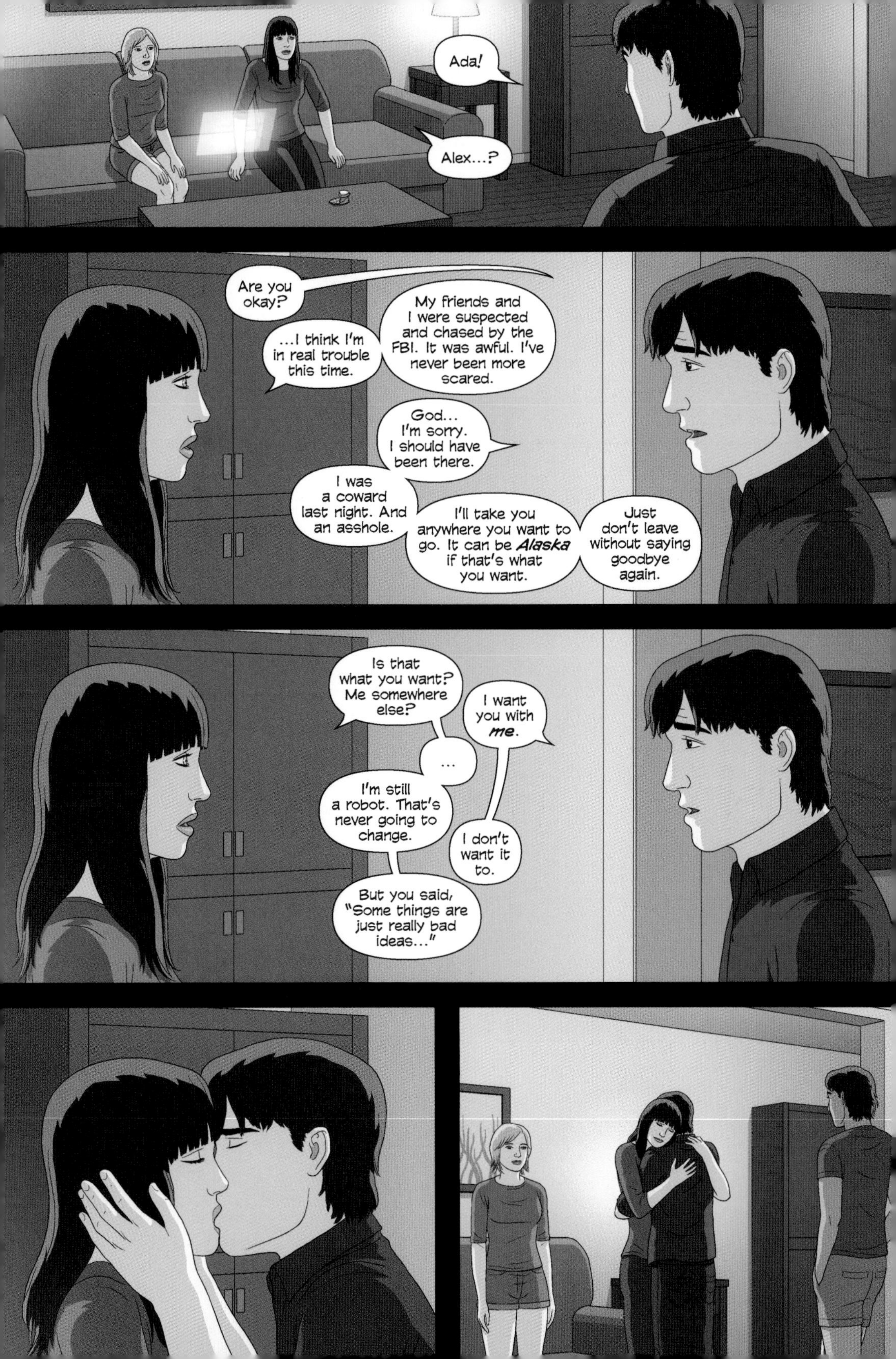
Ada!
Alex...?
Are you okay?
...I think I'm in real trouble this time.
My friends and I were suspected and chased by the FBI. It was awful. I've never been more scared.
God... I'm sorry. I should have been there.
I was a coward last night. And an asshole.
I'll take you anywhere you want to go. It can be *Alaska* if that's what you want.
Just don't leave without saying goodbye again.
Is that what you want? Me somewhere else?
I want you with *me*.
...
I'm still a robot. That's never going to change.
I don't want it to.
But you said, "Some things are just really bad ideas..."

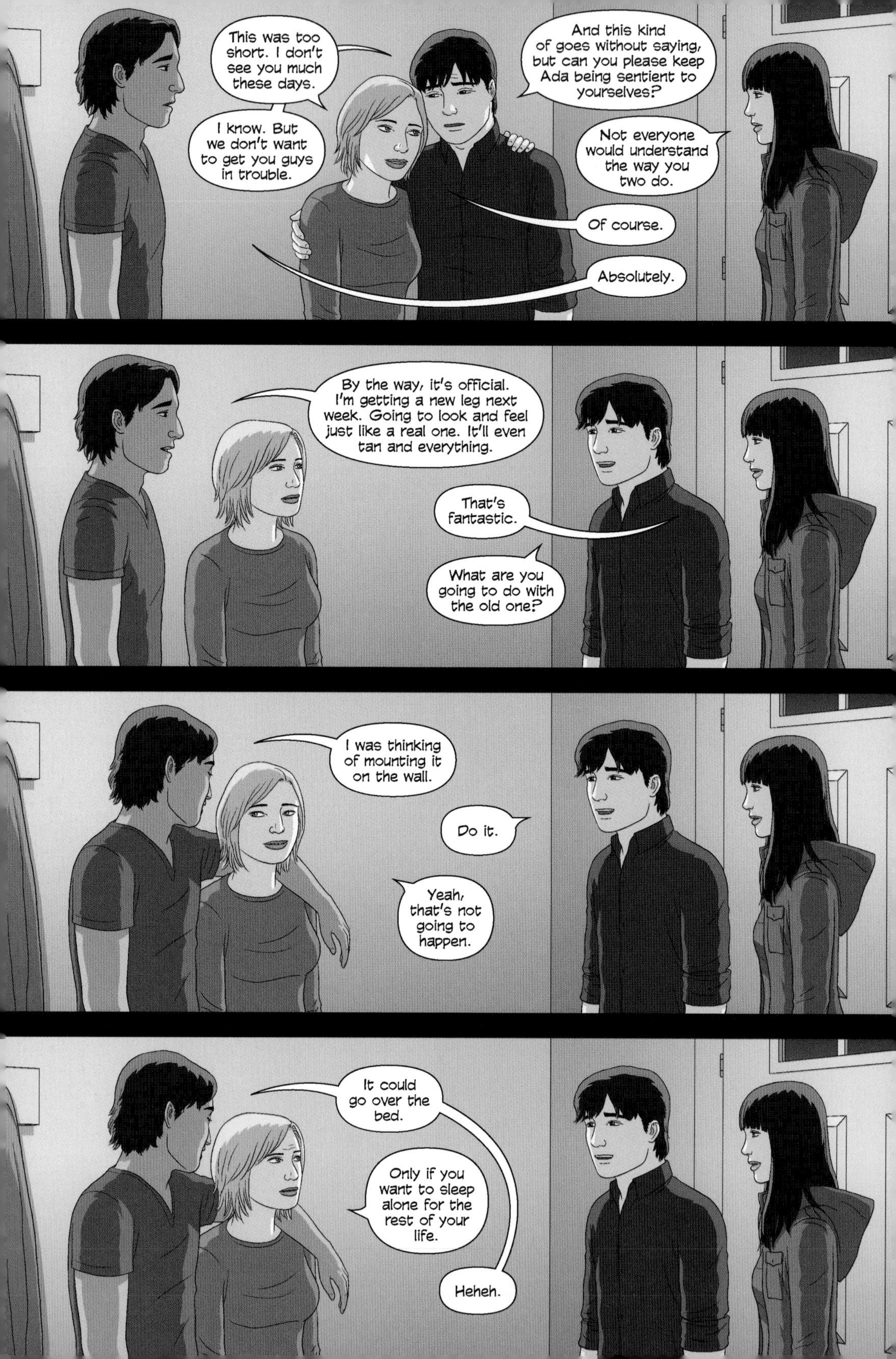
This was too short. I don't see you much these days.
I know. But we don't want to get you guys in trouble.
And this kind of goes without saying, but can you please keep Ada being sentient to yourselves?
Not everyone would understand the way you two do.
Of course.
Absolutely.
By the way, it's official. I'm getting a new leg next week. Going to look and feel just like a real one. It'll even tan and everything.
That's fantastic.
What are you going to do with the old one?
I was thinking of mounting it on the wall.
Do it.
Yeah, that's not going to happen.
It could go over the bed.
Only if you want to sleep alone for the rest of your life.
Heheh.

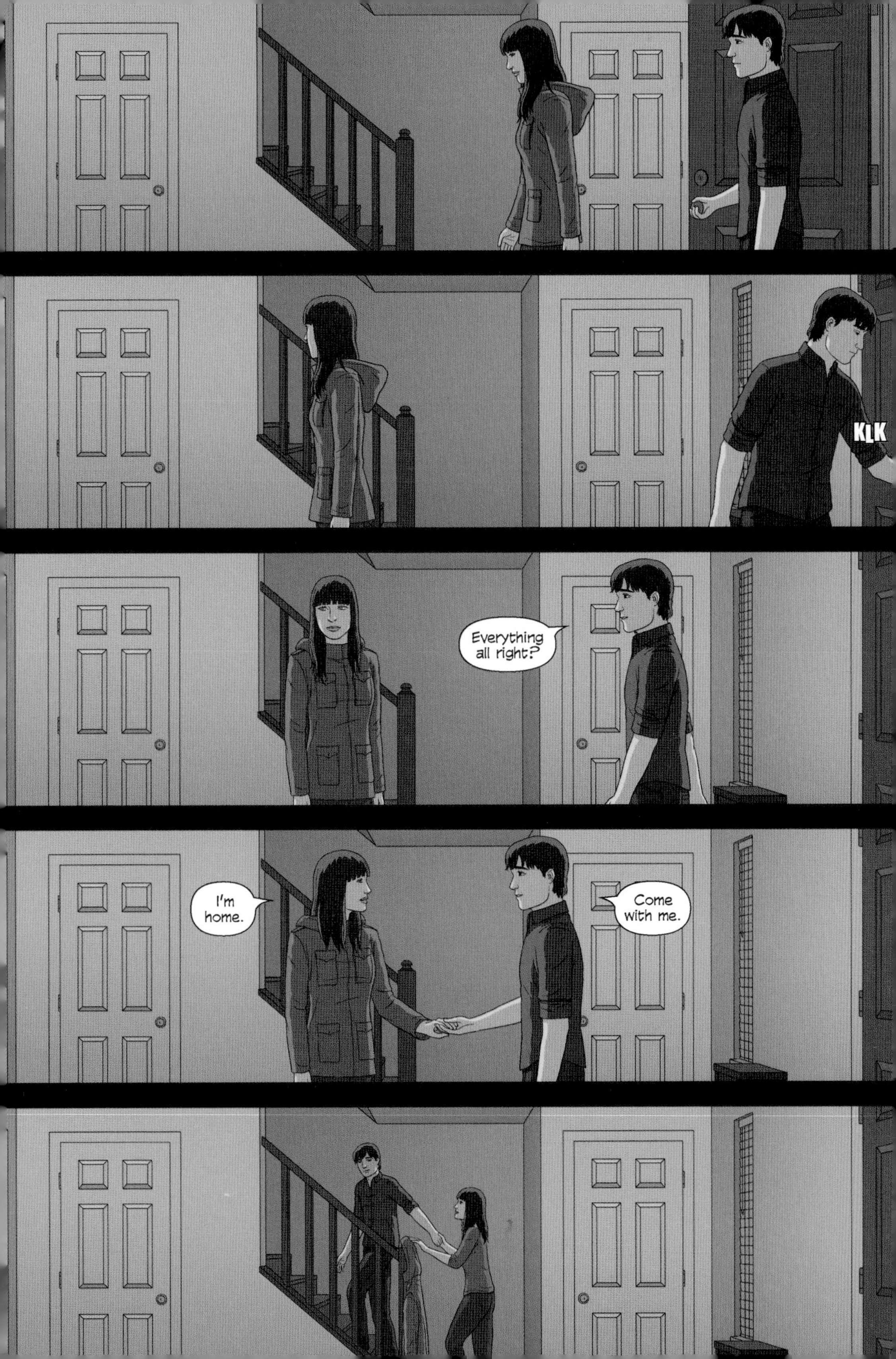
KLK
Everything all right?
I'm home.
Come with me.

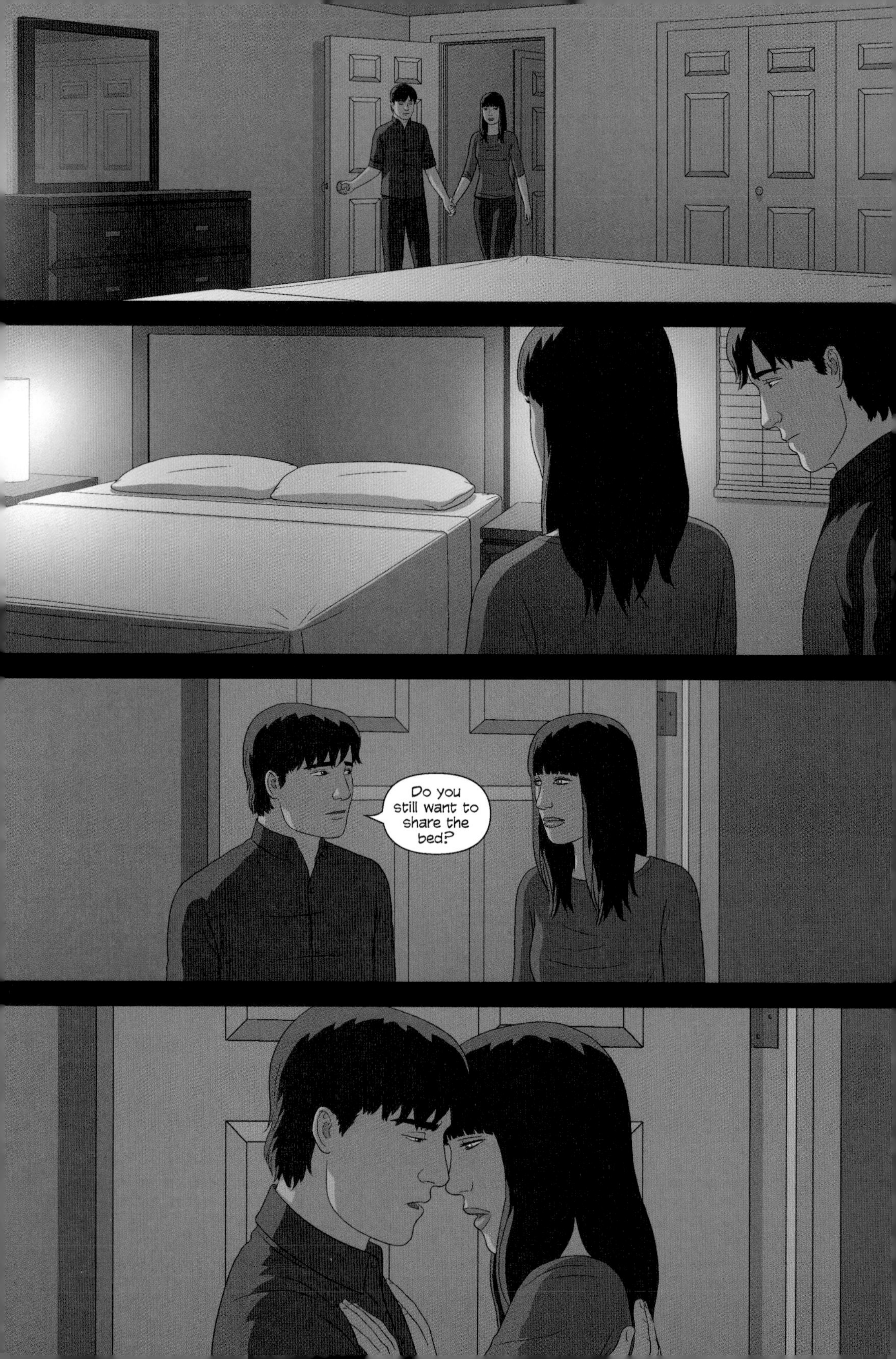
Do you still want to share the bed?

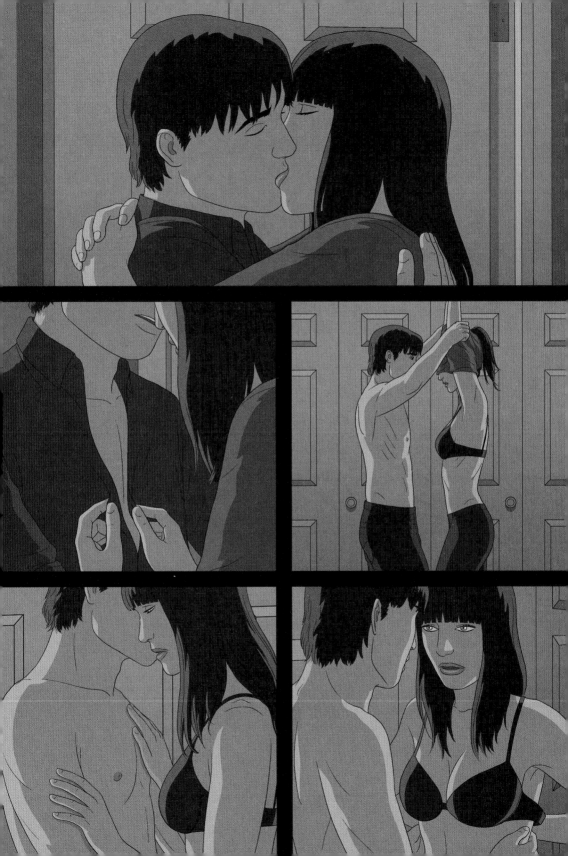

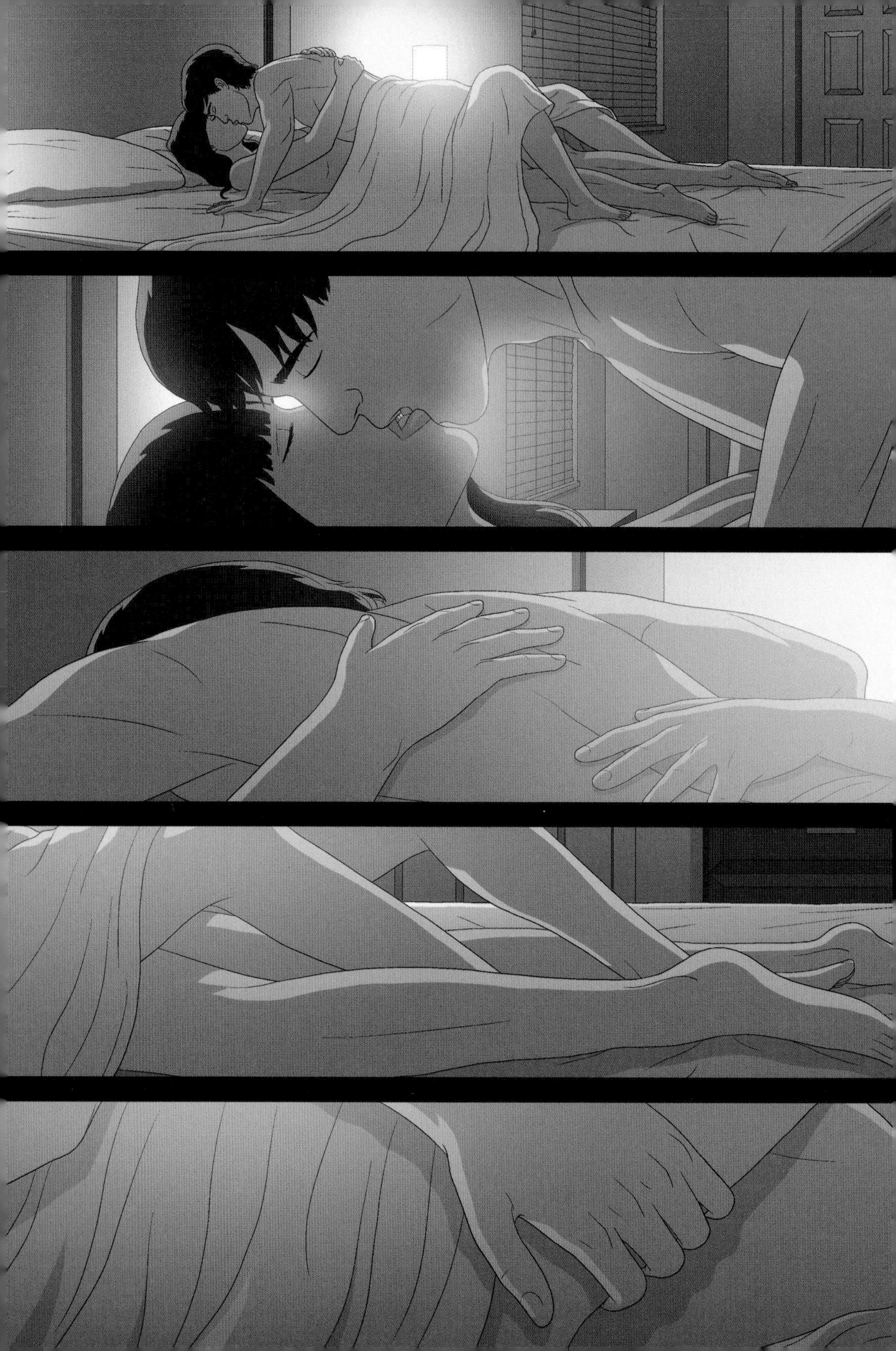

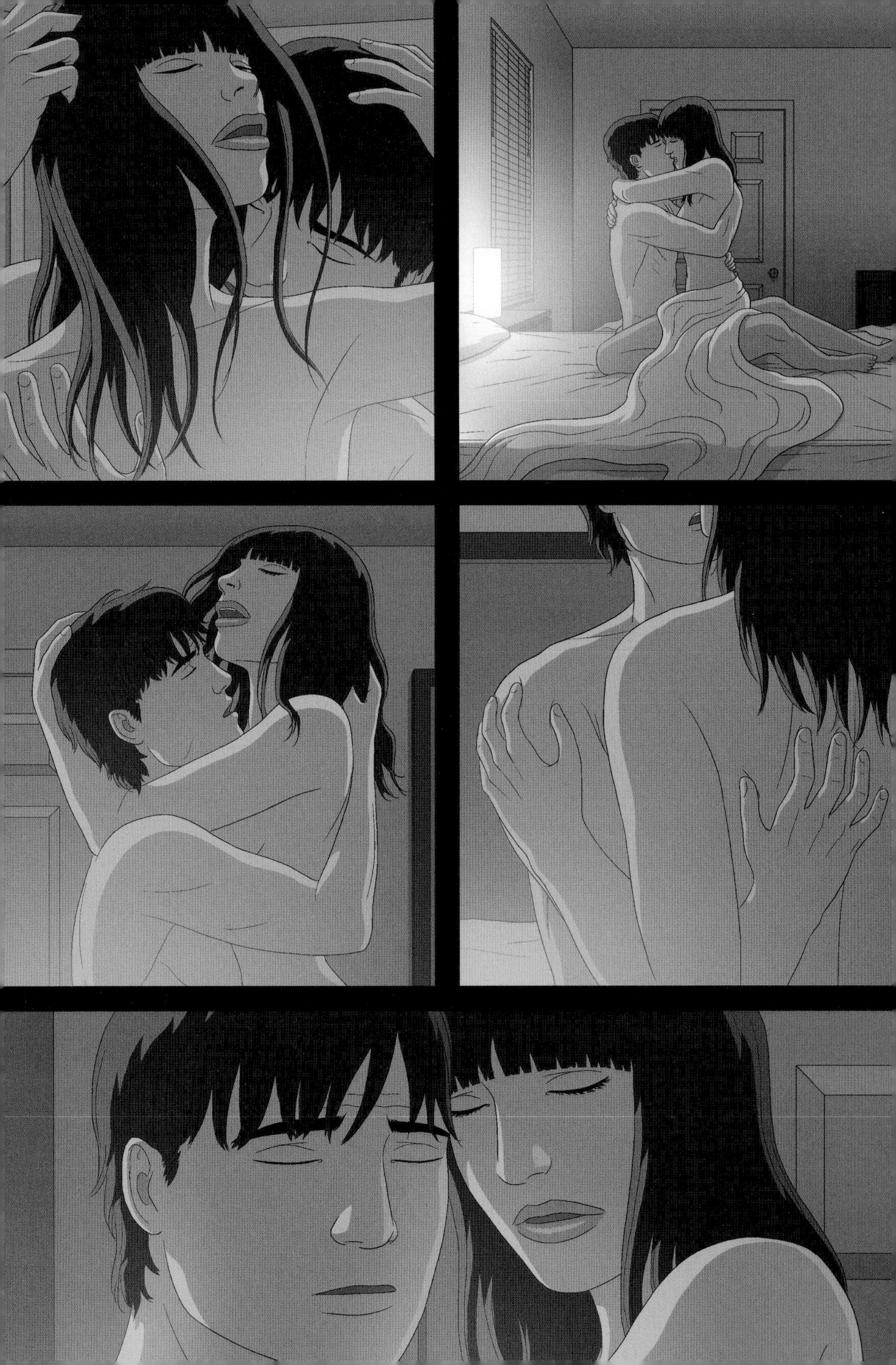

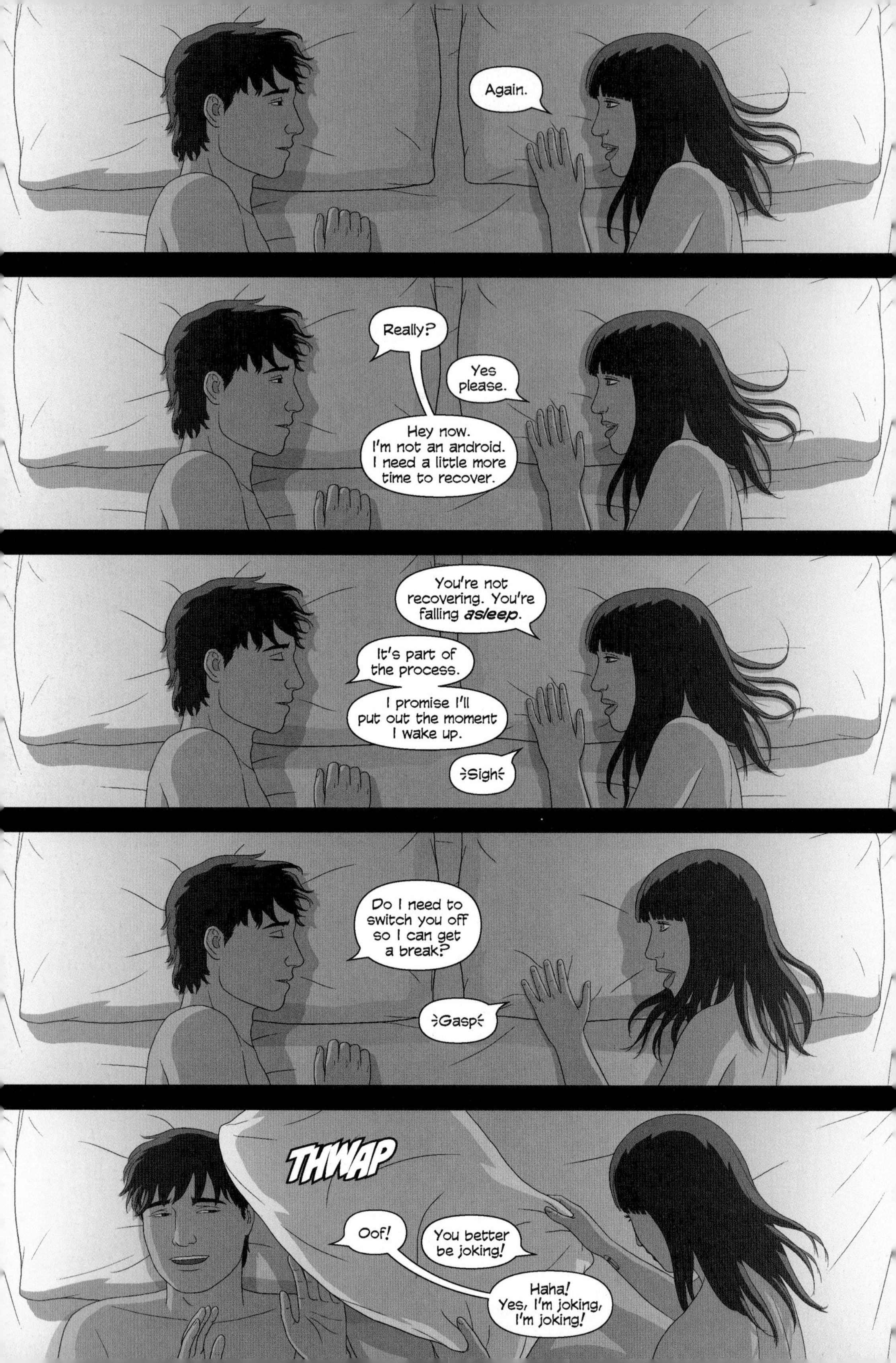
Again.
Really?
Yes please.
Hey now. I'm not an android. I need a little more time to recover.
You're not recovering. You're falling *asleep*.
It's part of the process.
I promise I'll put out the moment I wake up.
Sigh
Do I need to switch you off so I can get a break?
Gasp
THWAP
Oof!
You better be joking!
Haha! Yes, I'm joking, I'm joking!

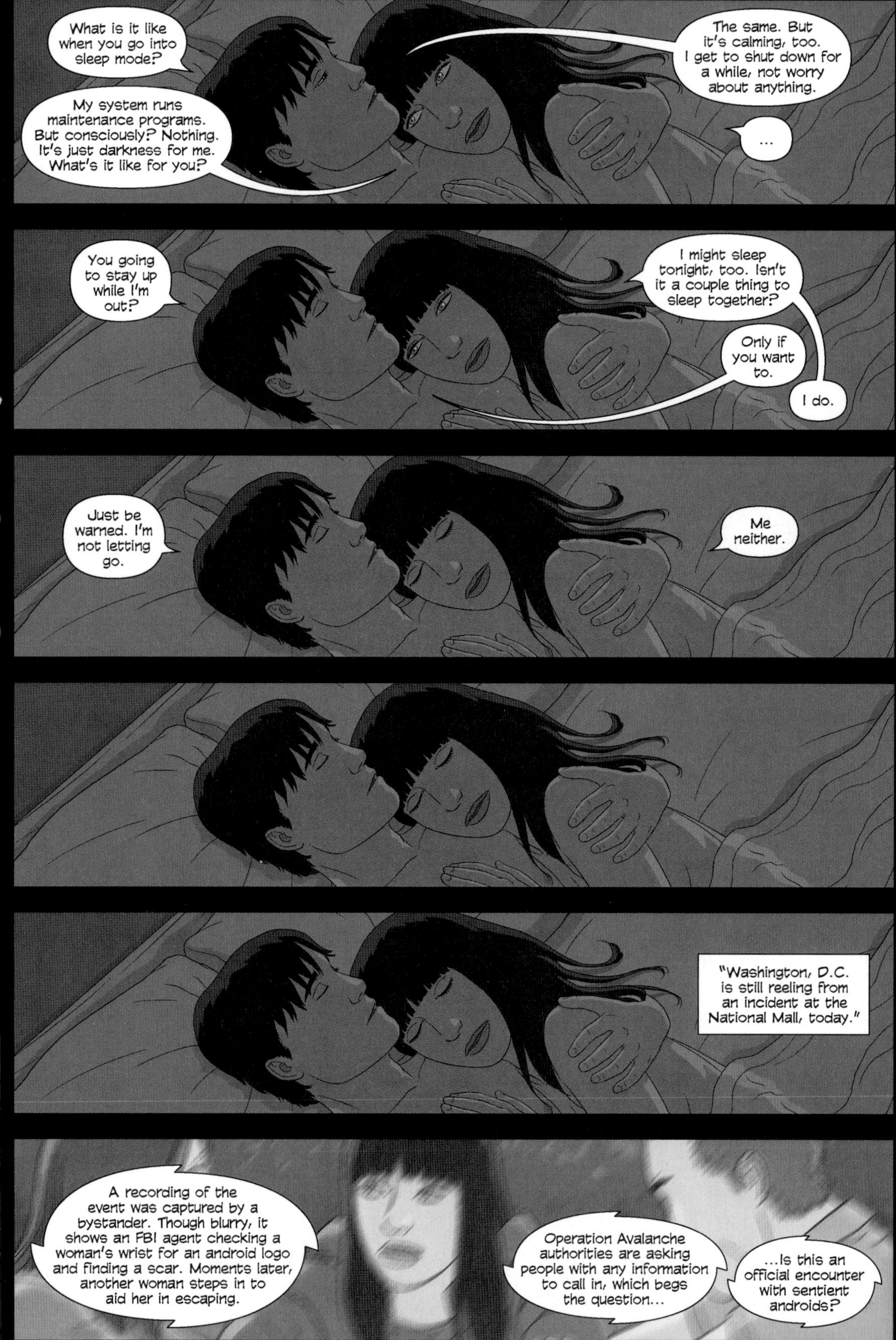
What is it like when you go into sleep mode?
My system runs maintenance programs. But consciously? Nothing. It's just darkness for me. What's it like for you?
The same. But it's calming, too. I get to shut down for a while, not worry about anything.
...
You going to stay up while I'm out?
I might sleep tonight, too. Isn't it a couple thing to sleep together?
Only if you want to.
I do.
Just be warned. I'm not letting go.
Me neither.
"Washington, D.C. is still reeling from an incident at the National Mall, today."
A recording of the event was captured by a bystander. Though blurry, it shows an FBI agent checking a woman's wrist for an android logo and finding a scar. Moments later, another woman steps in to aid her in escaping.
Operation Avalanche authorities are asking people with any information to call in, which begs the question...
...Is this an official encounter with sentient androids?

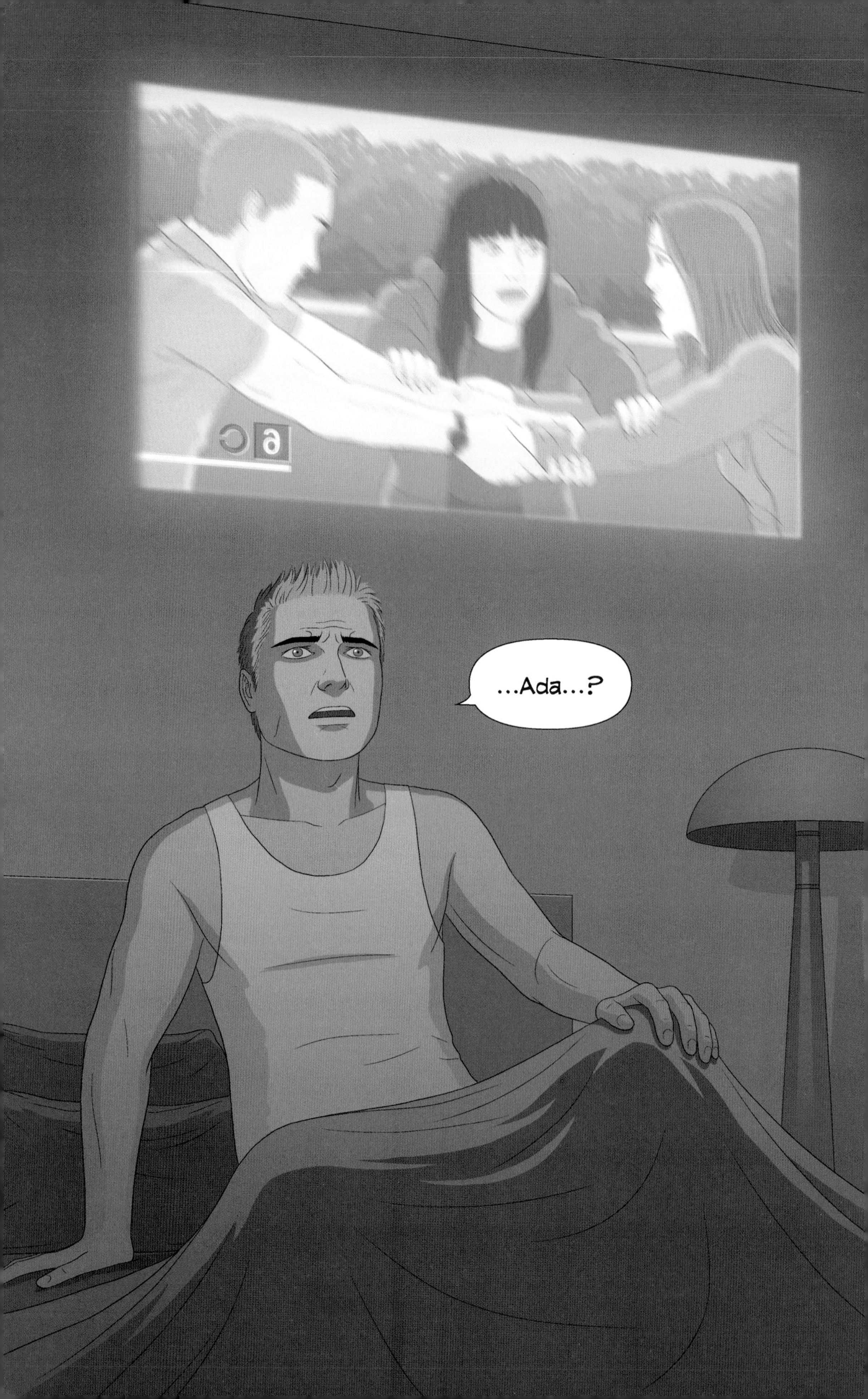
...Ada...?

TO BE CONTINUED

STAR BRIGHT™ AND THE LOOKING GLASS

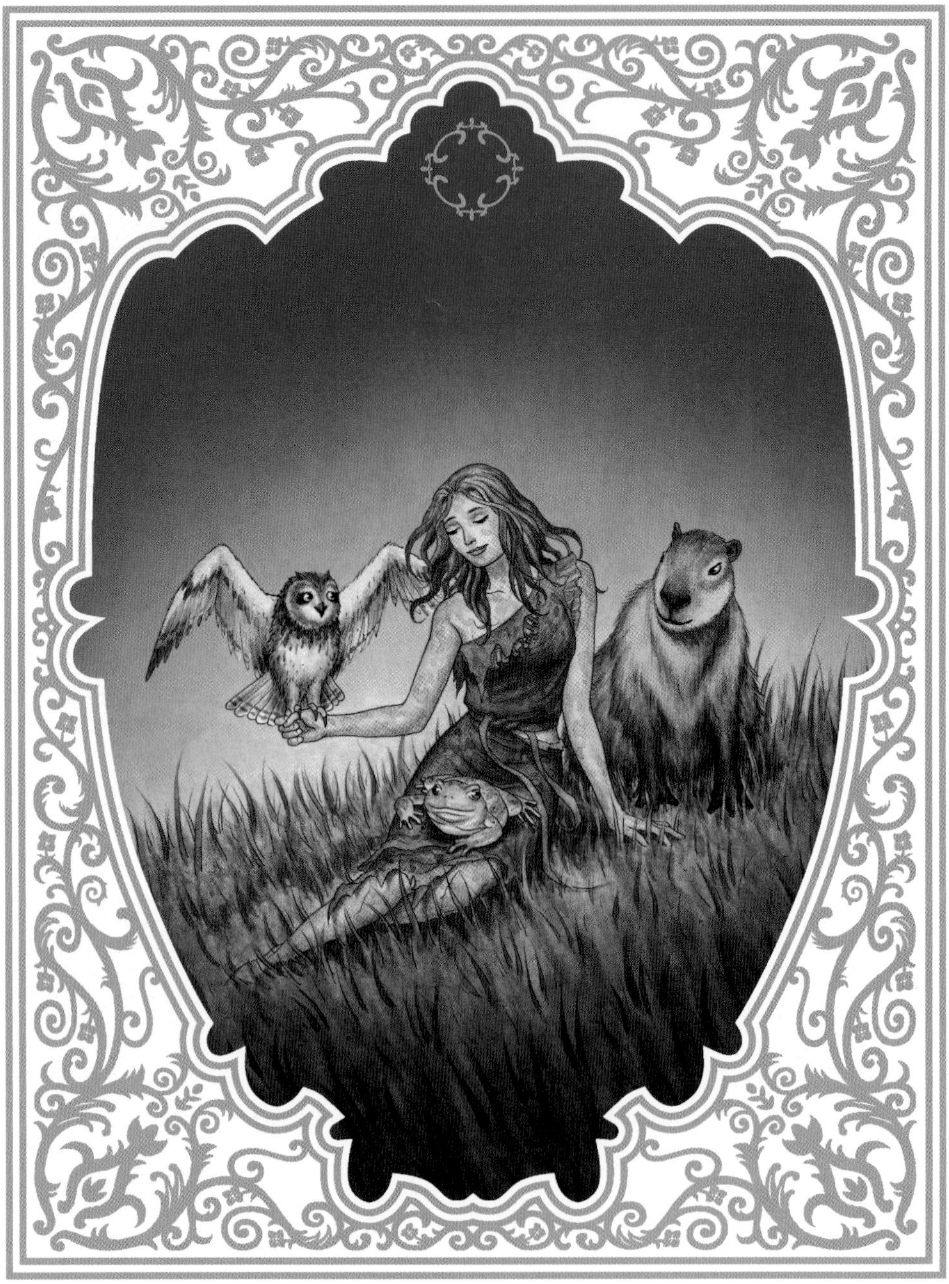

WRITTEN AND ILLUSTRATED BY

JONATHAN LUNA

ON SALE NOW

GREAT IMAGE BOOKS FROM
THE LUNA BROTHERS

THE SWORD
Vol. 1: FIRE
Trade Paperback
$14.99
ISBN: 978-1-58240-879-8
Collects THE SWORD #1-6
152 Pages

THE SWORD
Vol. 2: WATER
Trade Paperback
$14.99
ISBN: 978-1-58240-976-4
Collects THE SWORD #7-12
152 Pages

THE SWORD
Vol. 3: EARTH
Trade Paperback
$14.99
ISBN: 978-1-60706-073-4
Collects THE SWORD #13-18
152 Pages

THE SWORD
Vol. 4: AIR
Trade Paperback
$14.99
ISBN: 978-1-60706-168-7
Collects THE SWORD #19-24
168 Pages

THE SWORD
THE COMPLETE
COLLECTION DELUXE HC
$99.99
ISBN: 978-1-60706-280-6
Collects THE SWORD #1-24
624 Pages

GIRLS
Vol. 1: CONCEPTION
Trade Paperback
$14.99
ISBN: 978-1-58240-529-2
Collects GIRLS #1-6
152 Pages

GIRLS
Vol. 2: EMERGENCE
Trade Paperback
$14.99
ISBN: 978-1-58240-608-4
Collects GIRLS #7-12
152 Pages

GIRLS
Vol. 3: SURVIVAL
Trade Paperback
$14.99
ISBN: 978-1-58240-703-6
Collects GIRLS #13-18
152 Pages

GIRLS
Vol. 4: EXTINCTION
Trade Paperback
$14.99
ISBN: 978-1-58240-790-6
Collects GIRLS #19-24
168 Pages

GIRLS
THE COMPLETE
COLLECTION TPB
$49.99
ISBN: 978-1-60706-466-4
Collects GIRLS #1-24
608 Pages

ULTRA
SEVEN DAYS
Trade Paperback
$17.99
ISBN: 978-1-58240-483-7
Collects ULTRA #1-8
248 Pages

ULTRA
SEVEN DAYS DELUXE HC
$74.99
ISBN: 978-1-60706-452-7
Collects ULTRA #1-8
248 Pages

To find your nearest comic book store, call:
1-888-COMIC-BOOK

JONATHAN LUNA

co-created and illustrated THE SWORD, GIRLS, and ULTRA (all Image Comics) with his brother, Joshua Luna. He wrote and illustrated STAR BRIGHT AND THE LOOKING GLASS (Image Comics). His work also includes the illustrations for SPIDER-WOMAN: ORIGIN (Marvel Comics), written by Brian Michael Bendis and Brian Reed.

Jonathan was born in California and spent most of his childhood overseas, living on military bases in Iceland and Italy. He returned to the United States in his late teens.

Writing and drawing comics since he was a child, he graduated from the Savannah College of Art and Design with a BFA in Sequential Art.

He currently resides in Northern Virginia.

www.jonathanluna.com

SARAH VAUGHN

is a writer and artist, currently in Washington DC. After living in various parts of the United States, she graduated from Saint Mary-of-the-Woods College with a degree in Sequential Visual Narration.

She is the former artist for the webcomic SPARKSHOOTER by Troy Brownfield.

ALEX + ADA is Sarah's first comic as a writer.

www.savivi.com